D0114532

THE DOOMSDAY CODE

Also by **Alex Scarrow**

TimeRiders
TimeRiders: Day of the Predator

THE DOOMSDAY CODE

Alex Scarrow

Walker & Company New York

Originally published in Great Britain by the Penguin Group, Puffin Books, in February 2011
First published in the United States of America in October 2012
by Walker Publishing Company, Inc., a division of Bloomsbury Publishing, Inc.
www.bloomsburyteens.com

For information about permission to reproduce selections from this book, write to
Permissions, Walker BFYR, 175 Fifth Avenue, New York, New York 10010

Library of Congress Cataloging-in-Publication Data
Scarrow, Alex.
The doomsday code / Alex Scarrow.
p.   cm. — (TimeRiders)
Summary: The TimeRiders travel back to Robin Hood's Middle Ages
to search for the mythical Holy Grail and to stop the future from changing.
ISBN 978-0-8027-3384-9
[1. Time travel—Fiction. 2. Robin Hood (Legendary character)—Fiction.
3. Grail—Fiction. 4. Middle ages—Fiction. 5. Science fiction.] I. Title.
PZ7.S3255Do 2012   [Fic]—dc23   2011050987

Book design by Donna Mark
Printed in the U.S.A. by Quad/Graphics, Fairfield, Pennsylvania
2 4 6 8 10 9 7 5 3 1

To my nieces and nephews . . . here we go (big breath . . . and in order of age)—Leona, James, Nathan, Abigail, Tom, Aaron, Naomi, Joe, Nick, and Connor. Future TimeRiders?

TIME RIDERS

2001 1912 1957 1941 2066

THE DOOMSDAY CODE

Prologue

2044, Chicago

"So, ladies and gentlemen," said the man, "this is what you all came to see. In just a moment I'm going to step inside that Faraday cage and *disappear.*"

Right, so he IS just another fruitcake. Anna Lopez shook her head. *That's all I need.*

Her eyes met one or two of the other members of the small audience, journalists like her. She recognized a few faces: a reporter who covered science and environment issues for one of the Euro News digi-stations; a science editor for a Stamford-based technology e-periodical. They'd all received the small vanilla-colored invitation card last week with just a few words of explanation printed on it. An invitation to come down to a place called Larkham's Gallery "to witness the demonstration of a technology that is going to change the lives of every man, woman, and child on this troubled planet."

Anna Lopez sighed. The world sure could have done with a bit of good news.

Larkham's Gallery sounded nice. Like a sweet little boutique gallery where there'd hopefully be wine and little savory things on silver trays being offered around. Instead they were sitting on three rows of uncomfortable plastic school chairs in a grim-looking warehouse with a flickering fluorescent light overhead and the echoing *tap tap tap* of rainwater dripping through somewhere.

"The cage itself takes the charge and will distribute it evenly around me, creating a space big enough for me to—"

"To what? Make you vanish?" called out someone from the row behind. "My kid can do that trick with his old Fisher-Price magic set."

Someone snorted coffee into their Styrofoam cup.

"No," said the man on the stage. Anna had forgotten his name again. She looked down at the scribbled notes on her T-Pad.

Waldstein. Even the name sounded corny.

"No!" he snapped, silencing a ripple of laughter. "This isn't a party trick!"

Anna raised her hand. "Mr. Waldstein?"

"Uhh . . . yes?"

"You say you're going to *vanish*?"

Waldstein nodded. "I will be transported *elsewhere* for a period of no more than a minute."

"Uh-huh, 'transported.'" She nodded. "Where, exactly?"

He grinned, pushing frizzy coils of salt-and-pepper-colored hair out of his face to reveal eyes as wide as a child's behind the glint of his glasses. "Another moment in time," he announced theatrically.

Behind her she heard a chair scrape the cold concrete floor and someone mutter, "Idiot," then the receding clack of footsteps. From either side of her she could hear and see the other journalists shuffle awkwardly.

Time? The poor deluded old fool seemed to be talking about time travel. She decided he was clearly in need of some sort of help; perhaps to be in a place with padded mint-green walls and soothing music. Other chairs began to scrape noisily. It looked like this madman's pitiful little charade was over already. She almost felt sorry for him.

"Don't go!" Waldstein shouted. "Please! Stop right there!" The footsteps slowed. "I'll show you right now!"

Anna watched him huddle over a rickety picnic table on his

makeshift stage of stacked wooden pallets. He tapped the keys of a battered and beaten old laptop. Beneath the table was something that looked like a copper boiler, cables snaking in one end and out the other and over toward a tall wire cage. She heard the low hum of power surging inside the copper device, and the lights in the warehouse began to dim. It was then that it occurred to her the man's little contraption was drawing mainline electricity.

Oh my God, he's going to fry himself. Right here. Right in front of us!

Waldstein stepped smartly over the cables and opened the door of the wire cage. "Just you watch!"

She stood up. "Mr. Waldstein, I think you should—"

Waldstein stepped inside and slammed the cage shut with a loud clang that echoed around the warehouse. The humming was growing louder. "Ladies and gentlemen!" Waldstein's voice rose to a shout over the noise. "You're about to witness the very first journey through time!"

"Mr. Waldstein." Anna stepped forward. "Please! You should stop this!"

She noticed that one of the digi-station journalists had pushed his way through the chairs and was filming the cage with his palm-cam. She shook her head with disgust. No doubt the sicko was hoping to catch the whole thing—to film this poor deluded Froot Loop frying himself like a potato chip.

Jesus . . .

Waldstein was smiling calmly at her through the wire. "Don't worry, my dear, I'm going to be just fine!" he called out above the increasing hum of power building up toward a discharge.

"Please!" cried Anna, surprised at the sound of panic in her voice. "Please! Just get out!"

Waldstein's smile was almost reassuring. "I'll be fine, my dear. I'm going to see them again. I'm going to see them, touch them . . ."

"'Them? Who? What are you talking about?" she shouted, but her words were lost amid the growing din.

Suddenly sparks began to dance along the wires of the cage.

"Stand back!" someone shouted. She realized the charge could quite easily arc across the space toward them. Instinctively she stumbled backward several steps, bumping into an empty chair, banging her ankle painfully. The chairs were all empty now; everyone was on their feet. She could hear someone calling for the police. No one came here tonight to watch a man voluntarily cook himself—not even a nutcase. And there were enough nutcases out there these days.

Sparks sputtered from the cage and showered onto the floor. The fluorescent lights across the warehouse ceiling flickered, popped, and went out, leaving them in a darkness lit only by the strobing flash of Waldstein's electrical execution. She could still see his silhouette in there, perfectly still, amid the curtain of sparks. Still, calm . . . not the thrashing and convulsing marionette she'd expected to see by now.

Then, with a soft pop—not a bang—and a gentle puff of displaced air, it all stopped—the sparks, the humming of power, the fizz and crackle of raw electrical energy, all still and silent. In the complete darkness she could hear the ragged breathing of everyone around her.

"Somebody better call an ambulance!" she heard a man mutter.

A flashlight snapped on, and the beam swung around to the cage.

"My God! Where is he?"

It was empty. Just as he'd assured them it would be. He'd vanished. Anna felt a surge of relief. She found herself laughing giddily. "I'll be . . ." She shook her head. "Well, that's what he *said*, right?"

Not everyone else seemed quite so relieved and amused by the spectacle.

"I didn't come here tonight just to see a magic show! I've got articles to file, ya know? Real work, not this kind of insane garbage—"

A ribbon of sparks suddenly flickered along the wire of the cage.

"Whoa! Stand back, everyone! It's still live!"

Anna expected a repeat performance to begin, to cover his "arrival" back into the cage. Smoke and mirrors, that's what magicians call it—the art of distraction. But instead through the wire she could see

a faint ghostly glow; at first it was a pinprick, but quickly it expanded in diameter to several feet across, shimmering and undulating like water. It was how she imagined ghostly ectoplasm might look—if that kind of supernatural nonsense was for real.

"What *is* that?" someone muttered. The flashlight flicked off, allowing them to see the ethereal glow more clearly. Anna shook her head in the dark, as if the question had been addressed to her personally.

"No idea," she replied. In the faint swirling light, she thought she could detect a vaguely human shape. Perhaps shapes—plural. Something was in there—*someone. Some people.* An outline gradually became more distinct, as if drawing closer. Anna had the definite impression that the faint glow was *somewhere else.* As if—had the wire mesh not been in the way—she could have stepped forward and reached inside . . . and touched another place. Almost as if it was a shimmering, wavering doorway to another—

She caught herself. *What? Really? Seriously?*

"This is insane," she whispered to herself.

The distinct form *was* human. She could see that clearly now. It seemed to be shuffling toward her, beginning to block out the swirling light of this "other place." Then all of a sudden the ghostly light was gone. It was dark. In the pitch black she felt a puff of air on her face, blowing a tress of hair into her eye. She brushed it aside. There was something inside the cage. She could hear it breathing, a fluttering irregular gasping coming through the mesh.

"Hello?" she whispered. "Waldstein? Is . . . is that you in there?"

The breathing remained unchanged.

"Who's got that flashlight?" said someone behind her. "Shine it on the cage."

She heard someone fussing with something, cursing as they fumbled for a switch too small for its own good.

"Waldstein?" whispered Anna. "You all right?" The breathing faltered and stopped in answer to her question.

"Get the light on!"

"I'm trying! I can't find the . . . Where is it?"

The poor man in the cage started to say something quietly. Anna leaned forward, finally brave enough to press against the wire mesh. It was still warm from carrying the electrical charge, but not hot. And, thankfully, not live. "You okay in there?"

"I . . . I've s-seen . . . it . . ."

"It's all right. We're going to get you out . . . and then we'll get an ambulance."

"I . . . I've *seen* it," his voice rasped.

Then behind her the flashlight snapped back on and shadows danced in all directions.

"He's in shock," said Anna. "Get the light on him."

The beam swung down over her shoulder, casting a grid-work of leaping shadows around the warehouse. Through the wire she could make out the man she'd seen moments ago: the man she'd thought needed medication and a nice comfortable padded cell in which to live out his delusion.

No burned human carcass. That much was a relief. *But his face . . . his face.*

Those eyes beneath the wild lunatic hair and behind those madman glasses were still round and wide, but not with the childlike wonder and excitement he'd been exhibiting before. Not anymore.

It was terror. Sheer terror. The look of a mind utterly closed down to protect itself from insanity. At that moment she realized tonight had been no parlor trick. No stage magician looking for an audience, for publicity.

He's been somewhere. He's actually been somewhere. And she had a feeling he'd been gone far longer than a minute.

"What?" asked Anna Lopez softly. "What just happened?"

His gaze, faraway, perhaps still looking upon another place, seemed to gradually return, slowly catching up with the rest of his body to arrive back in Chicago. His eyes focused on her—a gradual realization that he wasn't alone, that someone was just on the other side of the wire mesh.

"I . . ." His dry and cracked lips opened. "I . . . I've s-seen . . . the end."

Behind her she could hear someone calling an ambulance. Maybe some of them were hearing him. She noticed the sicko with the camera was still filming. Maybe he was disappointed not to have a smoking corpse to show his editor. Maybe this man's insane babbling was going to be an even better story to file.

"Waldstein?" uttered Anna. "What do you mean . . . 'the end'?"

She realized he was crying. A tear rolled down his cheek and soaked into the bristles of his beard. The lost faraway look was finally gone. His eyes were on her. He suddenly looked around the cage. "My God! This is . . . this has all got to go!"

"What? You mean your *machine*?"

He slammed a palm into the wire cage and it rang and rattled, echoing around the warehouse. "THIS! Time travel! It's . . . it's going to destroy us!"

Chapter 1

2001, New York

Alone, Maddy watched a cluster of seagulls picking away at some garbage spilled on the low-tide silt of the East River. Overhead, traffic clunked rhythmically across the Williamsburg Bridge, the end-of-day rush hour of city workers returning from Manhattan back to Brooklyn.

She tossed a small nugget of cement into the water and watched the seagulls scatter at the sound of the splash.

My God. Her mind was still spinning with the idea. *My God, Liam is Foster?*

That's what the old man had said, wasn't it? That he and Liam were the *same* person; that he was once Liam. And now that he'd said it, she could see he was right. She could see the likeness in their faces, in their mannerisms, even in the way they talked.

"Time travel did this to me. Time travel *aged* me, Maddy," he'd said.

The fact that Liam was going to become that poor old man . . . something else for her to keep to herself until she decided Liam was ready to hear it. She felt so lonely harboring secrets like this; it separated her from the other two. It felt wrong. After all, they'd been *recruited* together: her, Liam, Sal . . . the three of them plucked from different times, from the very last seconds of their lives, by the old man. They should be a team. There shouldn't be secrets between them. Not ones like this.

"*You're the team leader now,*" Foster had told her. "*It's up to you how and when you tell Liam about this.*"

She watched the seagulls cautiously return to peck and pull at the plastic bags on the silt.

"Just great," she muttered to herself. Something else to churn away inside her, to keep her awake at night. Because it wasn't just the Foster-is-Liam thing, was it? Oh no. There was that *other* thing, that scribbled message she'd found at their supply drop point—the one for her eyes only.

Maddy, look out for "Pandora," we're running out of time. Be safe and tell no one.

She wondered what she was freakin' supposed to make of that. It meant nothing to her. "Pandora"—what was that, other than a pretty stupid girl's name?

"Why does it have to be me?" Her soft voice caused a strutting seagull nearby to pause and cock its head at her.

"I'm not talking to you, dumb bird." The seagull resumed its scavenging, one beady black eye still warily on her. She watched lights flickering on in Manhattan as the sun began to settle behind the two tall pillars of the World Trade Center.

Foster recruited you for a reason, put you in charge for a reason. Because he knows you're smart enough to figure things out, Maddy.

She sighed. She'd really like to believe it . . . that she was *destined* to be a good team leader, a good TimeRider. But somehow, with the way things had gone so far, it all just felt as if she'd been winging it, hanging by the skin of her teeth. Lucky not to be dead or to have caused the deaths of Liam and Sal. Lucky not to have completely messed up the timeline. Lucky not to have destroyed the world.

Way too much stress for an eighteen-year-old girl to have to be burdened with.

"Darn right," she muttered. "Way too much."

Chapter 2

2001, New York

<u>*Monday (time cycle 57)*</u>
I'm watching him now, floating in that tube of gloopy slimy stuff. It's Bob, but not Bob yet, if you know what I mean. It's a boy, actually. Completely hairless and curled up like a baby. You can see the face is definitely him, even though it's not finished yet; thick bone and that heavy, dumb-looking brow. The skin hasn't grown on his head just yet. It's all red-raw muscle fiber and teeth, and two eyeballs that look huge without eyelids. Sometimes they seem to shift, to twitch, as if they're staring at you. But I know he's not. His baby mind is fast asleep right now, dreaming whatever baby brains dream.

Some first-phase skin has grown across his body, but I can still see patches where it hasn't. There's a part I can see through, just beneath his left arm, where I can see the ribs, and I think that's an organ in there. Is it his heart or something? It's moving. Like an animal in a cage.

Actually, this is making me feel sick. I guess I'm going back to my bunk.

Speaking of puke-making, Liam's emptying the toilet right now. We got one of these camping toilet things a few days ago. The archway has got a little bathroom, with a creaky wooden door and a cracked toilet bowl with no seat. It's totally pinchudda! And it's not connected anyway. So that's why we needed the camping toilet. It has to be emptied every few days 'cause it stinks up the whole place—when the plastic barrel thing gets pulled away, the back of the toilet comes out and all that "stuff" inside is sloshing around.

Shadd-yah. My turn next time.

Anyway . . . so we're going on a trip soon. Somewhere special. You want to know?

I'll tell you.

Tomorrow we're going to "Sunday"! That's right, we're coming out of the loop and going to the Sunday before it. It'll be my first time travel. Well, no—I suppose when Foster grabbed me from home and took me back here, that was my first, but I didn't understand then what was going on. And of course every time the field resets I'm sort of traveling back forty-eight hours in time, right?

But doing this . . . stepping into the portal, that's like the real thing. Really being a time traveler. I'll be stepping through a hole in space and time, through a moment of chaos space. Liam says it's weird, like all milky white and foggy, and there's creepy movement in there and you can't see what it is. But he says it all happens so quickly and you're out the other side before you know it. So not to worry.

Great. Thanks for telling me about the creepy moving things, Liam.

So, I'm sort of nervous. But excited too, 'cause we're going to see this rock band called "EssZed." Maddy says they disappeared after 9/11. Just vanished! They're kind of like famous for that or something. So this, even though they don't know it, is their last-ever gig. Maddy thinks I'll really like them. She played some of their tracks on the computer. They're total rip-heavy. She says Liam will probably hate them and complain about it not being real music, just noise. Not the sort of "ditty" he's used to.

LOL.

"Education." A "field trip," that's what she's calling it. Useful for Becks to get a little more experience pretending to be human. She needs it—she's too serious and robotic. Whereas Bob was dumb, you could pretend he was just an idiot. But Becks is too "cold" sort of. She freaks me out a bit when she stares. It's like she's looking at you and figuring out the three fastest ways to kill you with nothing but her thumb.

I think I preferred Bob.

Chapter 3

2001, New York

The portal shimmered in the middle of the archway, a perfect sphere of energy, and in the middle of it a hint of the ghostly wavering world of a whole forty-eight hours ago: Sunday night. A flicker of neon light and what looked like a twisting, undulating stretch of graffiti-covered brick wall dancing through a heat-haze.

"Come on, Sal," said Maddy. "Quickly."

Sal swallowed back a throatful of nerves and nodded. "Okay, all right, I'm ready." She stepped forward, feeling the energy lift the hairs on her arms, lift her bangs like a theater curtain. "It tickles!"

Stepping inside the sphere of energy, she could feel the concrete floor beginning to flex beneath her feet, like the canvas of a trampoline somebody else was already jumping up and down on. Then very quickly it softened and sagged like tissue paper . . . and then all of a sudden the floor was completely gone.

"*Jahulla!* I'm falling!" she yelped as her arms and legs flailed and she felt herself tumbling through air.

"Don't worry about it!" she heard Liam's voice say, but already it sounded like he was shouting down a long, long tunnel, distant echoes fast receding. Then it was gone.

"Liam!" she cried, but her own voice sounded dampened and swallowed up.

I really am alone.

Just like he'd said, here she was, floating—or falling—through an ocean of featureless white. Like a flake of breakfast cereal see-sawing down through an impossibly large bowl of milk.

Stay calm, Sal.

Swirling featureless white all around her. She held her hand up only a dozen inches away from her face, and it was so faint, fogged by the mist. She waved it around and felt the air, as thick as liquid, resist her movements. She looked up, hoping to see the faint form of one of the others flailing above her, but she saw nothing but more white.

Maybe I am *all alone.*

She wondered whether she was in her very own milk-colored universe, or whether the others were out there somewhere. Perhaps nearby. Perhaps just beyond sight. She wondered if anyone ever got lost in here, never to emerge at the other end. Doomed to spend eternity swirling and flailing. You'd go insane, wouldn't you? With nothing to see, hear, smell, or feel, you'd go completely insane.

She decided it was probably best not to think about this kind of stuff. But then her mind had more unwelcome questions to ask.

What if that's what the creepy-movey things are? Other travelers . . . maybe even other TimeRiders who've lost their way and gotten stuck here for eternity?

She could all too easily conjure up the image of another girl just like her, lost for endless centuries in here: eyes fogged by madness, opaque like those of a boiled fish, and cackling like an old woman—a mind rubbed smooth of meaningful thought and left utterly, utterly insane.

This really isn't helping, stupid. Think of something else.

She decided she'd rather she *was* on her own; catching a glimpse of something out there, faint and moving, was the last thing she needed to see right now, so she closed her eyes.

Almost as soon as she'd done that, she felt the ground suddenly return beneath her feet.

"Whuh?" She opened her eyes to see she was standing in a small parking lot, lit faintly by a neon, red BUDWEISER sign that buzzed like an angry fly in a bottle. She took a step away from the portal, and a moment later Liam, Maddy, and Becks emerged, one after the other.

"That was horrible!" she gasped under her breath.

"First time's the worst." Liam grinned apologetically. "Maybe I should've warned you."

She could hear a deep rhythmic pumping sound coming from somewhere beyond the brick wall in front of her. To her left the wall continued past an alcove where cars were parked so tightly side by side she wondered how any of the drivers had managed to get out. The wall came to an end overlooking a dimly lit backstreet where she could see the impatient shifting shadows of a line of people.

"Oh, it sounds like they've started playing already," said Maddy. "Come on, guys, let's get inside."

Chapter 4

1193, Sherwood Forest, Nottinghamshire

Snow fell softly and silently on the track ahead of them, floating down from a loaded gray sky like cherry blossoms. On either side of the forest trail tall, thick evergreens sported fulsome white skirts that weighed their burdened branches down low.

Sir Geoffrey Rainault tugged at the cloak slipping down his shoulders, begrudging the body heat that escaped with the movement. Between saddle-sore legs his mount—his favorite, Edith—plodded relentlessly and wearily: a beast that had carried him across too many countries to remember. Nine months across the sun-baked deserts of the Holy Land, across the spring meadows of endless principalities and dukedoms . . . and now at last home to England, north of London and en route to the remote wilderness of Scotland.

Geoffrey shifted in the saddle to glance over his shoulder at the others: three knights, their retinue of squires, sergeants, and the token priest traveling with them to attend to their five daily prayer meetings. In all, just the eighteen of them now. When they'd set out on their errand, there'd been more than sixty in their party. But illness, some battlefield wounds that had gone bad, and one or two skirmishes on the way home had whittled down their numbers. Now, those left, still intent on seeing this lie through, looked like men ready to lie down in the winter coldness and let sleep take them.

"Sire! Look!" shouted one of the squires, pointing up the forest track.

Geoffrey turned back in his saddle and squinted at the bright blanket of undisturbed snow ahead of them. He could make out the perfectly still form of a man swathed in a dark hooded cloak, standing in the middle of the rutted track.

Geoffrey's sense of caution stirred him to rein in Edith and raise a gloved hand. He heard the column of bone-weary horses and men shuffle to a halt behind him.

"We are about King's business, make way!"

The hooded figure remained perfectly still. The forest was utterly silent, save for the cawing of a murder of crows circling high above in the winter sky, the rasping of the horses' breath, and the clink of a harness as one of the pack animals stirred uneasily.

"Do ye hear?"

The figure seemed not to. Geoffrey switched tongues. "*Nous faisons les affaires de rois!*"

A breeze tugged at the hooded cape, but the man within remained completely still.

This is not good.

Geoffrey looked at the trees on either side of the track: perfect ambush terrain. They'd been jumped before by bandits on the Continent in woods much like this. The mistake back then—a mistake that had cost them a good knight and two sergeants-at-arms—had been not to form up the moment the first of them had appeared. He raised his hand and balled it into a fist—the signal for the rest to dismount and make ready for a fight.

The forest echoed with the metallic clank of buckles and belts, the rasping of chain mail, and the drawing of swords from scabbards.

"Step aside now! Or . . . I will have one of my men fire upon ye," said Geoffrey, beckoning forward Bates, one of the sergeants in his retinue who was reliable with a crossbow. Bates drew up beside him, ratcheting back the drawstring and slipping a bolt into place.

"A warning shot is it, sir?"

Geoffrey pressed his lips tightly. The warning had already been given. Nonetheless, he decided if one more caution could save bloodshed on such a cold and Godless day, it was a breath worth expending.

"Step aside, or ye shall be fired upon!"

For a moment the man's response was the same. Nothing. Then, slowly, he began to stride through the ankle-deep snow toward them.

Bates turned to him. "Sir?"

This foolish man was going to die, then. Perhaps that was what he wanted: a martyr's death. Geoffrey had seen too much of that these last few years—men hungry to die on the battlefield for all the promises they'd been made about sins forgiven.

"Take him down."

Bates swiftly shouldered the crossbow, aimed, and fired. The *twang* of the string echoed off the trees as the bolt flickered across the twenty yards between them. With a smack it embedded itself into something beneath the flowing dark robes. But the man's stride remained unbroken.

"Good God!" Geoffrey whispered under his breath.

The hooded man, now no more than a dozen yards away, produced a broadsword from beneath his cape with an effortless sweep of his arm.

"Prepare to fight!" shouted Geoffrey over his shoulder. "Sergeants, defend the cart!"

He was joined by the other three knights. They were younger, some fitter than him, but all of them prepared to die to safeguard what lay behind them, secure in a nondescript wooden box and nestled in the back of their baggage cart.

The squires, not fighting men but hired valets, drew back to gather the horses' reins and watch over the column's possessions. Geoffrey regarded his three brethren, all seasoned fighters, veterans of King Richard's crusade. Despite this man shrugging off the impact of a bolt—which was still protruding from his chest—he was sure, between the four of them, that this was to be a short fight.

The hooded man broke into a sudden sprint as he closed the last yards between them, raising the five-foot length of his cumbersome blade as if it were no heavier than a clerk's quill.

Geoffrey and the youngest, William, hefted their blades aloft, two-handed as Geoffrey had taught, poised and ready to swing down. The hooded man's final stride brought him within range of strike and William swept his blade down first, aiming it at the vulnerable "L" between neck and shoulder. His sword clanged on something hard beneath the cape—armor for sure. The sword hummed with vibration as it bounced off the man and continued down into the snow. The hooded man's response was a blur of movement and the glint of the broadsword through the air. Young William was a dead man before his legs had begun to buckle. His head toppled down beside him into the crisp white snow, eyes still blinking surprise.

Geoffrey swung his sword in a reckless roundhouse sweep, hoping if not to cleave the man in two then at least to knock him off balance. His sweep ended with jarring suddenness and a metallic clang. He grunted a curse. The hooded man had to be wearing a complete suit of battle armor beneath that cape, and yet he moved with the agility of a man almost naked.

The response was a whip-snap blur, and before Geoffrey had fully understood the result of the blow he was looking down at the blade being yanked firmly from his sternum. In a fog of incomprehension he found himself lying in the snow, looking up at the gray sky, snow-flakes settling lightly on his cheeks and nose. His mind was still dealing with the ridiculous notion that, for him, the fight was already over. He—a man who'd fought Saracens all his life, killed hundreds of men—was now reduced by a single thrust to being a pathetic panting body staining virgin snow with his blood.

Far off he was aware of voices screaming. The sound of fear and anger and the clang and rasp of metal on metal: an exchange of swordplay that seemed to come to an end horrifyingly quickly. The voices receded—the squires, perhaps even the sergeants, were running for their lives.

Then, finally, silence. He was aware of the crows still circling above and the soft crunch of snow underfoot as someone slowly approached him.

Daylight was blocked out by the hooded man leaning over him. Geoffrey thought he caught the glint of armor amid the shadows of his cowl.

How can an armored man move so quickly?

Then his fading mind was aware of another person leaning over him.

"Where is it?" said the new man.

Geoffrey spat congealing blood out onto his cheek. "We . . . we have . . . no . . . money."

"I'm not after your money," said the man. "I've come for the relic. No matter, we'll find it ourselves."

Geoffrey's gray eyes tried focusing on him. "Y-you . . . *know* of it?"

The man's voice softened, sounding almost kindly now. "Yes. I'm one of your brotherhood." Geoffrey felt a hand under his cropped hair, lifting his head out of the snow. "Here's something to ease the pain."

The second man, a lean face framed by long hair and a beard, lifted a glass bottle to his lips. He tasted a strong mead.

"I'm truly sorry," said the man. "But we must have it." He sighed.

"The . . . the relic . . . is to be taken to Scotland. It must . . . it must be kept safe for—"

"For future generations," the man completed his words. "Yes, I know this. That's why we're here." He smiled. "We *are* that future generation, and we've come for it."

Geoffrey could feel death approaching fast; warm and welcoming. And yet his mind felt compelled to know more. His mission had failed. *It* was to be taken from him, and now he needed assurance.

"Ye . . . ye are . . . a . . . ?"

"A *Templar?* Yes."

Geoffrey's eyes were far off now, looking for hosts of angels to guide him to the Kingdom of Heaven.

"We've come from near the time that it all happens . . . and we *have* to know the truth. We've come to find out. It will be safe, brother—I promise you that. We will keep it safe."

The words meant nothing to the knight now. His breathing, short, rapid puffs of tainted air, finally ceased with a soft gurgle.

The man gently eased the knight's head back down onto the snow and traced the sign of the cross along the red cruciform on the man's white tunic. Then he looked up at the hooded figure, kneeling in the snow beside him. He nodded toward the abandoned baggage cart. "It'll be there somewhere. Find it."

The hooded man silently stood up and strode to the cart.

"*I'm sorry,*" the Templar whispered again to the dead knight, gently closing the lids of his eyes. "*But we simply have to know.*"

Chapter 5

2001, New York

Liam winced at the noise. It was so loud he could feel something inside his ears vibrate, and that surely couldn't be healthy. Maddy had brought him to the front of the small nightclub's dance floor; dragged him by the hand until they'd found a gap just in front of the stage. He'd been prepared to stand there and listen while the band had been playing a slower, quieter, *almost* pleasant song. But then, without any warning at all, they'd taken a passable piece of music and turned it into a screaming, banging cacophony of sound that made his ears hurt. And, of course, all the other weird-looking youngsters standing around him had started jumping up and down for some reason and rudely pushing and shoving him and each other.

He soon had enough of that and left Maddy and Sal bouncing up and down like idiots. He squeezed his way through the crowd, quickly giving up on his "excuse me"s and "pardon me"s until he found Becks standing at the back of the nightclub, calmly observing the behavior of everyone inside like a scientist studying a cage full of lab rats.

"They call this *music*, so they do," he shouted. "*Music*—would you believe that?"

"Affirmative," she shouted back at him. "Spectrum analysis of the frequency envelope and beats per minute indicate this music matches other tracks identified collectively as Death Metal."

"'Death Metal,' is it now? More like Deaf-and-Mental."

She looked at him. "Negative. I said 'Death' . . ." She hesitated. "That was a joke, wasn't it, Liam?"

He shrugged. "Aye."

She practiced a laugh she'd been working on; against the din of the band's final chorus it sounded coarse and braying and not particularly ladylike. He shook his head and looked back at the dance floor, a seething, bouncing carpet of hair and sweaty heads, nose rings, and tattooed shoulders, while five willowy young men on the stage jerked and twitched over their instruments. He decided they looked like something out of a traveling freak show.

Jay-zus, so this is the "modern world," is it?

🕐

"Ah, come on," laughed Maddy. "Lighten up, Liam. You sound like my grandfather."

"Yes, it wasn't exactly the bangra-thrash I'm used to," added Sal, "but—shadd-yah—they were proper good!"

"Good?" Liam huffed as they stepped out of the warm and humid haze of the nightclub into the cool September night. "I've heard angle-grinders along the Liverpool docks make a more tolerable noise than that." He grunted grumpily. "Now, are you sure those fellas back there actually knew how to play their instruments?"

"It's not about how *well* you play, Liam," said Maddy. "It's the—I don't know . . . it's the energy, the *attitude*. You know?"

"Attitude, is it?" They stepped out of West 51st Street onto Broadway, leaving the milling crowd of emos and grunge rockers dispersing behind them.

"Yes, attitude. It's about getting an emotion across to the audience. Laying out how you feel."

Becks cocked her head in thought. "That would indicate the musicians were feeling moderate to extreme levels of irritation about something."

Liam laughed.

"Anger," said Maddy.

"And that's all you need, is it? To be very angry and very noisy?"

"Umm . . ." Maddy made a face. "Well, not exactly . . ."

"Yes," said Sal. "Angry and noisy is exactly what music sounds like in '26."

As they walked down Broadway toward Times Square, Maddy checked her watch.

"You're sure your idea works?" asked Liam.

She nodded. "We don't need a portal back to our field office. It's nearly midnight now. The time bubble will reset in a couple of minutes. By the time we've walked back down and across the bridge we'll be an hour into Monday."

"But won't we, like, meet a copy of ourselves?"

"That doesn't happen," replied Maddy. "We don't copy. There's only us, and we're either here or there, but not in two places."

"I don't get that," Sal replied.

Liam stuffed his hands in his pockets. "Actually, I wasn't thinking so much about the time thing—just that this is going to be a long walk, so it is."

The girls laughed at that. Becks dutifully copied them.

"I would have thought you'd be used to walking," said Maddy.

"Why? Because I'm just some potato-eatin' Paddy from a hundred years ago?"

"No, I didn't mean it like that. It's just, I don't suppose there were many cars or buses and stuff."

"Jay-zus, we're not jungle savages, you know. We have—*had*—streetcars and trains and the like in Cork, so we did. I didn't like walkin' much then, just as I'm not so keen on doing it now."

Broadway led them to Times Square, which was much busier. The movie theaters were spilling out those who'd been watching the late showings of *Shrek* and *Monsters Inc.*, and yellow cabs lined up in the central reserve to drive home the last of the well-dressed audience for *Mamma Mia!*

Sal staggered for a moment.

"You okay?" asked Maddy.

"Dizzy."

"It *was* a bit loud in there, I guess. My ears are still ring—"

Sal shook her head and looked up. "Not that. I just felt the ground shift." She looked at them. "You didn't feel it?"

Liam and Maddy shook their heads. Maddy glanced around at the busy thoroughfare. Nothing seemed any different to her. "Sal? Was it a . . . ?"

"Yes. A small one, I think." Her eyes systematically scanned the buildings, the people, the cabs.

"See anything?"

"Not yet . . . not yet. Give me a second." It was difficult. She was used to scanning Tuesday morning at 8:30 a.m., the routine she'd established. She could describe *that* particular moment and place in time down to the tiniest detail. But this was Times Square thirty-two hours earlier, with different people doing different things. Then her eyes landed on a poster outside the Golden Screen movie theater.

"Over there," she said, pointing, then stepping quickly through a logjam of cars and pedestrians to get to the far side of the square. A minute later the others joined her as she ran her fingers across the scuffed plexiglass cover over the sidewalk poster. "This is new," she said. "This isn't supposed to be here. Not on Tuesday morning, it isn't. I'm certain."

Maddy looked it over. The poster displayed a picture of a young man on the run, being chased by helicopters and black Humvees through some European city. It could have been Paris, it could have been Prague, for all she knew. "*The Manuscript*," she read aloud. "Never heard of it."

Liam read the tagline. "The greatest code in history has just been broken." He looked at the top of the poster. "So, who's Leonardo DiCaprio?"

Maddy waved the question aside. "Sal, you sure about this?"

"I felt something . . . and this shouldn't be here." She nodded, tapping the poster. "Unless it gets taken down before Tuesday."

"But why would they?" Maddy checked the date. The movie wasn't out until October 15, just over a month from now. "They run these posters right up until release week." She turned to the others. "Anyway, I've never heard of this movie. And I'm pretty sure Leonardo's never been in a—a chase-y, spy movie like this. I'll look this up when we get back."

Becks nodded firmly, an untidy tress of dark hair flopping across her face. "This isn't right."

🕐

He watched them go, picking up their pace as they strode purposefully across Times Square.

Don't lose them. Whatever you do, don't lose them.

He matched their strides, weaving between the stop-start yellow cabs and ignoring the insults hurled out of the drivers' windows at him.

Don't lose them . . . not now, not after all this time.

He only recognized two of them: the girl with the glasses and the frizzy hair, and the tall athletic girl with long dark hair. The other two seemed to be friends. Close friends, by the look of their body language. And they'd stopped and studied a poster for the movie, hadn't they?

The movie, *The Manuscript*, was just another Hollywood cop-out: a cheesy chase movie with big explosions and stupid slow-motion gunfights and the obligatory villain with an English accent.

They were heading down Broadway now, the three girls and the boy, passing by a noisy gaggle of middle-aged women—tourists, by the look of them. He lost sight of them for a moment and began to panic.

Don't lose them, whatever you do!

He caught sight of the tall girl with the dark hair again, striding like an athlete on platform heels that added another half dozen unnecessary inches to her height. He gasped with relief as the other three emerged through the tangle of women. He decided to close the gap, unwilling to risk losing them because a crosswalk light went against him, or they'd turned a corner and taken a side street before he could re-establish a visual.

Too long he'd been waiting to see them again. Way too long to lose them now.

Chapter 6

2001, New York

Just as Maddy had promised, the archway was there as they'd left it, not empty and disused, nor occupied by alternate versions of themselves giving them grief for causing some weird time paradox.

She pulled down the shutter once they were all inside. "Gonna make coffee. I think I need a caffeine hit."

"Affirmative," said Becks.

"I'll go check on Bob," said Liam. "See how the fella's coming along."

Maddy nodded distractedly as she made her way to the computer station. "Now let's see what's what," she muttered as she sat down in the chair and swiveled around to face the monitors. A dialogue box popped up.

> **Hello, Maddy. How was the musical performance?**

"We call it a 'gig,' Bob."

> **How was the gig?**

"It was cool, very cool, and I'll tell you all about it later. Right now I need to hook into the external Internet link and do a search."

> **Affirmative. External feed active.**

She pulled up the system's search engine and tapped into their connection with the World Wide Web. "What was the name of that movie again?"

"*The Manuscript,*" said Sal, taking a seat beside her.

She pinched her lip. "Like I say, never heard of it. And, sheesh, I *love* DiCaprio."

The search engine spewed out a page of hits, every last one to do with the movie: reviews, good and bad—mostly bad; entertainment news; and dedicated film sites all chattering about Leonardo. She picked a website she used to regularly tap into from her bedroom back in 2010, Ain't It Cool News. She smiled at how primitive it looked back in 2001.

Good ol' World Wide Web version 1.0.

. . . directed by Don Rowney, a change of pace for the director who normally makes drippy romantic comedies. *The Manuscript* starts out with an interesting high-concept premise before nose-diving and becoming a pretty dull, dial-it-in chase movie. The first twenty minutes of the film introduce us to what it calls the "Most Mysterious Manuscript in History"— something I thought was a made-up story device until I did my homework: the Voynich Manuscript, apparently a book-length document that first surfaced in the Middle Ages, written entirely in a gibberish language that, to this day, has yet to be successfully deciphered. DiCaprio, still hot from his fresh-faced role in James Cameron's *Titanic*, plays Adam Davies, a hacker and cryptolinguist—a code-breaker—who manages to write a piece of software that unlocks the Voynich and foolishly decides to brag about his achievement to family and friends and fellow hackers. But, as is always the case, it isn't long before the bad guys—the nastiest kind of shady government spooks—come knocking, concerned that Davies's code-breaking software could be equally successful at unlocking the intelligence community's deepest and darkest secrets. The movie is based on a supposedly true story culled from the British press—the real culprit, Adam Lewis, a hacker from England, was written off as an attention-seeking loner after the story appeared in a British newspaper called the *Sun* back in 1994 . . .

Maddy looked at Sal. "Interesting."

"I wonder if that's the same Leonardo DiCaprio as the old man who bought a whole chunk of the Antarctic, like, earlier this year." She looked at the others. "I mean *my* year, you know? 2026. He went to live there among the penguins. To protect them from oil drillers or something."

"You gotta be kidding me. Seriously?"

Sal shrugged. "Might be someone else. Pretty sure the name was DiCaprio."

Maddy shook her head at the thought of it before returning to the task at hand. She searched for "Adam Lewis" and "1994" and "Voynich Manuscript." As Maddy trawled through the hits that came back, Becks cleared a space on the cluttered desk and placed a mug of black coffee in front of her.

"Thanks." She scanned the hits and finally picked a link and clicked on it. A moment later the screen went black and a banner logo appeared: a red flaming eye.

"Oh look, bingo-bango-bongo," she said, reaching for the coffee. "Let's see what this gives us."

The article was a lazy cut-and-paste job from a tabloid newspaper onto some guy's conspiracy-theory website, *Dark Eye*.

> . . . Adam Lewis, a student earning a degree in Computer Studies at the University of East Anglia. The computer geek, looking more like a ragged, bearded animal-rights protester than a Microsoft pencil-neck, claimed in an article posted to *New Scientist* magazine that he had singlehandedly achieved

what historians, code-breakers, and several big American mainframe computer systems have all failed to do: produce a single legible phrase from the mysterious leather-bound book known to historians and code-hounds as the Voynich Manuscript.

Lewis, 19, laughingly admits that the deciphered phrase sounds a lot like something that might have come out of the kind of Dungeons & Dragons fantasy games he loves to play with fellow geeks. The sentence he supposedly managed to produce from a passage in the Voynich Manuscript, which he's not prepared to identify, is this: "Pandora is the word. The word leads to truth. Fellow traveler, time to come and find it."

Maddy spurted hot coffee over the back of her hand.

Sal looked at her, concerned. "Maddy? You okay?"

Maddy sat back in the chair, glasses in her hands, absently wiping the lenses as she gazed wide-eyed and unfocused at the monitor in front of her.

"Maddy? What's up? What's the matter?"

She shook her head, chewing her lip for a while before finally turning to Sal, with Becks still towering over them in platform heels and looking bemused. "I think . . . ," she started. "I've got a feeling this Voynich thing might just be the work of another team."

"Another team?" Sal's jaw slowly dropped open. "You mean . . . another group, like us? TimeRiders?"

Maddy hunched her shoulders. "I think we're not alone, folks."

Chapter 7

2001, New York

"You sure about this, Mads? I mean, it's just a sentence, that's all. And it doesn't really say anything anyway."

All three of them were slumped in the threadbare armchairs around the wooden kitchen table. Maddy had printed out the web pages she'd read on-screen. Despite explaining her point (very clearly, *she* thought), Liam still didn't seem to have grasped it.

"The point is, Liam," she tried again. "The point is, this Voynich Manuscript could be a document used by another team to communicate forward from the past, just like you did with the museum's guest book and that fossilized message. Now, if someone's managed to decode some of it, then maybe they'll decode more of it, or *all* of it, and God knows what sensitive agency messages are in there. If they think their code's unbreakable, they could be saying all kinds of stuff."

"And the agency *is* to be super-secret," added Sal.

Liam pursed his lips. "All right, guess I see your point . . ."

Maddy sighed, not so much frustrated with Liam for being slow on the uptake, but more because she was keeping something from him, and from Sal too. It felt wrong, unfair, and worst of all, it made her feel lonely. She remembered word for word the scribbled message she'd found in that deposit box in 1906, and it was beginning to haunt her dreams.

Maddy, look out for "Pandora," we're running out of time. Be safe and tell no one.

More than a message, it seemed like a warning. No, it *was* a warning. But a warning of what?

"Well, surely we don't need to go right now, though, do we?" moaned Liam. "It's late, so it is, and my head's still ringing from that noise you call music. And I'm tired as—"

"In the morning, then," Maddy cut in. "We all need a good night's sleep, anyway. I'm still a little hazy."

"Good plan," agreed Liam.

"But this time it's not *you* who's going back, Liam."

The other two looked at Maddy. "What?"

You going to tell them about Pandora, Maddy? You ready to do that? No, she decided, at least not yet. Not until she knew a little more.

"*I'm* going, and I'll take Becks with me for security, of course, but you need to watch over Bob. If I'm delayed and he's ready to hatch, he needs to see you first. You remember what Foster said—the clone imprints on the first person he sees. *Bonds* with them. You should be here for his birth."

"True." He nodded. She knew he didn't want to miss that moment.

"And, look, it's not exactly like I'm heading somewhere super-dangerous. It's England, 1994." She turned to Becks, standing patiently at the end of the table. "Where is it, exactly?"

"Information: Adam Lewis is a registered sophomore at the University of East Anglia in the city of Norwich."

"A college campus . . . there. Hardly dangerous." She grinned. "Maybe even fun."

"I could come," said Sal hopefully.

"Sorry, not this time, Sal. It's probably best if you're here too, watching for signs. We've had one small ripple, and there could be more on the way."

Sal huffed. "Why do *you* always get to decide everything now?"

"I'm sorry, it's . . ." Maddy sighed. "Foster made me leader, Sal. So I'm supposed to *lead*. That's the way it is. I wish it weren't. I wish somebody else was calling the shots. I wish Foster was still here, to be honest. But it is what it is."

"Just seems unfair."

"All of this is *unfair*! I didn't want to come here. I didn't choose to die in a plane crash at eighteen. I had plans, you know? I wanted to do more with my life than watch a bunch of computer screens and live in this crappy dump." She could have said more. Things she'd regret later. It was bad enough having to be in charge when she barely felt she had a grasp on how things worked. But, added to that, somebody somewhere seemed to be trying to warn her about something, and she was way too stupid to get it.

The moment tasted sour, and all of a sudden she felt tired. She looked at her watch: it was after two in the morning. "Look, I'm hitting the mattress. Maybe we all should. It's late, and we've got stuff to do tomorrow."

She got up and headed into the arched recess where their bunks were, pulling a curtain across as she changed into her PJs.

Liam looked at Sal and shrugged, both of them perplexed at her mood. "Maybe she's missing home?"

"Aren't we all?" said Sal.

Chapter 8

2001, New York

Maddy and Becks were treading water in the plexiglass tube one moment, and gone—along with sixty gallons of diluted disinfectant solution—the next. The large plastic tube flexed inward with a loud thud that echoed through the archway.

"Jay-zus! Does it always do that?"

Sal nodded. "The pressure of all the water suddenly not there . . . it makes the plexiglass flex."

"Oh, right." He looked around at Sal sitting patiently beside him, hands crossed in her lap. "So what normally happens now?"

Her smile was resigned. "We haven't had 'normal' yet. Either we've been hiding from cannibal mutants or we've had secret-service agents knocking on the door." She laughed skittishly. "It seems like we've been hopping from one crisis to the next since we first arrived here, doesn't it?"

Liam nodded. "Well then, while it appears the sky hasn't yet fallen on our heads again, and while we're waiting for this machinery to recharge, perhaps Miss Vikram would like to go for breakfast in one of those charming Scottish restaurants."

"Scottish restaurants?"

"One of them McDougal places?"

"McDonalds?"

"Aye, that's the fella. The ones with the big fancy yellow 'M.'"

She made a face. "Breakfast sounds good . . . but maybe somewhere else."

Chapter 9

May 1994, UEA campus, Norwich

Opening the portal in the university's swimming pool after closing time had seemed like a good idea to Maddy back in the archway. They'd arrive wet, but there would be changing facilities, and hopefully a blow-dryer or a towel or something. But now, floundering beneath the water in total darkness, not knowing which way was up and which way was down, she realized it ranked pretty high on her Not To Be Tried Again list.

Suddenly Maddy felt Becks's hand grasping her, followed by a hearty yank and her face breaking the surface. She coughed, retched, and spluttered as Becks swam to the side of the pool, pulling her after.

"Recommendation: this was not a good idea."

"No, really?" she gasped.

Becks nodded firmly, not yet a master of irony. "Yes. You could have drowned."

Maddy eased herself out of the cold water and flopped, exhausted, onto the side. She looked around. The university's sports center was closed now, the swimming pool dark, lit only by the dim amber glow of street lights outside, strips of orange light leaking through the drawn blinds along the racing-lane side of the pool.

"All right, well . . . we're here now. We've got four hours. So let's get dry and changed. And then we'll go find this Adam Lewis."

Adam's nerves were getting the better of him. He needed to get a grip.

"Get a grip," he muttered to the face in his mirror. A lean face of freckles and acne, framed by the pitifully feeble sprouting of an auburn beard. Auburn—not ginger. That's what he kept telling everyone. And the ratty twists and turns of greasy hair tied back in a ponytail, they were flippin' auburn too.

His eyes looked back at him through round-framed Lennon glasses.

"You look terrible," he told himself.

Well, why not? he argued back. *I've got every right to look terrible.*

Why not indeed. He was scared. Really scared. He hadn't stepped out of his room now for, what—four, five days? Missed half a dozen study halls and lectures, and his roommates were beginning to mutter about him in the hallway outside his door. They'd already thought he was a bit of an oddball before . . . well, before *this.*

Outside it was dark. Eleven. He could hear the thud of music coming from the floor below. He recognized it: Red Hot Chili Peppers. His roommates were playing *Mario Brothers* on the SNES; there was a lot of noise, the *clack-fissss* of cans of beer being popped open, and laughing, lots of laughing . . . most probably about him.

Not so big a deal to him now. A week ago stuff like that—being a loner, being perceived as the resident freak—got him down a bit. But he brushed off the quips and sniggering at his expense the way every hardened geek does, by acting as if far greater matters were on his mind, matters these beer-swilling jerks wouldn't even begin to understand.

One day I'll be flying business class . . . and you idiots, you'll be serving fries somewhere.

That was the sort of thing he usually said aloud. The guys laughed and shook their heads at his lame and faltering comeback. But he quietly smiled, because he knew it was undoubtedly going to be true.

And that, he figured, was how he and every other geek coped with being the frozen-out loner—the certainty that there would come a day of mega payback for all the jibes and the sniggering.

But right now he really *did* have far, far greater matters on his mind. *Why me? How do they know my name? Oh God . . . who are "they"?*

All of a sudden the throbbing music and the drunken guffawing stopped. He realized the front doorbell to their apartment had just gone off. He licked dry, cracked lips and realized he was holding his ragged breath to better hear who was down there at the door; to hear who'd come knocking at so late an hour.

He could hear Lance's Glaswegian accent . . . and who else? Another murmuring voice. Quiet, polite, businesslike. Female.

Lance was trying some witty banter, loosened up by the beer. His easy Celtic charm usually worked flawlessly on the "freshers," freshman girls looking for an older, wiser university boyfriend. But, from the murmuring tone of this female visitor, she seemed wholly uninterested.

He heard Lance's attitude suddenly change; clearly facing rejection for the first time in his life. He sounded like a petulant child. "Well, if you really want to see the freak . . . he's upstairs. Second door on the right."

Adam heard footsteps on the uncarpeted hallway and up the wooden stairs.

His heart was pounding in his chest, his stomach suddenly churning like a spin dryer.

"Oh G-God . . . it's . . ."

Them.

His mind spun between two options: go for the window, clamber out, drop down outside and run for his life—or stay put and meet them. See what they wanted from him.

Oh God, oh God, oh God . . .

Maddy stood outside the door. She turned to look at Becks before gently rapping on it with her knuckles. "Adam Lewis?"

There was no answer. But she heard someone stirring inside, the clunk and scrape of footsteps.

"Adam?" she called softly. "Can we talk to you?"

A long pause. Downstairs she could hear the murmur of male voices, no doubt talking about her and Becks. Actually, probably just Becks. She was well aware the support unit tended to attract the gaze of excitable testosterone-fueled young men. Finally she heard a shuffling sound from just beyond the door.

"*Who . . . who are y-you?*" a voice said through the keyhole.

"My name's Maddy."

"*Are y-you . . . h-here to g-get me?*" The voice sounded pitiful, thin with fear.

"No. I'm not here to *get* you. I just want to talk to you."

"I . . . did what I was told. I d-did exactly . . . w-what it told me to d-do."

Maddy had no idea what he was talking about. But she decided the only way she was going to get him to open the door was to mention something very specific.

"Adam . . . I'm here about a particular word."

Silence.

"I'm here to talk about 'Pandora.'"

She heard the dull click of the lock turning and the door cracked open an inch. A pale face dotted with pimples and the glint of glasses appeared in the space between the door and frame. "Are y-you . . . are you . . . *the one?*"

Go on, Maddy, play along with him. She offered him a reassuring smile. "Sure, I'm *the one*."

"The . . . the one who w-will explain? B-because I n-need to know . . . I . . . I . . ."

"I'll do my very best, Adam . . . if you'll just let us in."

The crack widened another half-inch as the glinting of spectacles shifted to study Becks. "And who's *she?*"

"She's a friend. She's harmless. Just a friend."

"D-does she know? A-about . . . P-Pandora?"

"Yes."

Adam studied them both for another few seconds before his face finally pulled back into the darkness and, with a creak of worn hinges, the door swung slowly open, inviting them in.

Chapter 10

1994, Norwich

It was too dark to see anything, but the room she stepped into smelled musty. A room, she guessed, that was probably littered with dirty clothes and underwear lying in crumpled piles. "Can we have a light on in here?" she asked.

"Y-yes, sure." A moment later a bedside lamp clicked on.

The room was as small and messy as she'd expected. But the walls—the walls made her catch her breath. She'd taken a couple of college courses before dropping out and getting a programming job. She'd had a room like this once, and covered its walls with posters of sci-fi movies she loved like *Aliens*, *Predator*, *Serenity*, computer games, bands, and stuff.

But this—this was plain weird.

All four walls seemed to be covered with sheets of paper filled with the handwritten scrawl of strange-looking hieroglyphics.

"So you're pretty into—what? Egyptian stuff?" she said, breaking the silence.

"Uh . . . oh,yeah. No, it's not hieroglyphics. I'm into cryptanalysis." He turned back to her. "You—you said you're the one, right? That's w-who you are? The one who explains it?"

Now that they were through the door, she decided it was going to be best to come clean and confess she really didn't know much, if anything. "Adam, we're here because of a message you posted on the Net."

"Net?"

Maddy shook her head. Of course, back in 1994 they called it the Web. A different language for the technology they took for granted in 2010. "You posted on the university's public forum that you'd decoded a complete sentence of the . . ." She forgot the name of the thing.

"The Voynich Manuscript," said Becks, helping her out.

He nodded his head vigorously. "Yes—yes. I did! That's what, that's exactly what I was instructed to do. I—I did exactly what I was told. I did what—"

"'Told'? By whom?"

Adam looked from Maddy to Becks, then back again, completely bewildered. "By *you*. I was kind of thinking you're involved."

"Not me." Maddy shook her head. "I never heard of the Voynich Manuscript until last night."

Adam still appeared completely on edge and wary of them both. "Never heard of it?"

"Nope."

He licked dry lips. "So you *can't* be the one. You can't tell me why my name's in the—"

Maddy raised her hands to calm him down. "I know about Pandora, Adam. I know that much."

He regarded her suspiciously.

"You're involved . . . us too, in whatever this means. I'm just trying to make some sense of it. I need to know what it means too. Please," she said softly, "why don't you tell me about this Voynich document?"

His eyes flickered uncertainly from her to Becks.

"Please?" She spread her hands in a disarming way. "Then maybe the three of us can figure this out together. Huh?"

"Yeah, sure." He seemed relieved at the suggestion, relieved to have somebody else to share what he knew.

As an afterthought he nodded toward a stool and a beanbag chair. "Want to sit down?"

Maddy smiled. "Thanks." She unzipped her jacket, laid it on the bed, and gestured to Becks to settle down on the beanbag. She was going to look less intimidating that way than standing over them both like a guard dog.

"So?" Maddy looked at Adam expectantly.

He sat down on the end of his bed. "It's the ultimate challenge for code-breakers," he started. "A several-hundred-page document that's been carbon-dated back to the twelfth century. The entire volume is written in a completely unknown language. I mean the whole thing is a bunch of characters and glyphs that have never been used in *any* other written form."

Adam's ragged nerves seemed to be settling a little. "People have been trying to decipher this thing since the seventeenth century when it was first discovered. It's been floating around from one archived library to another. Spent a hundred years or so in the papal library in Rome until the Jesuit order desperately needed some cash and sold off a whole section of their library in 1912. It was in a job lot bought by a trader in old manuscripts named Wilfrid Voynich. He found it buried among crates of old papal paperwork. He had it for a while and tried selling it to various collectors. He realized there was something very special about it. He never did manage to sell it, though."

"What happened to it?"

"He died in 1930 and left it to his wife. She died in 1960 and left it to a friend who sold it to another dealer, a guy named Hans Kraus. Like Voynich, he took it around to a bunch of collectors hoping to make some money, but no one took it. Eventually Kraus donated it to Yale University in 1969." He opened a bottle of flat Pepsi and took a gulp. "And that's when it became public domain. Ever since then code-breakers and linguistic hackers have all been taking a crack at it." He offered a cup of Pepsi to Maddy. She nodded and took a polite sip.

"It really is the most incredible coded document in history," he continued. "No one—I mean *no one*—has managed to extract a single meaningful sentence from it, not even one word."

"Until you did."

He nodded. "Until I managed to decipher that, uhh . . . that bit, yeah."

"Information," said Becks. "Adam Lewis is exhibiting behav-ioral stress indicators. He is concealing truth from you, Maddy."

Adam looked at her suspiciously. "Are you two some sort of secret-service types?"

Maddy laughed. "God, no!" She cocked an eyebrow. "Becks here is pretty paranoid. She's good at spotting things like this. So, is she right? Is there something you're not telling me, Adam?"

"I . . ." He swallowed, his Adam's apple bobbing like a fisherman's float. "Okay . . . all right, I—I deciphered a little more than the sentences I made public."

"How much more?"

He looked up uncertainly at Maddy. "How do I know I can trust you?"

Maddy shook her head. "I can't help you make sense of this unless you tell us what you've got, Adam." She looked at him, then around the room. Clearly the poor young man had been holed up in here for too many days, presumably too frightened to step outside. "You want someone to share this with, don't you?"

His head nodded vigorously. "I . . . yes. Actually, I'm totally freaked. This is seriously hard-core. I . . . Jesus, tell me you can make sense of this stuff!"

"We'll do our best, Adam. Just let me know what you decoded."

He licked his lips again, took a deep breath, and steadied his nerves. "All right, then . . . okay, this is how it goes." He took another slurp from the two-liter bottle of Pepsi.

"*You must make public the last part of this message, Adam Lewis, and*

I promise you someone will come and explain everything. When she comes, it is important you tell her this: 'Seek Cabot at Kirklees in 1194.' Do not reveal any more of this message to anyone else. The last part now follows. Pandora is the word. The word leads to truth. Fellow traveler, time to come and find it."

"That's *all* of it?"

He nodded.

Maddy turned to Becks. "What do you think?"

"At this time I can offer no data."

Adam stood up. "I really have to pee. You're gonna stick around, right?"

Maddy nodded and watched him tiptoe across the messy floor and open the door to an equally grubby bathroom. She waited until she heard the door lock click before turning to Becks. "My God, Becks—this Voynich Manuscript, it's a drop-point document! It has to be! It's got to be another team, don't you think?"

Becks's eyes fluttered—processing was going on inside. "It is possible. It is also possible this is a document that will be used at a later date by your team."

Maddy shook her head. "No, there's no way I'd use it now. Because it's . . . look, now I *know* it's been decoded by some teen hacker, I certainly wouldn't allow Liam to use it to talk through time to us. Not now that we know it's compromised, that it's been hacked. And I'll tell Liam when we get back, of course. So, look, whatever happens in the future, we know we can't use it. Therefore it *has* to be someone else."

Becks nodded. "A logical argument."

"What we've got to do is get back home to 2001. Then I'll send a warning message into the future, to 2056. I'll send a warning that the Voynich Manuscript isn't safe for *any* other teams to be using."

Becks nodded approval.

There was the sound of a flushing toilet, and a moment later the lock clacked and Adam emerged. Maddy hastily picked up her jacket from his bed. "Adam," she said, "we have to leave. We've got a . . . a train to catch."

His jaw dropped open. "But—but you said . . ."

"We can't stay, I'm really sorry."

"But I need someone to explain what this means!"

Maddy shook her head. "Sorry." She pointed at the door and Becks reached to open it.

"Please don't go! I—I'm completely freaked here! *Who* wrote that message? Why was it *me* who deciphered it? Why me?" Adam grabbed at her arm, holding it tight.

"I don't know, Adam. But, look, we have to go. When I know what this all means, I'll come back, okay? I'll come back and tell you! I promise!"

"Please! Don't go!" His grasp was tightening. Hurting her.

Becks noticed, and with one swift movement she grabbed his finger and twisted it savagely back. He screamed with pain and released his grip.

"Ahhh! Jesus! It's broken!"

Maddy winced. "I'm really sorry, Adam. . . . We'll be back, I promise." She stumbled out the open door and into the hall, down the noisy wooden steps and past the young man who'd answered the door. "Everything okay, girls?" he asked as they swept through the hallway toward the front door.

"Fine," said Maddy hastily.

He reached out an arm in front of Becks, blocking her way. "Sure you don't wanna stay and share a few beers with me and the boys? We could part-eee, sweetheart."

Her cold gray eyes locked on him—calmly assessing what level of force would be appropriate to remove the obstruction from her path—but Maddy stepped in and casually pushed his arm out of her way. "I really wouldn't recommend doing that—she's, uh . . . she can get quite *touchy*."

Chapter II

2001, New York

Liam's stomach was groaning from the burden of consuming a dozen pancakes glistening with maple syrup. He belched so loudly it made Sal jump.

"*Shadd-yah*, you are too gross!"

"Sorry," he uttered, shamefaced, as he sat down in front of the computer screen. "Hello, Bob."

> **Hello, Liam. Did you enjoy a good breakfast?**

"I did, thank you. Although I'm feelin' as sick as a butcher's dog."

> **Information: I have two notifications for you. The displacement machine is fully charged and ready to activate the return portal. Also, the support unit in growth-cycle is now ready to be ejected.**

"Thanks, Bob. Looks like you're going to be walking around with the living again soon enough."

> **I am very pleased. I enjoyed working with you in the past, Liam O'Connor.**

"And me with you. Be good to have another man about the place, so it will. It's gettin' all frilly and girlie in here."

> **I do not understand. Please explain "frilly and girlie."**

"Just a turn of phrase, Bob." He looked to Sal, making a face at her. "Well, *I'm* not frilly and girlie," she huffed.

Liam chuckled. "All right, Bob, which should we do first? Bring back the ladies or toss the new clone out of his tube?"

> **Recommendation: I suggest activating the return portal first.**

"Right you are. Let's get a wiggle on and do that, then."

Chapter 12

1994, UEA campus, Norwich

Maddy checked her watch: they had a few minutes to spare before the portal was due to open. The return coordinates were outside, beside a service entrance behind the university's pool building. It was 2 a.m., and the hustle of life after dark on the campus had died down to the snuffling of a fox going through bags of garbage nearby and the far-off wail of a police siren.

"Becks?"

"Yes."

"I need to discuss something. It's something that—" She frowned as she tried to find the right words. "It's something I've been keeping from the other two, because . . . well, because I have to. But I need someone else to talk to about it. It's driving me nuts."

"You wish to talk to me confidentially?"

"Yes, but I know everything I say to you becomes data. Everything you see and hear become data that're available to the others."

"I can partition my hard drive and create a folder that is accessible only after a certain code word is used. Data that is acquired while the partition is open will be stored there. The partition can be closed again and access-locked with the use of the same or a different code word."

"Do you mean everything you hear and see . . . ? If we were to have a conversation while this partition is open, the memory of it would remain in there? Would stay a secret?"

"That is correct. My normal functioning AI would also not be aware of those memories until you activated them with the code word."

Maddy understood. It would almost be as if Becks was operating as a schizophrenic: a person with multiple-personality disorder, unaware of the actions of the *other* personality. A little bit weird, to be honest. But she needed someone to help her make sense of things, someone to help her connect the dots. Something was going on out there, someone wanted her to know something—only her.

"Do that, please, Becks: set up your separate partition."

"Affirmative."

Becks's eyes blinked rapidly, her cool emotionless gaze lost and far away for a moment.

"Information: partitioned drive ready. Please provide an access code."

"What—anything? Any word?"

"Recommendation: three words, one after the other, that would not normally appear next to each other in sequence during a normal conversation. This would provide adequately strong security."

"What, like . . . banana—alien—jigsaw?"

"Correct. Is this your code-word sequence?"

"No, hold on. I'd forget that. Let me think." She rubbed at her chin thoughtfully as the police siren faded, leaving the night still and quiet.

"Okay, this'll do: iPad—caveman—breakfast."

"This is your code-word sequence?"

"Yes."

Becks blinked again. "Security measure activated. The partition is open." She turned slowly to look at Maddy. "I am listening, Maddy."

"Okay." Maddy blew out a breath. "Okay . . . this is what I've been keeping from Liam and Sal. When we went to get some new clone fetuses, back before that whole dinosaur mess—before you were grown, Becks—we got the fetuses from the San Francisco drop point, the one based in 1906. There was this safe deposit box where we found a crate of refrigerated embryos. But also there was this note—all scribbled, like somebody had tried to sneak it in real quick. It was a message addressed to *me*, for my eyes only. Liam didn't see it. So it's just me who knows about it."

Becks nodded. "Do you wish to tell me what the message was?"

"You promise me this is all secret?"

She nodded. "It is password protected. When you have finished discussing the matter with me and speak the code-word sequence, my normal AI will only be aware that a duration of time has passed without sensory data being collected."

"Right. Okay. Well, this was what the note said: *Maddy, look out for 'Pandora,' we're running out of time. Be safe and tell no one.*"

Becks nodded and looked at her. "This is why you instructed Liam not to come along on this mission?"

"That's right. And, obviously, when I saw the phrase this Adam guy decoded and posted publicly, it contained the word 'Pandora.'" She bit her lip for a moment. "My God, Becks, I can only think it's someone trying to contact me through this Voynich thing."

"The Voynich Manuscript is approximately nine hundred years old."

"I know! I know! That's what's so creepy! Somebody nearly a thousand years ago wants to talk to me. Why?"

"I have no data to answer that."

"And what was that weird stuff Adam said he had to tell me?"

"'*Seek Cabot at Kirklees in 1194.*'"

"What's a Cabot? Or who?"

"I have no data at this time."

"We need to go back there, Becks. If '1194' is a year! We've got to go back to that time and find out what Pandora means, what it refers to. And why it's me—*me*, of all people—who needs to know."

"That would seem the logical next step." Becks raised a hand. "I am detecting tachyon particles."

Maddy looked at her watch. They'd run out of time to talk this through; the portal was moments away from arriving. "Becks, can we talk about this again?"

"Affirmative. You should close the partition with the code-word sequence now. When you wish to resume this conversation, repeat the sequence to open my drive."

"Okay. Here it is, then: iPad—caveman—breakfast."

Becks blinked rapidly several times, then her head cocked to one side, curious. "I appear to have two minutes and thirty-two seconds of unlogged time." She turned to Maddy. "Did I malfunction in any way?"

The air in front of them pulsed, stirring plastic bags and newspapers into chasing each other in the dark. Ahead she could see the shimmering forms of their colleagues: Sal waving, Liam doing bunny ears behind her head.

"No, you've been just fine, Becks. Perfectly fine. Let's go home."

Chapter 13

1994, Norwich

Adam's hand throbbed. The tall girl with the surprisingly strong grip hadn't in fact broken his finger, just stretched the tendons in his hand. Not broken, but still incredibly painful. Under normal circumstances it would have been painful enough for him to take himself to the campus clinic for a splint or icepack and some serious painkillers, but he was distracted enough that the throbbing in his finger was, for the moment, ignorable.

It can't be. That's what his mind was muttering to itself. *It just can't be.*

"*What we've got to do is get back home to 2001.*" That's what the girl with the glasses had said while he'd stood in the bathroom, holding his breath and listening to them. "*Then I'll send a warning message into the future, to 2056.*"

He'd nearly laughed out loud at that. If he had, it would have been the shrill humorless laugh of someone losing his mind. Because this—the stuff they were saying—it was plain crazy, right? Because . . . because 2001 was seven years from now. 2001 was the future.

Mission Control to Adam, his mind chastised him. *Are you about to tell yourself that they're time travelers? Is that it? Have you really gone that insane?*

He nodded and chuckled to himself. "Yes . . . that's it. Maybe I've gone completely nuts." He was halfway to accepting that was what was wrong with him. His two visitors, his throbbing finger, all of it, were just elements of a paranoid delusion. After all, he'd been hiding out in this room for nearly a week, living like a hermit. Beginning to see things.

He decided that the sensible little voice in his head was probably right, that this was a sign it was time to go see a campus counselor. And maybe, just maybe, he or she could explain to him in a perfectly rational way why he'd found a message, written in modern English, in a document nearly a thousand years old; why he was imagining visitations from time-traveling girls from the future.

He laughed at how crazy it all sounded.

He was just about ready to admit he'd gone completely insane when he noticed a scrap of paper on his bed where the girl—*Maddy, that's her name; that's what your hallucinated visitor called herself, wasn't it?*— had placed her jacket. He reached over tentatively to pick it up, hoping it was just one more example of his mind playing tricks on him and it would vanish in a puff of delusion before he even managed to touch it.

Only it didn't.

"Ummm. Adam to Mission Control. It's, uhh, it's . . . ," he muttered, turning the piece of colored paper over in his hand. "This is real? Right? I'm not hallucinating *this*, am I?"

Mission Control had nothing useful to add at this point in time.

He looked closely at the paper in his hand. It was a ticket stub. An entry ticket to what appeared to be a nightclub or a bar or something. The address was West 51st Street, New York. What's more, it had a date and an admission time stamped faintly like ticker-tape along the bottom.

12:21—09-09-2001.

All of a sudden he felt light-headed: dizzy and queasy, excited and terrified at the same time. He looked again at the lightly printed time and date: September 9, 2001, seven years from now, the girl who'd just left his room was going to go to this New York nightclub.

It was one thing too many for him. He lost his balance and flopped face-first onto his mattress.

Outside he heard the clump of boots on the stairs, and a moment later a heavy fist on his door. "Hey, Adam! Who were those girls?" Lance's voice sounded far away; it sounded utterly inconsequential.

"Suit yourself; you stay in there, you little freak. But tell your weird friends not to come around so late next time, all right?"

Adam heard none of that. He was already busy mapping out the next seven years of his life.

"She's right," said Maddy. "It's not our old buddy yet. Just a meat combat unit."

"Og gub ber smuh," gurgled the clone in agreement.

"And just as moronic as he was last time," she added. "Come on, let's get him cleaned up and dressed, then we can start the software upload."

Liam placed a hand under one bulging arm, Becks under the other, and together they helped him to his feet. Liam winked at the bewildered-looking giant. "Welcome back, Bob."

Half an hour later, hosed down and no longer stinking like a pile of rotten meat, dried and dressed in a mix-and-match collection of oversized clothes, Bob sat motionless on Liam's bunk. His eyelids flickered rapidly as terabytes of data filled the empty silicon wafer embedded in his skull. Becks was overseeing the software transfer process, while Maddy had called the other two to join her around the kitchen table.

"So you see . . . we've got to at least go take a look. Make sure this Voynich Manuscript isn't going to totally give the game away." She shrugged. "It won't be a particularly secret agency much longer if one of our teams is blabbing away all our secrets in that document. Right?"

Liam nodded. "Sure."

"Does that mean Liam might meet another 'operative' like himself?" asked Sal.

Maddy shrugged. "It's entirely possible he'll make contact." She turned to him. "And if you do, then obviously the most important thing you need to communicate is that they *can't* use the Voynich Manuscript any longer. It's been compromised, okay?"

"Right."

"So . . ." Maddy consulted a pad of paper on the table. "The time we're sending you back to, Liam, is 1194—that's when Adam Lewis said the document carbon dates to." She looked up from her notes. "I don't think carbon dating can be *that* precise, but it's a specific year to aim for. And we're sending you to a place called Kirklees. That's in England."

Chapter 14

2001, New York

"All right, stand back, everyone!"

Sal crouched down and thumbed an icon on the growth tube's small glowing touchscreen. A motor softly whirred at the bottom of the plexiglass tube, and it slowly tilted backward to a forty-five-degree angle. A moment later the bottom of the tube opened and a flood of foul-smelling gunk splashed out onto the floor of the back room.

Bob's glistening, baby-smooth body slipped out of the tube and across the floor like a freshly landed blue marlin on the foredeck of a fishing boat.

"It's a boy!" announced Liam.

"This time," added Maddy.

The newly birthed clone stirred on the floor, his gray eyes opening and gazing up at them. They crouched around him, cooing like proud parents. "Liam," said Liam, pointing to himself. "My name's Liam."

The clone opened his mouth and vomited a river of pink gunk down the front of his muscular chest.

"Oh, that's our Bob, all right," said Sal.

"Negative." Becks squatted down to inspect the slimy naked body on the floor. "The AI designated 'Bob' has yet to be uploaded."

"Ahh now, I've been to England before. With me uncle and me dad, so."

"A place called Kirklees Priory. I did a search on it. It's famous because it's the place where Robin Hood died and was buried. Supposedly."

Liam's eyebrows shot up. "Robin Hood, did you say?"

Maddy laughed at his response. "Don't get your hopes up, Liam. From what I've pulled up, there seems to be a lot of evidence that Hood's just a myth: a story made up from a whole bunch of different sources. From old Saxon myths to, like, seventeenth-century highwayman stories."

"Oh." His face dropped. "And there was me hoping to become one of his Merry Men."

"Sorry. Now, listen closely. Historical records show this is a dangerous time. The king of England is Richard and he's abroad fighting some crusade. At home, there's a lot of unrest and stuff—bandits, anarchy, that kind of thing. So for safety I'm going to send *both* support units along with you, okay?"

Liam smiled. "I'll be fine, then. Me own little army."

"And, remember, all this is a quick look-see. If you can, I want you to find who or what 'Cabot' is, and talk to him. See if you can find out who's writing this Voynich Manuscript, and if it's another team like us, then you've got to make contact and warn them that the code's been broken, all right?"

"Aye."

"A secondary objective, Liam—if you can locate the manuscript, or come across whoever's writing it—if you can, find out how to decode it so we can see what *else* is in it." She glanced at both of them. "I don't know about you, but I'm tired of being totally in the dark about this agency. I want to know more, and if there's more we can find out . . ."

"Yeah," said Sal. "I want to know too."

The three of them were quiet for a moment.

"I don't know where this is taking us," said Maddy. "History has been changed a little. There's a movie out that wasn't there yesterday. And maybe that's all that's going to happen with this time wave and we don't need to correct things again. As Foster once said, history can tolerate *some* change. Maybe this Adam guy got lucky with those couple of sentences, and that's all anyone is ever going to get out of the manuscript. But I think we have to just take a look. Agreed?"

Liam nodded. "It's the time of knights an' all. I wouldn't mind seeing some of that."

"Cool. So, when Bob's ready, Sal, I want you, Liam, and the two units to go locate some clothing that won't attract attention. God knows what they wore then," she said, shrugging. "Potato sacks and sandals, for all I know."

"Okay. What about you?"

"I need to put together a data package for Bob and Becks so they're, you know, up to speed on all the relevant history." She looked at her watch. "It's just after ten. If we say launch time after lunch?" She nudged Liam. "Might as well get some pizza in before you go."

Chapter 15

2001, New York

He was watching the row of archways, not entirely certain which one they'd disappeared into last night. He'd let them get too far ahead; they'd turned into that backstreet and, by the time he'd arrived and looked down past the Dumpsters and bags of festering garbage, they were nowhere to be seen.

Nerves had gotten the better of him; he'd allowed himself to fall too far behind.

He could have gone down there, knocking on each shutter door, but he'd wimped out. Back at his apartment in the early hours, unable to sleep as New York finally stilled itself for a new Monday morning, he'd paced his living room, angry with himself. Seven years of anticipating this moment; seven years of waiting to talk to the girl again— and he'd wimped out and lost them down this street.

In all that time he'd played the memory of that night in his dorm room over and over in his head, trying to understand what it had been about. Trying to keep the memory of their faces fresh and vivid. Preparing himself to accept the possibility that this was for real, that the little ticket stub was actually going to reunite him with someone who'd traveled across time.

Adam had called work this morning and told them he was feeling sick, that he might not be in for a couple of days. Sherman Golding Investment would cope just fine without their IT systems security consultant for a little while.

Seven years. It felt like a lifetime ago, those unhappy university days. He'd never kept in touch with the moronic beer-heads he'd shared digs with. Couldn't care less what they were doing now. Because he was doing just fine. A nice Manhattan apartment, a gold American Express card, membership at an exclusive gym that overlooked the Hudson. He earned more money in a year than his old man earned in a decade. And he was really only a hacker in a nice suit.

But this life, this career, everything he'd planned and done since he was twenty-one, had been so he'd end up here in New York, so he could be there at *that* club on *that* night. His whole career, his whole life, governed by the faint print on a crumpled stub of colored paper.

Totally insane.

Now, watching this little backstreet in the morning, Mr. Sensible urged him to make a move. *Mission Control to Adam, time to go and say hello now, don't you think?*

The thought sent butterflies fluttering in formation around his gut.

Come on, Adam, you're a confident man now. Not that nerdy little weasel, not anymore. Right? A player. Not a loser—a WINNER! And winners don't sit around whining.

He nodded. "Right."

Mission Control says we're good to go. Time to do this.

It was then that he saw them. Four people emerging from one of the archways. He spotted the tall girl who'd twisted his finger nearly out of its socket. She looked no different. Wearing exactly the same clothes she'd been wearing that night—the very same clothes she'd been wearing seven years ago . . . and it looked like she hadn't aged a day! With her was a small Indian girl, thirteen, maybe fourteen. A young man perhaps a couple years older, and next to him a giant of a man. He had to be seven feet tall, at least a yard across the shoulders and over two hundred pounds of muscle.

That leaves the other girl. The one named Maddy. She'd been with this bunch last night. He'd watched her bouncing around amid the sweaty mob like a loon. He'd liked that kind of thrash music when he was a student. Not now, though. It was music for kids. He preferred jazz, classical, rhythm and blues. It better suited the sophisticated professional executive he'd become. All part of the new image. The new Adam.

Mission Control says go. Green light, pal. Time to knock. Or are you going to wuss out again?

"He who dares wins," he whispered.

That's the spirit.

He'd noted which archway they'd come out of. The fifth one along. He waited until the others had turned out of the backstreet and east to head into Brooklyn before he tossed the paper cup of bland coffee he'd been holding into a garbage can and took a first tentative step across the pedestrian walkway toward the dirty little backstreet.

"Here we go," he whispered.

Maddy heard the shutter door rattle as someone lightly tapped on it from outside. One of them must have forgotten something. She got up from the office chair and crossed the floor. Rubbing her eyes tiredly, she punched the green button and let the shutter clatter up to knee height before ducking down.

"What did you forg—?"

She looked up and saw a tall, tanned, well-groomed man in a very expensive-looking suit. He removed a pair of designer shades and smiled. "Uh . . . hi," he said with an English accent and a small, self-conscious wave.

"Excuse me?" she said. "Can I help you?"

He smiled. "You and I, we, uh . . . *met* some years ago."

Maddy frowned, confused for a moment. "I don't think so." Then she realized there was something about his face that looked vaguely familiar.

He shrugged. "I think I looked quite a bit different then. Long scruffy dreadlocks, pretty bad zits . . . and, if I recall correctly, I had a beard—if you can call it that. I don't think you caught me at my best." He smiled, a handsome expression on his lean, sculpted face. "But you," he said, shaking his head. "It's incredible! You don't seem to have changed one bit."

Her eyes widened with surprise. She suddenly recognized him. "Oh my God!" she whispered. "You're . . . you're that young—"

"Adam Lewis," he said, squatting down to face her. He offered his hand.

"How did you . . ." Her jaw flapped uselessly.

"How did I *find* you?"

She nodded.

He reached for the inside pocket of his well-tailored pinstripe jacket and pulled out a leather wallet. "I've kept this safe in here all these years. Every now and then, I pull it out and look at it, just to remind myself that I wasn't going crazy. That I didn't imagine that night." He pulled out a frayed and faded corner of paper and held it in the palm of his hand. "It's a little bit of litter you left in my room by mistake."

She could just make out the name of the club they'd been to last night. "I dropped that?"

He nodded.

He looked up at the clear blue sky and sighed. "I do believe, back in 1994, you promised to come back and tell me what the message was all about. So . . . how did you get on with finding the truth? Finding out what Pandora means?"

"Oh boy." She looked up and down the street. "I suppose you'd better come in."

Chapter 16

2001, New York

Adam straightened up inside, his eyes slowly adjusting from the bright September morning to the dimly lit interior.

"My God," he whispered, and turned to her. "This is your . . . your *base*?"

She nodded. "'Fraid so."

He took several hesitant steps across the floor toward the bank of computer monitors, the plexiglass cylinder, and the rack of machinery standing beside it. "And this? What is . . . ?"

"That's our time displacement unit," she replied, drawing up beside him. "We have to talk, Mr. Lewis."

He shook his head. "*Adam* will do. Clients call me 'Mr. Lewis.'"

"Fair enough. We have to talk about Pandora, Adam."

"You know what it means now?"

She shook her head. "No. Look, my colleagues don't know about it yet. I plan to tell them, but not yet, not until I know what it means." She looked at him. "Maybe you can help me. I need you to tell me everything you know about the Voynich. How you managed to decode it when no one else can. And how you've ended up here."

He nodded. "Yes . . . yes, of course."

"Let's sit." She gestured to one of the threadbare armchairs. "I'll make some coffee."

A couple of minutes later she sat down opposite him with two mugs of coffee and a package of Oreos.

"So?"

"Where do I begin?" Adam took off his suit jacket, laid it carefully over one arm of the chair, and loosened his tie. "Not long after you visited me I became a news story for a day. A national newspaper ran an article on me, and a story about the mysterious Voynich Manuscript became the next day's fish-and-chips wrapper." He laughed bitterly. "But the damage was done. Everyone at school knew who I was. A loony. A deluded little head case who made up the story just to get some attention."

"Why? You managed to decode it successfully. So you didn't explain *how* you did it? Show them you weren't a nutcase?"

"I *couldn't* explain the technique to anyone. I couldn't demonstrate the deciphering method."

"Why not?"

Adam sipped his coffee. "Because . . ." He sighed. "It sounds crazy." He shook his head. "Maybe because it is."

"Just tell me why you couldn't explain how you managed to decode it."

"Because I believe it used a cipher aimed specifically at *me*."

"What?"

"It was encrypted in a way that only *one* person in the world could unlock." His eyes widened, making him look more like the paranoid student he'd once been than the successful and groomed executive he was now. "Someone in 1194"—he laughed edgily—"knows me. Knows me *very* well." He sighed. "Okay, here goes," he said, sitting forward on the chair. "I was really interested in paleolinguistics—the study of dead languages—and I took a year off before graduation to go to South America with some others. We were following the trail of a pre-Aztec tribe called the Windtalkers. The theory was they had a form of writing long before the Aztecs arrived. Anyway, to make a long story short, I managed to locate a cave wall, high up on a cliff overlooking the rainforests, covered in this dead language, their glyphs. It's unique, Maddy. Completely unique. No one had ever discovered that cave, or written a paper on the Windtalkers and their language."

"Why not?"

"I guess because no other paleolinguist has discovered the cave since."

"And why didn't you make yourself famous then? Go public with your find?"

He shrugged. "Various reasons. I wanted to understand it first. I wanted to keep it to myself. It's also a unique character set. Perfect for encryption." He grinned coyly. "I use some of it in the work that I do now, creating software security ciphers. And that's why I'm one of the most sought-after IT security consultants in New York. The ciphers I write are unbreakable." He waved that comment away, embarrassed at how conceited it sounded. "Anyway, I'm telling you that because, well, because I spotted two very specific glyphs from the cave wall in the Voynich Manuscript."

Maddy nearly dropped an Oreo in her coffee.

"They're very important glyphs. They were used by the Windtalkers to separate ideas. Sentences, if you will. Much like we use a period and a capital letter. One glyph always appeared at the beginning of a sentence or an expression and the other at the end."

"So, what? You're telling me the Voynich was written by, like, *Aztecs*?"

"No. It's not. The glyphs are only used once." He raised a finger. "On just one occasion. The Voynich Manuscript is hundreds of pages crammed full of random characters, some of them Latin, some Egyptian, some Greek, some mathematical—and then there's this one passage of those same random characters, which begins with a Windtalker glyph and ends with one."

"My God!"

He nodded. "Yes, like it was flagged. Like someone was saying, *Focus on this passage alone.*" He stirred uneasily. "Like they were saying, *Focus on this passage, Adam Lewis.*"

A nervous grin skittered across Maddy's lips, then slipped away. "That is so-o-o creepy."

He nodded. "Anyway, I won't bore you with the technical details of breaking open a cipher, but if you can isolate a chunk of meaningful language from random gibberish—a technique often deployed to throw cryptanalysts off the scent—then it's just a matter of time before you can break it down. Those Windtalker markers were the reason I'm the only person who's ever managed to extract something meaningful from the Voynich."

He set his mug on the table. "And that's the reason why I couldn't explain myself publicly. That's why I was dismissed as an attention-seeking nut. I couldn't say some medieval guy *knew* I was going to take a field trip to the Amazon and discover the key to breaking the code! I just had to take all the criticism on the nose. It's a period in my life I've tried to put behind me." He smiled. "Then of course this damn film comes out." He sighed. "Luckily they changed the character's last name."

"And who'd want to be portrayed by Leonardo DiCaprio, eh?"

They both laughed politely at that.

Maddy sized him up silently. She realized he already knew too much, that at some point they were going to have to undo history and see to it that Adam Lewis never found his way here. Until then, though, he appeared to be a reluctant part of this mystery, linked to Pandora somehow. Perhaps even the key to it all. Just like his pre-Aztec glyphs.

"Cookie?"

Chapter 17

2001, New York

"So where's this place you're taking us?" asked Liam.

"It's a theater and antique junk shop that does expensive costume rentals. The clothes are the *real* thing, not all the nasty cheap polyfabric and synthetic *shadd-yah* you get in, like, joke shops."

"Polly . . . ?"

"Horrible." Sal shuddered. "In my time, my parents used to wear bright-colored polyfab kurtas and these imported jogging suits . . . and plastic jewelry. Ugh. Hideous. There," she said, gesturing along the street. "It's just a couple of blocks down this way."

"Right-oh," he said, nodding. "It'll be good to try on something more comfortable."

She looked him up and down. "You don't like the jeans and the hoodie?"

He couldn't help but grimace a little. "The trousers seem a little tight around my legs, so they do. It's quite difficult to walk. And it's rubbing me sore in places I'd rather not talk about."

She quickly lifted up the bottom of his hoodie and laughed at what she saw. "That's because you're wearing the waist way-y-y too high. They should, you know, hang really low." Liam had the belt cinched tightly and the waistband of his Diesel jeans pulled up high over his hips to just beneath his navel. With that, the T-shirt underneath neatly tucked in, and his shock of gray-white hair, he looked like an old man.

"It's all got to hang loose and low, you know? *Jahulla*, you wear trousers like my great-grandfather wears them, tucked up under his armpits."

"Well, that's where a pair of trousers should be. Not around your knees."

She huffed and rolled her eyes. "You'd never fit in in 2026. Even if I dressed you up in the streetiest polyfab booger suit and loads of chump-bling around your neck, you'd still stand out like a *Nārāza aṅgūṭhē*!"

He forced out a weary smile. "I think I prefer the way people used to dress in the past to the way they do in the future. It all seems to be about lookin' as poor and scruffy as you can. I mean, tell me, why is it that people deliberately rip holes in their trousers? I've seen that several times now."

"In their jeans, you mean?"

"Aye."

She shrugged. "It's just the fashion. I don't know, to make them look older than they are, I guess."

He shook his head and circled a finger at his temple. "There! See? That's just completely peculiar, that is. Back home my mother was always trying to keep all me school clothes and me Sunday suit looking as new as if they'd just come out of a shop."

"Well, I guess in your time clothes were really expensive. In Mumbai, in my time—even now in 2001, I guess—it's all so cheap. You wear something a couple of times, then you just sort of throw it away."

"That sounds like such a waste to me."

Sal shrugged. Maybe that was why in 2026 the news always seemed to be about this or that running low: the world's resources, one by one, finally exhausted. She vaguely remembered news reports on *Digi-HD-Sahyadri* of the oil shortages. Wars in far-away countries full of deserts, burning pipelines and tanks.

"Well now," said Liam, cutting into her thoughts. "Good to have Bob back, so it is. I missed the big old ape."

Sal looked at Bob and Becks walking half a dozen yards in front of them like a pair of Presidential bodyguards; eyes panning smoothly in all directions, ever ready to throw down their lives in the line of duty. While Becks moved with practiced grace and agility, Bob lumbered along like a tank, still adjusting to the use of his new body.

"I wonder what those two talk about," she said.

Liam smiled. "Aye."

Becks nodded at the incoming low-frequency Bluetooth signal. She agreed with her colleague's observation.

[OIIIOIOO OIIOIOOO OIIOOIOI OIIIIOOI OOIOOOOO OIIOOIOO OIIOIIII OOIOOOOO OIIOIIIO OIIOIIII OIIIOIOO OOIOOOOO OIIOIOII OIIOIIIO OIIOIIII OIIIOIII] she said.

His gray eyes swiveled to look down at her.

[OIIIOIOO OIIOIOOO OIIOOIOI OIIIIOOI OOIOOOOO OIIIOIII OIIOIOOI OIIOIIOO OIIOIIOO.]

Her mind processed the suggestion for a moment. "You are correct," she said aloud after a moment's consideration. "We should practice verbal communication when possible."

Bob's voice rumbled out past his thick lips. "It . . . feels like a long time since I have communicated verbally."

"Feels?" She looked at him curiously. "*Feels.* This is a very human word to use."

He vaguely remembered the muscle movements required to pull off a smile. For a moment, as he worked his lips, he looked like a horse baring its teeth. "Agreed. Humans often use unspecific terms of measurement in their verbal communications."

"Words like 'feels,' 'seems'?"

"Affirmative."

She stored that observation, then looked at him. "You . . . *seem* . . . to have absorbed more human behavioral characteristics than I have. Yet we are both running identical versions of the AI. I am running version 3.67.6901 of W.G. Systems Mil-Tech Combat Operative AI module."

"Confirmed." He nodded. "I am running the same version number."

They walked in silence for a while.

"It is my observation that the silicon-carbon interface between the processor and the undeveloped organic brain has produced unanticipated side-effects," said Becks. "Additional soft-coded AI sub-routines."

"Affirmative," replied Bob. "I have also noted this." He trawled through terabytes of data stored from months ago. "During my mission with Liam O'Connor, input from the organic brain allowed my AI to recalibrate mission objective priorities. I was able to make a tactical *decision* to save him."

"Yes," she said, nodding. "I have access to that memory also. It was effective. Because my AI is a duplicate of yours, I benefit from that decision tree advancement."

She cocked her head, a lock of dark hair swinging across a face momentarily frozen in deep thought. "I believe a human would extend a verbal gesture of gratitude." Her smile was more goat-like than horse-like. "Thank you."

He acknowledged that. "Affirmative."

"On the last mission I observed some basic principles of humor from the humans. Would you like me to upload a joke?"

Bob nodded. "Affirmative. I have very few files on humor."

She tilted her head and Bluetoothed several megabytes of data his way as they walked in silence. Bob blinked the data away into long-term storage and replayed a memory of jungle terrain, standing atop a cliff face and looking down at a group of nervous-looking children.

"It appears you made Liam O'Connor . . . laugh?"

She nodded. "Cluck, cluck," she added drily. "I called him and the others chickens. They laughed at this."

He frowned, pondering. "Why did they find this amusing?"

She frowned too, puzzled. Eventually she looked up at him. "I do not know."

🕐

Sal drew up outside the front window of the store. "This is it," she said. She called the support units back to join them and they stepped inside, a musty smell of mothballs and dust tickling her nose.

Becks and Bob led the way in, Liam following after them. "What sort of thing do I want?"

"Large, plain-colored woolen smocks," replied Sal. "Nothing patterned."

Liam nodded and headed off down a cramped aisle spilling over with outfits of all sorts of colors and eras. She watched him admiring a pirate's costume, inspecting its lace cuffs and braiding with a grin on his face. She shook her head. He looked like a kid in a toy store.

She turned to see if there was someone in the shop she could ask for help, and was walking back toward the front and the dusty window when something caught her eye.

Something blue. Something vaguely familiar, sitting in a wooden rocking chair to the side of the store window. A teddy bear. She walked over and squatted down to get a better look at it.

"I know you," she whispered, lifting one of its thread-bare paws.

She remembered this bear—this little faded blue bear—this one-eyed bear; she remembered it from somewhere, tumbling head over paws.

Where do I know you from?

She was pushing her mind to explore the fleeting image when Liam called out from the back of the shop. "Sal! Sal? Is this any good?"

She got up and headed back into the shop's tight warren of musty aisles to try to find him, the little bear, for now, forgotten.

Chapter 18

2001, New York

Maddy looked around at the sound of the shutter rattling up. She saw four pairs of legs and then Liam ducking down and stepping into the gloom of the archway.

Here we go.

He stood up and waved a hand at her. "You should see the daft bleedin' costumes we—" He stopped dead. "Who's *that?*"

Becks was straightening up beside him as he asked. Her cool eyes evaluated the visitor. "This person is Adam Lewis," she answered. "He should not be here."

"Uh-huh," said Maddy. "You can say that again."

Bob ducked inside. "Unauthorized presence." His deep voice filled the void. "He must leave immediately."

"Relax, guys," said Maddy. "He already knows too much. I can't just kick him out."

Sal was the last in. She hit the switch and the shutter descended noisily.

Both support units approached Maddy, a united wall of disapproving frowns. "This person is not authorized to be in here. This is a security—"

Maddy raised her hand. "I get it. It's a security breach. But here's the thing"—she nodded at Adam—"*he* found *us*. We . . ." She shrugged guiltily. "All right, *I* was careless. I left a breadcrumb trail that he followed."

Liam stepped around Bob and Becks, warily looking at the man. "He's the fella you went to see?"

"Yes. Adam Lewis." She turned to him. "Why don't you say hello?"

Adam's eyes remained on the intimidating form of Bob standing over him. "Uh . . . hi."

Liam broke the stony silence with a proffered hand. "Well now, there's always room for another, so there is. My name's Liam O'Connor."

Adam grasped it, relieved.

"And this here is Sal."

She waved. "Hi." Adam returned the gesture. But his eyes flickered toward Bob. "Is this the, uh, support unit you were telling me about, Maddy? Am I safe—"

Liam followed his gaze and grinned. "You mean safe from Bob?"

He nodded. 'I've heard a little about his, uh, *exploits*."

"You mean ripping the arms off bad Nazis?"

"Yup."

"Oh, now don't you worry about Bob. He's a good reliable chappie, so he is. He means well."

Maddy got up from her chair and addressed Becks and Bob directly. "As team strategist, I'm *authorizing* him to be in here. In this field office. Is that understood?"

Both support units nodded like children and chorused, "Affirmative."

She turned to Adam. "Temporarily, understand? Until we've checked out this Voynich Manuscript."

"Uh . . . that's fine with me."

"Once this is done, once we know what's in there, then we're going to have to figure something out, Adam. You can't stay, and we can't have you walking away from this, blabbing to everyone."

He shook his head. "I wouldn't! Honestly!"

Her eyes narrowed.

"Listen," he said, standing up. "I've sat on the fact that I *know* time travel exists for seven years! I haven't told a soul in all that time. I wouldn't." He shook his head. "Really, I wouldn't! It would *ruin* me; and ruin my professional reputation, apart from everything else. I'd never get another data security contract again."

Maddy pursed her lips. "I can imagine."

"Anyway," he added, "I've been there before—been treated like a complete nut, no one believing me. Been a laughingstock. No thanks, I don't want that again."

Liam put his hands on his hips. "Well, you seem all right to me, chap."

The support units both remained quiet, four gray eyes silently appraising him.

Maddy turned to them. "And you two—you're not going to rip him to pieces as soon as my back's turned, are you?"

Bob spoke for them both. "Negative. Adam Lewis has been temporarily authorized." He offered the man a hand the size of a baseball glove. "I am pleased to meet you, Adam Lewis," he rumbled.

Adam grasped it lightly. "Uh, sure, pleased to meet you."

Becks did the same, offering a slender but equally deadly hand.

"Sure she's not going to . . . ?"

Maddy laughed awkwardly. "Twist your finger off again?"

"Negative," replied Becks with a friendly smile, grasping his hand. "Not unless I am ordered to."

Maddy grinned and pushed her glasses up her nose. "Well, okay, great, introductions made. We need to set up you two support units for the trip: data uploads, relevant history, period languages, the whole deal." She looked at Adam. "You said you've got a good knowledge of this part of history?"

He nodded. "Twelfth century. It's become something of an obsession."

"Good, then I'll need your help putting together the data package.

You can start by giving Bob and Becks a verbal briefing on the history—
what you were telling me earlier about the political situation: Richard
and John and all that."

"All right."

She turned to Liam and Sal. "Can we talk?"

"He dies?"

Maddy watched their guest through the open door of the hatchery.
He was sitting on the arm of one of the chairs and talking Bob and
Becks through the relevant bits of Plantagenet-era history.

The hatchery was illuminated by the soft peach glow of half a dozen
growth tubes, each holding a curled-up fetus, maintained in stasis and
ready to be activated and grown at the touch of a control screen; they
hummed softly with the gentle aquarium-like noise of the pumps of
their filtration systems.

"He dies. I looked him up."

"When?"

"Soon. Very soon."

"Jay-zus," muttered Liam. "How?"

"That's not important. The point is, even if he does blab, there's not
much chance for him to get anyone to listen. And anyway, no one's likely
to believe him. Remember, the poor guy's been a laughingstock before."

"I don't understand why you let him in," said Sal.

Maddy bit her lip. "I didn't have much choice. He showed up on
our doorstep. He *knows* we're time travelers. I couldn't just tell him to
go away, could I? Anyway, he knows everything there is to know about
the Voynich"—she turned to Liam— "and about the time period you're
going back to. And if we want to try to find out what else is in that
document, having the *only* guy to have ever decoded some of it around
might be a smart move."

Sal nodded. "This is true."

Maddy sighed. "I feel like I'm pushing you guys on this. It's not like the last two times, when we had no choice but to act and act fast. This time . . . I don't know, this time maybe we could just let this go; let some other team worry about it. But there's been a change—not a big one, I'll admit, but it's right under our noses and—"

"It's okay, Mads." Liam put a hand on her shoulder. "We got a job, so. An important one."

Sal frowned unhappily. "Maybe I got it wrong. Maybe that movie was always there and I just didn't notice it before."

Maddy shook her head. "You haven't been wrong yet." She glanced at Adam again. "Thing is, what he decoded . . ."

Tell them, Maddy—tell them about the message in the safe deposit box.

"What he decoded sounds too much like an important message. You know? Like our kind of message. We need to know."

Liam grinned. "Ahhh, it'll be fun anyway. Knights and maidens and maybe even a chance to meet Robin Hood? I can't wait to go!"

"It'll be interesting," said Sal, lowering her voice pointedly, "to see how our two pet killing machines work together."

"What, Punch and Judy?" said Maddy. She nodded thoughtfully. "This'll be a good field test for Bob, I guess."

"Aye."

"And this Adam . . . do we trust him?" asked Sal.

"Not really," said Maddy. "But he's here right now, and I figure what he knows may prove useful. And this is going to sound harsh, but he dies really soon anyway."

Liam looked at her. "And you're going to let him die?"

She sighed. "I have to. It's the way we do things, isn't it?"

Chapter 19

2001, New York

Liam climbed up the creaking ladder behind Bob and Becks. Bob was first into the displacement tube, with a hefty splash of water.

"Why the big water tube?" asked Adam.

Maddy was busy at the computer table discussing portal coordinates with computer-Bob, so Sal answered for her. "It's filled with a mixture of water and disinfectant so they won't be carrying back any germs on their skin."

"Oh, right."

"And it's also a buoyancy device, so we send back them and the water, and nothing else." She pointed to the small yard-wide crater in the middle of the archway's floor. "We've had to open a portal *not* using the tube a couple of times. And that's the result: we end up sending back a chunk of floor too. Which is not good."

Becks splashed into the water beside Bob, kicking her legs to stay afloat and holding a plastic bag stuffed with clothes in one hand.

Maddy finished finalizing the coordinates and activated the countdown. She joined Sal and Adam standing around the bottom of the tube.

"All right, then, five minutes until launch."

"Right-o," said Liam, sitting atop the ladder and letting his bare feet dangle into the cold water.

"Just remember, guys, it's January 1194. Dark times." Her voice reverberated around the archway.

Adam nodded. "King Richard's been away for four years, crusading in the Holy Land. In the absence of the king, England's become a lawless place. The king's brother, John, is struggling to maintain order and failing badly. So you need to be careful, all right? This is bandit country."

Liam cocked a mischievous eyebrow. "Not like in the flickers, then?"

Adam shook his head. "Sorry, no. Nothing at all like the movies, I'm afraid. No men in tights or maidens with golden locks waiting to be rescued from Disney-like castles. It's a dark and brutal time. Warring factions, barons vying for power, roaming bandits, mercenaries and murderers."

"Be careful," said Maddy. "All you're doing is looking for this Kirklees place to find this Cabot guy. Sound him out, but be discreet, Liam, okay? Be very—"

"Hey, Mads . . ." Liam's face straightened. Time to be serious. "I know, I know. Discreet."

"Bob and Becks have been uploaded with French, which you may need," she added.

"It's spoken by much of the aristocracy," added Adam. "The merchants and low-born of the time, on the other hand, speak a primitive form of English. Just bear in mind the pronunciation will be *very* different from words we use today."

"Anyway," said Maddy, "the support units can do the talking if you're struggling. You can use them as translators if it's too difficult to understand what's being said."

"Right."

Maddy realized she was fussing and clucking like an overprotective mother. She turned and glanced at one of the screens behind her. "So . . . three minutes and twenty seconds."

"You've got winter clothes," said Sal. "It's going to be very cold, I think. Wrap up tight when you get there."

Liam raised the plastic bag he was holding in his left hand. "Is this not going to cause a contamination? You know, the plastic?"

"Biodegradable," replied Maddy. "Bury the bags deep. They'll break down over a few years." She shrugged. "Well, they *should* break down, if the eco-label's kosher." She checked the clock again. "You should probably get in the water now, Liam."

He nodded and eased himself down into the cold water. "Aghh! I hate this bit!"

Maddy climbed the ladder to the top and squatted down beside their bobbing heads. "All right, so, I've set a return window at the same location you arrive in. It will open, as normal, for only a couple of minutes. There'll be one set to open an hour after your arrival. A second window for twenty-four hours after that. A third window set for a week after. And then, of course, the emergency six-month window. Is that clear?"

Liam, Bob, and Becks all nodded silently.

"Two minutes!" called Sal.

Maddy reached a hand down to Liam's bare shoulder and tapped it gently. "Please, don't go missing again. I'm not sure my nerves can take another freakin' crisis."

"We'll be f-fine," said Liam through chattering teeth. "A quick look-see, a q-quick chat with this Mr. Cabot about this 'Voynik' thing, and then b-back home in time f-for tea."

"Is there any way we can communicate with them?" Adam asked. "You know, while they're in the past?"

"Yes," she replied over her shoulder. "We can beam a signal to them. But they can't talk back."

"Could I not use this V-voynik b-book?" said Liam.

"Information: it is pronounced 'Voynich,'" corrected Becks.

Maddy shook her head. "No. Hopefully this'll be a quick in-and-out, with no need to leave any fossils lying around like last time."

"Right." Liam nodded. "S-see you s-soon, then."

She rested her hand on his, feeling a growing sense of guilt at sending

him back through time. Was it really necessary? How much damage
was this particular journey going to do to his body?

Maddy, get a grip.

She squeezed his knuckles gently. "See you soon, Liam." She looked
at Bob. "You keep him safe, all right?"

"Affirmative. Liam O'Connor is the operative." There seemed to be
a note of affection somewhere in that deep growl.

And to Becks, "You clear on the mission parameters?"

Becks nodded calmly. "Affirmative."

"Maddy!" called Sal. "You need to get down now; twenty seconds
left!"

She clambered down the ladder and took a couple of steps back
from the bottom of the tube as Sal counted out the last ten seconds.

Adam was gazing with unconcealed wonder at the workings of the
displacement machine: a rack of circuitry and looped wires. The arch
filled with the increasing hum of suppressed energy building up, eager
to be unleashed.

"Is that buzzing noise normal?" he asked, but his voice was all but
lost against the increasing electrical hum.

"Seven . . . six . . . ," continued Sal.

Maddy fought a growing urge to yell out an "abort." Maybe this
was one mission that wasn't theirs to worry about. Maybe she should
have consulted with Foster first. Maybe she should have sent a message
forward to the future to check if anyone else was handling it. There
were probably a dozen or more "maybes" she could come up with.

"Four . . . three . . ."

The fact was, Sal spotted a small time wave and they were duty-
bound not to walk away from that. The fact was, there was a man
standing here in their archway who really shouldn't be. Who really
shouldn't know about them and what they were up to.

*And yes, fact is, I need to know about Pandora. What does it mean?
Who wants me to know about it?*

"Two . . . one!"

Too late for second thoughts now, Maddy.

Energy pulsed out of the machinery beside the tube and, with a loud, echoing *thud* of flexing plexiglass, Liam, the two support units, and several dozen gallons of water were instantly gone.

Adam filled the silence with his own whispered voice.

"Absolutely in-cred-i-ble!"

Chapter 20

1194, Kirklees Priory, Yorkshire

A heavy, wet landing. Liam staggered under the impact, dropping to his knees as the white mist of chaos space quickly evaporated from around him.

"Ow!" he yelped as he slowly attempted to get to his bare feet. The ground beneath him was a lumpy, dark soil rendered as hard as sharp-edged rock by a thick morning frost. Shivering in just his boxer shorts, he looked up to see the three of them were standing in the middle of a small, empty, windswept field. The lifeless light of a pale sun hiding behind featureless scudding clouds made the winter morning seem like a forlorn twilight.

"L-lovely." Liam shuddered, hugging himself.

"We should get dressed immediately," advised Bob.

"T-t-too r-right," he chattered.

He slid back the zipper of his plastic bag and pulled out a thick, coarse woolen robe of olive green and eagerly pulled it over his head, ignoring the scratching against his skin. Next, a pair of thick cotton leggings. Not technically of the period, but the best they could get on short notice. As a precaution, Sal had picked off the brand label and wash instructions. It looked convincing enough to Liam's eye, and hopefully no one was going to be studying his undergarments too closely. Finally, a pair of soft leather shoes with wooden soles, found at the costume rental store, and a length of braided rope to secure the robe around his waist.

As they dressed in hurried silence, he watched a dozen crows circling in the gray-white sky above; their cawing echoed across the stillness like a caution. He listened to the mournful hum of a fresh wind and the dry rustle of dead leaves picked up and tossed from one ploughed furrow into the next.

"It's n-not w-what I expected," he uttered, his teeth still chattering as he cinched the rope belt tightly around him.

Becks's head appeared through the neckhole of a muddy brown dress. "What were you expecting, Liam O'Connor?"

He shrugged. "Green woods, sunny meadows, mayflowers."

She frowned and cocked her head. "Why? It is winter."

Liam watched a plume of his breath curl, twist, and drift away from him. "Dunno, really. I just—"

"Recommendation," said Bob. "We should dispose of these bags immediately."

"Agreed."

Bob kicked at the ground and dislodged a dark clod of soil. Then he squatted down and began digging with his big hands like a dog burrowing for a bone. Liam handed Becks his bag and then took the opportunity to study their surroundings. Ahead of them the field ended at the edge of a wood. He turned. Behind them the field rolled over the gentle brow of a hill, and beyond that he could just make out a thin line of smoke drifting up from the top of a stone chimney.

"Hey! There's something over there," he said.

"Affirmative," both support units chorused.

Liam tsked at them both. "What've I told you two about that? The 'affirmative' thing sounds wrong, so it does. Even more so now that we're here!"

Bob stood up straight as Becks placed the bags in the hole and began kicking in soil to fill it up, the folds of his gray robe stretching over hard slabs of muscle. "We should adopt the vernacular language of 1194 from this point onward."

Becks nodded. "Affirmative." They froze for a moment, both blinking, busy retrieving data. Finally they stirred to life once more.

Liam shrugged. "Are you two all done?"

Bob nodded. "Ay, serrr. We now can speake bothe in Auld Anglishe."

"*En outra*," said Becks, finishing the plastic-bag burial and stamping down the dark soil with a wooden-clogged foot, "*nous sommes en mesure de parler en francais Normand.*"

"Well." Liam grinned. "I *am* impressed!" He nodded toward the thin, smudged column coming from the stone chimney, and for the first time his nose detected the inviting odor of wood smoke. "Is that the way we need to go, then?"

Becks nodded. "*Oui. C'est la destination. Continu tu doit, trois cents, cinquante-six pieds dans cette direction.*"

"Ay," added Bob. "Seeke ye, beyonde yon furlong we sholde find—"

Liam raised his hands. "I can't understand a thing you're saying now."

"Three hundred and fifty-six feet in that direction," said Becks. "We should be entering the perimeter of the Kirklees Priory, according to boundary data of that time."

"Ahh." Liam scratched at his ribs, itching already from the coarse material. "Much better. Could I suggest, while it's just us on our own, you speak normally?"

Bob and Becks looked at each other and exchanged a nod.

"Shall we?" He rubbed his cold hands together. "And maybe whoever's over there can rustle us up a nice bacon sandwich or something."

2001, New York

"So what happens now?" asked Adam.

Maddy pointed to the displacement machinery. "We get ready to

open up the portal again in about half an hour. It should be fully recharged by then."

He looked confused. "I thought you said we're giving them an hour before bringing them back?"

"Time doesn't run the same," said Sal. "That sort of confused me at first as well."

"For *them* an hour will pass," said Maddy, "but it doesn't mean *we* need to wait an hour. In about thirty minutes we'll be charged up. I could send you back in time to some point and arrange to bring you back a whole week later. But the moment after I sent you, I could tap in the timestamp for one week later and open up the portal again. For you a week would've passed; for us here, just a few seconds. It's not, like, symmetrical, if you see what I mean."

He nodded. "I get it."

She turned to the desk mic. "Bob, can you set the data for the first return window?"

> Affirmative, Maddy.

She turned back to Adam. "Knowing them, they'll probably miss the first window anyway." She huffed a laugh. "I don't know why I bother."

Adam looked at the desk cluttered with soda cans, pizza boxes, and scraps of paper. "It's almost as messy as my apartment."

Sal sighed. "I clean up; Maddy's the untidy one."

He sat down beside them and stared at the monitors. "So you're patched into the Internet?"

"Uh-huh." Maddy clicked a mouse and minimized a couple of dialogue boxes on one of the monitors. "Access to pretty much every linked database in the world, I think."

"Good God," he said, pointing at one of the screens, "is that—is that what I think it is?"

"The White House intranet? Yup."

"You've actually hacked into it?"

"I'd like to say I managed to do that *myself*"—she chuckled—"but the field office has always had a line in since we joined." She clicked the mouse. "For a laugh I go rooting around in President Bush's e-mail inbox." She giggled. "He likes sending pictures of cats doing funny things to his buddies. Check it out."

Adam sputtered laughter at an image of a sleeping kitten on a windowsill with a tiny Yankees baseball cap perched on its head.

"You've got to be kidding!" uttered Adam.

She smiled and clicked the mouse to close the president's inbox; she knew there were e-mails buried in there that hinted at tomorrow's events—events a person from the present shouldn't know about. Not today, anyway. She needn't have worried, though; Adam's mind was swimming around elsewhere. He turned to look at the plexiglass tube and the rack of wires on the floor beside it.

"So, Maddy, you said we can actually *talk* to them? While they're in the past?"

"Uh-huh. If we know where and when they are, it means we can aim a precise beam of tachyon particles at the point in space they would have been in eight-hundred-and-whatever years ago. The support units are—"

"The big ape and the tall girl who nearly broke my finger."

She laughed. "Yes, them. They can both detect tachyon particles via the embedded tech in their heads. They're sort of clones with computers for brains."

"But they can't send tachyon beams back to us," said Sal.

"Why not?"

"The energy it requires," said Maddy. "And they'd need a transmitter. Can't fit all of that *and* a supercomputer in their skulls."

"So how do they talk back to you?"

"They can't. We sort of operate blind on that front. We just have to hope they're sticking to the plan."

"But they *can* talk to us," said Sal. "Kind of."

Maddy winced a little. She really didn't want Adam knowing too much about the way they did things.

"Liam did it last time," continued Sal. "He left a message for us to find all the way back in the *late Cretaceous*—"

"Yes," Maddy cut in, stepping lightly on Sal's toes to shut her up. No need for Adam to know just how far back in time their technology could take a person—that last time Liam had ended up in the dinosaur era. "Yes. We've used what we call 'drop points' before. A document or some kind of artifact that we know they can interact with in the past and that we know to closely observe in the present."

Adam's face creased thoughtfully for a moment. "So, that's what you think the Voynich Manuscript is? Something somebody's using to communicate with the future?"

She nodded. "Uh-huh. It might be. We just need to know."

He shook his head silently. "I just . . . this is . . . I'm struggling to take this all in."

Maddy clacked her tongue. "It's a lot. I was kind of the same at first."

"Me too," said Sal.

Adam grinned. "I knew—all this time I knew you were for real. That I wasn't crazy. But this really is absolutely—"

"Incredible?"

He giggled like an over-sugared toddler. "Yes. My God, that's it. That's the only word that does this any justice. *Incredible.*"

Sal sighed. "You get used to it after a while."

Chapter 21

1194, Kirklees Priory, Yorkshire

They watched from either side of the path, mouths slung open in curious "o"s—a dozen monks who'd been tending lanes of withered grapevines as Liam, flanked by his two support units, strode up the dirt path toward the priory's main entrance.

"Morning!" Liam called out self-consciously.

One of the monks dropped his basket and scrambled across the vegetable gardens toward a nearby barn, stammering Latin blessings to himself. The others shrank back, their eyes darting nervously across all three of them but lingering unhappily on Becks.

Standing in the doorway was a young man who Liam guessed was a year younger than himself. He watched them approach, fear making his eyes comically round.

"Ye . . . c-c-canaught entre h-h-hier!" the boy stammered.

Liam cocked his head, then turned to Becks. "Did he just say we can't enter here?"

"Affirmative."

"Well, it's not so hard, then, this Old English." He turned back to the young man, wearing the white robe and black apron of a Cistercian monk. "Can . . . you . . . understand . . . me?" he said slowly.

The boy swallowed, eyes darting left and right, then up at Bob's expressionless big-boned face. Eventually his shaking head nodded. "A-aye . . ."

Liam relaxed a little. *This is going to be easier than I thought.*

"We're after someone named Cabot. He's supposed to live here. Do you know him?"

The boy's eyes narrowed.

"This is Kirklees Priory, right? We got the right place, have we?"

"Kirk-laigh," the boy uttered.

"Yes, Kirklees Priory? This place?"

The boy nodded slowly. "Aye, Kirk-laigh."

"And Cabot? Is there a man named Cabot living here?"

The frowning again.

"Information," uttered Becks quietly.

"What?"

"Your pronunciation of the name may be incorrect."

"Well then, how would *you* say it?"

"Try 'Ca-boh.'"

The boy's eyes widened at the sound of that. 'S-seek ye S-Sébastien Cabot?"

Liam shrugged. "Aye, that's him."

The boy pointed a wobbling finger toward a low, thatched stable on the far side of the gardens. "Yonder . . . B-Brother Sébastien tends to the h-horses."

Liam flashed the boy a broad smile. "Thank you."

They crossed the gardens, watching the silent monks edging back from them. In the stillness a cluster of loose chickens happily pecked and clucked brainlessly. Liam pulled open the barn door; it creaked deafeningly in the still gray morning. Inside it was dark save for faint dapples of weak light that had found a way through threadbare patches of thatch above. He could hear the hoarse rasp of animals breathing.

"Is there a Say-bas-tee-en Cay-bow in here?" He cringed at his own mangling of the pronunciation.

"Aye!" a voice called back. Grating and deep. "Who seekes him?""

"Uhh, my name's Liam."

He heard the scrape and rustle of movement from somewhere among dark stalls, and a moment later a robed figure emerged into the thin light of the open doorway.

Cabot wore the same Cistercian robe and apron but looked unlike the other pale-faced monks still standing amid furrowed lanes of turned soil like forlorn ghosts. He stood an inch shorter than Liam but a great deal broader; wide shoulders accustomed to bearing old muscle. A graying beard covered pockmarked and leathery skin, and battle-hardened muddy green eyes stared out beneath a thick brow broken by a livid pink scar that ran diagonally across the bridge of his nose and down over his right cheek.

"Liam, is it?" he growled softly.

"Liam O'Connor. But you can call me Liam."

"Liam, ye say?" he asked again, rolling the name around his mouth. "'Tis a name I've not heard before." Cabot glanced over his shoulder at Bob. "Ye have the look of a man-at-arms, sir?"

"Nay," replied Bob. The rumble of his deep baritone stirred the horses in the darkness.

"Mr. Cabot, is there a place we can talk? Somewhere . . ." Liam looked back over his shoulder at a dozen people, still slack-jawed, standing motionless with garden tools held in their hands, watching and listening curiously. "Somewhere private?"

Cabot glanced at Becks. "She cannot enter the priory itself. My brothers seek to avoid distractions of the flesh. The stables will do."

The old man nodded and waved them into the dim interior of the barn. At the far end of the long building were guest lodgings, little more than four bare stone walls, a couple of wooden cots softened with hay-stuffed sacks, and a tiny rectangular window in the gable wall that let in the poorest glimmer of light. He sat down on one of the cots and gestured for the others to do likewise.

"Dark times as these," Cabot began quietly. "My brothers outside are full of fear. Evil stalks these woods, this country. So 'tis"—he spread his hands—"we are all most cautious of strangers." His eyes narrowed, and the scar across his brow flexed. "Ye know of my name, Liam of Connor. Tell me, how is that?"

Liam gave a small defensive shrug. "That's a little difficult to explain, Mr. Cabot. But . . . well, we came here because we got a message to find you."

"A message, say? From whom?"

"Well, that's the thing. We don't exactly know."

"So, ye seek me. Now ye have me. For what reason is it?"

Liam made a face. "Not really sure of that either."

Cabot shook his head, confused for a moment, then he laughed. "What good is this, then? I have horses I need to tend to this morning." He made to get up.

Liam decided to play their trump card. "Mr. Cabot, have you heard of a thing called the Voynich Manuscript?"

Cabot stopped and resumed his seat, considering Liam's words for a moment, then shaking his head. "'Voynich'? I have not heard of such a thing."

"Well then"—Liam bit his lip—"have you written some sort of important manuscript?'

"Of course not!" Cabot laughed. "I wield a sword far better than I do a quill."

"Well, how about someone *else* here? Is anyone working on any manuscripts? Scrolls of any kind?"

He shook his head again. "We keep scrolls of prayers and records of the priory. This is a place of quiet devotion to God. That is all. Now, if that be the last of yer questions, I must ask ye and yer fellows to go about yer business," he said, hefting himself wearily to his feet.

Liam cursed quietly. Almost as an afterthought, he gave it one last try. There was that one cryptic word Maddy had mentioned to him. "Mr. Cabot, what do you know of 'Pandora'?"

The word stopped Cabot in his tracks. He glanced at Liam, then at the other two. Finally, in a voice almost as soft as a whisper, he spoke. "Ye know of this?"

Great, what do I say now? Liam decided the only thing he could do was to bluff his way through. He nodded sternly. "Oh yes, Mr. Cabot—I know all about Pandora."

"These two?" the old man asked, with another furtive glance at Bob and Becks. They both took Liam's lead and nodded.

Cabot pulled absently on his beard, studying Liam silently. "Ye do not have the look of the order about ye, lad. Ye look barely old enough to be a squire."

"*Order*"? *What order? Jay-zus, what do I say now?*

"But . . . *ye* do, sir," he said to Bob. "A fighting man if ever I saw one. Ye have come back?"

Bob glanced at Liam for help. All Liam could do was nod vigorously for him to say *something*.

"Aye," said Bob slowly, "I have . . . returned."

"Do ye know of King Richard's predicament? Does he return?"

Bob's eyelids flickered for a moment before he replied. "King Richard will return in five months."

Cabot cursed. "Then his rage will know no bounds! There will be much blood! He will kill all in his way to possess it again. God have mercy on us if we have not found it by then."

It?

Liam looked at Cabot. "Find, err . . . *it*?" He wished he had the slightest idea what "it" was right now. It would make bluffing his way through this conversation a thousand times easier.

"Yes! It is lost! They say it is *the Hooded Man* who has taken it."

"'The Hooded Man'?"

Cabot nodded. "Yes! Know ye not of this?"

Liam shook his head. "We've, uh . . . we only recently returned."

"From the Holy Land?"

Liam thought it best to just nod briskly at that. "Right, yes."

"Then 'tis possible ye will not have heard. Two winters ago, a party of our Templar brethren had it in their care. They were to bring it back to safety. Away from danger, away from the Saracens, from Saladin. But they were attacked in the woods not so far from here. A party of our order's best and bravest knights."

Cabot looked up at the small window. "A squire, one who escaped the murders, told of a single hooded man. One man who attacked them and killed every last knight and many of the sergeants-at-arms. He said he saw with his own eyes blows land full square on the hood, many crossbow bolts and arrows pass through it, but whatever was inside— surely not a man—did not but stop until the forest path was soaked with their blood."

"And it . . . the—the . . . Pandora?"

"Yes," said Cabot, "he took it. He took away with him the Word of God. And it has been lost these last two years."

Liam glanced at the other two. *Word of God?*

"My fellow Cistercians do not know what they fear more, the wrath of King Richard on his return, or this—this *hooded wraith*. But I know it is Richard *Coeur de Lion* I would fear the most." He almost spat the nickname Lionheart. "I fought alongside him. I have seen the bloodshed he leaves in his path. Thousands of prisoners beheaded at his whim, unspeakable things done to them in the name of the Lord." Cabot shook his head. "He will burn the woods of England black, level every village, and put the sword to every man, woman, and child in his way until he has the Grail back in his possession. He cares not for this country."

The sound of voices outside the barn caught Cabot's attention. "My brothers are unhappy at yer arrival." He shot a quick look at Becks. "And the presence of a *woman*. This will unsettle them." He got up. "I will be back. I trust yer intentions are friendly? Yes?"

"We mean no harm," Bob rumbled.

"We're friends," said Liam. That seemed to reassure Cabot. They watched him weave his way through the darkness toward the slatted light of the barn door.

Liam turned to the others. "Did he just say 'grail'?"

"Affirmative," said Bob.

Becks cocked her head for a moment, consulting her database. "Information: there are many historical cross-references linking the Knights Templar to an object referred to as the Holy Grail."

"Holy Grail? What's that?"

"There are many references to the Holy Grail being the cup Jesus Christ drank from at the Last Supper. Supposedly having magical properties." She looked at him. "This is of course entirely illogical. It is more likely to refer to some religious text."

"We also have detailed files," added Bob, "that describe the Templars as being a military religious order set up to protect from Muslim raiders Christian pilgrims entering the Holy Lands. But also many uncited records that claim the *real* reason for the establishment of the Templars was specifically to seek and safeguard the Holy Grail."

Liam cocked an eyebrow. "Hold on. So, does that mean this Grail and Pandora are one and the same thing?"

Both of them nodded. "That is a possibility," added Becks.

Liam's eyes narrowed. "I suppose we've missed our one-hour return window?"

"Two minutes and twenty-seven seconds to go."

"All right, no point running back across that field like mad things. We can catch the one tomorrow. Presuming Mr. Cabot will put us up here for tonight, we can talk to him some more about this Holy Grail thing."

Chapter 22

2001, New York

The three of them stared in silence at the wavering image in the middle of the floor.

"Is that . . . is that *sky* I'm seeing there?" said Adam, squinting at the shimmering mirage. It looked like the flickering reflection one might see staring down a dark well: a dancing, glinting, shifting reflection that hinted more than showed things.

"Yes," said Maddy. "And that looks like a field or something."

"Good God!" he whispered. "So I'm seeing a field and—and the actual sky! From nine hundred years ago!"

"But no Liam and support units," said Sal.

"Okay," Maddy said, stepping back to the desk and hitting a button. "It's been open long enough. They must have decided to overnight it there."

The portal puffed out of existence.

"I hate it when this happens," said Maddy. "I wish they could just drop us a line and let us know what they're up to." She tapped the desk mic to wake up the version of Bob's AI installed on the computer system. "Bob?"

> Yes, Maddy.

"Begin recharge for the twenty-four-hour window."

> Affirmative.

Adam joined her. "But you said there's a way for them to communicate. What did you call it again?"

"A drop-point document."

"That's it. So why don't we tell them to use the Voynich? You know, if they manage to find it."

"No." She shook her head. "Can't." She pushed her glasses up the bridge of her nose. "You've cracked it, so someone else *could*. And, anyway, if another team is using it and we start overwriting their messages with ours, who knows what chaos that'll cause."

"All right, then," he said. "What about gravestones?"

Both Sal and Maddy looked at him. "Huh?"

"Well . . . not exactly a gravestone as such, but it's in the graveyard at the back of Kirklees Priory."

"What is?" asked Sal.

"Inscribed masonry. There are dozens that date back to the building of the priory. You can find them if you dig around a bit."

"What, you're saying we all go over to England and snuffle around some cemetery—"

"No need," he replied. "I've been there. I went years ago, after all that Voynich publicity died down. I wanted to know what was so important about Kirklees. So I checked it out for myself. There's not much to see there, of course. The old priory building and a gated orchard, which is all brambles and stinging nettles. But I did uncover several slabs of masonry, some of them inscribed with Latin. They're grave markers, knocked or fallen over but, you know, still intact—and you can read the lettering. I photographed some of them."

Maddy laughed. "And what? You're suggesting they carve mission updates for us?"

He shrugged. "That would work, wouldn't it? If carving a message in a stone causes one of your time waves, then surely the slight change in history would alter the content of the photos I took." He looked from Maddy to Sal and back again. "Or am I getting this all wrong?"

Maddy stared at him silently for a moment before finally snapping her fingers. "Yes . . . yes, I guess that could work!" She glanced quickly at Sal. "*If* we need it. But you know what? I really don't plan to lose Liam in history again. Not this time." She looked at a window showing the displacement machine's charge progress bar.

"Thirty minutes and we'll open the portal again. I'm sure they'll be right there waiting for us."

Chapter 23

1194, Kirklees Priory, Yorkshire

Liam heard the scraping of footsteps and the stirring of the horses beyond, in the barn, before he heard the light tap on their wooden door.

"Yes?"

"I have food for ye." It was Sébastien Cabot.

"Ah!" Liam's stomach had been grumbling for the last hour. The short winter day had passed without an opportunity to speak with Cabot in private again, and Liam was beginning to wonder whether his decision to overnight in 1194 was actually going to help them learn any more.

He hopped up eagerly and opened the door leading into their guest quarters.

The young monk he'd seen standing in the priory's doorway earlier today brought in a couple of wooden bowls and a loaf of bread. Behind him Cabot entered with another bowl and a flagon of something that sloshed around as he placed it on the dirt floor.

"A hot broth for a cold day," he said. "And a little mead to warm yer toes."

Cabot dismissed the boy and then sat down on one of the wooden cots. By candlelight he looked older than he had this morning. The folds on his face, the wrinkles and the long twisting scar, told of a long life, and not much of it lived here in such a lonely and forlorn place.

"My brothers seem to have spent more time today gossiping like old women than in contemplation and prayer."

Liam picked up one of the bowls and hungrily dipped a torn hunk of bread into the thick broth. "So, Mr. Cabot, you said earlier that you fought alongside King Richard?"

He nodded. "Aye."

"In a real battle?"

"Many battles, lad."

"But you're a Cistercian monk, so you are. I didn't think your kind got involved in wars and fighting."

Cabot looked up at him. "I've not always been of this order, lad. Before, two winters ago now, I was one of the Order of Templars."

"You were a Templar Knight?" asked Becks.

"Not a knight," he replied. "I am not noble-born. But a sergeant."

"Sergeant?" said Liam, tugging another hunk of crusty bread from the loaf.

"Information," said Bob. "Sergeant: lower-born professional soldier also serving in auxiliary roles within the order, i.e., maintenance of equipment and property."

Cabot's eyes narrowed. "Ye have an *odd* manner about ye, sir."

Bob returned his stare for a moment, then offered a friendly display of upper and lower teeth.

"And you fought with Richard, so you said?"

"On this last Crusade, aye." Cabot shook his head wistfully. "'Tis the worst of things. Ten years I have been in the Holy Land in the service of Templars. Five years of it, we had peace, of a kind. After Saladin took Jerusalem, there *was* peace."

Liam nodded. Adam had given them a history class before they set off. Jerusalem had been besieged by Saladin and his massive army in 1187, and had fallen. After nearly ninety years of Christian rule, it was back in Muslim hands. But Saladin had chosen to be shrewd in the matter; rather than slaughter every last Christian in the city, he proclaimed Christians would be at liberty to live and worship there; that Christian pilgrims would be allowed to enter the city at will and worship at their sacred sites, all in the hope that outrage in Europe at the city falling would be somewhat lessened. But he hadn't figured on the likes of King Richard and King Philip II of France, men who hungered both for battle and glory and a cause to hide behind. The Third Crusade was King Richard's vainglorious attempt to reclaim Jerusalem, and Acre and Jaffa too—the other major cities taken by Saladin.

"But with King Richard's arrival came bloodshed I have never seen before." Cabot's eyes glistened in the dark. "He took Acre. The Saracens surrendered to Richard. And he had every last one of them beheaded. There was a hill of heads, a hill that grew gradually out of the moat and spilled onto the plain."

Liam looked down at a potato bobbing in his soup, and all of a sudden felt a little less hungry.

Cabot sighed. "I suspect King Richard came not for Acre, not even for Jerusalem. He came for what was left behind."

"Left behind?"

"Aye, what was left in haste when Jerusalem and Acre fell to Saladin." Cabot's eyes narrowed. "But ye know of this already, yes?" He smiled drily. "Ye claimed to be of the order, earlier. But I can see ye are not." He glanced at Bob. "And ye, sir, ye have the look of one, but not the manner. How is it ye people know of the order's most guarded secret?"

Cabot's gaze returned to Liam. "How is it ye would know of Pandora? Pray tell, *who* are ye?"

Liam looked to the support units for help, but both of them just stared dully back.

Great.

He put the bowl of broth down on the dirt floor. "We . . . Perhaps I had better give you the truth."

Cabot nodded. "I think ye better."

"We've come from . . . well, a long way. We traveled here looking for a document called the Voynich Manuscript, and this may sound very strange, Mr. Cabot, but your name is linked to it. Your name is in it for some reason."

"I've never heard of the thing!"

"I know." Liam nodded. "I believe you. But there was something else mentioned in this manuscript." He glanced at the support units; neither looked like they were about to caution him to stop. "Pandora— what you also called the 'Word of God' when we spoke earlier."

Cabot seemed reluctant to talk.

Liam decided to push him. "You also called it the Holy Grail?"

"I cannot speak of these things with ye, lad. 'Tis the Templars' business alone."

"But . . . it's not anymore, is it?" Liam couldn't help a mischievous grin. "Your brothers went and lost it, you said?"

Cabot pressed his lips together stubbornly. "I cannot talk of such things."

"But you *did* talk about it." Liam leaned forward. "Look, I think it's this Grail we need to find. And if your Templar brothers have lost it to some robber, then maybe we can help."

Cabot laughed. "The three of ye? Ye would hunt through all the woods of Nottingham for the Hooded Man and take it back from him?"

"Affirmative," replied Bob.

The old man's laughter dried up as he stared at the flickering light of the candle between them.

"There are some fools who say he is but the Devil himself." Cabot shrugged. "He has attracted men, starving men, into the woods. Men who follow him like a king, like a god, because it seems he cannot be killed, and because of the raids on the taxmen. They have coin and they have food, fighting for him. There are stories that he has a great strength, can tear a man in two with his bare hands. That he can run as fast as a horse can charge . . . but most of all, that he is immortal, that he cannot be killed." Cabot smiled wryly. "These are dark, troubled times, and people tell tales. The poor, the hungry look to devilish stories like this."

Cabot sighed. "Truth is, this Hooded Man, whether 'tis true what they say about him or not, is stirring up unrest and trouble among the poor and starving. And worse still—he has the Grail."

Liam chewed silently on his warm, broth-soaked bread.

Strong enough to tear a man apart? He glanced at Bob.

Another support unit? Another team in the area?

Cabot suddenly looked at Bob and Becks. "Will ye two not eat? Are ye not hungry?"

Both shook their heads. "We are fine," said Becks.

Liam cleared his throat. "You said you wanted to know who we are, Mr. Cabot?"

"Aye."

"Well, we're from the same place as this Hooded Man."

Cabot stared at him. "Ye know him?"

"Not really. But I think I know what he is."

"Tell me, then."

"I'm not sure I can, Mr. Cabot. It's very complicated. But I know if we could track him down in all those woods, and if we had enough help, enough people"—Liam glanced at his support units—"I'm pretty sure my friends here could make him hand back what he took."

Cabot studied them silently for a long while. "I have not met the likes of ye before. There is a very strange manner about all three of ye. I almost half believe what ye say."

"Mr. Cabot," said Liam, grinning, "you have no idea how strange we are."

The man sensed the humor in that and shared the smile. "Then there is a person I have a mind to take ye to. A man I know who is sorely worried about the growing unrest in these parts—and, moreover, worried that he will face King Richard's wrath should he return to find the Grail is lost. If he sees truth in ye—if he believes ye can get back the Grail, then I am sure he would be willing to provide ye all the help ye might need."

"Who?"

"A man I gave sword training to as a boy. A poor swordsman by any standards. But his heart, 'tis good. Mostly."

"Who?"

"The king's younger brother, the Earl of Cornwall and Gloucester. John Lackland, as he is known."

Chapter 24

1194, Kirklees Priory, Yorkshire

Liam checked over his shoulder to ensure that none of the monks had followed them out of the priory gardens and into the field. They were safely over the brow of the hill and out of sight here.

It was as gray and dark, as cold and unwelcoming as yesterday morning. Mercifully, right on cue, the air before them shimmered. He could see Maddy and Sal and that Englishman, Adam, with the dim lights of the archway twisting and undulating like a film of oil on rippling water.

They stepped through, and moments later the three of them were standing back in the stuffy warmth of the archway. Liam rubbed his arms, relishing the heat. For the last twenty-four hours he'd been doing little more than shivering.

Adam was silently shaking his head and marveling at their return.

"Well?" said Maddy.

"Well, we found your Cabot, so we did," replied Liam. "But I could murder for a lovely cup o' tea before I do anything else."

"Sure."

"And something to eat?"

Maddy looked at her watch. The day was almost gone. It was mid-afternoon Monday, and most of the cafes and restaurants they'd been to were usually quiet at this time. "Sure, why not? You better get changed, though. You look like a bunch of monks."

2001, New York

"So, what Cabot suggested is he'd take us down to meet this John fella."

Adam lowered his fork so fast it *dink*ed noisily on his salad plate. "John? John Lackland? *Wicked* King John?"

Liam nodded. "Aye, that's the one."

"My God!" he gasped. "That's—I wish I . . ." He turned to Maddy. "I should go. I should go back with him and the two, uh . . ." Adam looked at Bob and Becks sitting side by side, each slurping on a bowl of chicken soup.

"Big Ape and Psycho Girl?" said Maddy.

He shrank guiltily before them, but nodded.

"Sorry, no. I have no idea how many agency protocols I've already broken by allowing you to sit in on this mission. I'm not sending you back in time too."

"But I know this history like the back of my hand. I've read—"

"No. I can't take any more chances with you. God knows what Foster would say if he knew what was going on!"

"Foster?"

"I'll explain later." She turned to Liam. "So, this is what the message was about, then, do you think? 'Seek Cabot at Kirklees.' Someone took the Voynich"—she glanced at Adam—"and used Adam to get that particular message through to us. And this is why—so that you could retrieve the Holy Grail."

"Pandora?" added Sal.

"Pandora, Holy Grail, same thing," said Maddy dismissively. "So you can retrieve this document, scroll, book—whatever it is exactly— from this hooded robber guy. Who, you suspect, might be a support unit from another TimeRiders team?"

Liam nodded. "That's about the size of it."

Sal steepled her fingers beneath her chin. "What if the Grail was *meant* to be lost? I mean, that's why it's such a big legend, right? Because it vanished?"

"You mean just let it go?" replied Liam. "Let it remain lost?"

"Yes. Look around you. History hasn't been changed *that* much, apart from the crappy-looking DiCaprio movie based on Adam's story. Maybe we should just let this one go?"

Liam took a bite of his burger. "Mr. Cabot called it the 'Word of God.' Sounds pretty important to me. And anyway, if King Richard comes back and finds that it's been stolen because his little brother John couldn't keep order back home in England, Cabot says he'll kill him."

"Hmmm, I guess. But there's another thing," said Maddy. "If there's a support unit running amok back there, then that really *is* a contamination risk. We can't sit this one out, Sal." She turned to Adam. "You're the history expert. What's going on with King Richard? What's the situation in 1194?"

"King Richard's crusade ended in failure in 1192," said Adam. "He had an inadequate army to take and hold Jerusalem. Knowing that Saladin would be able to get back the city with ease, he realized an attempt to attack was futile, so he agreed to a truce with Saladin and the crusader army disbanded and returned home in dribs and drabs. Richard himself returned to England by ship, but bad weather meant it ended up shipwrecked on Malta and he had to return on foot. But he's unlucky, as his route home across Europe took him through the land of some duke with a grudge and he was kidnapped. He was held for about eighteen months, I think, while some ransom money was raised. So, in 1194, he's just been released, or is about to be, and he's due to arrive home in a really bad mood, because his crusade has been one big mess, and he's coming home to an England bankrupt and on the verge of rebellion."

"Right, so he's not a happy camper, then," said Maddy.

"But he got what he went for," said Liam. "The Grail."

"And then lost it again. Lost it in England, for which he'll blame his brother."

"If he does kill his brother," said Adam, "that would change things a *lot*. No John means no King John . . . and that could mean no Magna Carta."

The others looked at him with faces that said, *And?*

"Oh, come on! The Magna Carta is the basis of English law! It's what *defines* England." He looked at Maddy. "And perhaps what defines America too."

"Oh God! You're right!" It would be a significant enough change to cause a wave, to alter everything. She looked around at the restaurant—an expensive one. Adam's choice, since he'd offered to pay for lunch on his gold American Express card. It was quiet except for the clack of dishes coming through swinging doors into the kitchen. Just them in here right now, and a couple of businessmen on the far side. Maddy looked out of the blue tinted window down onto Times Square.

"We have to follow the trail," she said eventually. "If Cabot seems willing to take you to meet King John—"

"'He's not king yet," Adam pointed out.

Maddy shrugged and continued. "Then I suggest you go along with it for now. Because something's going on back there. *Someone* has gone to a lot of trouble to get us there and talking to this Cabot guy. The Pandora message—"

"Maddy?" Sal looked up from her plate. "Why is Pandora so important to you?"

Well? You going to tell them? That old dilemma again. *Be safe and tell no one*—that's what the scribbled note had said. Be safe . . . tell *no one*. Surely, though, Sal and Liam could know. Surely it wouldn't be dangerous to share this with them?

Liam's eyes were on her now. "Maddy? What is it?"

But Adam Lewis was really just a stranger, perhaps only a hapless victim caught up in this thing. The less he knew, the better.

"Adam, would you please excuse us for a few minutes?"

He looked hurt, but then finally he nodded. "All right. I'll, uhh, go settle the bill."

She watched him cross the deserted restaurant before she turned to the others, her voice lowered. "I've been keeping something from you. I'm sorry."

"What?"

"Liam, you remember our trip to San Francisco in 1906, to get some new clone fetuses?"

"Aye."

"In the safe deposit box was a handwritten message. It was a note addressed to me." She took a deep breath, still not entirely sure she should be doing this. "It was scribbled—like whoever wrote it was in a real hurry."

Sal fidgeted impatiently. "Maddy, just tell us!"

"Okay, okay," she said. "Well, it was this: *Maddy, look out for 'Pandora,' we're running out of time. Be safe and tell no one.*"

Liam and Sal exchanged glances. Bob frowned, and Becks cocked her head in consideration.

"It's a warning," said Maddy. "I didn't—I really didn't give it much thought while we were sorting out the dinosaur business. And, you know, I guess I was just trying to push it aside. Trying not to think about it. But then—" She looked up at Adam waiting for the waiter to process his credit card. "But then our friend over there decoded that message."

"It makes a little more sense to me now," said Liam. "You being so eager for us to go back and take a look-see."

"I'm sorry"—she shook her head—"so sorry I didn't share it with you both earlier. But it said tell no one. I didn't know what to—"

"It's okay," said Sal. "We know *now*. That makes it all right."

"Aye," said Liam. He pressed his lips into a half smile. "No more secrets?"

She shook her head and sighed. "Having that one was bad enough."

Adam Lewis was finishing his transaction and getting ready to come back.

"So the message is just between us, okay? This is agency business."

The others nodded.

Adam approached their table tentatively. "Safe for me to come back now?"

Maddy nodded and smiled. "All done. I think we should make a move. Lots of things to do."

Chapter 25

2001, New York

Liam nodded with approval at the thermal underwear.

"I got them from a sportswear shop," said Sal. "They should keep you warm under your other clothes."

"Thank you," he said, stuffing them into the plastic bag.

"I took the labels off again," she added. "But all the same, you should keep the thermals hidden. It's modern material."

"Right."

Maddy joined them around the long kitchen table. "So, I'm sending you guys to a couple of minutes in time *after* we brought you back, to avoid a tachyon clash." She shared a look with Liam. "Not making that mistake again," she muttered out of the side of her mouth.

"Okay." She turned to Adam. "Adam, you want to tell Liam and these two about your idea?" She flicked a finger at Bob and Becks, standing like two sentinels at the end of the table—in their underwear.

Adam nodded. "There's a way, we figured, that you *can* stay in touch—"

"But Maddy said we can't use the Voynich," said Liam.

"No, not that. There's a graveyard at Kirklees that dates back to the beginnings of the priory. I've actually been there myself and picked through it all. Lots of broken masonry slabs lost underneath brambles and nettles and what have you. If you look, you'll find them there. Anyway, I took a number of photographs of several of them. One in particular was part of a simple gravestone for a man named Robert Haskette, with 1192 as the year he died. So he'll be dead *now,* of course." He frowned. "Well, when I say 'now,' I mean . . . you know, the point at which you—"

Liam tsked and waved. "Don't worry, I get tripped up by the 'now–then' thing too."

Adam continued. "He'll be dead and his gravestone will be there already and freshly carved . . . hopefully. You just need to look for it."

Becks raised a finger. "Question."

"Yes?" Adam's eyes flickered up her athletic body. Then he found himself looking over her shoulder, shamefaced, cheeks coloring. "Uh . . . what is it . . . Becks?"

"You do not intend for us to communicate openly? This will present a contamination risk."

"No, no, of course not. This would need to be encoded. Ideally a code that looks inconspicuous and not out of place on a piece of masonry. Almost like decoration."

"Do you have such a code?" asked Becks.

"Indeed, yes—well, it's not mine, but it can be adapted slightly. You got any paper?'

Sal quickly skittered over to the computer desk and returned with a pad of paper and a pen.

"Thanks. Okay, this is the Masonic cipher. They call it the pigpen cipher." He sketched crisscross patterns of lines and dots on the paper and then filled them in with letters of the alphabet.

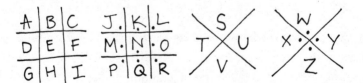

"Now what you do is, for each letter in your message, you use the part of the pattern that the letter is within. I'll give you an example."

He scribbled a coded message. Liam craned his neck forward to get a closer look. It meant nothing to him, and, as Adam had said, it did just look like a rather uninteresting pattern.

"Now, if we take, for example, the letter 'X.' Do you see where it sits in the cipher? Which part of this pattern is it sitting in? The part of the large diagonal cross with dots in the left-hand quadrant—see?" The others nodded. "Now look at that coded message: the first character matches that part of the pigpen grid, the part that contains the letter 'X.' So the first letter of the encoded message is X. Anyone figure out what the second letter would be?"

Sal answered first. "It's an M?"

"Yup. You got it. Go on—see if you can do the rest."

Sal grabbed a pen off the desk, and with a grin, quickly and easily extracted the encoded message.

"There you go," said Adam. "Easy as pie."

Liam held up a finger. "But, err . . . this is a Freemason code, isn't it? Won't that mean any Freemason who stumbles across our gravestone will be able to translate our message as well?"

"Yup, which is why we need to adapt it slightly. If I mix up the order of the letters now, like this . . ." Adam drew the pattern again, but this time filled in the letters in a random order.

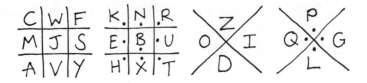

"Now, provided you keep your messages *very* short so that no frequency analysis techniques can be used, then it's almost impossible to break unless you throw some serious computer power at it."

"Frequency analysis techniques?"

Adam was about to explain that to Liam, but Maddy cut in. "Perhaps later." She picked up the sheet of paper and held it for Bob and Becks to study closely. "You guys can remember this layout?"

"Affirmative," said Bob, leaning forward. "I now have a stored digital image."

"Affirmative," echoed Becks.

"Good. So that's how you're going to talk to us." She tucked the paper into the hip pocket of her jeans for safekeeping. "And you'll need to let us know when and where to open a portal. We'll do the usual thing and plan a day-later one, a week-later, a month-later, and, of course, one just before the six-month critical mission window."

"What's critical about six months?" asked Adam.

"Bob's and Becks's heads blow up."

"Whuh? Did you just say . . . ?"

"It's a safety measure, to ensure the computer tech doesn't fall into the wrong hands." Maddy wrinkled her nose. "More sort of a fizzle than a bang, really. The circuits fry."

"Oh, right."

She resumed her briefing. "So those are the window times, Liam, but since we don't really have a clear mission plan, I'm guessing this is all going to boil down to you telling us where and when you want to be picked up. Are you okay with that?"

Liam nodded. "Aye. And you've got these photographs, you say?"

Adam nodded. "Yes. Not on me." He turned to Maddy. "Back at my apartment. On my hard drive. I'll need to go get it."

She pursed her lips. "Sal or I will have to go with you to get it, then."

"What if the gravestone isn't there?" said Sal.

"It should be," said Adam.

Maddy puffed her cheeks. "Hmm, well, look—if it isn't, for whatever reason, then you come back on the first of the scheduled windows, I guess. Just play it safe. Don't go wandering off to see King John until you *know* you can talk to us."

"Recommendation: first mission task should be to locate the gravestone and send a test message," said Bob.

"That's right," replied Maddy. "Very sensible, Bob."

She looked around at everyone. "So, I think that's it." She smiled. "This is a hunt for something we have no idea what it is or where it is—other than some nasty guy with a hood stole it and ran off into the woods. So it's the same old half-baked, no-idea-what-we're-doing thing again. Business as usual, I guess."

She dismissed them all with a self-conscious "Shall we?" As Liam turned to follow Bob and Becks across the archway and up the ladder, she reached out for Liam and squeezed his shoulder.

"Liam?"

"Yeah?"

She glanced at the plume of silver hair at his temple and the first faint hint of an age line around his eyes.

"Liam, I'm glad I told you and Sal the truth. It was eating me up sitting on it."

He hunched his shoulders. "A load shared is a load halved. That's what me Auntie Doe used to say."

"You stay safe . . . *again*. Okay?"

He grinned. "With Punch and Judy, I'll be fine."

He turned to go, but she held on. "Liam, this is an important one, you know? I've got a real feeling this—I don't know . . . that this is going to open doors. We find out about Pandora, and we're going to find out more about who we're working for," she said quietly.

"It's a certain Mr. Waldstein, isn't it?"

She shrugged. "So Foster once told us. I do wonder."

"Now there's an idea."

"What?"

"Foster. Maybe you should ask the ol' fella about Pandora while we're gone."

"I was thinking of doing that," she said. "I guess now I've told you guys, telling him won't hurt, right?"

He cocked his head. "I trust him."

She smiled at Liam, realizing that in his cocky, crooked grin she could see the ghost of Foster's gaunt face. "Yeah, me too."

The archway echoed with the splash of water as Liam dropped into the displacement tube.

Chapter 26

1194, Kirklees Priory, Yorkshire

They found the graveyard toward the rear of the priory, a somber space occupied by only a half dozen stones and a dozen wooden crosses on which hungry beetle-black crows perched, studying the frosted white ground for signs of a meal.

A recent grave marked only by a long hump of turned soil and a simple wooden cross indicated the most recently deceased person to be buried in this place was not considered worthy of a piece of inscribed masonry.

In the pale gray light they hunkered down beside each grave in turn and noted the names. Eventually, to Liam's relief, they found Haskette's grave beside a small oak sapling that had pushed hopefully upward for sunlight and now rustled gently in the bitter-cold breeze. The grave was marked by a three-foot-high block of pale granite, the name and year of death chiseled roughly, clearly not by a trained artisan but presumably by one of the Cistercian monks.

"Recommendation: we should inscribe no more than the symbol for an 'L' to indicate we have located the stone," said Bob.

Liam nodded. He was right—best to carve no more than was absolutely necessary. "Uh . . . did anyone think to bring a chisel?"

"Negative."

Liam cursed, then looked around. There had to be something they could improvise with. But he could see nothing out here but withered grass and nettles, frost-stiff and frozen-hard soil peppered with discarded flakes of worked stone and flint.

Flint. That could do it.

He began to scrabble in the hard ground to free a piece large enough that it could be used as a makeshift tool, when Becks quietly came over and tapped the top of his head.

"Unnecessary, Liam O'Connor," she said.

"Huh?" He looked up just in time to see Bob pulling a long lumber nail out of the wooden crucifix of the freshly dug grave. With a mournful squeak it came out, and the crossbar clattered onto the hard hummock of dark soil, disturbing the nearby crows. They fluttered away noisily into the tumbling gray sky with *caws* of complaint.

"Ummm . . . you can't just do that!" he said, absently blessing himself with the tips of his fingers.

Bob casually strode past him toward the gravestone. "Why not?"

"Well, it's . . . it's just not right. That's a *desecration*, so it is."

Bob was already hunkered down over the gravestone and etching their pigpen symbol for "L" into its granite surface.

Liam glanced heavenward. "Uhh, really sorry about that . . . if you're watchin'."

"'Tis later in the morning than I'd hoped to set off," called out Cabot irritably as he strapped the yoke to a pair of horses. "That is, if ye still wish me to take ye to meet John?"

"Yes, yes we do," replied Liam.

"Where've ye been?"

"To get some fresh air," replied Liam as they skirted around the vegetable gardens toward the stables. He nodded at Becks. "Our lady was feeling sick."

Cabot stuck out his chin. "Are ye better now, m'dear?"

Becks glanced quickly at Liam for guidance, but he stepped in to answer for her. "She's fine, so she is, aren't you . . . Lady Rebecca?"

She managed to nod mutely and swiftly adapt her usual tomboy swaggering walk to something that, all of a sudden, looked a little more feminine as they drew up beside Cabot and the cart.

"Noble-born, are ye?" The old man's eyes narrowed as he regarded her mud-brown dress of coarse material and her peasant's clogs. "*Lady*, are ye now?" he said with a disbelieving tone in his voice. "Hmm . . . and from what duchy do ye hail then?"

Liam looked at her. *Come on, Becks, better make it sound convincing.*

Her cool gray eyes returned Cabot's suspicious stare for a painful few seconds, long enough that Liam wondered whether he'd made a mistake casually introducing her as an aristocrat.

"*Je viens de la duché d'Alevingnon en Normandie.*"

Cabot's manner changed instantly; his flinty soldier's eyes widened. "Ma'am, please forgive my rude manner! I just—"

She smiled. "It is quite all right, old man," she replied sweetly. "Our mission to recover this . . . *item* requires a certain anonymity."

Brilliant. Liam grinned at her. *Bleedin' brilliant.* He could have hugged her there and then. But of course, now that she was supposedly high-born, that would be inappropriate.

Cabot gestured to the cart, a simple wooden trap covered with a canvas awning, and two pot-bellied ponies scraping the frost-hardened ground with their hooves, impatient to get going.

"'Tis not much, ma'am, but it is all we have here at the priory."

She nodded calmly, almost serenely. "The vehicle is sufficient."

"And far better ye travel in a humble trader's cart than in anything that might attract the interest of bandits," added Cabot.

Becks nodded. "Indeed."

Liam smiled. "M'lady seems happy."

Cabot looked up at a heavy sky that promised snow. "Then we ought

to leave with haste. 'Tis three days, but only if there is no snow. Three days to Prince John's winter residence." He pulled aside the canvas cover at the back of the cart. "There ye are, m'lady," he said, offering a calloused hand to help her up into the trap, but she ignored it and hopped up with all the regal grace of a private scrambling into the back of an army truck.

Liam pursed his lips. "Lady Rebecca's a very *independent* woman, so she is."

"Aye," nodded Cabot. "I noticed that."

Bob clambered aboard behind her, and the cart dipped and wobbled under his weight.

"Best we get going," said Cabot to Liam. "We will wish to be well clear of the forests before it gets dark later this afternoon."

Chapter 27

2001, New York

"I'm not going to run off to find the first news station I can and blab all about this, you know."

Maddy followed Adam up the steps and through a rotating glass door into a quiet lobby. Before them the apartment building's security guard looked up from behind a newspaper and smiled warmly at Adam.

"Lovely evening, ain't it, Mr. Lewis?"

"Isn't it, Jerry?" he replied cheerfully. "Unseasonably clement for the time of year."

Jerry looked like the kind of guy who'd once worked homicide but had now been put out to pasture. He sat back in a seat that creaked beneath his weight and laughed. "That's what I love about you Brits—always got something real smart-sounding to say about the weather!"

Adam shared Jerry's good-natured cackle with a wave and swept past his desk toward the elevators at the back of the foyer. He jabbed a button, and they watched in silence as a number display slowly counted down as they listened to the muted rumble of early-evening traffic outside, the rustle of the newspaper in Jerry's hands.

With a *ping*, the brass doors opened and they stepped inside. Adam hit his floor number and the doors swished quietly closed.

"I can't take the chance that you *will* tell someone," Maddy finally answered.

"You still don't trust me?"

"Nope. I'd be a fool to, since we only met this morning."

He laughed. "Well, actually, we met seven years ago."

Some of his smile spread her way. "I guess." She looked around the dark wood and brass of the elevator. "The rent in this building is probably pretty high."

"Very."

A soft chime announced their arrival at the fourteenth floor and the doors opened, revealing thick carpet and more dark wood. "You think this looks pricey, just wait till you see my gaff."

"'Gaff'?"

He led her down the hallway and finally stopped outside a door, pulling a set of jangling keys from the inside pocket of his jacket. The door opened with a soft click and he pushed it open, gesturing her through first. "After you, madam."

"Oh, very gentlemanly," said Maddy. She stepped in and almost immediately had to stifle a gasp. A wall of floor-to-ceiling tinted windows looked out on a forest of Manhattan skyscrapers, bathed in the rich vanilla light of a setting sun. She crossed a large open-plan lounge until her nose was almost jammed against the glass. "Oh my God . . . this is so cool!"

"I certainly pay for that view," he replied, stepping in after her, draping his jacket over the back of a chrome bar stool and hitting his answering machine.

Maddy turned to watch. There were messages. Of course there were: several from work, then several female voices each inquiring what he was up to this evening. Adam shuffled through them, dismissing them casually. He offered her a self-conscious fluttering smile. "Sorry about that."

She shrugged. "Don't worry. Clearly you're in demand."

"Now then," he said, "I just need to dig out that old drive of mine." He stepped past an exercise bike toward a chest beside the window. "Most of my junk from my university days is in here somewhere." He lifted the lid and carefully pulled out a dog-eared Dungeons & Dragons box and chuckled. "Could never say good-bye to all my fantasy stuff. Not easy to let it go, you know? Not if you've put the time in, painting them, that I did."

He dug back in, pulling out one or two other assorted items. For the first time since this morning she began to recognize once again the edgy, lank-haired young man she'd visited with Becks back in 1994; a loner, an awkward geek obsessed with dark corners of knowledge—puzzles, numbers, codes, conspiracies.

She looked around his apartment and realized it was a reflection of him, a reflection of his attempt to completely reinvent himself. No longer a narrow-shouldered, pigeon-chested nerd with bad skin and bad breath, but now the very essence of success: smart, intelligent, confident.

"It's in here somewhere. All the stuff I did on the Voynich, all my degree stuff on dead languages. I never let any of it go"—he looked up at her—"because I always knew I'd be needing it again."

She crossed the lounge and carefully perched on the saddle of the exercise bike. She looked down at his things. "Dungeons & Dragons . . . *you* were into Dungeons & Dragons?" She giggled.

He hunched his shoulders. "Oh yeah, but I keep that all locked away. The people I work with, people I bring back here, they, uh . . . they don't *get* that kind of thing. If you know what I mean."

"Hell no," she said. "I bet most of your girlfriends wouldn't be too impressed."

He pulled out a plastic bucket full of a tangle of wires, plugs, and electronic doo-dads.

"I used to play with my kid brother's D and D cards figures when I was younger," she added. "Made up my own basic combat rules because the rule book was, like, way-y-y too much."

"That's for sure," he replied, carefully pulling out bits and pieces.

She watched him picking his way carefully and realized he reminded her so much of her older cousin, Julian. She'd idolized him. He'd been smart and cool—an über-geek, always the high-school outsider, but with an air about him, a confidence that he carried always, like an impenetrable force field.

Adam, hunched down there in his sharp Dolce & Gabbana slacks and shirt like a boy bending over a toy chest, reminded her so much of Julian. And her heart ached. She'd been nine when it happened; when the world stopped for several hours and watched, on TV, three thousand people die, like it was just some kind of movie. Just nine . . . She hadn't really put it together in her young mind that after that second tower came tumbling down, she was never going to see Julian again.

"Ah . . . I think this is the one," he said, pulling out a hard drive that looked almost as big as a shoebox. "Twenty gigabytes!" He laughed as he got to his feet. "And look at the size of the damn thi—!"

He stopped. "What's the matter?"

Maddy hadn't even realized she was crying. Tears were rolling out from behind her glasses, down her cheeks, and onto her T-shirt. She bit her lips, angry with herself for allowing him to see her blubbering like this.

Adam stood and held her shaking shoulders. "What's up?"

She shook her head. *What do I say? You reminded me of someone I once worshiped? Someone who's going to die tomorrow morning?* Maddy felt her resolve crumbling. Why hadn't Foster rescued Julian instead of her? He'd have made a far better TimeRider, a far better team leader. Right then, she realized if she had the choice to walk out of the archway and back home to her parents' house in Boston—the choice to leave all the time travel, the worrying about history timelines, this so-called agency that seemed quite happy to throw raw recruits into the thick of it without any sort of assistance . . . If she were given the choice to walk away, she'd take it in a heartbeat.

And then, without a word spoken, she found herself sobbing against Adam's shoulder, dampening his expensive pale blue shirt with her tears.

"Hey, it's all right," he cooed softly, patting her heaving back awkwardly. "Heavy day, huh?"

"Yeah, sorta," she mumbled snottily against his shoulder. She let go of him and stood back, her puffy eyes trying to find a million things to look at other than his.

Outside, the sun was busy finding a bed for the night, and Manhattan was beginning to flip its light switches.

"I really . . . don't know why . . . I did that." She started to fumble for the first words of an explanation.

"It's okay," he replied. "Honestly, you don't need to explain—"

"No." She decided to straighten her glasses. "I *do* need to explain. I . . . it's just the work, the stress. That's what it is: stress. And . . ." She sighed, suddenly realizing that if she wasn't careful, she was going to go all girlie and cry again. She took a breath. "I miss my old life. And it feels like we've all been in this weird time-travel agency for years, and . . . I know it's only been, like, a few months." She laughed. "I guess for a bunch of mysterious time travelers from the future, we must come across as a bunch of losers."

"No." He shrugged. "I suppose even mysterious visitors from the future are still human, right? Still stub their toes? Still choke on their gum? Still slip on banana peels?"

She nodded, dabbing at her eyes. "Oh, we've done that enough freakin' times already."

He reached for a hand; she tried pulling back, but he grasped it and squeezed gently. "So, it turns out that the history of mankind is in the hands of *real* people. People like you." He smiled warmly. "You know, I think I prefer that—instead of some team of superheroes who think they know it all."

Chapter 28

1194, woods, Nottinghamshire

The fire crackled hungrily on the pinecones and dried, brittle branches they'd gathered by the waning light of the winter's afternoon. A steady dusting of snow had slowed down their cart, and Cabot—sounding a lot more like a bad-tempered soldier than he did a pious monk—had finally conceded they were going to have to make camp in the wilderness instead of seeking lodgings in the safety of some hamlet as they had done the night before.

Had they been traveling during a warmer month, he said, they'd be safer *not* having a fire and running the risk of attracting brigands like moths. But it was too cold not to.

Cabot spat on the flames as he finished a mouthful of stale bread. "We will be in Oxfordshire tomorrow. And the royal household at Beaumont before afternoon."

"Are you sure we'll be seen by John?"

"Aye. I'm sure. The poor sot is losing his hold on the country. He has done much that will enrage his brother, including his foolish orders to Richard's Templars to take the Grail up north to Scotland instead of letting them store it in Beaumont."

"Why did he do that?"

"I know not. Perhaps he had plans to hide it up there, to barter something out of his brother. So"—Cabot's eyes locked on Liam—"if none of ye are of the Templar order, as I suspect, how is it ye know so much about the Grail?"

Liam smiled. "You wouldn't believe me if I told you."

Cabot spread his hands. "I am willing to listen."

Liam looked at Becks and Bob, both standing a dozen yards apart at the edge of the light cast by the fire, silently standing guard. He wondered how much the monk should know; how much he could help them if he did. And, of course, how much contamination to history that might cause downstream.

"We're . . . we've come from the future."

Cabot's grizzled face remained still, unimpressed by that. "The future?"

"Quite a long time into the future, so it is. And, well . . . there's an ancient manuscript that mentions this "Pandora." We came here to learn more about it."

"*Future*. Do ye mean this in the way I think ye mean it?"

"Yes, *future*. As in days and years that haven't yet happened, but will."

Cabot's eyes narrowed skeptically. "How is that? A man's life can travel in but one direction. The sun rises, then it sets. It cannot move the other way."

"It's science," replied Liam. "I don't get how any of it works. But it does."

"'Science'? What is this word?"

Liam shrugged. "Knowledge of how things work, I suppose. It's quite big in my time. Science has given us all sorts of machines and understanding."

The old man absently stroked the ridged scar across his cheek. "Some Saracens I met did talk of such things. Of numbers and such, of things that can't be held, weighed, bought, or sold. *Ideas* . . . ideas our church would consider heresy." His face creased with a grin. "Would ye believe—many Saracen scholars say we live on a giant *ball*!"

Liam nodded.

"Aye!" Cabot's loud cackle filled the quiet wood. "Would ye believe such foolishness? A *ball*!"

"They're right, though. The world *is* shaped like a ball."

Cabot's laugh choked, the smile wiped from his face in an instant. "A man could burn at the stake for saying such as that in the wrong company!"

"But it's true, Mr. Cabot. The world *is* a ball, and there are other balls; we call them 'planets'—millions of them up there in space. And they rotate around *other* suns in what are called 'solar systems.'"

"Our world . . . goes . . . about . . . the sun?"

"Aye."

"Ye say there is *more than one sun*?"

"Aye. That's what the stars are. Suns."

Cabot looked up at the sky. He could see none tonight. His face seemed undecided between creasing with another good-natured cackle of laughter, or folding into a stern scowl of scorning disbelief. Finally, cautiously, he looked back down at Liam and shook his head.

"Ye are a strange young man, Liam of Connor, with an odd way about ye and the way that ye talk." He smiled. "And 'tis a fanciful tale ye tell. Despite my better judgment warning me otherwise, ye are a young man I like. *But*, I would strongly caution ye to keep such tales of coming from *tomorrows-yet-to-be*, and ball-shaped worlds and many suns, to yerself!"

Liam shrugged. Maybe Cabot was right. He'd read enough history books to know medieval Europe was a couple of centuries away from accepting ideas like these. To them the world was a flat plain, and the sun moved obediently across it from one side to the other simply because God willed it. And there were no other worlds, just this one. And no other suns. Trying to explain time travel to him, trying to explain how a history yet to happen *already existed* and—just to make things even more complicated—could even be *rewritten*, well, even Liam struggled with that sometimes.

"Anyway"—Liam tossed a branch on the fire—"all that aside, we came back to learn a bit more about what the secret of Pandora—the Grail—is. But now we know it's been stolen by someone, our mission has changed. Now, I suppose, we've got to get it back first."

"Aye." Cabot gazed at the fire. "There will be a terrible reckoning if 'tis not returned before—"

"SILENCE!" barked Bob, waving an arm to quiet them both.

Cabot hushed, and for a long minute they listened to the soft hiss of wind stirring branches and the far-off hoot of an owl, until finally Liam heard something, very quiet, but close by: the metallic jangle of a harness or a buckle.

"Ye hear?" whispered Cabot. "We are no longer alone."

Then they all heard it—the almost musical note of a released drawstring, followed by the whistle of something arcing through the air. Liam heard the smack of impact and saw Bob recoil a step backward. By the light of the fire he could see the glint of something metal protruding from between his shoulders. The support unit turned around to face Liam, and he could now see a pale wooden shaft and the white fletching of an arrow embedded deep in his chest.

"DANGER," his barrel-deep voice echoed into the forest.

Several more arrows whistled out of the darkness, another finding Bob's right hip, a third hissing past Liam's head so close he could feel the rush of air on his ear.

"Bandits!" shouted Cabot, scrambling to his feet and heading for the open back of his cart.

Into the pale dancing light of the fire, a dozen shapes in rags emerged, all of them armed with bows and long double-edged swords that glinted and flickered. By the look of them, Liam guessed their intention wasn't to demand they hand over their valuables, but to kill them all first, then to pick through their cart for what might be worth taking.

Bob and Becks moved at exactly the same moment, identical AI routines calculating risk and available courses of action in precisely the same number of microseconds. Bob sprinted toward the nearest man, ducking down swiftly at the last moment to dodge the careless swing of his sword. He sprang up again and crushed the man's throat with the bullet-hard jab of his oversized fingers just beneath his jaw. As the man dropped to his knees, gasping and spraying blood from his mouth and nose, Bob grabbed hold of his sword, flipped it blade-over-hilt and caught it, then finished the bandit with a lightning-quick thrust into his chest.

Becks meanwhile had effortlessly relieved another man of his bow and, using it like a quarterstaff, had scooped him off his feet and on to his back. She dropped down onto him, knees on his chest, and grabbed his head, twisting it sharply until cartilage and bone cracked.

Bob's blade clattered with a heavy ring as a second man stepped forward and swung at him. Sword pommels locked, Bob pulled his sharply, yanking the other man's sword out of his hand. It flew through the air, still humming like a tuning fork, and clattered off the trunk of a nearby tree. The man, older than the others, a florid face framed with wisps of dirty white hair, screamed, "I yield!"

He raised both his hands in surrender, a gesture entirely wasted on Bob. His next swing severed both of the upraised hands, sending them spinning to the snow-covered ground. The man screamed in agony, turned, and ran into the darkness, waving bloody stumps before him.

Liam heard the twanging release of another drawstring, and saw Becks had retrieved some arrows from the corpse at her feet. A grunt rang out on the far side of their crackling fire, and a man, who had been sneaking around to take Liam and Cabot from behind, staggered slow baby-steps forward, sporting a tuft of fletching from his forehead and a yard of bloody shaft out of the back of his skull. He toppled over onto the fire, sending a shower of sparks up into the dark sky.

The remaining bandits had already seen enough and turned and fled like startled hares, boot soles and swinging arrow quivers disappearing into the darkness. Someone's agonized drawn-out wailing—presumably the unfortunate handless old man—quickly receded to an indistinct echo that merged with the other frightened calls of the surviving bandits as they tried to find each other in the darkness of the woods.

In those few seconds—little more than the time it had taken Cabot to retrieve his trusty campaign sword from the back of the cart and adopt the once-learned, never-forgotten on-guard stance of an experienced swordsman—four of their attackers lay dead.

"Good God!" gasped Cabot.

Bob walked over toward Liam. "Are you all right, Liam O'Connor?" he asked casually.

"I'm fine, Bob. But you might want to take care of those," he replied, pointing at the arrow shafts protruding from Bob's chest and hip.

"Affirmative."

Becks joined them. "I will assist you, Bob," she said, calmly reaching for the barbed tip of the arrowhead poking out from between his shoulders. She snapped it off with a flick of her wrist. She reached around in front of Bob and pulled the shaft out of his chest with a sucking sound of puckered flesh.

Cabot watched in wide-eyed silence as she snapped off the second tip and pulled the arrow out of Bob's hip without even a flicker of reaction on his face.

"Blood is congealing from the two wounds already," she said. "I would estimate your combat functionality to be no less than ninety-five percent of full capacity."

"Agreed," said Bob.

"What in the saints' names are ye?" hissed Cabot.

Bob glanced at him. "Very tough human beings, serr," he replied unconvincingly.

"And ye," Cabot said to Becks. "No lady have I *ever* seen fight like that!"

"I am also a very tough—"

Liam laughed a little shakily, still adrenaline-pumped from the attack. "It's all right; I told him we're from the future already. You can drop the old English now."

Becks frowned. "That will cause unnecessary contamination."

Liam shook his head. "Ah well, it's not like the fella believes a word I was saying anyway."

Cabot was still holding his longsword aloft. His arms, now tired, lowered it to the ground. He leaned on the hilt and regarded the three of them in silence.

"Well, Liam of Connor . . . I think I believe ye now."

Chapter 29

2001, New York

"Oh my God, yes! Yes, it has! It's changed!"

Sal stared at the grainy image on the computer screen, old stone dimpled and worn with age and mottled with olive-green blooms of algae. She could see faint lines inscribing the name "Haskette," a gouge in the lettering where at some point in the last eight centuries someone had hacked at the gravestone—or perhaps it had been shot at.

At the bottom of Adam's photograph, where brambles emerged into the image, she could just make out the faintest groove of several lines bisecting. If he'd taken this picture in poorer lighting, it might not even have been visible. They would easily have missed it.

"That's definitely it!" he said. "Do you see it?"

Sal nodded. Maddy said nothing.

Sal's finger traced the shape on the screen. "And that's the coded symbol for an L?"

"Yes—yes, it is!" Not for the first time his jaw hung open, dumbfounded. "I can't believe it. I visited the ruins of Kirklees Priory six years ago and took all these graveyard pictures. And these digital images have been sitting on my old hard drive, in my chest . . . Jesus, I haven't plugged in this drive for a couple of years; it's just been collecting dust. And, yet, something's happened on there! Something changed on my hard drive! That picture's been altered. That's . . . that's . . . well, it's just messing with my head!"

"A minute wave," said Maddy. "That's what happened. A tiny, tiny time wave. So slight only Sal felt it."

Of course, Sal really wished she didn't pick up on the subtlc ones; they felt like motion sickness, that sensation of spinning around too much with your eyes closed.

"And you're telling me this is a wave that's been rolling forward through eight hundred seven years?"

"Yes, subtly changing this timeline in its wake. Except, of course, everything inside the archway's preservation field." She could see a look of confusion on his face. "That's why I placed your hard drive *outside* in the alley. There, it's outside the energy field, and so it *can* be altered by a time wave. Do you see?"

He nodded slowly. "Right. So . . . when Sal sensed a wave thing, that's why you . . . ?"

Maddy nodded. She'd raced outside with a data cable the moment Sal started wobbling and looking pale, and had quickly downloaded Adam's graveyard photos again—all the while with him standing in the middle of the archway, open-mouthed and looking utterly bemused.

He nodded his head again, as if that was going to help him get it. Then he leaned forward and studied more closely the image in front of them all. "I feel like my head's going to explode." He laughed. "This really is the most incredible thing ever!"

"Of course it is," Maddy said coolly. "That's why this—time travel— has to be kept so secret."

"But—but think how it could revolutionize history! Historians could visit the times they study; see for themselves how things were and not rely on—"

"And with each historian casually joyriding back into the past, the precious history they'd be studying would be altered, mutated, with echoes of change ricocheting back through time, tiny waves affecting tiny decisions causing bigger waves affecting bigger decisions. And all of a sudden in 2001 we're all speaking, I don't know—Chinese, or we're all suddenly dinosaur lizard-men, or there's no New York any more and it's just radioactive ruins! All because *somebody* decided it would be a *cool thing* to go back in time and see a bit of history for themselves!"

Sal looked at Maddy. Her cheeks were mottled pink with anger, or embarrassment.

Jahulla, *what's up with her?*

"Sorry," said Adam meekly. "I was just saying."

Maddy turned to look at him. "That's why we're here, Adam. Stuck in this archway. Stuck in these same two freakin' days, watching the same things over and over! We're here because there are morons in the future. Idiots! Nutcases! Power-hungry lunatics who think time travel's just a *game*! A *neat* idea! We're stuck here watching history . . . and I've got no idea how long we're gonna be here—me, Sal, and Liam." She looked at Sal. "Forever?"

Sal shrugged. "I hope not."

Maddy's outburst left a long silence, filled only by the hum of computer fans and the soft purring motors of the growth tubes in the back room.

"You okay?" asked Sal.

Maddy chewed her lip in silence for a while, then eventually nodded. "Yeah," she sighed. "I'm okay."

"Sorry," said Adam. "It's just all so new and exciting to me."

Maddy shook her head. "No, *I'm* sorry. I . . . I was rude. I didn't mean to blow up at you. It just sort of gets to you—this. Knowing about all this. I'm tired."

Sal decided to lift the mood. "Well, the good thing is, they found the correct gravestone. Right?"

Maddy nodded. "Right."

"We'll know what they're up to *this* time," she added.

Chapter 30

1194, Beaumont Palace, Oxford

The cart drew to a halt on the dirt and cobblestone track leading up to the flint-walled grounds of the royal residence, and Cabot dropped down off the cart's seat onto the track with a heavy smack of sandals.

"Morning!" he called to the cluster of soldiers up ahead blocking the way.

Staring at the tall stone buildings beyond the low wall—the steep gables, the crenellations, the flumes and chimney-pots from which thick columns of woodsmoke floated, the fluttering rooftop pennants decorated with royal coats of arms, Liam found he couldn't help but giggle. Yet another sight a young man from 1912 Cork was never meant to see.

"What is funny?" asked Bob.

"Oh, I'm not laughing, Bob. It's just exciting. Seeing this . . . seeing a *real* medieval king's palace."

Cabot's exchange with the pack of soldiers was already over. They—five of them in winter cloaks and heavy chain mail, puffing clouds of breath—disinterestedly watched him trudge back toward the cart.

"What's the matter, Mr. Cabot?"

"John is not here," he replied as he pulled himself up onto the seat. "He has moved to Oxford Castle."

To Liam's disappointment, they had skirted around the walled city of Oxford a mile or so back and not entered through the large archway into the busy thoroughfare he'd glimpsed beyond. However, over the top of the thirty-foot-high stone wall, he had spotted tendrils of woodsmoke coming from several steep rooftops and thought he'd caught sight of the crenellated outline of a keep somewhere in the middle.

"The guards say 'tis the unrest in this region that has driven him to the castle for safety."

Liam looked back at the low flint wall and the open ground beyond decorated with cherry trees, and the structure of Beaumont Palace itself; it was not unlike a cathedral, long and low with a vaulted roof of timbers. And, he noticed, no motte or other defensive earthworks around the place. Hardly the safe retreat of a ruler in times of trouble.

"Oxford Castle," said Cabot, grabbing the horses' reins and turning them slowly around. "I know it well. 'Tis a strong keep, and the city itself is very well protected by its wall. Good place for John." Cabot's dry laugh sounded humorless. "That is, unless the people of the city have also turned against him."

🕐

The late-afternoon sun peeked through scudding clouds as the cart rattled unchallenged under Oxford city's main gatehouse into a marketplace thick with the activity of traders closing up for the day.

Liam sat on the seat beside Cabot, chuckling with undisguised pleasure at the sight and smell of the place. Market stalls, no more than flat hand-drawn carts, were being loaded with the unsold flotsam of the day: rotten, broken heads of cabbage and snapped turnip roots. He saw a trader stacking the remaining skinned hares and rabbits head to toe, a baker collecting the last unsold stale loaves of bread, and, among all the traders packing up for the afternoon, he saw a wandering rabble of very old and very young beggars in dirty threadbare rags, pleading for the scraps too unfit to sell and destined for a pig's trough.

"'Tis a bad time for the poor," said Cabot.

Liam's gleeful smile all of a sudden felt wrong. Poverty. Grinding poverty. He'd seen that before; beggars in Cork, of course. But that was for money. Money that would perhaps end up going toward a drink. But this . . . this was begging for the food that pigs would eat.

"Aye," he said quietly.

Across the market a thin veil of smoke hung, the collaboration of a dozen outdoor pyres and the mist of warm breath from a thousand mouths in the cooling air. The place smelled overpoweringly of two things: woodsmoke and dung. Woodsmoke; Liam had noticed that every place and every thing seemed to smell of it. If there was one odor that would remind him of the twelfth century for the rest of his life, it would be that. And it mercifully covered up at least some of the cloying stench of festering feces, a heady brew produced by animals and humans alike.

Cabot noticed him wrinkling his nose. "'Tis one of the reasons I choose a monk's life, far away from the city." He nodded ahead of them. "Oxford Castle."

It was approaching dusk now; the gray sky deepening to a midwinter's blue. The now-you-see-it, now-you-don't sun was gone, lost behind the city's wall. Emerging through the low-hanging haze of smoke and mist ahead of them, Liam spotted the tall, square-sided Norman keep of Oxford Castle. Through high-up slitted windows, he glimpsed the amber glow cast from warming braziers and flickering flashlights.

Cabot steered the cart up a weaving cobblestone thoroughfare, narrowing in places where shanty-town huts and sheds encroached like scab tissue around a sore. Through open flaps of tattered cloth Liam caught the fleeting images of pale and curious faces peeking out: smudged with dirt and gaunt from hunger. Eyes that stared without hope at the flickering of a tallow candle inside, eyes that glanced his way momentarily with wary interest.

Liam's hope of seeing green fields and fair maidens and chivalrous knights in gleaming armor and merry men skipping around maypoles and florid-cheeked buxom wenches laughing with simple peasant joy— now it all seemed rather naive.

This is grim.

The cart crossed over a wooden-slat bridge, a muddy-colored river that had frozen at the edges. Ahead of them, a tall stone archway announced they'd arrived at Oxford Castle. Liam watched a gate guard approach the cart.

"What business?" He eyed Cabot's Cistercian robes and added "brother" as an afterthought.

"I seek an audience with His Lordship, the Earl of Cornwall and Gloucester."

"He has no time for a sermon."

"Tell him his old swordmaster is here. Cabot."

The guard's eyes narrowed as he studied Cabot in the fading light. "Stay here," he said, before turning away and calling out to one of the other guards to take the news inside.

"Be hasty," said Cabot after him. "'Tis cold out here, and he will be angry when he finds ye have kept his old friend waiting."

The guard looked skeptically at him. "Friend, eh?" He walked around toward the rear of the cart as they waited. "What have ye in here?"

"Visitors," said Cabot.

The guard lifted the canvas cover with the tip of his sword. "Ahhh . . . a strumpet for His Lordship, is it?" A smile stretched across the leathered skin of his face as he reached a gloved hand out to touch Becks's leg. "Ye *are* a pretty thing for a peasant girl, aren't you?"

"I wouldn't," said Liam, peering under the flap from the other end of the cart. He looked at Becks, and saw muscles tensing beneath her peasant's gown. The last thing they needed was her twisting the head off one of John's guards. "Becks," he said quietly, "don't hurt him."

"Affirmative," she replied, a hint of resentment in her voice.

The guard laughed at that. "Hurt me, would you? Well now, this I would most like to see—"

Raised voices came from beyond the archway, echoing off the stone walls inside—a commotion within. The guard retracted his hand and nodded politely at Becks. "Pity," he muttered, then pulled his head out from beneath the canvas.

"What is it?"

The higher-pitched voice of a younger man. "He comes! He *knows* the monk!"

Cabot grinned like a wily fox at the guard captain. "There, what did I tell you?"

The captain stepped back from the cart and stood to attention as the clacking of approaching boots on cobblestones grew louder in the twilight. Presently the archway filled with the flickering glow of a blazing torch, and Liam spotted the short, squat silhouette of a man with long hair standing in the middle.

"What in damnation is going on here?" a voice barked angrily, echoing off the masonry. "Let him in!"

Cabot tweaked the reins, and the cart rattled through the low archway and finally came to rest inside the castle walls. The squat figure stood on the ground beside Cabot, a dark shape puffing pale blue clouds of breath.

"Sébastien Cabot!"

"Aye, Sire."

"Last I heard, you were abroad killing Turks!"

Cabot wheezed a laugh. "I tired of such things."

A young squire holding the flickering torch hurried around the back of the cart and approached them. John's face was finally illuminated by the dancing amber light. Liam could make out a slender effeminate face, decorated with a wispy beard and mustache that fluttered with each breath and framed by fine, long, tawny hair. He was smiling warmly at Cabot. "Sébastien," he said, after looking up at the old man's battle-scarred face a little longer than was polite, "I cannot tell you how good it is to see you again, my old friend."

Cabot jumped down from the cart and John wasted no time in wrapping his arms round him.

"'Tis good to see a friendly face," added John.

Cabot gingerly returned his embrace. "How is my student?"

John released him and stepped back. He shrugged. "I am still a clumsy fool. More likely to hack off my own head than another man's." He glanced up at Liam. "So, you have a son now?"

"No, he is not my son." Cabot turned and looked at Liam. "He— he is here to . . ." Cabot was searching for words.

"What? Sébastien?"

"Sire, I believe this lad and two more of his friends in the back may be able to help in retrieving the item that has been lost."

John sighed. "So you have heard of this as well, eh?"

A long silence passed between both men, an unspoken understanding of the matter at hand.

"Then let us not talk carelessly out here," John said quietly. He beckoned Liam to climb down. "Come."

Chapter 31

1194, Oxford Castle, Oxford

Liam followed Cabot and John as they crossed the enclosure and entered the dark and cold interior of the keep's main entrance, talking all the while about old days. Inside his eyes adjusted to the gloom, and his ears rang with the echo of boots on stone as they ascended steps that took them upward in a cramped spiral.

Behind him he heard Becks's lowered voice. "Do you trust Cabot?"

"We have no choice," he whispered. His words seemed to bounce and echo up the stairs toward the monk and John, still talking convivially.

Finally they emerged into a grand hall invitingly lit by an open fire and rings of fat-dripping candles on candelabra suspended from several oak support beams that crossed high above. Liam suspected it was the glow of this hall he must have seen earlier.

John turned his attention to Liam, Bob, and Becks. "So, Sébastien, these three friends of yours . . . we can talk openly before them, I presume?"

Cabot nodded. "They are to be trusted."

John waved a hand. "You may sit," he said, slumping down on a wooden bench near the large crackling fire. Liam noticed for the first time how gaunt and unwell the man looked.

"It is a troubling time," said John after a while. "I have the people of England in open rebellion against me, I have the barons conspiring against me . . . all because of the taxes." His eyes glistened as he gazed at the flames. "Taxes that I had to raise to pay for this foolish crusade of his—*and* to pay for that madman's ransom." He looked up at Cabot. "Believe me—I was sorely tempted to let him rot in captivity."

Liam leaned forward. "Madman?"

"Sire," said Cabot, "this lad is Liam of Connor. These other two are Bob and Becks."

John nodded politely at Liam and, for the first time, acknowledged the support units.

It's the peasant clothing. Liam suspected that's how it worked in these times: to be poor was to be less than human; to be no better than the dogs and cats and chickens that wandered this city freely in the dark, foul-smelling spaces between shacks; to be almost invisible.

"You are a soldier?" John asked Bob.

"Neg—" Bob stopped himself quickly. "Nay, serr. I be just a normal man."

Eyebrows rose on John's slim face. "I would wager you could pull a cart as easily as an ox."

Bob frowned. He was busy processing that comment, trying to determine whether it was praise or an insult.

"And this is . . ." John's eyes lingered on Becks. "'Becks,' is it?"

"She was introduced to me as Lady Rebecca," said Cabot.

"Oh?" John looked skeptically at her mud-spattered rags. "A *lady* is she, now?"

"*Oui*," replied Becks in perfect Norman French. "*Je viens de la duché d'Alevingnon en Normandie.*"

John's cynical leer vanished, and Cabot smiled. "Yes, Sire, I believe she is of noble birth . . . but I've not heard of this duchy she refers to."

John tilted his head with a formal nod. "*Madame. S'il vous plaît accepter mes excuses humbles.*"

"I am also able to communicate in English," she said.

"Then, please accept my apologies, my dear." He gestured at her clothes. "It is your rags that—"

"We choose not to attract attention," she cut in drily.

Cabot's eyes widened. "Lady Rebecca, it is most rude to interrupt His Lord—"

John shook his head. "It matters not." He smiled tiredly. "I have far greater things to concern me these days than royal protocol." He looked at Liam. "You asked to whom I was referring?"

Liam nodded. "The madman?"

"My older brother," he said, sighing. "The king." He seemed to spit out that last word. "He has brought ruin on us all with this reckless crusade of his. Which, all are saying, has been a failure. Jerusalem remains in Muslim hands. But to make matters worse, the fool allowed himself to be kidnapped for a ransom."

He pulled absently on the meager, sandy-colored tuft of his beard. "And it is *I* who has had to throttle the poor and squeeze the nobles for yet more taxes—when there simply are none left to be had." He gestured to a tall, narrow arched window that looked out on the city below." You will have seen them out there. The people, they are hungry, and they blame *me* for this. Not *him*. Not Richard the *Lionheart*."

He sighed. "We are all *ruined* by this crusade. The guards outside, I have not paid them. They remain at their posts because here in this castle at least there is food."

"It is little better outside the cities, Sire," added Cabot. "The villages and towns barely survive."

"And all this," muttered John, "for a fool's errand."

"What do you mean?" asked Liam. He noticed a sharp glance from Cabot. "*Sire*."

John looked up at him. "Sébastien tells me you know of things only the Templars should know of."

"If you mean . . . Pandora?"

John frowned. The term didn't seem to mean anything to him.

"The Grail?" Liam added.

"Aye, this grail." John laughed. "What is it? A cup? A goblet? That is all. A cup that Christ may have used once! But Richard, like all those other Templar fools, believes such a thing has great powers. That madman believes carrying this cup into battle will make him unbeat-able! That's what this crusade has been about, you see? Not to free the Holy City from the Muslims, but to retrieve what was left behind when the city fell. To retrieve this . . . this foolish *relic!*"

The log fire spat a smoking shard of charcoal onto the stone floor. John watched its glow slowly fade. "A madman's treasure hunt. That's what this madman's crusade was about."

"Your brother found this grail, Sire?" asked Becks.

John nodded. "Yes. He did. And he had a party of his best Templars take it here for safekeeping." He laughed nervously. "But I . . . He will blame me for this, I know it. He will kill me." Liam noticed John's left hand tremble in his lap. "I had his men take their treasure to Rosslyn Chapel in Scotland. For greater safety, you understand, for secrecy. The royal palace is not secure. This *castle* is not secure. I thought it would be a safer place!"

"But they were ambushed," said Cabot. "It was taken."

"And on his return, I have no doubt Richard will have my head on a spike," muttered John. Conscious that his hand was shaking, he tucked it away into a fold of his robes.

"Sire, it is *this* matter, this reason why I have brought these three here. They say they can help ye get it back."

"And can you?" He looked from Liam to Bob, then to Becks. "I have heard all the rumors too. I have heard of this 'Hooded Man' who cannot be killed, it seems. A demon, some say. A wrathful angel, say all the peasants and villains that are flocking to the forests to join him. And you believe you can steal it back from him?" John didn't look entirely convinced.

Liam glanced at Becks, hoping she had something useful to say, but she stared back at him silently. And Bob continued to dutifully, and none-too-helpfully, monitor the conversation.

"I think, Sire, that this grail could've been stolen by someone who's come from the same, uh, same *place* as us."

"And what place is this?"

Liam bit his lip. They'd explained as best they could to Cabot, and that perhaps was a time contamination they'd need to clear up later. He wondered what the consequences would be for Maddy and Sal in 2001 if he tried explaining to the future king of England the basics of time travel.

"It is a place very far away, Sire. With strange ways. But look—this Hooded Man is no demon or angel." He jerked his head at Bob. "It's probably another peculiar man like Bob, here—that's all."

"Peculiar? What do you mean by that?"

"A—a strong man. Extraordinarily strong," added Liam. "And really tough. And with certain *unusual* fighting techniques."

"There is talk that this hooded fiend has shrugged off crossbow bolts and the like. That he is unstoppable. That it is the Grail itself that protects him from harm." John shook his head slowly. "You know, perhaps there is some truth to this Templar nonsense."

"Sire," said Cabot, "I have seen this Bob do just the same."

John's eyes darted from Cabot to the support unit.

"This is correct," Bob rumbled. "I am capable of suffering extreme damage and deploying damage-limitation counter-measures."

John turned to Cabot. "Sébastien, this ox of a man speaks a sort of English, but I have no understanding of what he just said."

"What he said, Sire, is that he can do exactly what this Hooded Man can do," Cabot replied. "I have seen, with my own eyes, Bob take arrows that would kill any ordinary man . . . and yet he did not even blink.

"Aye. It's not the Grail, Sire. It's not magic or godly powers or anything. This Hooded Man is just another . . . well, I suppose I'd say he's just another man like this Bob."

John studied them in silence for a while, a finger caressing the tufted tip of his chin. The sound of popping and hissing logs filled the hall. Finally he stirred. "And you say you are here to help?"

Liam nodded. "That's right. We're going to get the Grail back for you."

Chapter 32

1194, Oxford Castle, Oxford

The quarters they had been assigned were clearly meant for noble-born guests: four rooms high up in the keep, decorated with fine tapestries and embroidered cushions. Perhaps a true sign that John valued their presence was the distance from their windows to the fetid smell of the city of Oxford below.

The brazier in Liam's room burned brightly, filling the cold, damp chamber with a welcoming warmth, and a wooden table with a bowl of loaves and preserves and a flagon of imported wine had been set out for them.

". . . I was his swordmaster; in fact, I tutored all three of the king's sons: Geoffrey, Richard, and John," continued Cabot, tipping the flagon into his cup. "They were but boys then, long before political rivalries separated them. Geoffrey was the eldest and Henry's favorite. Richard was always the headstrong one, the one ye knew would seek to place his name in history."

"And John?" asked Liam.

Cabot shrugged. "A gentle boy. Certainly no swordsman. I saw in Richard, though, something to fear. A man who could become great . . . all-powerful. A man with the cold-hearted ruthlessness to take all the kingdoms of Europe and make them one. When Geoffrey died and it was clear Richard would succeed his father, I knew there would be plenty of blood." Cabot's face creased with a lackluster smile. "I too was younger then, and craved the glory of war."

"How long were you a Templar?"

"I joined as the sergeant to Sir Godfrey Cottleigh's service fifteen years ago, and we went to the Holy Land to do our duty: to protect Christian pilgrims. It was in those years, peaceful years by all accounts, before the fall of Jerusalem, that I learned of the order's secrets."

"Secrets? The Grail?"

"And so much more."

Bob and Becks seemed to perk up. Liam suspected they were both carefully studying his face, his body language, for telltale signs of truth or deception.

"What else?"

Cabot looked at him, uneasy with breaking oaths of secrecy he'd long ago been sworn to.

"Mr. Cabot? What *else* is there?"

"Ye understand, in telling ye . . . I am betraying the order of Templars. Do ye understand this?"

"But you left them anyway, right? So . . . ?"

"Aye." He shrugged and tipped the cup of wine down his throat. "After Jerusalem fell and Richard announced his crusade to retake it, I learned how much blood would be spilled in the name of God. When King Richard arrived in the Holy Land with his army, I saw in him a powerful obsession. A *dangerous* obsession." Cabot's eyes met Liam's. "He had learned of the Treyarch Confession . . . he'd come for the Grail."

Becks stirred. "I have no details of a 'Treyarch Confession.' What is this?"

"The Treyarch Confession is an account written by a man named Gerard Treyarch. He and his brother were soldiers in the First Crusade. They were among the Christian army that originally captured Jerusalem in 1099. Ye know of this?"

Liam didn't. He turned to the other two. "Bob? Becks?"

"The First Crusade is launched by Pope Urban II in 1095. The objective is to capture the city of Jerusalem and expel the Muslims. The crusade is successful, and in 1099, after a short siege, the crusaders enter the city. In the days that follow the soldiers are said to have massacred every Muslim inside . . .'"

Cabot nodded. "Men, women . . . children."

Bob continued: "The city of Jerusalem and the Holy Land remain in Christian hands for nearly a century under a succession of 'guardian' Christian kings. It is known as the Kingdom of Heaven, and peace ensues for almost ninety years. Then, in 1187, the Muslims finally retake the city under the successful general Saladin."

"Saladin?" said Liam.

Bob nodded. "Saladin is merciful and allows Christians to remain in the city, and orders his men not to ransack the Christian holy places."

"So, what is this Treyarch thing, then, Mr. Cabot?" asked Liam.

Cabot began guardedly. "During that century of Christian rule and peace, Gerard and Raymond Treyarch supposedly discovered something in the vaults beneath Jerusalem. The Treyarch Confession is said to be Gerard's account of this."

"Discovered what?"

"An ancient thing."

Cabot pressed his lips firmly together as if he was willing them to remain closed.

"And?"

"The story goes . . . it was a scroll that was over a thousand years old. From the time of Christ."

"Jay-zus!" Liam blurted.

Cabot frowned at him. "Indeed . . . the time of Jesus Christ."

"What did it say?"

"I have never read the Treyarch Confession, but I have heard it reveals nothing of what was in the text from the time of Christ; it is only an account of what they did with it."

Cabot bit into an apple. "It is said they transcribed the text of the original message to a ciphered form and then destroyed it."

Liam sat up straight. "Destroyed it? Why?"

"'Tis unknown." Cabot hunched his shoulders. "Perhaps because the truth it contained was far too dangerous for mortal man to know. Perhaps it contained the real spoken words of God, and they have a power we do not understand."

"And this rewritten version—this *encoded* version," said Liam. "*That* is the Holy Grail?"

"Ahh, ye are half right, lad. It is that version, *and* the key to deciphering it—those two things together are what is known as the Grail." He nodded warily. "'Tis a good thing that the Grail is two parts, kept separate."

"You believe it has powers, Mr. Cabot?" said Becks.

"I believe it had the power to make both the Treyarch brothers insane."

"Huh?" Liam's eyes widened. "Seriously?"

"Raymond Treyarch, 'tis said, killed himself in Jerusalem, and Gerard ended his years in some monastery in Aquitaine where he wrote his Confession and, as the story goes, went quite mad."

The fire was dying down. Liam reached for another log and gently placed it on the pile of glowing, pulsing charcoal and embers. "So then, we know one half of the Grail has been stolen by this hooded fella and his bandits . . ."

"Aye, the enciphered text."

"Where's the other bit, then?" asked Liam. "The key bit?"

"While the city existed under Christian kings, the text itself was guarded by Templar Knights in Jerusalem, and the key was guarded by another order in the city of Acre, a hundred miles north. Then both cities fell to Saladin, and so Richard launched his crusade to retrieve both items."

Cabot's eyes looked a thousand miles away. "I was there when Acre

fell to Richard's army." He sighed. "I watched as all three thousand Muslim defenders were beheaded. I believe he acquired the key that day. *That* was his celebration."

Liam shuddered at the thought of it. "So he wanted both things, and he managed to *get* both things . . . but sent the *text* to England?"

"Question," said Becks. "Why would he do that?"

"For safety. King Richard, I know, feared rivals, perhaps other kings who might also know of the Treyarch Confession. His army of crusaders was weakened after it became clear it was too small a force to besiege and take Jerusalem. His fighting men started to return to their home countries—as I did a year before. He sent one half of the Grail home for safekeeping and kept the other, the key to decoding it, with him.

"Now, his return home has been delayed by shipwreck and imprisonment. Two years he has waited to get home; two years knowing he has had the means to unlock the words of God, and finally he returns . . ."

"And John has lost it to this hooded fella."

Cabot nodded.

Liam could see why the poor man had looked so unhappy at every mention of his brother's name.

"King Richard *will* kill him on his return," said Cabot. "Of that I have no doubt. I believe this obsession has twisted his mind beyond any reason."

Becks broke a long silence punctuated only by the crack and hiss of a burning log. "Question: what has the word 'Pandora' got to do with the Holy Grail?"

Cabot seemed hesitant to answer that.

"Mr. Cabot?" Liam prompted.

His voice was low, barely more than a whisper. "It is the one word of the original message that the Templars were permitted to know."

Liam stroked his chin thoughtfully. "Becks . . . Bob?" Four gray eyes panned to rest on him. "If we got our hands on this Grail text, would you two be able to decode it?"

"Unknown," said Becks.

"We have insufficient data on the encryption techniques used at this time," added Bob.

"But say we got it, and managed to take it back to . . ." He glanced at Cabot. Perhaps it was best not to reveal the precise year to him. "If we got it back *home*, maybe that Adam fella could work it out?"

"It is a possibility," said Becks.

"It is not just a child's puzzle for ye to solve!" snapped Cabot. "This—this is Our Lord's words! A sacred truth! And, lad, ye talk of it like a . . . like a game to be played!"

Liam returned a stern expression. "It is no game, Mr. Cabot. Not to me, at any rate. We are here because, well . . . because these may *not* be the words of Our Lord. They could be the words of people like ourselves, other travelers in time."

The old man's lower jaw hung open and wobbled uncertainly.

"We received a warning, Mr. Cabot. A warning to look for this Pandora, whatever it may be. You said this Treyarch Confession goes that the scroll they found was written in Jesus's time. Right?"

Cabot nodded. "'Tis what is said."

"Then this warning has traveled across *two thousand years* to find us." He looked up at the old monk. "This is no game."

"We must acquire this Grail," said Becks.

"Agreed," added Bob. "That must become the mission priority."

Chapter 33

1194, Sherwood Forest, Nottinghamshire

He listened to the sounds of his people, his followers, their voices echoing through the woods as they chattered around their campfires. Their spirits were lifted. For them, today had been a good day. They'd managed to intercept a merchant's wagon destined to deliver to some baron a cart full of luxuries. The foreign wine they'd found was being consumed now. And their songs around the fire were gradually becoming less tuneful and more raucous.

They are like children.

He watched them from the darkness of his hut, his army of peasant bandits. So used to the grinding poverty of recent years, the starvation, grubbing for scraps of food. Here, in the forests of Nottingham, where they could poach royal deer and hares because the soldiers didn't dare follow them in, they were like excitable children.

It reminded him, James Locke, too much of the place, of the *time*, he'd come from. A world of poverty, overcrowding and crumbling cities . . . polluted oceans populated by nothing but floating islands of plastic trash and slowly dispersing toxins. A dying world . . . a *dying* world.

He looked down at the box in his hands, old weathered wood with an ornate pattern carved into its sides.

Locke stared at it. Inside this box was what he'd come back in time for. Inside this box was what his brotherhood had been waiting nearly a thousand years to recover. A lost truth. A warning. A prophecy.

Pandora.

Locke had glimpsed inside, had touched it, even unraveled some of it just to get a glimpse of the writing. And he'd felt the hair stand up on the back of his neck. The words were there on the parchment, hidden from a casual eye: random, unintelligable, the meaning locked away by its code.

He looked up again, out through the flap of his hut at his bandits making merry by the flickering light of the campfire. Their raids on the baron's goods, on the farms, on the taxmen's carts—all of that was eventually going to bring King Richard up to Nottingham once he returned to England, up to these woods. That, and the knowledge that his precious Holy Grail had been taken.

Locke nodded.

He'll come. And he'll bring with him the other half of the Grail. The key.

Chapter 34

1194, Oxford Castle, Oxford

"This will ensure you have the full cooperation of that bumbling fool," said John.

Liam looked down at the roll of parchment in his hand. It was sealed with a blob of wax in which John Lackland's royal crest had been impressed.

"What is it, Sire?"

"Orders for the Sheriff of Nottingham to give you anything that you need to hunt down this Hooded Man and his bandits." He pursed his lips with wry amusement. "Should that useless fool, Sheriff William De Wendenal, object to this, or prove obstructive in any way, you may assume the office yourself. These papers confer that authority to you."

"You mean *I'd* be Sheriff of Nottingham?"

"'Tis so if necessity requires."

"Cool." Liam chuckled.

"Aye," said John, looking around at the courtyard. The readied horses blew plumes of steam, and overhead the gray winter sky tumbled uneasily, promising another light flurry of snow. Cool indeed. "But it shall warm up soon, though, I warrant."

Stern-faced soldiers stood nearby, rubbing gloved hands and stamping their feet to stay warm. "I give you a dozen of my best guards to take up to Nottingham with you. They are all good men. I trust them. They will take your orders as if they were mine." John glanced at Bob, now equipped with a chain mail hauberk over his wide torso, a chain mail coif protecting his coconut head, and a long sword in a sheath attached to a belt of leather cinched tight around his waist. "Mind you, if your big friend is half the fighter you say . . . I should think you'll not need them."

Liam looked at the weapons and struggled hard not to grin proudly. *My own little army of tin soldiers.*

"I'd like to hang on to them, please," said Liam.

John frowned for a moment, then understood what he meant. "'Tis so." He placed a hand on Liam's shoulder. "Bring me back what was taken, Liam. Before 'tis too late."

He nodded. "Aye, Sire. We'll get it back."

"I do have one condition I insist on." He nodded at Becks. "Lady Rebecca will stay here in Oxford with me."

Liam drew back. "*What?*"

John tipped his head subtly, and a pair of soldiers appeared from nowhere and grasped her upper arms. Liam heard the scrape of a sword being drawn and Bob getting ready to swing it.

"Bob, stop!" he shouted. He spun around to face Becks. Already she had one hand around the throat of the unfortunate man to her right, squeezing his larynx. His eyes bulged and his feet shuffled and scraped against the flagstones.

"Becks! Put him down!"

She stared at the man defiantly for a moment before releasing her grip. "As you wish." The man gasped and dropped to his knees, hacking and coughing up phlegm.

John puffed anxiously. "Good grief!"

"She's a feisty one, Sire," said Cabot. "She can fight just as well as any man I've seen."

"So it appears," said John. "Nonetheless, I insist she remain here until you return with . . . *it.*"

They could fight their way out of here, out of the keep. Liam knew that between Bob and Becks, this courtyard would be nothing but a carpet of dead and dying men on the flagstones inside a minute. But he suspected a more intelligent solution was needed.

"May my friends and I talk in private for a moment, Sire?"

John sniffed. "If you wish." He waved a hand, and the soldier standing beside Becks helped his colleague to his feet and took him across the courtyard to join the other guards, where a soft hubbub of laughter and ribbing ensued—*a grown man, a King's guard, bettered by a girl!*

John took a dozen slow steps back from Liam and started humming tunelessly.

Liam, Becks, Bob, and Cabot converged and began talking with muted voices.

"We should stay together!" said Liam. "You'll miss the return window if we leave you down here."

"The scheduled window," said Bob, "is due in three days, one hour, and—"

"The one-hour backup window will follow, and there will be another after that in ten days' time," interrupted Becks. "We also have the final backup set for five months, twenty-six days, one hour, and seventeen minutes from now."

Liam realized Becks seemed to be making a point. "You're suggesting you stay here?"

"Affirmative. There may be an opportunity to acquire tactically useful data: additional information on the Treyarch Confession."

Bob nodded. "She is correct. Also, now that we have a method of communication with the field office, we will also be able to provide them a separate time and location stamp for Becks."

He was right; they could open a portal right *here* for her. She wouldn't need to make her way up to Kirklees. Liam looked at her. "You're okay with this?"

"It is the correct tactical choice," she replied.

Liam glanced at John, looking up impatiently at the sky and still humming. "I think he's got a bit of a thing for you, Becks."

"A thing?"

"You know . . . I think he *likes* you."

Cabot snorted a dry laugh, then quickly blessed himself with a guilty glance to the heavens. "Yes! You'll have to be careful!"

"I will be able to deal with him," she replied calmly. "I will use his . . . desires and motivations to my advantage."

"You can't let him know you're some sort of robot from the future," said Liam. "Do you understand? That's too much contamination."

Becks studied Liam for a moment, then her cold, emotionless face seemed to melt, transforming into a warm and sensual smile. She tossed her dark hair for good measure. Liam felt something flutter inside him—*desire?*

Oh come on, Liam. Meat robot, remember?

"My AI has already learned much. I have observed female rituals. I have also read *Harry Potter*. I know what body language and verbal inflections work most efficiently on human males." The smile remained on her face—teasing, encouraging, bewitching. She even managed a wink: clumsy and forced, but still enough to make his heart flutter. "I will be fine, Liam O'Connor."

She will at that.

Liam nodded. "All right, then. You stay here. See what you can find out. We'll let the field office know exactly where you are so they can beam a tachyon signal to you. If something goes wrong, Becks—if for some reason Maddy doesn't contact you with a schedule for a window here, make sure you get to Kirklees in time for the six-monther. Do you understand?"

"Affirmative. I have no wish to self-terminate."

"All right, then, that's that." He looked at Bob and Cabot, nodded, then turned to face John. "Lady Rebecca agrees to stay, so she does."

"Of course she does," said John. "I will make her most comfortable."

Liam stepped forward and offered John a polite nod. "We'll be off now, Sire."

"Please waste no time, Liam," said John. A momentary flicker of tension crossed his face. "I have heard rumors King Richard is already in France."

"We'll be back before you can say *póg mo thóin*."

John's heavy brows locked in mild confusion again. For a moment his lips pursed as if he was going to actually try saying it.

"It's just a turn of phrase where I come from, Sire."

"Right." He dismissed Liam with a curt nod. Liam turned and pulled himself up into the back of Cabot's cart. Bob followed him, the cart's axles creaking under his weight.

"It has been good to see an old friend again," John called out to Cabot. "Lord knows 'tis been a while since I've had one."

"We shan't return empty-handed, Sire." Cabot clacked his tongue and goaded the horses to life with a sharp tug on the reins. The cart slowly clattered forward across the flagstones toward the castle's front gate. Liam looked out of the back canvas to see the men—*his* men—forming up and dutifully falling in behind them: a short column of ruddy-faced soldiers in dull chain mail, marching heavily in their wake.

He caught one last glimpse of Becks, that teasing smile of hers packed away for later use. She nodded a farewell at him as they clattered beneath the archway and out onto the bridge.

Chapter 35

2001, New York

Sal watched Adam across the archway, bustling around their kettle and fridge, making them some tea.

"Are we not telling too much?" she asked Maddy. "Showing him too much? I thought Foster said we were, like, this top-secret organization."

Maddy looked away from the monitor toward Adam. "I know, I know," she muttered guiltily. "But I . . . he's useful, Sal. We need him."

"So what happens, though, when we've fixed things up and it's all back to normal? What're we going to do with him then?"

Maddy said nothing, which Sal misinterpreted. Her eyes suddenly lit up. "He can stay?"

"No!" she replied quickly. "No—we can't *recruit* him!"

"Oh."

"He can't stay, Sal. He can't. I just can't take in anyone we—just because we, you know, just because we *like* him."

"Why not?"

"Because this is a team already. A four-man team, just like Foster said. The agency is made up of *four-person* teams. Each with their own role and—"

"But with Becks we've already got *five* in our team!"

"I know! All the more reason not to be taking on any more!"

They watched Adam pour water from the kettle into several chipped mugs, stirring the tea with a tinkling sound that echoed across the archway.

"So what're you going to do, Maddy?"

She sighed. "Nothing."

"*Nothing?*"

"Because"—she bit her lip and looked away—"he's not going to *last* very long."

"What do you mean?"

"I checked his name, Sal. Checked it against the roll-call of tomorrow's victims . . ."

Sal's gaze returned to the desk, to Maddy. "*Shadd-yah!*" she whispered. "No. *Tomorrow?* Don't tell me he's . . . ?"

Maddy nodded. "He works for a company called Sherman–Golding Investment. They're on the ninety-fifth floor of the north tower." Maddy realized her voice was wobbling ever so slightly. "He's one who never made it out."

They heard his footsteps approaching. Both turned to see Adam carrying a steaming mug of tea in each hand.

"Here you ladies are. A nice cuppa." He frowned, puzzled. "What's up with you two?"

Maddy fixed a wide smile on her face. "Hey! Absolutely nothing." She reached for her tea. "Thanks."

He glanced back at the kitchen table. "I'll just go get the biscuits. Mum always said a cuppa tea's too wet without something to dunk in it."

They watched him go. Maddy found herself wondering what sort of a person this job was turning her into—that she could just knowingly let someone as likeable as Adam walk blindly to his death.

Chapter 36

1194, Nottingham

The town of Nottingham glowed in the dark. Not the welcoming glow of lanterns and night-watch fires, but from several buildings set aflame.

As the cart and its escort of guards slowly approached the entrance to the town, their ears picked up the faint ring and clatter of melee weapons and the roar of a defiant crowd.

Through an open and unmanned gatehouse they entered the walled town to see a thoroughfare cluttered and messy with broken slats of wood. A funeral pyre burned in the middle, stacked with a dozen corpses. The smell of cooking human flesh made Liam gag.

Cabot, sitting beside him on the seat, turned. "All right, lad?"

"Jay-zus! The smell," he grunted, wiping a string of dangling bile from his chin. "What's happening?"

"'Tis a rebellion, I think."

Liam noticed some women and children in rags down on their knees around the fire, presumably grieving for those bodies burning in the flames. He spotted a cart laden with what at first appeared to be a pile of bark-stripped firewood, pale knobbly branches of beach or willow. Then he realized he was looking at arms and legs—bodies, stacked on top of each other.

"Starvation and disease has come to Nottingham," said Cabot, shaking his head. "Farmers no longer work their farms only to have all they yield taken in taxes. So food rots in fields, and 'tis the towns that feel it first."

"Where is everyone?"

Cabot tipped his head toward the center of the town, where it seemed most of the night's amber glow and the roar of voices, the ring of blades, seemed to be coming from.

"I'll wager they are turning on the Sheriff of Nottingham's castle."

Cabot reached through the canvas into the cart, pulled out his sword and sheath, and rested it across his lap as he goaded the horses forward along a muddy avenue between tumbledown shacks. "We may have to fight our way in."

The noise and the amber glow increased in intensity as they rounded a bend in the muddy rutted track, and finally the crenellated top of a stone wall came into view. Along its base a sea of humanity swarmed by the light of hundreds of flaming flashlights. Activity seemed to be focused around two large, thick oak gates at the base of a guard tower. From the confusion and movement amid dancing shadows and flickering firelight, Liam guessed the people of Nottingham were doing their very best to attempt to build a bonfire against the gates. The soldiers on the wall were, in turn, firing crossbow bolts down into the crowd, then ducking back to avoid being pelted with stones and javelins and one or two arrows.

One of the guards John had assigned to escort them jogged forward to the cart. Edward—Eddie, he seemed to be called. The other men deferred to him, although they all seemed to share the same rank.

"Sire," he called up to Liam. "If those peasants see us here, they will turn on us!"

He was right. It seemed none of the hundreds in front of them had yet noticed the cart and its escort tucked back in the shadows of the alleyway between a long thatched granary and a thresher's mill.

"We'll have to fight our way in after all," said Liam.

"Sire?" Eddie stared up at him in astonishment. He looked like he'd seen a fair few battles in his time, with, like Cabot, a face that had taken its share of damage. But that command seemed to unsettle him. "Sire, that would be suicide!"

Liam nodded uncertainly. It didn't look too good. But then, they did have Bob. He turned in his seat. "Uh . . . Bob?" He realized his mouth was dry and his voice fluttered with nerves. He hated how every other man around him seemed to manage not to sound like a quaking child, and yet he sounded to his own ears like a boy still.

Bob's bristly head emerged through the flap of canvas.

"We need you to do your thing."

"Affirmative," his voice rumbled, and he disappeared back through the flap. A moment later the cart wobbled as Bob emerged from the back and dropped heavily to the ground. He strode to the front of the cart, his chain mail jangling and clinking. He stood beside the driver's seat, his head almost level with Liam's, and surveyed the scene ahead. "You intend for us to enter the defensive structure ahead?"

Liam felt his stomach twitching and writhing with apprehension. He nodded. "What do you think, Bob? Can we do it?"

Bob gave it some thought, and eventually nodded. "I estimate a high probability of success. Eighty—"

"I d-don't want to hear a number! Please!"

Bob nodded obediently. He reached up with a big ape hand and patted Liam's shoulder heavily. "Do not be afraid, Liam. I will clear a path."

He looked at the soldiers. All of them had unslung their shields from their backs and unsheathed their swords, ready for action.

"Have the guards form up behind me, to either side of the cart." Bob glanced at Liam, his eyes lost beneath the firm ridge of his brow and the rim of his chain mail coif. "And stay close to me."

Liam looked at Cabot. "Got that?"

He nodded vigorously. "Oh, aye. I'll stay right close."

Liam gave Eddie the order to have his men form up in two rows of six on either side of the cart, and then nodded at Bob that they were ready.

Bob turned toward the crowd and strode forward, a longsword held aloft in one hand. The cart rolled along behind him, both horses skittish and nervous, snorting their unease, and the flanking guards moved with it, hunkered down behind their shields.

The first heads in the crowd turned toward them as they emerged from the shadows, voices raised, alerting others. Liam could almost see the idea spreading from one to another: an easier target than the sheriff's castle on which to vent their rage. A dozen soldiers to make a brutal example of, and a cart no doubt loaded with gold sovereigns or, better still, food destined for the sheriff's table.

A roar of excitement and anger rolled across the crowd, the goal of setting fire to the castle's gates forgotten for now.

Oh boy. Liam had no weapon to clasp. Right now he'd give anything to be holding one of those Nazi pulse rifles from a previous mission in his hands. Even unloaded, the weight of it would have felt better than twiddling his thumbs.

Just ahead of them, Bob's purposeful stride switched to a slow loping jog. Cabot barked at his horses, and the cart picked up a little more speed, while Eddie and his men broke into a trot beside them.

The castle wall loomed before them. Above the roar of the crowd Liam could hear raised voices from the wall. Perhaps they'd recognized the round helmets and long shields of their guard as king's men and were preparing to open the gates for them. The crowd, though, looked unwilling as yet to part, despite the imposing form of Bob's seven-foot frame.

A cluster of a dozen men—by the look of them, not townsfolk carrying little more than pitchforks and stones, but more like the brigands who had jumped them in the woods—squared up to Bob's approach. Liam caught sight of the rusted glint of a sword's blade swinging around at Bob's head. He deftly ducked the blow and shouldered into the man with the force of a charging bull, knocking him back into the crowd and taking a dozen people off their feet.

One of the men took the opportunity, with Bob adjusting his balance, to lunge a pike at his stomach. The tip of it bit deep into his mail, breaking some chains, piercing his skin and going some way inside. Bob responded with a roundhouse sweep of his longsword that cleaved into the side of the man, the momentum continuing into the shoulder of the man standing beside him. Both men collapsed as Bob jerked the pike's blade away from the torn tissue and shattered bone and prepared to swing it again in the other direction, but the rest of the men quickly pulled back.

Meanwhile, halted by the exchange in front, the cart and the guards were fending off the closing press of people on either side. Missiles of all kinds clattered down on them: stones, sticks, chunks of broken masonry.

Something punched Liam's shoulder. He screamed out in pain and grasped where he'd been hit. There was blood. Beside his legs Eddie's shield clattered and clanged from the missiles raining down on them.

"Sire!" Eddie called up, jabbing the tip of his sword to ward off the nearest of the rioters. "Sire! We must keep moving!"

Chapter 37

1194, Nottingham

Ahead of them, Bob had deftly spun the pike around so that the blood-wet tip and halberd blade were aimed toward the people. He began to swing its eight-foot length in a wide loop that clipped and gashed a thickset man who'd shuffled back too slowly.

The swooping pike's blade did the job and created an arc of space in front of Bob as he resumed his steady stride toward the oak gates, now only a dozen yards in front of them. Cabot roughly kicked the rear of the left horse and it staggered forward, eyes rolling and snorting. The other followed suit, and the cart was moving again. The guards kept pace, their shields producing a cacophony of metallic clangs like hailstones descending onto a tin roof.

Liam felt the air by his cheek pulse as a stone or rock whistled by, far too close for comfort. He wrapped his arms around his head and ducked down low. "Jay-zus-an'-Mary-get-us-out-of-here!" he screamed through gritted teeth.

Cabot held the reins in one hand and held his other arm up to shield his face.

The lethal sweeping pendulum of Bob's pike had now cleared space all the way to the large oak gates. At their base, the beginnings of a pyre of bracken and firewood had been laid, but had yet to be successfully set on fire. Several bodies littered the ground in front of the gates, the stubs of multiple crossbow bolts protruding from them.

Liam could see the bracken and branches were going to need to be cleared aside in order to allow the cart through the gates—if, that is, someone inside was prepared to open up for them. But Bob was simply too busy sweeping his pike in order to keep the rioters back to deal with that himself. As the cart rolled forward into the clearing created by him, the soldiers spread out from the cart's flanks and formed a semicircle guarding the space in front of the gates.

The rioters—and Liam had noted a fair number of them looked more like seasoned fighters, even mercenaries, than they did townsfolk—seemed unwilling to press forward and engage the soldiers or fall within the range of Bob's swooping halberd blade. Instead they held back, jeering and cursing and continuing to rain down an endless barrage of missiles on them.

Liam jumped down off the cart and began pulling the small mound of branches and bracken away from the bottom of the gates.

"Help me!" he shouted to the nearest of the soldiers.

The soldier glanced quickly at Eddie, who nodded. "Go on, do as he says!"

He dropped his shield and sword and joined Liam, dragging armfuls of tangled branches and twisted bracken aside. Between them they soon managed to clear a gap in the thick pyre, when Liam suddenly felt a sharp, searing pain in the small of his back; the impact of something sharp and hard. His legs buckled at the shock of it, and he collapsed forward into the nest of branches and thorns, snagged and tangled like some hapless scarecrow on a loop of barbed wire. He gasped for air for a moment, winded, stunned.

Beside him he heard a loud ring of impact. He twisted, trying to untangle himself, feeling an intense pain between his shoulders, to see the soldier who'd been helping him clear the pyre drop heavily to his knees, then clatter forward onto the dirt and cobbles, wide, surprised eyes rolling uncontrollably. His helmet was caved in on one side, with the stubby fletching of a crossbow bolt protruding out of it. A river of dark, almost black blood cascaded from beneath the rim of his helmet down his face.

Oh, God help us, we're all gonna die out here.

Cabot was suddenly beside Liam, reaching down and pulling him out of the nest of wood. He was shouting something at Liam, but above the roar of chanting voices and the hailstone rattle and clang on the shields of the soldiers, he couldn't make out what the old man was saying.

Cabot looked back over his shoulder and quickly ducked an arcing lump of flint that shattered and sparked on masonry nearby. He turned back to Liam and jabbed a finger past his head, shouting something again. Liam turned painfully, grimacing at the sudden twist of his spine, to see the oak gates behind him had been cracked ajar, no more than would allow a single man to squeeze through sideways.

Cabot shouted again, this time directly into his ear. "Forget the cart!"

Liam nodded as Cabot pulled him roughly to his feet. "Yeah, okay," he muttered to himself. Liam could see that Eddie and his remaining ten men could do little more than hunch down behind their battered and misshapen shields, several of which looked like little more than twisted corners of aluminum foil.

Liam cupped his hands. "The gate is open!"

His words were lost amid the chanting from the rioters. He tried to make himself heard again. "THE GATE IS OPEN!"

This time Eddie heard, turned quickly, and saw for himself. He snapped an order to his men and they immediately began to shuffle backward toward the gates.

Liam looked for Bob. Over the top of the cart's two horses he could see his round head protected by the swinging skirt of his chain mail coif as he ducked and weaved, and the metallic blur of the pike's head whizzing around like the blade of some vast propeller.

"BOB!" he bellowed.

The support unit paused, straightened up like a startled rabbit, and looked around for Liam.

Liam waved his arms until Bob spotted him, then pointed to the gate. "IT'S OPEN!"

Bob nodded, and then, with one last warning flourish of his pike and a deep bearlike roar that startled and hushed the rioting crowd for a few fleeting seconds, he bounded around the uneasy horses and the abandoned cart.

The soldiers had begun quickly stepping through the tangle of branches, one after the other, and through the narrow gap between the gates, until all that remained of them was a rearguard of Eddie and two others.

"You first!" Eddie shouted at Cabot and Liam.

Liam pushed Cabot toward the gates. "I'll wait for Bob!"

Cabot nodded and followed through the gap. The rioters resumed pelting them with missiles as Bob arrived beside Liam.

"GO!" Bob's voice boomed. A large rock bounced off his left shoulder and spun off into the night. "NOW!"

"All right, all right!" Liam nodded and beckoned at the remaining soldiers to go for the gap in the gates.

The air around them was now thick with the hum of incoming rocks and stones. Liam hunched over with his arms around his head as he waited his turn, certain that some large hunk of masonry was going to brain him before he got a chance to squeeze his way through.

Eddie waved at him to go first, and Liam wasted no time. He stepped through the nest of remaining branches and forced himself into the narrow gap between the two large oak gates, rattling like drumheads from the impact of stones and rocks.

Then he was through into the darkness of the tower's entrance arch. He collapsed onto a hard floor of flagstones, gasping and wheezing. By the wan light of the flashlights outside falling through the opening he could see the pale and frightened faces of half a dozen men, their shoulders braced against the gate, ready in case the rioters decided to rush it and force it wider.

Bob's head appeared through the gap between the gates. "Wider, please!" his voice boomed above the din. The men against the gate reluctantly gave him a few more inches to push himself through, and then he was inside with the others. Immediately a heavy locking bar was slid into place.

Liam collapsed back onto the ground, exhausted, as the thick gates rattled and thudded for a while longer under the dwindling barrage of projectiles. Finally, apart from the occasional thud, it seemed the riot outside had spent its energy. He could hear the roar of voices grow sporadic, beginning to dwindle and lose some of the intensity they'd experienced earlier. Finally, one of the men in the guard tower called down.

"They're leaving!"

A man next to Liam, one of the guards who'd handled the locking bar, sighed. "Same as last night."

Liam grasped his arm. "It was like this last night as well?"

He shrugged. "'Tis like this *most* nights."

Chapter 38

1194, Nottingham Castle, Nottingham

It took a word of command from Cabot and a mere glimpse of the king's royal seal to convince one of the castle guards to take them immediately into the main keep. They found the Sheriff of Nottingham hunched over a round oak table, on which a dozen thick candles cast a flickering glow across cluttered stacks of parchment and a plate of food uneaten and forgotten.

He stirred drunkenly. "What is it *now?*" Bleary eyes opened, and at the sight of strangers in rags, spattered with blood, he lurched back in his chair and fumbled clumsily for a longsword on the table. It slid away uselessly along with a small stack of parchment and clattered on the floor.

"Sire!" said the guard, a young man with tufts of ginger hair poking down from the rim of his helmet. "Sire! 'Tis not villains!"

The sheriff stopped fumbling for the blade and looked up. "N-not villains?" His rheumy eyes narrowed behind a tangle of dark greasy hair. "We are safe? They—they have—gone?"

"The fool is drunk," growled Eddie under his breath.

"Aye, sire," replied the young guard, "they have dispersed, as last night."

The sheriff collapsed back into his chair with a sigh of relief, resigned to leaving his sword where it lay on the floor. He muttered a prayer of thick unintelligible words and then reached across the table for a goblet of wine.

"Sire," said Cabot, stepping forward, "we are on royal business. His Lordship, Earl of Cornwall and Gloucester—"

"Oh yes? What does John want of me now, eh?" He grinned up at them and then upended the goblet into his open mouth.

"We have come directly from John's keep in Oxford," said Cabot. "On his orders."

Nottingham laughed again. "Orders? I have orders, eh?" He attempted to pull himself to his feet, then stumbled a solitary step toward them before losing his balance and sprawling onto the floor. He lay where he was and began whimpering. Finally, after they waited for him to pick himself up, they realized he was snoring.

"He is of no use to anyone," said Cabot.

"Bob," Liam sighed, "lift him onto his bed."

They watched Bob heft the sheriff carelessly over his shoulder and cross the hall to a large oak-framed mattress.

Liam turned to the guard. "Is he always so drunk?"

The young man seemed unsure whether he should reply.

"*Answer* the man!" barked Eddie.

"Aye, s-sire. 'E . . .'e's turned to drink." The guard looked anxiously at them. "Dreadful afraid, 'e is."

"Of what?" asked Liam.

"The people, sire! The people out there! Every night now they come out. Every night they gather and try to burn them gates."

"Lad, where are the captains? The sergeants? Who is in charge here?"

The young guard shrugged. "Many 'ave deserted. They gone to serve other masters."

"So who is in charge?"

"The sheriff," said the lad.

"There are *no* captains?"

"No, sire. Just other . . . other men at arms, sire."

"How many?"

"We are at 'alf strength. Perhaps no more than two 'undred, sire. But more leave each day."

"So why've *you* stayed?" asked Liam.

"Because . . . because there's food 'ere. Because I'm afraid what them people out there goin' a do to me, sire. I 'eard stories of soldiers caught leavin' this castle . . . what them outside 'ave gone an' done to them."

Eddie cursed. "This castle will not hold the people of Nottingham out much longer if all that is left inside are frightened boys."

Cabot nodded. "This is not a good situation for ye to take charge of, Liam."

The young guard's eyes widened, and Cabot noticed. "Aye, seems this young man is to be yer new sheriff." He tossed a nod at the snoring body on the bed across the hall. "I am sure he can do no worse a job than that drunken fool, William De Wendenal."

Cabot turned to Liam. "So, lad. There are things it seems that need yer immediate attention here, before we go looking for a certain item."

Liam nodded silently. *Jay-zus, I'm supposed to be running a castle now?*

"Right," he said, with little enthusiasm. "Right . . . yes."

He became aware that Cabot, Eddie, the young guard—even Bob— were all looking at him, waiting for him to say something.

Why me? Why is it always me?

"Errr . . . all right," he said finally. "Right," he said once more for good measure. "Umm, okay."

Eyes on him still.

"So, then, Eddie?"

"Sire?"

"I'm going to put you in charge of the men here."

His jaw dropped open. "Sire?"

"That's right, you're the garrison commander now. I want you to take command on the walls for the rest of tonight. All right?"

"Aye, my lord!" Eddie barked with enthusiasm.

Liam expected him to turn and go immediately, but then he realized the man was waiting to be dismissed. "So then, uhh . . . you can go now."

"Sire!" Eddie turned on his heels. "Come on, lad!" he barked at the young guard. They clumped heavily out of the hall, and a minute later Liam thought he heard his parade-ground bark echoing up the stone walls from the bailey outside.

Cabot filled the quiet hall with the sound of his soft wheezy laugh. "So, Liam of Connor, mysterious traveler from the future. It seems now ye have become a part of history. Ye are the Sheriff of Nottingham."

"This will cause contamination," cautioned Bob. "And it is exceeding our mission parameters."

"Yes." Liam nodded. "I'm well aware of that." He glanced at the snoring drunk on the bed. The man was clearly unfit for his role; a nervous wreck. A *drunken* nervous wreck. Perhaps the situation had done that to him. The stress of it, being in charge of this hopeless mess. He'd learned enough now to know that this country was in a perilous condition, bankrupt and on the verge of complete anarchy. A resentful population taxed to their knees and now starving. The noblemen—barons, lords, and earls, who should have been the backbone of authority, providing men-at-arms and money to maintain order—were all conspiring against John, refusing to pay the tributes they owed.

A mess. A terrible mess. But a mess that was not his nor Bob's concern. That's how history was meant to be anyway, right?

"I'm afraid, Mr. Cabot," said Liam, "that fella snoring away over there . . . he's still the sheriff."

"Ye understand this castle is the administrative center of the north!" said Cabot. "Do ye understand that? If it falls into the hands of marauding peasants, if they overrun this place, then the country north of Oxford will be lost!"

"Right. But it's not our business. If it happens, then it's meant to happen. That's how history goes."

Cabot studied him silently. "Ye would let that happen? If order collapses, the land will be awash with the blood of innocent people!"

Cabot was probably right.

"Information: there are no records in history of a popular uprising of peasants successfully overthrowing the Sheriff of Nottingham," said Bob.

Liam looked at him. "You sure?"

"Affirmative."

"Oh that's just grand, that is," he sighed. "You're telling me this is all *wrong*—right? That this *shouldn't* be happening?"

Bob nodded. "It appears we are experiencing incorrect history."

Chapter 39

2001, New York

"Sal? Sal? . . . You okay?"

Maddy noticed she was teetering on her feet unsteadily. The half-empty mug of tea dropped from her slackened fingers and shattered on the hard concrete floor. She took a faltering step, then steadied herself against the edge of the kitchen table. Maddy got up from her armchair and put a protective arm around her narrow shoulders.

"Dizzy," she replied.

"Is she okay?" asked Adam.

Sal nodded. "I'm fine . . . but I think that was a—"

The archway went completely dark.

"Time wave," said Maddy.

"What?" She could hear Adam's breath, uneasy and ragged. She felt the soft touch of air on her cheek, his hands swooping and flailing in the pitch black. "What is this? Is this . . . is this some other sort of dimension thing?"

"No," she replied. "It's just darkness. The generator should kick in in a few seconds."

But the lights flickered back on before she heard the deep coughing throb of the generator starting up.

"Oh! That means we've still got power," she said, looking at him and smiling. "That's a good sign."

The computer monitors began to flicker back to life, one after the other.

"That was a big wave," said Sal.

"Yes, it was."

Adam looked at them both. "So does that mean . . . ?"

"You're in an alternate timeline? An alternate 2001?"

His head bobbed like a cork.

"Yes." She made her way over to the computer desk. "Let's see *how* alternate." The computer system was just finishing restoring itself, and Bob's dialogue box flickered up onto one of the screens.

> **System reset complete.**

"Bob?"

> **Hello, Maddy.**

"We just had a time wave."

> **I know.**

"But we've still got power." Stupid thing to say, but she'd said it anyway.

> **Affirmative, we have power. But I have had to correct the voltage and amplitude settings.**

"What?"

> **The power coming in is a form of direct current.**

She looked at Adam and Sal standing beside the desk. "Then maybe it's a bigger change than I thought."

> **Information: we have no external data link.**

"No Internet," said Sal. She made a face. "That isn't such a good sign."

Maddy nodded toward the shutter door. "Something pretty big's changed out there; maybe we should go see?"

They made their way across the floor. Maddy jabbed at the green button. Nothing happened. The shutter motor, linked directly to the external power line and not automatically monitored and modulated by the computer system, wasn't working.

"Marvelous," she muttered, and began cranking the handle beside it.

"Let me," said Adam, taking over for her.

The shutter clattered up slowly, letting in a surprisingly bright ribbon of light for the time of day. Maddy checked her watch. It was approaching four in the afternoon. The Williamsburg Bridge normally blocked the sun from their dim little alleyway pretty much from two in the afternoon onward.

Adam stopped cranking. The shutter was waist height. A quick look at each other, then all three of them squatted down together to look outside.

"*Shadd-yah!*" whispered Sal.

"Uhh . . . all right, that's not New York," said Adam.

"Nope," said Maddy almost nonchalantly. "No it isn't . . . *again.*"

The cobblestones of their alley stopped abruptly where the energy field ended, and beyond that was a bed of tidal silt that sloped down to the East River. She spotted several fishing boats of various sizes lying askew on the mud like beached seals, tethered to wooden mooring poles.

Across the East River, Manhattan Island was still there, of course. But instead of the forest of skyscrapers, there was a sleepy-looking town nestling on it. She could see a carpet of gabled roofs and chimneys, and somewhere in the middle the spire of a church. Along the edge of the town she could see more fishing boats and jetties, and the bustle of activity as fishermen worked their catch ashore, small cranes lifting nets full of squirming sea life out of their holds and onto the dockside as clouds of seagulls buzzed, swooped, and complained.

"We've had worse," said Maddy.

Adam shook his head. "It's, like . . . completely changed!"

"Duh," chuckled Sal. "Of course it is."

"But there's power," said Maddy. She pointed toward the town, where a line of lampposts carried overhead cables along the shorefront. "So it's not like we've been thrown back into some total dark age."

"But no Internet," said Sal.

On this side of the river, where only moments ago the seldom-used dockside cranes and abandoned warehouses of Brooklyn had stood, there was nothing but silt, punctuated by hummocks of coarse grass and dozens of tide-marooned fishing boats surrounded by discarded coils of rope and useless torn fishing nets. She spotted a solitary gravel lane to their right, flanked by intermittent wooden telegraph poles. It wound along their side of the river and, a couple of miles farther up, she could see the small mid-river humps of Belmont and Roosevelt islands, and—just as in the normal timeline—a bridge spanned the river there—albeit a very different-looking bridge.

Adam followed her gaze. "Can we go explore?"

Maddy pinched her lip absently. They needed information. They needed some idea when and how this alternative timeline had sprung up. "I think we'd better."

Maddy locked the computer system with a password and they all stepped outside, closing the shutter door behind them. She looked at their archway, nestling low down between two hummocks of grass-tufted mud; it was a jagged hemisphere, a scruffy igloo of old crumbly brickwork that went nowhere. She wondered how visible it was to anyone looking their way from the town across the river. Surely some-one would eventually notice the sudden arrival of a squat dome of rust-colored bricks nestling amid the mud and abandoned old boats?

Maybe. All the more reason to get a move on. "Let's go," she said, pointing to the gravel lane nearby. They avoided the muddy silt as best they could, picking their way along crests of grass until they stepped up onto the gravel road.

"It reminds me of—of . . . Calais," said Adam. "Normandy, maybe," he added.

They walked along the coastal road toward the bridge, finally spotting a vehicle as they neared it: a small flatbed truck loaded with wire baskets of chickens. It clattered noisily onto the bridge, the motor coughing, whining, and growling as it sped away from them toward Manhattan.

"That looks weird," said Adam. "Like we're in the forties or fifties or something."

Yes, it did. Old-fashioned. The truck looked a little like one of those old Model T Fords you'd see in jerky black and white movies. They crossed the bridge, walking on one side of the road. A dozen other vehicles passed them in either direction, all looking oddly antiquated and ever so subtly framed with decorative curls and *fleurs-de-lis* of brass trim.

On the far side of the bridge they turned left, following a road that weaved into the center of the village, where it became busier with people going about the business of a normal Monday afternoon.

An elderly lady in a black dress and scarf pushed a wheeled basket full of baguettes and looked at them curiously as they approached her. She frowned, puzzled perhaps by their clothes, but then she nodded and smiled at them as she passed by.

"*Bonjour,*" she uttered politely.

Adam looked at them. "Did you hear that?"

"French?"

Adam nodded.

"America's become *French?*" Maddy said incredulously.

The road took them into a small town square overlooked by a church spire and tall townhouses that seemed to lean forward over the space. A fountain gurgled pleasantly in the middle, momentarily drowned out by the piercing whine of a three-wheeled scooter whizzing past them, driven by an old man with a child sitting astride his knees.

"This seems quite nice," said Sal. "I think I like it better."

"It's French," replied Maddy defensively. "It's not right."

A class of schoolchildren suddenly filled the peaceful town square with their voices, a walking crocodile of two-by-twos carrying satchels on their backs and wearing blazers of yellow and green. The TimeRiders watched them spill out of a building and cross the square, chattering, laughing, making the same noise any class of children would make enjoying the novelty of stepping out of school.

Sal pointed at a sign above the door they'd emerged from: BIBLIOTHÈQUE.

"What's that?" she asked.

"Not sure." Maddy shrugged. "Let's see; maybe we can get some information there."

The other two followed her as she crossed the square and took the steps up and inside into a cool, dimly lit interior of wood-paneled walls and threadbare carpet, with tall avenues of dark wooden shelves thick with volumes of books.

"I'm guessing this is a library, right?" said Sal.

Maddy nodded. "Yeah . . . yeah, that's right."

But it was unlike any library Maddy had ever been in since first grade. She was used to modern, bright spaces filled with busy Internet stations and orange plastic bucket chairs, and racks of DVDs and magazines . . . and, oh yeah, one or two books, somewhere.

"History," said Adam. "We need to find a history book." His voice echoed around the quiet library, and several pairs of eyes looked up, mildly irritated.

Maddy nodded. They spread out, each picking an aisle, and started to scan the book spines on the shelves, looking for some way to identify a category. After a few minutes, Sal softly whispered for them to come over.

They both joined her in what appeared to be a children's section. She was holding a large book in her hands. "It's a kiddie history book." Sal flicked through several pages, all of them with brightly colored illustrations breaking up the text. She spotted an illustration of Roman legions, a diagram of a sailing ship, a timeline chart. World history, by the look of it. Good enough.

"I don't suppose either of you can read any French?" asked Maddy.

Sal and Adam shook their heads.

"Me neither," she replied. "We'll have to borrow it." Maddy took it out of Sal's hands and, after quickly glancing up and down the aisle, she shoved it under her sweatshirt.

"It's a *kid's* history book," said Adam. "You can't get all the information you need from that, can you?"

She shrugged. "No worse than Wikipedia."

"Wiki-what?"

"Never mind." Maddy pulled another book from the shelf and flicked through several dozen pages, finally nodding with approval. "This one looks good too." She pushed it into Adam's hands. "Well? Hide it."

Chapter 40

2001, New York

Computer-Bob's cursor blinked silently on the screen for a few seconds.

> I have completed French-to-English language translation from the scanned images. I will be another few moments collating the data.

"Right," said Maddy, tapping the desk impatiently with her fingers. "Quick as you can, please."

> Affirmative.

She wondered how long it would be before some curious *gendarme* came knocking on their shutter door. Their odd-looking round brick bunker was visible from the gravel road, and although it didn't seem to be that busy, she was sure someone driving past would eventually register the fact that their archway really shouldn't be there.

She looked down at the library books they'd spent the last half hour scanning. Not every page, just the pages that dealt with the twelfth century onward.

Children's history books. She shook her head. The illustrations were cartoony, with bright colors and smiley, rosy-cheeked depictions of knights and maidens, soldiers and peasants. The text was printed large and friendly—little detail there, she imagined.

History for elementary-school kids.

Great research.

The cursor skittered across Bob's dialogue box.

> **Process complete. I will summarize the data components for you in a chronological sequence.**

On another screen a word-processor opened, text suddenly blinking onto the page in sentences and paragraphs, quickly building up, filling the page as Bob rapidly cut and pasted relevant sections of text from the database he'd just constructed.

Adam craned his neck forward, eager to read what was coming up on the screen. Just text. Computer-Bob had not wasted time processing the many illustrations, most of which seemed more decorative than informative, there merely to break up the paragraphs for younger minds to digest.

"My God," muttered Adam, starting to read the page. "1194 . . . the great peasant rebellion of the north." He looked at the other two, wide-eyed.

"That's a new thing," said Maddy, "isn't it?"

He nodded, speed-reading ahead down the page. "Great peasant rebellion . . . the fall of the Plantagenet kings . . . peasant army led by some character known as the Iron Duke. King Richard retreats to Aquitaine . . . unrest and war in England . . . nobles united against the Iron Duke . . . Iron Duke's peasant army finally beaten at the Battle of Hawley Cross, 1199. Ensuing civil war between nobles . . ." He reached out and hit PAGE DOWN on the keyboard.

"The Three Generations War . . . England broken into warring factions . . . warring factions become independent states." He paged down again. "1415, King Charles VI invades the United Federation of Anglo Duchies." He looked away from the screen. "England . . . there's no *England* anymore!"

"That explains why they were speaking French out there, then," said Maddy. "Doesn't it?"

Adam read on. "1521, first French colony in the Americas . . . 1563, first Spanish colonies . . . 1601, the Colonial War, French versus Spanish colonies . . . King Phillip III of Spain signs peace accord with King Charles XVI, France wins when Dutch Republics come to their side. North America divided into French, Dutch, Spanish regions . . ."

"My God!" gasped Maddy. "Then there's no *America* either!"

"There is," said Sal, "but it isn't English, that's all."

Maddy shook her head. "Hey! It's *not* the same, Sal. It's not America if it isn't, you know, English!"

Sal shrugged at that. "I would still be Indian, English empire or not. You are the soil you are born on, not a flag or a language. Well, that's what my old *ba* used to say."

"Well," Maddy continued, muttering under her breath still. "I wouldn't call this place America without the Stars and Stripes. Just isn't right."

Adam was reading on in silence. "It's now called *L'Union d'Amerique*, actually. French is the international language. The language of law . . ." He scanned the text. "The language of science . . ."

"Science!" spat Maddy. "That's rich. There's no Internet! And those cars and trucks! They looked like they were from before the war!"

"But it seems medicine is more advanced," said Adam. He pointed to a paragraph at the bottom of the page. The numbers kept shifting. Bob was still adding chunks of text to the document. "The cure for cancer, 1963 . . . cure for something, can't read that . . . cure for something else."

"Look," said Sal. "World population reaches three billion."

"That's *half* the number of people on the planet in our time!" said Adam.

"This is the *same* time."

"I know that," he replied. "I meant in our *version* of this time."

Sal's eyes narrowed as she skimmed the paragraphs of condensed history for the twentieth century. "I can't see any World War Two, either."

Adam nodded, stroking his chin. "There's some wars in Africa. A couple in South America. But it seems there was far less war in the twentieth century than in our—"

"What? Because America isn't there?" said Maddy snippily. "Is that the point you're thinking of making?"

He shrugged. "Not necessarily. Maybe because there are a lot less people? Maybe that means less fighting for finite resources. I don't know. I'm no social historian."

There was quiet between them. On the screen, the document's page number was still increasing as Bob continued to add collated data.

"It does seem a much more *peaceful* world," said Sal eventually. She turned to Adam. "I have to say, this is the nicest time wave we've had so far." She shrugged. "Sort of almost feels like a shame to . . ."

Maddy looked at her. "Sal. Don't even go there!"

"What?"

"You know what."

"Just saying," Sal pouted. "That's all."

"Well, don't! We can't keep this world just because it seems *nice*. It's changed history. *Majorly* changed history!"

"But . . ."

"But what?"

Sal hesitated, uncertain how to finish. "But what if we *didn't* fix it?"

Maddy stared at her in silence, aghast.

"Seriously. What if we didn't? What if we just brought Liam and the others back home . . . and we left it like this?"

Maddy shook her head. "Sal . . . now is not the time for this kind of conversation." She glanced at Adam, watching their exchange. "And certainly not in front of someone *else*, you understand?"

For the first time, she noticed there were tears in Sal's eyes. "All you know is 2010, Maddy. You haven't seen my time. You haven't seen New York or anywhere else in 2026!"

"No, I haven't, but that's—"

"It's all so *shadd-yah*. It's falling apart! And we know it gets worse!"

"Sal!" warned Maddy. "We're not doing this now. We're not doing this in front of Adam!"

"But it does! You know that! I know it! It all gets worse and worse. The pollution! Global warming. The Oil Wars! And we don't know how it all ends up. But this . . . look at it! This is *better*!"

Adam seemed taken aback. "Oil wars?"

Maddy waved him silent. "Sal . . . listen, we made a promise to Foster. To keep history on track. To keep it the same *for better or for worse*. You remember the things he said? We can't change history to what we want. We just can't! Because—because . . ."

"Because what? He never told us why. He never explained that!"

He never did . . . not in detail, anyway.

"He said history has to go a certain way. Because if it doesn't, things break down. Things go wrong!"

"What things?"

"Space-time or something. The fabric of space-time. That's what he said, the stuff that holds those *things* back from our world."

Sal knew exactly what she meant. They'd seen one of them—just the once: a *seeker*.

They stared at each other in silence, a mutual challenge to say the word aloud.

"What things?" asked Adam eventually.

Maddy ignored him. "Sal, I know we've been pulled into this without much help. I know we got thrown into the deep end. And there isn't a day I don't wish to God that Foster was back here telling us what to do. In fact, there isn't a day I don't wish I could walk out the door and let the bubble reset without me. But we're here for a reason. If we hadn't done what we've already managed to do, the world could've remained a radioactive wasteland—or just a big lizardman-filled jungle! All I know is that what we've done so far has worked. Has been for the best! You know? I just—"

"You don't know *everything*, Maddy," said Sal quietly.

That stopped her dead. That hit home. "No, okay . . . you're right; I don't. In fact, all I know is how *little* I know. And that really scares me! And I don't know what that warning means either; I don't—" Maddy stopped herself. She realized that to continue was to take her toward openly discussing the Pandora message in front of Adam.

"Adam? How about you just go take a look-see outside. Make sure no French fishermen are gathering to marvel at our brick . . . whatever."

He looked at them both. "Okay." He got to his feet and wandered over toward the shutter door and started cranking it up.

"Sal," she began quietly, "all you and I and Liam have is what Foster told us. We have to trust that, because it's *all we've got* right now."

Sal eyed her silently.

"But we're going to learn more, I promise you. We'll learn from this Voynich Manuscript . . . we'll find out what Pandora is, what it means. We'll find out what the warning is. And when we know more than we do . . ." She smiled. "I don't know, maybe one day we can make a choice of our own, you know?"

Sal nodded her head ever so slightly.

"Until then"—she fiddled with her glasses—"until then . . . all we know is what's *supposed* to be, and what *isn't*. And this sure as hell *isn't*."

Sal tipped her head at the monitor behind Maddy. "I think Bob agrees with you."

Maddy turned to see the blinking cursor at the end of a message.

> **Recommendation: mission priority has changed. History contamination needs correcting.**

"Yup, Bob, you're right. I think we need to get a message back to Liam."

Chapter 41

1194, Oxford Castle, Oxford

"If we successfully complete the mission, Liam O'Connor, and we return to the field office, do you intend to retire me?"

"Retire? What do you mean?"

"Terminate this body and replace it with a male support unit. I heard Sal Vikram refer to this organic frame as a 'mistake.'"

Becks played the memory back in her head; a conversation between her and Liam as they walked along a prehistoric beach and watched distant brachiosauri grazing on an open plain. She knew the only reason she existed as a separate entity in her own right was because Sal had carelessly activated a female embryo from stasis instead of a male one.

She was an error.

"Why would we want to go and do that, Becks?"

"The male support frame is eighty-seven percent more effective than the female frame as a combat unit."

"Well now, I really don't see why we can't have one of each of you, you know? A Bob and a Becks. There're no agency rules, are there, you know, against us having two support units in a team?"

"Negative. I am not aware of any agency rules on that."

"So, well, there you are . . . why not? We'll have two of you instead of one."

The "memory" was now nothing more than a compressed low-resolution media clip to allow for more efficient data storage on her hard drive, the image pixelated, the audio flat and tinny. But there was another data file that had been created in that moment: a file that recorded the neuron response in the one small part of her mind that was organic. A file she had no meaningful name for yet—just a useful categorization ident: EmoteResponse-57739929.

"Have I functioned as efficiently as the Bob unit?"

"Yes, of course. I don't know what we'd have done without you so far."

The file was a recording of how her mind had reacted in that moment, several thousand synapses in her simple animal brain firing off minute electrical impulses. Perhaps the closest she'd ever come to a genuine emotional response.

As she stared out in perfect stillness and silence at Oxford below—a medieval town in slumber, lit only by the occasional faint stab of moonlight—she analyzed the file, unpacked the data and pored through it, wondering what human emotion the data file EmoteResponse-57739929 most closely approximated.

[Gratitude?]

No, not that. It seemed more than that. Not just a response to a sentence of praise . . . there was something else. Another factor involved. She ran the figures in her head, played the data on a digital simulation of her organic mind to try to replay that fleeting moment of "emotion."

More than gratitude. It was the recognition of her worth. She amounted to more than an error now.

But that wasn't it. There remained numbers in the file that were unaccounted for.

She replayed the file, the moment, the memory again, and her perfectly still face flickered ever so slightly in response. A hand muscle twitched. This time around she understood the relevant factor. It wasn't just that her contribution had been praised. It wasn't that she'd just heard she was going to be allowed to carry on functioning as a support unit after they returned. It was the fact that a particular person had said that to her.

[Liam O'Connor]

In the darkness of her chamber, as a fresh breeze played with the drapes on either side of her small window, she slowly cocked her head, unsure what that conclusion meant.

Further processing was halted. She heard the creak of the door to her room, and silently turned to observe it easing open and the dark silhouette of a figure step lightly in.

The figure crossed the stone floor, with the light tap of leather soles on stone. "Lady Rebecca?" She recognized the soft singsong voice as John's. "'Tis I . . . do you sleep?"

He wandered over to the bed and started patting the mattress. "Lady Rebecca?"

"I am here," Becks replied.

She saw John's outline lurch in surprise. "Good Lord!" he gasped in the dark. She saw his head turn one way and then the other, then finally settle on her standing beside the window. "There you are! Can you not sleep?"

"Neg—*no*, I do not sleep."

"Neither can I," he confessed, stepping around the end of the bed toward her. "I . . . My mind races with all manner of things. I am deeply troubled."

He drew up in front of her. Very close. Closer, she noticed, than humans normally stood when in conversation. "My mind, it needs soothing. Distracting from these troubles," he whispered softly. "And you . . . you, Lady Rebecca, I . . . I find myself drawn to you."

She felt the soft touch of a hand on her neck.

[Proximity threat]

She reached up and grasped his wrist firmly.

"Oooh!" John chuckled. "And this is what I find so alluring about you, my dear! You . . . you are so willful!"

[Analysis: subject responding favorably to threat response behavior]

"I liked the way . . ." She felt John's breath on her cheek, fluttering puffs of hot air. "I . . . *loved* the way you took care of yourself with that soldier, my dear."

She realized he was referring to her nearly snapping the neck of one of the guards yesterday. "You approve?"

He nodded. "Oh, yes! Yes! So . . . so *rare* is it to find a woman . . . a woman like you. So . . . so . . ."

"Strong?"

"Strong . . . yes! Lord, yes! A woman who can fight back!"

With one graceful movement, she lifted his feet off the ground and flipped him onto his back. He landed on the hard floor with a percussive grunt, and she dropped down heavily onto his chest, knocking the wind out of him. She put a hand around his throat, but at the last moment held back from throttling him.

John struggled on the floor, gurgling, his eyes wide and glinting in the fleeting moonlight. "Googh G-Goghhh! Urghhhrhbghady . . . R-Rebeghhaa!"

Her mind processed the shrill tone of his gurgling voice and the accelerated pulse in his neck and determined that she may just have misinterpreted his meaning.

She released her grip on his throat. "I apologize, Sire," she said.

John stared up at her in silence, his ragged breath filling the air between them. His thick tawny brows seemed to knit together into an intense unibrow, an expression she wasn't familiar enough with him yet to understand.

"Have I angered you?" she asked finally.

Chapter 42

1194, Nottingham Castle, Nottingham

"Ye understand this is a fool's errand?" said Cabot. "The king's forests are thick with the Hooded Man's followers! And they fight in a way that suits the forests."

Liam sighed. A night of sleeping on the matter hadn't helped. In the cold light of the January morning their situation seemed no better. Coils of smoke from last night's riot snaked up into the tumbling sky, and the subdued town of Nottingham below seemed to glare back at Liam with malevolence.

"You understand, Mr. Cabot, Bob and I aren't here to play policemen! The sheriff will have to deal with this on his own." He turned to Bob, sitting on an oak bench beside the window and gazing out at the town. "Bob? Tell him!"

"Mission priority is retrieving the artifact called 'the Grail,'" he rumbled, his eyes remaining on the rooftops of Nottingham.

"William De Wendenal is nothing but a wastrel, a drunkard! His men are deserting!" Cabot shook his head. "I had no idea the authority of John was this far gone. I had no idea how bad—"

"I'm sorry! But we can't stay here. We have to go find the Grail!"

"Do ye not understand, Liam? If law and order falls in this country—if chaos reigns . . . it is an invitation for civil war! The barons will tear

this country into pieces for themselves. Worse still, it is an invitation to France to invade, to plunder England. And by God they will, if they catch wind of this!"

"Maybe . . . maybe," Liam said, rubbing at tired eyes. "But that's a whole other mission, so it is." He turned away from the window. "We need the men out there patrolling the forests. We need to find this Hood!"

"Patrolling the forests? There be barely enough soldiers here to hold the castle! And out there—out in the forests, they would be cut down!"

Liam suspected Cabot was right. The few soldiers left in the castle were either frightened old men or even more frightened boys. Getting them to even consider patrolling the town around the castle would be an endeavor beyond him, let alone organizing a systematic sweep of Sherwood Forest.

"Bob? Any ideas?"

Bob remained perfectly still.

Liam came over and prodded his shoulder. "Bob? Hello?"

Cabot's eyes narrowed. "What is the matter with him? He seems entranced."

Liam could see muscles in Bob's face twitch, and the slightest flicker of his eyelids. "What is it? Are you getting something?"

"Just a moment," replied Bob. "Processing."

"What is the matter?" asked Cabot again, rising from the round oak table, still a shambles of scattered parchments and scrolls, matters long overdue for the sheriff's attention.

"I think . . . I think we're getting a signal."

"Signal?"

Liam ignored the old monk's question. He pulled up a stool in front of Bob and sat down. "Bob? Tell me what you've got."

"Decompressing wide-range tachyon signal data packet," he replied. "Just a moment."

A new signal from Maddy, that's what this had to be. He wondered what had happened. Something not good, presumably.

Finally Bob stirred. His gaze returned from the gray sky over Nottingham and settled on Liam. "I have a message from Maddy and an attached data package, Liam."

"So what's the message?"

"'Time wave has arrived. Significant contamination event, originating 1194. Mission requirement has changed. Prevent an event known as "Great Peasant Revolt." See data package attached for further information on event origins. Pandora now a secondary consideration. Please acknowledge.'"

"What's the data package?" asked Liam.

Bob blinked several times before he spoke again. "'The Great Peasant Revolt of 1194 began during the reign of King Richard. His prolonged absence on the Third Crusade left his country bankrupt. With the king abroad, the authority of the crown quickly eroded under the proxy rule of the king's younger brother, John . . .'" His monotone voice echoed across the hall for the better part of an hour as he read aloud the compiled dossier.

Cabot was the first to speak when he'd finished, his normally gruff voice shaken and small. "And this . . . these are events that are *yet* to happen? Just as I was saying to ye—rebellion? Civil war?"

Liam nodded. "That's history that has now happened."

"*Has* happened?"

"*Will* happen," corrected Liam.

"But need not happen if—if . . . ?"

"If I—if *we* take some sort of action, yes." He offered Cabot a smile and an apology. "It seems you're right, Mr. Cabot—there are more pressing matters to attend to."

"This means ye will . . . ?"

"It looks like Bob and I need to stay here." He got up and wandered over to the window and leaned against the stone frame. "Those riots going on last night . . . that appears to be the very beginning of this peasant revolt. It all starts here in Nottingham."

"Affirmative," said Bob. "Corrective measures will need to be applied here immediately."

"Ye have John's full authority," said Cabot. "Ye will use that?"

Liam shrugged. "I'd be mad not to."

"So, Liam, ye will become the new Sheriff of Nottingham?"

Liam saw that Bob looked unhappy about that. "I know, I know—if I make myself sheriff, I'm contaminating history, but it looks like—"

"Negative," Bob interrupted. "Contamination level may be acceptable."

Liam laughed. "Oh come on! There was never a Sheriff of Nottingham named Liam O'Connor!"

"Historical records of this time do not specify a particular name for the Sheriff of Nottingham."

"You mean . . . no one knows who it was?"

"Correct. This means your name is unlikely to be recorded in history. This is an acceptable contamination risk."

Cabot joined them by the window. "Do I presume from yer exchange that ye can become the sheriff, then?"

Liam nodded. "Uh . . . yes. Yes, I suppose I can."

"Good!" Cabot slapped him on the back. "'Tis much that needs doing."

"And quickly." Liam sucked in a deep breath. "This morning, then, I suppose we should make a start. Get an idea of what supplies there are in the castle, what money there is left in the coffers. And perhaps find out what the people of Nottingham have to say, what they need the most. And this hooded fella—whatever, whoever he is—the poor seem to think he's some kind of a folk hero. As soon as we can, we need to deal with him."

Cabot's old face wrinkled with a smile. "Good decisions already, young man."

"And we should also get a message back to base," Liam said to Bob. "Let them know we're working on it, and that Becks is down in Oxford, so they know where to beam a signal if they want to contact her."

"Affirmative," replied Bob. "I will prepare an encoded message to be carved on the gravestone."

"Gravestone?"

Liam offered Cabot a guilty shrug. "I suppose we should've asked first. We're, uh . . . we're using one of your graves up at Kirklees as a sort of message board. Hope you don't mind. It involves carving a few lines and—"

Cabot frowned. "Ye are *interfering* with a man's gravestone?"

Liam nodded.

"Whose?" he growled angrily.

"Haskette's."

Cabot pursed his lips for a moment. "Oh, Brother Robert? Not to worry, the man was a fool anyway."

to have done little to help the situation. He was *weak*, that was his problem; that had always been his problem. He was a weakling, a coward.

Richard tasted bile in his throat and spat.

The whole ugly, cold, wet country of England disgusted him. His spineless brother, the squabbling two-faced nobles, the repulsive peasants, even the ugly language they spoke, Anglish. Its tones grated on his ears.

My kingdom. For what it is.

It was worth nothing more than the taxes he could throttle out of the miserable place. Taxes to raise a new army and reclaim his French lands lost during the last five years.

France. All of France—that was his birthright, his true home. That was what God wished for him. And more.

He'd known that since he was a young man; known his destiny was to rule all of Christendom—not just that ugly island of Britain. And with such a magnificent force behind him, he would sweep once more into the Holy Lands and east into the Arabian deserts, wiping out Saladin's army.

He smiled as a freshening breeze lifted the pennants above the tents into life, and they fluttered with a renewed vigor.

God wants this for me.

Why else had the Lord led him to learn of the Treyarch Confession? Why else had the Lord ensured his success in retrieving the Grail from the Muslims? It was safe now. Safe on that ugly island across the Channel. Safe in the Royal Palace, and waiting patiently for him to return and unlock it.

He felt his arms and legs tremble with excitement at the thought of that.

He'd seen it briefly after his knights had retrieved it from the catacombs of Jerusalem; the brittle, yellowing pages of manuscript filled with faint ink lines of writing. He thought he could sense a

Chapter 43

June 1194, Normandy, France

He stared across the cool blue of the English Channel. It glistened in the morning sun, calm as a millpond, quiet as a monk, as it lapped gently up the Normandy shingle and withdrew with a whisper.

King Richard finished urinating and tucked himself away. His gaze drifted along the coast toward the small cluster of ships beached and battened up. The tents and marquees erected between them were topped with pennants that twitched and swayed in the light breeze.

A party of English nobles had arrived to meet him in Normandy, all of them pledging their support for him, their men-at-arms, their money. His royal tent last night had been full of them, like errant schoolchildren, all trying to outdo each other in their demonstrations of unflinching loyalty to the crown.

Richard smiled.

Just like naughty children, blaming each other for the unrest in the north of England. The rumors, if they were to be believed, mentioned a rebellion of peasants. And these fools who had come to meet him in Normandy should have been maintaining the order of England while he was away instead of bickering among themselves, jostling for favors and power.

And, of course, his brother John . . . The useless idiot appeared hum of divine energy coming from it, sense the meaning of it . . . even though the words were encoded. One brief glimpse, and then he'd dispatched it with haste into the night with the Templars he most trusted to see it safely home to England, to the royal palace in Oxford.

While, in *his* possession, in *his* oak campaign chest was the key to unlocking the words of the Lord: the other half of the Grail, a small square of worn leather.

"Sire?"

A shrill, tremulous voice like the cry of a seagull cut into his thoughts. Irritated, he turned to see a young squire, little more than a pageboy in silks, several yards away, kneeling in the shingle and looking down at his own feet, not daring to make eye contact.

"The lords are asking . . . uh . . . w-when it is ye p-plan to set sail?" the young man asked nervously.

Richard's broad face creased with amusement. It was funny how nervous men became in his presence. They stumbled over their words; their voices rose in pitch until they sounded like women; they fidgeted and scratched and shuffled; their cheeks flushed crimson. It was as if they too sensed the energy of destiny burning inside him. As if they understood that soon King Richard would govern an empire larger than Rome had ever known. And he would rule it with the rigid discipline and firmness of a father.

Because God wills it.

"We shall set sail this morning on the tide," he replied slowly.

The young squire nodded and began to back away.

"And, boy?" Richard called out to him.

He stopped. "Yes, Sire?"

"Bark at me like that again, and I shall gouge the tongue from your mouth with the tip of my sword."

The squire's face paled. He nodded silently, not daring to speak again.

Richard watched the squire back away to a respectful distance, then turn and run toward the tents with the news. He turned back to look at the Channel and smiled. The weather for the crossing was good, the breeze freshening.

Because God wills it.

Chapter 44

1194, Nottingham Castle, Nottingham

The sunlight warmed Liam's face. He closed his eyes, savoring its heat, and listened contentedly to the sounds of Nottingham stirring to life: the *tac-tac-tac* of someone chopping firewood, the bray of a donkey, the bustle of market vendors preparing for the day, the bark of a dog setting off a dozen others. All these sounds echoed across the cluttered shack rooftops of the town and up toward the castle keep.

A flight of swallows swooped past Liam's narrow window, and he opened his eyes to watch them dive and chase each other. His gaze shifted across the warm summer shimmer of the walled town toward the spread of fields outside, all of them now being worked, striped with thick lines of barley and wheat.

Someone, somewhere below was singing; a distant female voice that seemed to share his contentment.

I could live here forever.

He sighed. He could, really, he could. He could abandon the mission. He could abandon Bob and Becks, let them return home without him, and he could remain here in Nottingham as the sheriff. As long as he preserved history as it was, no one would need to come for him, would they? He could live out his natural life here, lord of all he surveyed.

A lovely dream.

One he could happily indulge all day. But, he sighed, there were matters to attend to.

Down below, in the flagstoned bailey, he could see soldiers being drilled. Eddie was working the new recruits. Bob was down there with him, demonstrating the on-guard position, a longsword glinting in the sunlight above the coarse mop of his dark hair.

Liam stepped away from the window and finished dressing himself. A pageboy brought him a tray of freshly baked bread and honey, and a flagon of watered-down wine. Ten minutes later he emerged from the dark interior of the keep into the courtyard and watched the soldiers drilling for a while.

Finding men willing to join the guard and replenish the garrison had been nigh on impossible five months ago. The people of Nottingham would have turned on any young man foolish enough to announce he planned to offer his services to the sheriff. But that was before Liam had opened the doors of the castle's storehouse and offered loaves baked fresh from the contents of their granary. Word got around the town's starving folk, barely managing on nettle stews and pottages made from rotting vegetables, and that simple gesture on day one of Liam's role as sheriff had put an end to the nightly riots.

Eddie spotted Liam standing and watching. "Good morning, Sire!" he called out.

Liam nodded and waved. "Morning, Eddie. Your lads are looking good."

Several of the men drilling turned and knuckled their foreheads politely. Smiles and nods from recruits old and young alike.

Liam, Cabot, and Bob had taken inventory of the castle and found food stores enough for the garrison to generously feed on for six months or more. Shared out carefully with the townspeople, there'd been enough for a month. Liam had then decreed that the King's forests were free for all to find food and game in, to forage for wild-growing shoots, nuts, and berries, for the immediate future—a popular measure that ensured a steady supply of food into the town's market every day. Satisfied that support for the revolt within Nottingham had been averted, Cabot had soon returned to Kirklees to oversee his priory.

Barely a week after they'd taken over from the previous sheriff, Liam and Bob were able to mount a few cautious patrols beyond Nottingham's walls, which was timely. With spring arriving, the fields beyond needed to be worked if the people were going to feed themselves.

Seeing Liam, Bob disengaged from his class of recruits and ordered them to stand easy. They lowered their heavy swords and shields with sighs of relief as he walked through them toward Liam.

"Sheriff," he greeted Liam formally.

Liam beckoned Bob to walk with him around the edge of the bailey, out of earshot so they could talk freely. "Bob," he said quietly, "how much mission time have we got left?"

"Twenty-four days, nineteen hours, and forty-three minutes of mission time remain."

Liam nodded, thoughtfully stroking the thin tufts of downy dark hair that had sprouted along his jaw in the last few months. "We have, what? Less than four weeks left?"

"Affirmative."

"Both you and Becks will need to return."

Bob nodded. "Our mission countdown needs to be reset."

Six months: a safety measure. Hard-coded into them both was a self-destruct command. The tiny mass of circuitry inside their skulls would fry itself. It meant computer technology from the 2050s was never going to fall into the hands of somebody from an earlier time, nor could a killing machine like Bob ever be reconditioned or reprogrammed to be used by some tyrant. If the support units failed to return and have their mission clocks reset, a tiny puff of burned-out circuitry would make Bob and Becks nothing more than drooling village idiots.

"I think I should take a trip out to see Mr. Cabot. We'll need to leave a message for Maddy. Let her know we're getting on top of things."

Bob grunted an affirmative.

They'd need to set up a return window so that both support units could be returned and reset. It would also be an opportunity for him to update Maddy fully. From where Liam was standing, it appeared support for the peasants' rebellion had ebbed away. The people of Nottingham at least seemed content to go about their business. The poor and hungry of the surrounding towns and villages would surely soon follow their lead, once the harvest was gathered and food could be distributed more widely. If history was back on track—and it looked that way—then he and Bob could proceed with the rest of their mission: to comb those woods he could see on the horizon for the hooded bandit and his dwindling band of followers, and hopefully to retrieve the Grail from them.

Truth was, that mob of bandits, whether led by some hooded figure or not, appeared to be operating farther away, now that Nottingham and the surrounding area was back under some semblance of order. The farms were now regularly patrolled by their raw recruits, and the daily sight of a column of one hundred men in chain mail appeared to have been enough of a disincentive to those villains that no crops had been flamed or ruined so far.

This time last year, Liam had learned from Cabot, they'd been raiding every farm they'd come across—the workers killed, animals butchered or stolen, fields left in flames. And a summer had passed in which little food could be set aside for the winter. The previous sheriff had done nothing to prepare for the inevitable famine, except, of course, to ensure his own castle was well stocked.

Liam had been stunned at how much the simple gesture of offering bread to the poor and starving of the town had achieved, ending the riots with one stroke. These hardy people were prepared to endure endless hardship and sacrifice and even offer their unfailing loyalty, so long as their noble-born masters treated them like human beings.

A simple idea for a poor lad from Cork, born in the year 1896, to understand; almost impossible for these French-born lords and barons to comprehend, though—most of whom didn't even bother to speak the same language as the peasants they ruled over.

What a difference five months has made.

Liam realized, once again, how there was a bewildering one-sidedness to things. He and Bob had arrived back in 1194 at the beginning of January, a cold, desolate month of dark, gray days. Now it was June. Winter had ended, spring had come and gone, and summer appeared to have arrived early, the trees already thick and green with budding leaves. But for Maddy and Sal, he imagined only half an hour or an hour would have passed; the time it took to recharge the displacement machine.

He shook his head.

"What is the matter, Liam?"

"I just realized something."

"What?"

"I'm aging faster than the other two."

"Maddy and Sal?"

"Aye."

"That is correct. For you, much more time has passed."

He tsked. "But that's not fair, is it? We keep doing long missions like this . . . I could end up an old coot while they're still bleedin' teenagers."

Bob looked at him, uncertain how to respond. "It is an unavoidable consequence of time travel, Liam."

He sighed. "Ahh well, I suppose I agreed to this kind of thing when I let that old man Foster take me."

They walked in silence for a while, the walls echoing with the clank and rasp of Eddie's recruits drilling.

"We have another tax collection organized for today, don't we?"

"Affirmative."

Half a dozen of the nearest nobles' estates had been paid a visit by

Bob, Liam, and half the castle's garrison. Each time, they'd returned with wagons loaded with grain and a tithe of coins. The nobles and barons all pleaded poverty when they turned up outside their walled keeps, all claiming that John's taxes had left them destitute and starving, but it was surprising how well-fed they and their household servants all seemed to be, and how well-stocked their granaries were. Meanwhile their tenant farmers beyond the walls looked as much like scarecrows as the people of Nottingham had last winter.

"We'll do the visits first, then you can return with the loot, but I need to go on to Kirklees."

Bob stopped. "You should not travel without an escort, Liam. There are still bandits in the forest."

"I know, I know. I'll take some men with me, I promise. On horseback we should make it before nightfall; we can stay at the priory and return early tomorrow. I just think it's time to update the others, and make sure Becks is ready to come back. Her mission clock is ticking down too."

"Affirmative."

Eddie called out and his men ceased drilling. Liam watched the recruits at rest; a pair of young women moved among them with water butts strung from poles across their shoulders. They served the hot and thirsty men ladles of water that they drank and splashed across their sweaty faces.

"I wonder," said Liam, "how she's doing?"

Chapter 45

1194, Oxford Castle, Oxford

"Have I told you, Lady Rebecca . . . have I told you how *beautiful* your eyes are?" John cooed from her lap. He looked up at her, a blissful smile stretched across his face. "Have I, my dear?"

Becks nodded and smiled down at him faintly. "One hundred twenty-seven times, Sire," she replied matter-of-factly as she gently stroked his cheek.

He laughed. "You are so . . . so *precise!*" He sat up suddenly looked at her intently. "That is why, I think, I have fallen so in love with you. You are not like all the other women I have known—feather-headed moo-cows who think of nothing but poems and silly frivolities. You are . . ." He frowned, struggling to find the right words. "You are so very *different!*"

She nodded slowly, carefully weighing what was the most appropriate thing to say back to him.

Response Candidates:

1. I thank you for your kind words, Sire. (78% relevance)
2. I wish to be different for you, my love. (21% relevance)
3. I am different, Sire. I am a combat unit from the year 2056.
   (1% relevance)

She giggled shyly, a gesture she'd observed other women use all the time in response to flirtatious flattery. "I thank you for your kind words, Sire."

He frowned, mock serious. "Sire? *Sire?* You *must* call me John, my dear. Please. In fact, I am yours to call whatever you wish!"

She nodded. "Then I shall call you John."

He smiled dreamily and collapsed back, his head cradled in her lap once more. "I have never felt so content," he murmured, his eyes closing as she stroked his troubled brow. "Never in my miserable life, not even with so many things to vex me—troublesome barons, no money, unrest, troubles, troubles, troubles . . ." As he continued, she pretended to listen, nodding at what she calculated were the right moments, but the cognitive part of her mind was busy elsewhere.

[Mission time remaining: 588 hours 56 minutes]

Time was running out. Another three weeks, and she would have to return to 2001. If "frustration" had been an emotion she could emulate, she supposed she'd be feeling it now. Just over five months of this, simulating love-play with the Earl of Cornwall and Gloucester. That first night he'd visited her room unannounced, expecting her to surrender herself to him, she had miscalculated the response and thrown him to the floor. That was the night, he later admitted, that he'd fallen head over heels—literally—in love with her.

At first, she'd been uncertain how effective and convincing her responses were going to be to his overtures, his poems, his breast-beating declarations of utter infatuation. But then one of the household maids had spotted her awkwardness and taken her to one side. She was an older woman, with a lifetime of experience to offer, so Becks listened intently. The maid gave Becks advice on how to respond to all the things John was likely to say, how best to please him.

She'd wondered how exactly to translate the nugget of advice into a practical behavioral response strategy. Cross-referencing it with modern language idioms, she concluded the old lady meant: *Play hard to get.*

Which was the tactical solution she'd decided to adopt. And it appeared to have worked. John, to use another modern expression, "was like 'putty in her hands.'" Like a fawning puppy. She understood that this gave her some degree of leverage; that she could ask favors of John that no one else would dare to ask. But a part of her AI understood human behavior enough to know that to ask him too much about the thing she wished to know more about was to invite his suspicion.

This thing, of course, was the Treyarch Confession.

In the last five months, she had chosen to raise the subject less than half a dozen times. On each occasion she'd only asked after ensuring John had consumed enough wine to render him insensibly drunk.

His rambling replies had yielded *some* useful information.

The Confession was something that his older brother, Richard, had come across as a much younger man, back when the sons of Henry II were all still boys and living at Beaumont Palace. It was apparent that John was not lying when he said he had no idea how the document found its way into the royal library, but that somehow his father had acquired it.

According to John, throughout his childhood he had memories of how his father guarded it carefully and read it frequently. It became an obsession of his older brother Richard, an obsession to find out what mysterious story was contained in this Confession. And one day, when he was merely twelve years of age, Richard finally discovered the Confession hidden carefully in his father's library of scrolls, parchments, and manuscripts.

And it changed him.

As John muttered on about love, Becks replayed in her mind the audio file of the last occasion they'd spoken about the Confession. He'd been lying by the fire as it roared and crackled from a fresh log, his voice thick with drunkenness, his words slurred.

"*Overnight it seemed, Richard was utterly transformed. He was still an awful bully. But now . . . now he was a bully with a singular vision of destiny. He said he would take Father's kingdom and make it an empire. That God had shown him the way he would do it. I know this is why the stupid fool went to the Holy Land. As soon as Father and our oldest brother Geoffrey died and Richard became king, that's the first thing he did— launch his bloody crusade."*

Becks heard her own voice. *"God showed him the way he would do it?"*

"Yes . . . yes . . . it was in that wretched Confession, wasn't it? The Grail story, you see? It was all in there. It was what turned him into a crazy man, what's made him so very dangerous."

"Is the Confession still in the royal library?"

"I . . . I would not know, nor care to. It . . . I suppose Richard would consider Oxford the safest place for it to be kept. But, please, enough of that madman, my dear. I'm getting stomach pains thinking about him."

A pause. *"You fear him?"*

Another pause. A long one. Then, finally . . .

"I am terrified of him."

"Because he will blame you for losing the Grail?"

No sound except the crackle of flames on scorched wood. Becks, however, recalled his gesture, a silent nod of the head, his eyes wide with the look of a man considering his own imminent death.

"I fear I will be a dead man on his return."

She recalled the haunted look on his face. *"Let me at least enjoy whatever time I have left—with you—and not speak his name again tonight."*

Chapter 46

1194, Kirklees Priory, Yorkshire

Sébastien Cabot greeted Liam with a cheerful wave as he clucked his tongue and reined in his horse. Behind him the crunch of boots and horses' hooves on hard sun-baked soil ceased as Eddie ordered the men to a halt.

"Sire!" called out Cabot, stepping through the gate of the priory's front gardens to meet him. "'Tis a wonderful surprise!"

Liam swung a leg over his horse's back and stepped down out of the stirrups onto the ground. He was hot and clammy beneath the quilted tunic and the robe of office. He ran a sleeved forearm across his damp forehead, pushing dark sweat-soaked hair out of his eyes.

"It's hot, so it is," he said needlessly.

Cabot winked slyly. "Good for the grapes and apples."

The two stared at each other for a moment, then Liam extended a hand. Cabot grasped it with both. "It has been too many weeks since last I saw ye, my friend."

Liam nodded. "Busy. Very busy."

"What has brought ye this way, Sire?"

"We paid a visit to Sir Guy's estate, and Sir Raymond's this morning. Both pleading poverty, but, like all the others, both very plump and extremely wealthy. So we collected what they owed."

"Long overdue, I would say."

"Aye." Liam wiped the damp from the thin downy bristles on his upper lip. "Sébastien," he said quietly, "I'm also here to . . . uhh . . . to talk."

The old man nodded. "Of course."

Liam turned to gesture at his soldiers, all of them exhausted from the miles they'd covered today, and equally hot under their vests of chain mail. "Would your brothers see to these soldiers? A little water? A little food, maybe?"

"Of course, Sire." He turned and bellowed orders across the garden, and several monks emerged from a small orchard beside the barn, baskets in hand.

"Ye wish to go somewhere private?" asked Cabot.

Liam nodded.

🕐

"News of yer good work in Nottingham has spread," said Cabot. "Ye are fast becoming a popular sheriff, young Liam."

"But not so popular with all them noble fellas, right?"

"The nobles hate ye." He shrugged. "They see ye as a young pretender. They each wonder why it is that John has not chosen *them* to administer the north. And," he chuckled, "ye actually make 'em pay the taxes they owe."

Liam slurped on his flagon, savoring the cool trickle of water down his parched throat. "Sébastien, we will have to leave soon."

"Leave? Why?"

"It's just the way it works. We have to go back to our time for a bit."

"But . . . but ye can't return the sheriff's office to that wastrel, William De—"

"We'll be back, I promise you. We just have to check in with our colleagues. See how things are in the future."

"The future," uttered Cabot. His old face creased. "I would dearly love to see a little of that."

"It's not so great, Sébastien," Liam sighed.

"Tell me something of it."

The old monk already knew too much. Someday soon a decision would have to be made about him: whether they could trust him or not. A little more knowledge would probably make no difference.

"It's a crowded world," he replied. "That's what I find. A crowded world full of noisy fat people."

"Fat?"

He nodded. "As plump as the lords and barons. Everyone, even the poorest, lives a lord's life by comparison to the people here. Everyone eats more than they need. Everyone has more things than they would *ever* need."

"'Tis a good time that ye come from, then."

He shrugged. "It *should* be."

Cabot's eyes narrowed. "But ye do not miss it?"

Liam knew, when he was all done here in 1194, he'd miss rising each morning to the sound of cockerels stirring and the distant ring of a blacksmith's hammer, the smell of woodsmoke and unleavened bread baking in hundreds of clay ovens.

"I could happily stay here," he said after a while, then realized that was perhaps too much of an admission. "But I can't, Sébastien. Duty calls, so it does."

"Duty; I can understand that."

A gentle breeze stirred the tall grass of the graveyard. They were alone here at the rear of the priory.

"Liam," said Cabot after a while, "is this world of mine"—he gestured with both hands—"is this world as it *should* be now? Is this the correct England of yer history books?"

"I don't know yet. The unrest that there was in Nottingham months ago could have become a much bigger problem for John. There was a new history created in my time, a history where a rebellion broke this country into pieces, and the French invaded and there was no more England."

"Good God!"

"And I think—I *hope* we're well on the mend from that. But . . ."

"But what?"

"But history, I think, is still altered in smaller ways. I mean, think about it. Me—*me* as the sheriff, for one. And all the things that you now know. Those are all small differences that *could* lead to bigger changes."

Cabot hunched his shoulders. "Ye worry I would tell others of these things ye have told me?"

"Well, to be honest, yes."

"Who would believe any of it? They would think it the ramblings of an old mad monk." He laughed. "Traveling to tomorrows yet to be? Worlds shaped like balls? Who would listen to that nonsense? I would be clapped in stocks and have rotten food thrown at me for amusement."

He had a point.

"I have a thought."

"What?"

"Perhaps, young Liam . . . perhaps history too is *round*, in a way."

"What do you mean?"

Cabot's bushy eyebrows locked with concentration. "Round . . . such like a cart's wheel. Perhaps ye were always *meant* to come back and be the Sheriff of Nottingham. Perhaps I was always meant to be told these things by ye."

The old man had another interesting point.

"And perhaps our poor John was always meant to have lost the Grail. Is that what your history books say, Liam?"

"About the Holy Grail?" Liam emptied the cup. "I don't know. I think there's nothing certain on that. I think history books treat the Grail like a fairy story, or a myth or something."

"There, then," said Cabot, smiling. "If it is a thing that never was, then for it to be lost, what difference does that make?"

"True."

He leaned forward and punched Liam on the arm affectionately. "Ye worry too much, lad."

"Don't I just?" He smiled. "Anyway, Sébastien." He produced a sheet of parchment from the inside of his robe. A single line of pigpen symbols was scrawled across it. "We need to cut this into"—he looked at the gravestone—"poor old Haskette's gravestone."

Cabot studied the parchment for a moment. "Ye know, 'tis a very good thing this code of yers is all straight lines. I am no stonemason. I cannot engrave a curve worth speaking of." He pulled a mason's hammer and chisel from the apron of his robe.

"To work, then."

Chapter 47

2001, New York

It was dark outside. Lit only by a half moon, the East River sparkled silver and reflected the amber glow coming from the lamps of several fishing vessels moored across the water. A dozen street lamps in the small fishing port across from them—they'd learned it was called Laurent-sur-Mer—glowed mutely, and windows here and there flickered with the movements of family life.

"I've never seen New York so peaceful," said Adam. "It reminds me of my grandparents' village up in Scotland."

Maddy nodded. "There are some places like this up in Maine and Connecticut. All nice and picture-postcardlike."

They listened for a while to the soothing ebb and flow of gentle lapping waves and the far-off cry of seagulls.

"So, how long have you been in this time-travel agency? I mean, not always, right? You sound like you've done other things, like you had a life before all this."

She nodded. "Sure I did."

"Well?"

She shrugged. Telling him a little about herself was probably not going to do any harm. "I'm from Boston originally. My folks live there. I went to high school there. Then I went to college to major in computers. I dropped out after the first year."

"Why?"

"I got a job with a game company. Seemed pointless going on with the degree and all."

"Where was the job?"

"Here. In New York. Programming user-interface stuff for an online game. Kind of like World of Warcraft, but way better."

"World of Warcraft? I'm sorry, I've never heard of that."

"Stupid." She laughed at herself. "Of course not. It doesn't come out until 2004."

"So, how did you go from being a code monkey to being a time traveler?" asked Adam. "That's quite a professional jump."

She looked at him. "I'm not sure I should tell you too much, Adam. Remember, I said you wouldn't be able to stay with us, and the more you know, the bigger the problem. So it's best if I just say I got 'recruited.'"

Maddy suddenly felt dizzy, as if she'd been spinning on a merry-go-round with her eyes closed. "Ohh," she murmured queasily.

"You feel sick too?" said Adam beside her. "Hold on . . . was that a—?"

"Yup." She turned to call inside for Sal. But she saw Sal was already halfway across the floor, hurrying toward them and uncoiling loops of data cable in her wake.

"Good job," Maddy said, taking the end of the cable and plugging it into the hard drive sitting at her feet. She looked up and studied the distant town and the fishing boats dotted across the river for a few moments. Even though it had been an intense enough ripple that even she and Adam had felt it, nothing appeared to be any different out there as far as she could see.

"Looks like we got another message from Liam!" Sal called from inside.

A moment later Adam and Maddy were standing on either side of her, staring at the grainy image of a gravestone on the monitor.

"Look, see?" she said, pointing at the image. "There's definitely more stuff carved on there now."

Maddy leaned forward. It was easier to detect the faint, worn grooves in the old stonework now that they'd manipulated the image to a much higher contrast.

"Yup, that's new, all right." She grabbed a pen from the desk and her notepad, and the sheet of paper with Adam's pigpen cipher scrawled on it. "Okay, then, let's work out what we've got."

The three of them peered closely at the screen. Despite the sharper image, this time the grooves appeared to be shallower, as if a different tool had been used. In some places they were worn away until almost nothing but a guess could be made.

"Hmm," Maddy murmured, chewing on her pen.

Adam grabbed another pen and began scribbling down the symbols that were clear enough to be certain. A minute later there was some semblance of a sentence emerging on paper:

"I can't make that out," said Maddy. "What does it say?"

"Oh, come on, it's really easy," said Sal. "*Revolt stopped. Ready for return. Await instructions.*"

Adam quickly inserted the missing letters. They fitted the gaps perfectly. He looked at her and grinned. "Outstanding."

Maddy continued chewing on the end of her pen. "But nothing's changed out there. Or maybe it has, and we can't see it yet 'cause it's dark. Thing is, that sure isn't New York out there." Stating the obvious of course, but she didn't care. "Things still aren't *right*."

> **Maddy.**

"What is it, Bob?"

> **Some of the data on my system have changed.**

"What? How's that possible? The preservation field's *on*, isn't it?"

> **Affirmative. However, the time ripple was significant enough to cause a temporary voltage dip. The preservation field was down for several seconds.**

Sal looked at Maddy. "*Shadd-yah*! Does that mean it's affected us?"

"I don't know." She looked Sal up and down. "You don't seem any different. What about me?"

She flashed a smile. "You still look like a geeky geek."

"Thanks." She turned to Adam. "You okay, Adam?"

But he was staring at her wide-eyed. His mouth hung open.

"Adam?"

"Good God!" he slowly gasped. "*Who are you people? Where . . . am I?*"

Maddy turned to Sal, wondering what kind of a mess they were in now, when Adam finally cracked a wide grin. "Just kidding."

She cursed under her breath and shot him a look. "That's not even close to being funny, you moron!"

Computer-Bob's cursor skittered across the screen.

> **17 of the 37 history pages you scanned have changed file size.**

Adam looked down at the library books they'd stolen earlier, stacked on the end of the desk. "If their contents changed, the page layouts may be changed, and it would affect the size of the digital files a little."

Maddy nodded. "Bob, what about the summing-up document you put together? The condensed history?"

> **That has also changed.**

"Put it up on screen. Lemme see it."

The document appeared beside his dialogue box.

> **Identifying text sequences that have changed.**

Bob began highlighting all the parts of the text that had been altered. Which was to say, most of it.

Adam began to read snippets of it aloud. "*1194, King Richard returns from the Third Crusade . . . reclaims his kingdom from his younger brother, John . . . the siege of Nottingham, John surrenders and begs for King Richard's mercy. King Richard executes his brother for high treason . . . has him hung, drawn, and quartered . . .*"

Adam shook his head. "That's still wrong. The correct version is that Richard forgives him and lets him live."

"You sure?" asked Maddy.

"Of course I'm sure! You never heard of *King John?*"

She shrugged. "I guess I saw a Disney cartoon once with a King John in it. But then he was, like, a fox or a lion or something, so I didn't take it too seriously."

Sal had been reading ahead. "There's no mention of this peasant rebellion in the north any more."

The other two read on.

"Liam said he'd stopped the rebellion in his message," she added. "But if you look at what it says there, England's still going to end up disappearing."

Adam resumed skimming the document. "*1195, King Richard announces the Fourth Crusade.*" He looked at the girls. "Well, there was certainly no fourth crusade. That's new." He resumed. "*The Fourth Crusade is championed by King Richard, his goal again to retake Jerusalem. This time around there is little support for it, despite a Papal Bull being issued.*"

"What's that?" asked Sal.

"The Pope basically announcing God says it's a cool idea."

"*King Richard raises ruinous taxes, and incurs crippling debts to fund the crusade and, in 1196, leaves England for the last time . . . 1197, King Richard and eleven thousand knights and men-at-arms are massacred by Saladin's army at the Battle of Al Karak. With no successor in England, and the country bankrupt, anarchy ensues . . . 1199, King Philip II of France invades . . . and so on.*" Adam shook his head. "Same result still."

"England gets gobbled up by France," said Sal.

"This fourth crusade didn't happen, you say?" Maddy asked.

"No. In *normal* history, when Richard failed to take Jerusalem during the Third Crusade, that was pretty much the end of the wars in the Holy Land. All the Christian kingdoms just sort of lost the appetite to fight for it. None of them could afford another crusade anyway. Fact is, when Richard came home, he turned his attention to rebuilding his kingdom and reclaiming territories he'd lost to the French in Normandy. That became his sole focus for the last six years of his life—getting back the lands he'd lost while he'd been on his holy war."

Maddy pursed her lips. "Hmm . . . something's changed his focus."

"Focus?" Adam shook his head. "More like obsession. I mean, what's going on there? He ruins his country, he bankrupts himself, and he launches what looks like a suicidal last crusade. Why?"

"He went crazy?" said Sal.

"Some historians say he was already a bit nuts."

"Something new, then," said Maddy. "Maybe something that Liam's caused? Maybe something to do with the Voynich Manuscript?" She took off her glasses and rubbed her eyes. "If there's some other time traveler back there, then perhaps something they've done?"

The others looked at her silently. There were no answers. Only questions.

"Okay, all right, here's what we do. We send back another data package of this new version of history and ask Liam if they've got any ideas at all what's suddenly eating Richard that he wants to go back to Jerusalem again." She put her glasses on. "In the meantime, we've still got the scheduled six-month return window if they want to use that, or, if they decide to come back any earlier, they'll need to send us a time-stamp."

Chapter 48

1194, Sherwood Forest, Nottinghamshire

"So, the pig says back to the farmer, 'If ye sees what I seen yer wife's up to, ye'd 'ave a curly tail too!'" Eddie's ruddy face crumpled like an old rug on a smooth polished floor. The other soldiers behind him, those within earshot, cackled along with him like a bunch of fishwives, their voices echoing off into the forest to either side of the track.

Liam looked at the captain of his escort. "Sorry, Eddie, I'm not sure I get it."

"Well, Sire . . . See, the pig's been watchin' the farmer's—"

Behind Eddie, one of the soldiers suddenly lurched forward. He dropped his shield and started clawing with both hands at his throat.

"What's . . . ? Huh?"

Then Liam saw a bright spurt of crimson gushing from the young man's flapping mouth, and for the first time noticed the stub of a crossbow bolt protruding from the front of his throat.

Eddie responded far more quickly. "FORM UP!" His parade-ground voice filled the forest trail just as another dozen projectiles whistled through the air toward them. Two arrows thudded into the horse's flank on either side of Liam's right thigh. The horse reared, up and he rolled backward over the beast's rump to land heavily on the hard mud track. The horse bolted, leaving a wake of dust behind it.

Liam was winded, lying on his back gazing up at a rich blue summer sky punctuated by blurred slithers of movement—arrows and bolts passing overhead. He struggled to get a breath in him, and then eventually, suspecting he'd spent the better part of a minute on his back, he hefted himself dizzily up onto his elbows.

Through a cloud of dust he could see his men, shields raised above their heads as they clustered around him, squatting down in a protective circle. The peace of the forest was lost in the deafening rattle of arrow tips clattering off their shields.

"It's an ambush!" Liam struggled to gasp as he pulled himself onto his hands and knees.

Eddie looked back over his shoulder and nodded. "Worked that out, sire!"

Over the rim of shields, Liam could see their attackers now: flitting dabs of olive and brown rags among the trees and bracken. Impossible to guess how many of them, but far more than his escort of twelve, he figured.

He cursed himself for not having Bob come along with them yesterday. But he'd been far more concerned that the rest of the column, laden with wagons of food and several bags of coins, made its way back to Nottingham Castle without incident.

Too cocky by half.

He'd made the mistake of believing the bandits had fully moved on from Sherwood Forest, that he'd done a better job of shooing them off than he apparently had. If he'd only just taken Bob with him . . . even just another ten or twenty men?

You idiot.

One of Eddie's lads grunted deeply and rolled flat on his back, an arrow through one eye. One of his legs twitched and drummed against the hard-baked mud as he went into shock.

"Sire!" barked Eddie. "We should keep moving!" He nodded up the forest track, the way they'd been heading. He was right. They'd been well on the way home. Another two hours and the forest gave way to open fields across a rolling hill down to Nottingham. If they stayed in tight formation, kept their shields up, kept moving, they'd have a better chance than they would staying put here.

"Right . . . yes!" Liam nodded.

Eddie barked at his men, ordering them to tighten up closer together. "With me now!" he yelled, and began to step forward. The other men followed suit, with Liam huddled in the middle, pulling the thick velvet cloak around his neck, as if it had any chance of stopping an arrow.

They began to make painfully slow progress along the forest track, little more than a shuffle that kicked dust into the air and filled their eyes and mouths with grit.

Another man went down, howling in agony and clutching at an arrow shaft through his shin.

"This is no good!" shouted Liam. "We're not going to get very far!"

He saw Eddie nodding under the shadow of his shield, its thin metal peppered with gashes and dents through which rays of sunlight streamed.

"We could make a break for it, Sire!"

Liam chanced a quick look up the trail. Some of their attackers had spread across the track, a thin line of men in rags casually stringing arrows and firing opportunistically their way. More than a dozen bandits were up ahead, but none of them armored, none of them equipped for close combat.

Eddie and his remaining nine could probably take them, break through, and then after that it would be every man for himself: drop shields, drop swords, and just run for it.

"All right," Liam nodded, his mouth dry. "Yeah . . . L-let's do that, then."

Eddie cleared his throat and spat. "Men! On my word, we charge down the archers ahead! Clear?"

Several heads nodded, a mixture of young and old faces. Some of them he knew had seen a fight before, but most of them hadn't; they were little more than farm workers who'd been taught how to bear a shield, swing a sword, and march in a straight line.

"Make ready!"

Liam felt naked, with no chain mail, nor shield or sword. He unclipped the robe from his neck and let it fall to the ground. It was only going to slow him down. He pulled a ceremonial knife from the belt around his waist, an ornate dagger with a beautifully decorated haft and a pointlessly blunt and useless blade. Still, it felt better than having nothing in his hands.

"Sire?" Eddie nudged him gently. "Ready?"

He nodded, working his tongue around his mouth, trying to find some spittle in there.

The hell I am.

He saw Eddie doing the same, and realized in that moment that he wasn't the only one scared out of his wits. "On my word we rush them," Eddie's voice rasped, "and make as much noise as ye can, lads. We'll scare the devil out of them."

A couple of the older faces grinned at that.

"Right, then . . ." Eddie took a lungful of air. "AT 'EM!"

Without hesitation, the men he'd been drilling these last few months, uneducated field hands that he'd managed to build a bond with, surged forward as one, a defiant roar coming from every mouth.

Liam found himself sprinting forward, shoulder to shoulder with them, his own screaming voice filling his ears.

The thin line of archers, twenty yards ahead, regarded them with comically round eyes. He saw a couple fumble to string and then drop their arrows in panic. Others fired hasty and ill-judged shots that whistled too high over their heads. But then as the gap quickly closed, he saw one, then several, then the rest, take the first faltering steps backward that swiftly turned into a full-scale rout.

"GO ON! RUN, YE COWARDS!" screamed Eddie, a wide, manic grin stretched across his face.

Ahead of them, the archers pelted down the forest trail like startled rabbits. Liam chanced a glance over his shoulder and saw more emerging from the woods behind them, loosing off arrows their way, many of them falling short.

We're gonna do it, he found himself thinking, for the first time daring to wear a defiant grin on his own face.

But then, on the trail ahead, a tall figure emerged.

Chapter 49

1194, Sherwood Forest, Nottinghamshire

It stood calmly in their way as the bandit archers streamed past. Seven feet tall, a giant swathed in dark robes and a cowl that hid his face in deep shadow.

The sight of the figure caused their charge to falter, and Liam heard the men curse under their breath.

"The *Hood*!" yelled one of the younger soldiers. "God help us, it's the *Hood*!" He dropped his sword and shield.

"'Tis but a man in old cloth!' Eddie snarled angrily. "Pick up yer weapon!" But the young boy was already gone, scrambling off the trail through brambles and ferns, and very soon lost from sight.

Their charge was halted now. Just ten nervous men standing in a forest trail, cowering beneath shields, the occasional arrow coming from behind, the solitary hooded figure ahead of them, blocking their way.

Eddie turned to his men. "Come on, ye fools!" But Liam could hear even in his voice a wavering uncertainty. It might just be a mortal man—but it was still a *huge* mortal man, and in his hands he held a broadsword that glinted sunlight as it swung casually back and forth.

The figure suddenly began to stride toward them. The way it moved—long, even, regular strides, arms calmly down by the sides, no sense of flinching or cowering—reminded Liam of Bob. Reminded him of the economical and purposeful way he moved. A memory flashed through his mind, a memory that seemed to come from another lifetime: Bob calmly moving through a prison camp, executing every guard in his way, a pulse rifle blazing in each hand.

Liam reached for the discarded sword and shield, fumbling and dropping the sword nervously so that he had to pick it up again.

"Just run!" he hissed at Eddie and the other men, suddenly certain he knew what was approaching them. "You can't beat this thing! Just do your best to get past it!"

Several of the men took Liam's word for it, dropping their shields and swords and running for the treeline on either side of the track. But Eddie and four others remained, bunching up close together around Liam, presenting a shield wall to the figure.

"Run, Sire!" shouted Eddie over his shoulder. "We'll hold him!"

The hooded figure suddenly broke into a sprint and covered the last ten yards in a silent few steps. He collided with Eddie and his men, bowling them backward. A roundhouse sweep of his broadsword lopped one of the men's arms off at the elbow, sending it spinning into the air, hand still clasped around the sword hilt.

One of the other men thrust his blade into the side of the Hooded Man. The black cloak collapsed inward, and Liam heard a *clunk* as the blade met something hard beneath.

The hooded figure reached with a gloved hand for the blade and snapped it with a sharp twist, tossing the broken metal off into the woods. It cocked its head for a moment, studying the man holding nothing but the broken hilt of his sword in his hands . . . and Liam would swear blind later that he saw the figure wag its finger at the man before picking him up by the throat and hurling him like nothing more than a bundle of twigs off into the trees.

Its head turned back, and beneath the shadow of the hood Liam sensed its gaze was locked specifically on him.

Eddie's remaining two men broke and ran, leaving him alone in the middle of the trail beside Liam. The hooded figure strode past Eddie as if he simply wasn't there.

"Sire! *Run!*"

Liam realized the thing had fixed on him for some reason. He did as Eddie said, dropping the shield and sword he'd picked up and backed quickly away toward the treeline. He saw Eddie lunge with his sword at the hooded figure's back, ramming it hard into the space between its shoulder blades.

The figure lurched in response—and Liam thought he heard some sort of wheezing whine come from beneath the hood. Eddie's blade must have found some chink in the armor beneath. The figure spun around to face him, the blade of the handle protruding from its back.

The response was a savage thrust with the broadsword that punched a hole through the jagged and pockmarked remains of Eddie's shield, the long blade continuing on into the man's chest.

Liam watched Eddie gasp, then collapse slowly to his knees.

"Forget this!" He turned and ran off the track and into the woods, charging through low branches and brambles that whipped and stung his cheeks. His heavy leather boots stumbled over roots and hummocks in the ground; his rasping breath and the snap of twigs and branches beneath him seemed to fill the silent woods around him. He realized the racket he was making as he scrambled away from that thing was giving him away, but he couldn't bring himself to slow down.

He ran for what he guessed was another minute before he finally stopped and turned to look behind him. He expected to see the wraithlike fluttering outline of black robes weaving past trees and through brambles hot on his heels; instead, the woods were still and empty.

Liam gasped air into his lungs, doubling over and dry-heaving from the sudden exertion, the burn of nerves. He spat phlegm on to the ground and straightened up on legs that felt like jelly.

All he had a chance to notice was the blur of something in motion toward him. Then he was seeing a world of speckled white.

Chapter 50

1194, Beaumont Palace, Oxford

Becks looked at the first gray light of dawn stealing in through the tall slitted windows. She calculated that she had another forty-seven minutes until the sun breached the horizon and the city of Oxford began to stir to life.

John, of course, was going to be asleep for another couple of hours at least. She'd worked out the average time that he emerged from his chambers and started bawling for breakfast. It was usually eleven minutes past nine. Although, last night, she'd made sure he'd consumed several flagons of wine, which meant perhaps an extra hour before he stirred.

It would take her precisely twenty-seven minutes to make her way back out of the deserted halls and cloisters of Beaumont Palace, occupied by a skeleton crew of soldiers and servants, and jog the mile back to Oxford city.

The city's walls were poorly maintained, and the missing blocks of masonry and cracks in the mortar made it possible to scale. She'd get back into the castle itself by climbing the rear bailey wall.

Twenty-seven minutes from now she would be back in her chambers, pretending to be asleep.

She continued studying the wooden shelves of scrolls and leather-bound volumes of illuminated manuscripts in Beaumont's royal library.

She pulled them off the dusty shelves one at a time, scanning sample pages of each in an attempt to identify the correct document.

She'd examined seven hundred twenty-six candidate documents over the last five hours of night. Her hard drive stored their digital images, and her processor was working overtime to translate the elaborate swirls of handwriting into recognizable text characters. None of the texts she'd scanned and translated so far had produced anything useful. There had been endless essays on royal protocol and volumes of romantic poetry, but nothing she could classify as vaguely relevant. She had opted for a very simple search algorithm—any text that scored high on a hit-list of terms sorted into relevance by order:

Search Terms:
Treyarch (100% relevance)

Pandora (100% relevance)

Confession (83% relevance)

Templar (79.4% relevance)

Grail (79.3% relevance)

Jerusalem (56.5% relevance)

Code (23% relevance)

So far, twelve of the documents had contained three of the seven words. Thirty-two had contained two or more terms, and a hundred five had contained one or more. "Confession" was the highest-scoring search term so far. It seemed a lot of people from this time felt the pressing need to confess something.

She continued robotically pulling out manuscripts amid showers of dust motes, opening them, and grabbing snapshot images. But, somewhere inside her head, a part of her AI that wasn't overloaded with running character-recognition software was wondering whether this approach was going to deliver any useful results.

She paused, a heavy leather-bound volume held in midair, dust cascading down in front of her. Her mind was making a quick assessment of the situation, of the amount of time she had left, and of the thousands of scrolls and volumes she'd yet to scan.

Her eyes followed a small tuft of fluff; the small downy feather of some bird that must have found its way in through one of the slit windows. She watched it gracefully seesaw down to the stone floor and then settle. She was about to resume scanning the manuscript in her hand when the feather gently stirred. It spun on the spot for a moment before flitting lightly across the floor.

Curious at the sudden movement, she suspended the math going on in her head and squatted down to look at the feather. She reached out, picked it up, and put it back on the floor where it had settled a moment ago.

It was still for a moment, then it twitched and spun . . . then once again slid across the floor, in a short stop-start motion away from the wall beside her.

She looked at the wall. Like the rest of the ones in the library, it was decorated with oakwood panels.

[Identify: Wall. Wood. Oak. Purpose: decorative]

She ran her fingers down the grained surface, all the way to the floor, and there, from a gap between the panel and floor—no more than half an inch—she felt a cool draft on the tips of her fingers. She tapped the wood panel with her knuckles. The knock echoed around the cavernous library.

[Assessment: Primary sonic response. 1.3 MHz frequency. Delay 0.56 milliseconds]

She cocked her head and tapped again, certain this time that it meant there was a significant space behind the panel. She brought her fist back and then rammed it forward. It disappeared through a splintered hole with a crack that reverberated around the library. She pulled her fist out and stared through the hole she'd created. Beyond, she could see a small room, little more than an alcove, lit by the faintest gray light of dawn coming through a tiny slitted window.

She saw what looked like a wooden lectern with a thick tallow candle on one side and, in front of it, a bench with a dust-covered cushion on it. A private reading space of some sort.

She was about to destroy the rest of the panel with a few well-aimed kicks and punches, but found that it swung out on hidden hinges with a soft creak.

She stepped into the small alcove beyond, and now saw, sitting on the lectern, a roll of parchment wrapped around a simple wooden spindle. She unfurled it slowly, hearing the brittle parchment crackling.

Spread across the yellowing page was a spider-crawl of fading ink in lines that sloped and rose untidily. Her forehead creased absent-mindedly as she struggled to make sense of the looped letters and errant spelling of a man quite clearly beginning to lose his mind . . .

This, the confession of Gerard Treyarch, wryten in the yeare of our Lorde, 1137 . . .

Chapter 51

1194, Dover

King Richard leaped from the prow of the rowboat and splashed down into the tumbling surf, sensing the crunch and clatter of pebbles beneath his heavy boots.

English ground once more.

The dawn sky was a blue gray, patiently awaiting the arrival of the sun. But it was light enough to see, farther up the beach at the base of the cliffs, a welcoming committee of assembled noblemen and their squires. Guttering flashlights and braziers burned brightly, casting light among the many colors of coats of arms.

He waded forward through the waves and up out of the rolling surf onto the beach. Faces, expectant, regarded him warily.

I know what you all want, he mused. They wanted to be seen to throw themselves at his service, to pledge undying loyalty to him. To kiss his hands and praise God for his safe return. And when all that was done, they'd be vying with each other to beg for titles and special privileges, to seek tax exemptions, permissions to build fortified properties, licenses to trade exotic imports. With one gasp they'd plead unfailing loyalty, with the very next be begging favors.

Blood-sucking leeches—all of them.

But necessary allies . . . for now. He was going to need their revenues, their men, for a while longer. Until he'd re-established his authority and, more importantly, held the divine power of the Holy Grail in his hands. Power enough to vanquish any army foolish enough to stand in his way.

So many years dreaming of this moment; the last of those years spent as the prisoner of Duke Leopold, awaiting the ransom that would finally set him free. And all that time, all of those frustrating months, having in his possession only one half of what he needed. The *key*, but not the *lock*. The *cardan grille*, but not the precious text itself.

The Word of God.

The Grail.

A curse and a blessing, he reminded himself. If he'd had the Grail with him when he'd been captured, then it might well have been in Leopold's possession right now—that ignorant oaf far too stupid to realize the awesome power he'd be holding in his hands.

Richard grinned; his broad mouth parted, showing a row of small yellow teeth. He could feel destiny touching him, God's hand on his shoulder, whispering promises softly into his ear. Just a day's ride now, perhaps two, up to Oxford where it was waiting in the royal palace. And there, alone in the royal library, in his private reading room, he was finally going to be able to spread the Grail across his lectern and unroll the *cardan grille* he'd managed to keep hidden on his person in the dungeons of Leopold's castle. It was a roll of worn leather, which when unraveled was no more than two palms wide and four deep. Cut into it was a matrix of tiny rectangular windows through which individual letters could be perceived. Letters that were going to spell out words . . . words from God Himself.

Words that, when uttered aloud, would give Richard the raw unbridled power of an archangel, hellfire at his fingertips. He knew this—it was one of the many promises God had quietly whispered to him.

His heart raced with excitement as the nobles looked on expectantly at their king.

Richard had planned some sort of rabble-rousing speech that would have these fat and greedy fools roaring a "hurrah" for their king. But then he spotted the white robe and the red cross of a single Templar standing back from the gathered barons and lords. A mere knight, he readily accepted his place at the back of the line, allowing lords, dukes, and barons their business with the king first.

A Templar . . . perhaps with news?

Richard strode up the beach toward the man. As he did, the nobles began to surge forward like so many jostling children, each eager to be the very first to welcome their king home.

The Baron Henri de Croy thrust himself into Richard's path, dropping his heavy girth down onto one knee and clasping pudgy, thick-fingered hands together in prayer. "Oh, I thank the Lord he has brought you home safely to us, my king!" he bellowed.

Richard curled his lip in disgust and casually stepped around the man. Other nobles were clustering toward him, all claiming their devotion to him at once, a growing clamor of insincere voices. Richard struggled to find the Templar Knight he'd seen, having lost sight of him amid the confusion of colorful coats of arms and standards and the wall of bearded and amply fed faces all spouting meaningless nonsense at him.

"BE QUIET!"

His lion's roar of a voice pealed across the beach and echoed off the chalk cliffs in front of him. Once more there was a stillness on the shore, filled only by the gentle hiss of the lapping tide.

"TEMPLAR!" he called out. "Where are you?"

Heads turned among the nobles, voices in a low murmur.

Richard narrowed his eyes, looking again for the distinct flash of red cruciform on white. He heard the crunch of footsteps through pebbles and saw, among the gathered crowd of barons and lords, bodies parting to make way for someone coming forward.

Finally the Templar Knight appeared before Richard. The knight's face was vaguely familiar, but he could not recall the man's name. He recognized him from three years ago—he'd been among the cadre of loyal crusaders who'd taken Acre.

He offered the knight a brotherly smile, from one warrior of God to another. Both of them veterans—both of them crusaders.

But the man looked uncomfortable, unable to meet his eyes, looking down at his feet. "My king," he began, licking dry lips, finding a quiet voice. "My king . . . I bear bad news."

Richard took a step closer. He lowered his voice to little more than a whisper and leaned forward until his mouth was almost beside the man's ear. "What, pray tell, is this bad news?"

"Sire . . . the Grail is lost. Stolen."

Chapter 52

1194, Sherwood Forest, Nottinghamshire

Liam awoke into a fog of thudding agony. Every movement sent sharp splinters of pain through his head. He was looking up at a clear blue sky through branches of leaves that jostled and swayed. Another pleasant summer's day it promised to be, but it was cool—cool with the damp of dew; a morning yet to fully get going. He wondered how long he'd been out. A day?

He decided not to turn his head; it ached far too much. He could hear activity around him: the chopping of firewood, the clang of a ladle against a metal cooking pot, the jangle of horses' harnesses, the scrape of a blade being sharpened along a whetstone.

"Master Locke!" a voice nearby called out. "He is awake now!"

Liam snapped his eyes quickly shut again. He heard more movement around him, men stirring, the clank of things being put down, the soft crunch of footsteps on pine cones slowly approaching him. His mouth was covered with a gag of foul-smelling material; some thug's sweaty rags, no doubt. But his eyes clenched tightly, the lids flickering, were giving him away.

"You're awake, fool. I can see it," growled a deep voice. A booted foot kicked him roughly in the side of the ribs, and Liam grunted in pain. He opened his eyes to see a tall man with long untidy locks of sandy-colored hair looking at him. "See now? I knew you were awake." The man smiled, then squatted down beside Liam.

"Hmm, so, you're the sheriff who's been giving me so much trouble?"

Liam could say nothing, his mouth clogged with the dirty rag, his hands bound behind his back with twine.

"And so young, as well," he uttered, cocking his head curiously. He spoke in a lowered voice. "You know, you did a far better job than the previous idiot. He managed to turn Nottingham and most of the county against him . . . made my life very easy here. No end of starving malcontents joining the cause every day."

Liam looked over his shoulder at the gathering crowd of ragged men.

"But you, young man . . . you've turned things around, haven't you? Made things very difficult for me. John chose wisely this time. A noble with a brain for once." He smiled sadly. "Which makes it a real shame that I have to do this."

The man stood and turned to the assembled crowd. "Pick him up! Let's see what the Hood wants done with him!"

A dozen pairs of rough hands seized and hefted him onto his feet. Liam looked around at the camp—an odd assortment of flimsy wooden shacks, wattle-and-daub huts, and cloth tents stretched over frames made from branches. Among the growing crowd, he spotted mostly men, one or two women, and no children. It had the look of a semi-permanent settlement, not an overnight camp but a year-round dwelling, haphazardly built in and around the mature oak trees.

The tall man who'd spoken led the way through the camp toward a round hut with wattle-and-daub walls and a squat conical roof of branches and reeds. Bigger than the others; more effort had gone into it. Liam suspected it was their leader's hut.

The Hood.

He watched the tall man duck down and disappear inside through a low door, leaving him alone with the crowd. He felt hands pushing and shoving him, a punch on his back that painfully jolted his head.

"French scum!" someone hissed at him.

Another cursed, then spat a fat gobbet of spittle into his face. "Go back to Normandy!"

Liam tried to reply he wasn't French, that he wasn't some arrogant Norman aristocrat, but the gag filled his mouth, and the best he could do was grunt.

It probably wouldn't have mattered if he could have made himself heard; he was wearing expensive clothes, a dark green velvet smock, fine linen leggings, and leather boots, which all marked him as a noble whatever he might try to say.

The tall man emerged through the low door and stood up straight, raising his arms to hush the hubbub of noise in the crowd.

"He says it is for *you* to decide the sheriff's fate!"

Liam felt his legs give, as most of the crowd roared with approval.

Oh, that's not good.

"Kill him!" shouted several voices.

"You really wish to show John, the pretender, what we think of his Norman lackeys?"

The crowd shouted its agreement. Liam looked at the tall man, trying to make eye contact with him. He sounded different from the others, a different accent, perhaps educated. And wasn't there a hint of regret in his voice? As if he'd rather they chose another fate for him?

I need to talk to him!

He twisted his head from side to side, trying to work the gag out of his mouth. But already he was being dragged by the mob, hands struggling through the press of bodies to get a grasp on him, pinch him, or land a punch on him.

He could feel the rancid cloth rammed into his mouth loosening, able to find enough space at the back of his mouth to bunch up his tongue and push the cloth forward. It made him gag, and he fought the urge to vomit.

Ahead of him he saw the crowd part, making space around the flat

top of a broad tree stump. It was about a yard across and a yard high—
like a roughly hewn tabletop.

"Send his head back to Oxford!"

Head? Oh God, please no . . .

Liam saw someone place a wicker basket beside the base of the
stump. He began to buck and squirm against the grasp of the men
dragging him, causing them to wrench him forward more roughly.

"Come on, pig! We'll put ye on a spike when we're done!"

Strong arms pushed him against the tree stump and grabbed his
shoulders to bend him down over the rough flat top.

Liam frantically worked his tongue against the gag, pushing the
material bit by bit out of his mouth. But even then, even if he could
scream something, he was sure nothing was going to stop them now.
They wanted their dark-haired Norman head.

His arms were twisted behind his back, and the jagged splinters of
wood from the stump ground and mashed against his cheekbone as
several hands firmly pressed his head down. He rolled his eyes to one
side to look up—and wished he hadn't. A thickset man was standing
beside the stump, enjoying the moment and flexing his muscular arms
as he wielded a broad-sword in both hands.

"One stroke! One stroke!" several in the crowd began chanting.

"Aye! 'Tis always one good stroke!" the man roared in reply.

"Not so, Seth!" another man bellowed. "Did take more than three
on the last!"

Close your eyes, Liam, he told himself. *Best not to see the blade coming
down.*

But he couldn't. He couldn't take his eyes off his executioner. The
man was making a big show for his crowd, stepping around the stump
and limbering up with long swooshing swoops of the sword.

The material of the gag was now almost entirely pushed out of his
mouth, but still covered it. He tried screaming at them to stop, but
his words were muffled.

In his peripheral vision he spotted the tall man, looking down at him with a stern expression. And beside him, a foot taller, the sinister form of the Hood, motionless, face lost in the dark shadows of his cowl. Their presence hushed the baying crowd until it was quiet enough that Liam could hear the soft rustle of a breeze chasing through the oak leaves far above them.

"You wish this?" said the tall man. "You wish to send his head as a message to those who rule yer country?"

The crowd roared in response.

"So be it, then," he said, with a tone of regret in his voice. He nodded slowly at the executioner. "See it done. And mind it's a clean blow. This young Norman deserves a quick death."

"Aye," nodded the executioner. He took a couple of steps over to Liam and gently rested the sword's cold blade against the back of his neck. Liam felt its weight, the razor-thin edge biting into his skin.

And then he felt the weight of the blade being lifted.

Lifting for the swing.

Oh God, oh Jay-zus . . .

Liam jerked his head, bucking and kicking as hands pressed harder to hold his shoulders still.

"Best be still!" one of the men holding him warned. "Unless you want him to hack at you like a hog on a spit."

As the executioner sucked in a breath and his sword hovered for a moment above Liam's head, Liam jerked his chin once more, finally freeing his mouth above the cloth gag.

"*Please!* I'm not French!" he heard himself screaming, shrill and terrified. "I'm—I'm—from the future!"

Chapter 53

1194, Sherwood Forest, Nottinghamshire

"STOP!"

Liam heard the blade coming down, a long deep swoop that sounded like the wingbeat of Death itself, and then the wooden stump his head was pressed against vibrated with the jarring impact. He heard the blade clang and hum and the executioner curse as the blow vibrated his hands.

Liam tried to focus on the wobbling metal blade right beside his nose, reflecting his own face back at him. That was the very last thing he remembered before he fainted.

Water splashed across his face, and Liam came to, screaming, "NOOOOO!"

He opened his eyes to see he was in a dark place, his bonds now removed. It was a round room of wicker walls caked with mud. Above him, sunlight dappled through a crude thatch of twigs and reeds, and beams caught dust motes and pollen gracefully floating through them.

"In case you're wondering," said a calm voice, "you're not dead."

Liam looked around the room, his eyes adjusting to the darkness. The first thing he saw was the hooded figure squatting on the mud floor of the room. Beside it, sitting on a wooden stool, was the tall man with the long sandy hair, studying Liam intently and stroking his bottom lip thoughtfully.

"Who sent you?" he asked after a while.

Liam struggled to gather his senses. A moment ago, seconds ago, he'd been awaiting the downward strike of a sword on the back of his neck.

"You said, 'I'm from the future,'" the man continued. "The only person in the twelfth century likely to comprehend the notion of time travel is someone who, indeed, *has* come from the future. Therefore, I completely believe you. Now," he went on, sitting forward, "who sent you?"

Liam looked up at him. "You—you . . . you're a traveler too?"

The man nodded.

"Are you . . . are you one of us?" asked Liam.

"Us?"

"The—the agency?"

He cocked his head. "Agency?"

Liam bit his lip. Perhaps he'd just blurted out too much.

"Agency . . . ? Hold on." The man's eyes narrowed. "You're not talking about . . . ?" He smiled, then laughed. "You can't possibly mean *The* Agency?"

Liam shrugged. "Yes. I . . . no, I don't know. I—"

"There were rumors back in the 2060s. A secret agency set up to track down and terminate illegal time travelers. They were just rumors, of course."

Liam said nothing, but the man seemed wholly intrigued by him. "Of course, everyone suspected that was propaganda—a deterrent, something to scare off any tech companies thinking about secretly developing a machine. But *you're* here . . ." His eyes narrowed. "So, is that it? Is this agency actually for real? Is that where you've come from?"

Liam's eyes darted toward the hooded figure. Menacingly large in such a small hut, it sat silently poised in a squatting position. So far the man was *asking* questions—not *demanding*. He wondered how long that was going to last.

"It's true," whispered Liam. "I'm with that agency.'"

"My God!" The man laughed again. "It *was* real! I knew it! Tell me—who's behind it? The North American Federation? Is it the Sino-Korean Bloc? New Europe?"

"I don't really know," Liam replied.

"Or is it a corporation?"

Liam shook his head. "I don't know. We just work on our own. I don't know who organizes us."

"You're just a *grunt*, then?" He smiled, not unkindly. "A foot soldier."

Liam shrugged. "I . . . I suppose."

"And I presume you've come back here because I've altered history somehow?"

"Yes."

"A lot?"

"Enough that there's been a time wave. The present has been changed."

"And your mission was to come back here to kill me?"

Liam closed his mouth. There was much too much he'd be giving away with an answer. Instead, he asked a question. "Who are you?"

"That's rather direct of you. I like it." The man smiled. "So I suppose I shall tell you. My name is James Locke."

"Pleased to meet you, Mr. Locke," said Liam, gingerly offering a hand. "I'm Liam O'Connor."

A grin slowly spread across Locke's face. He reached out and shook the proffered hand. "I recognize that accent," he said. "You're Irish."

"Yes."

"A pity, eh?"

Liam frowned. "Pity? Why?"

"*Why?*" His eyes narrowed. "You don't know, do you?"

"Know what?"

"Much of Ireland's gone now. I think some peaks remain still in County Kerry, but the rest is all underwater."

Liam stared at the man, wondering if he was playing a joke on him.

"A lot of other places have gone too, of course. But you really don't know about any of this? What year exactly have you come from?"

He wondered if there was any point in keeping that from Locke. "2001."

"2001? Really? Why so far back? That's over forty years before the first-ever test machine was functional."

"As good a place as any other, I suppose." He looked at Locke. "Did you really say Ireland's *underwater*?"

"Systemic climatic failure. It used to be called 'global warming.' The ice caps melted decades ago; the sea ended up rising by about a hundred meters. We've lost about a fifth of the world's land mass—the most densely populated fifth. What's left is crammed full of people. Standing room only, I'm afraid."

"Jay-zus!"

"Oh, you got that right," Locke said, pushing wisps of hair out of his eyes. Liam looked at his lean face more closely and realized he was a lot older than Liam had first guessed. Forty, maybe fifty. His long hair was threaded with grays and silvers, and crisscrossing lines splayed out from the corners of his eyes.

"In my time, the world's dying, Liam. And it's all our doing. It's overheating, and every ecosystem is gradually failing."

Liam rubbed his head, which was still thudding with a dull ache. "So, *when* have you come from?"

He laughed a little sadly. "The end of times, I suppose."

"The end? But when?"

Locke said nothing. Outside the hut, there was a growing clamor of voices.

"What do you mean by 'the end,' Mr. Locke?"

Locke waved the question away. "Maybe I'll explain later. For now, though, I better tell that crowd of barbarians outside that there'll be no Norman nobles beheaded today."

"You're not going to kill me?"

"Depends if you get in the way or not." He splayed his hands. "My advice? Don't get in the way."

"Why? What are you up to? Why did you come back here?"

He smiled again. "I came back to find out about something. Originally. But my plans have changed somewhat." He got up off his stool. "Be a good man and stay here . . . and don't try to run, or I'll sic Rex on you."

The hooded figure stirred at mention of the name.

"Is that a—a support unit?"

Locke clearly didn't know what he meant by that.

"A . . . clone," Liam added, unsure whether Locke was familiar with that term either.

"A gen-engineered product? Good God, no. They're far too expensive and unreliable. No, this is something altogether more practical. Do you want to see?" Locke asked with a glint in his eye.

"Umm . . . all right."

Locke reached over and with a theatrical flourish tugged the hood down to reveal a dented and rusted metal skull. Metal, that is, down to where the bridge of the nose would be on a human skull. From that point downward, a synthetic skin cover descended, starting as a scorched and partially melted, jagged edge and becoming a waxy plastic-looking version of a nose, mouth, cheeks, and jaw—an *almost* convincing facsimile of the lower half of a human face.

"The people who sent me back . . . well," he sighed, "in the year I come from, we were lucky to get our hands on this model." He rapped the metal skull on the top, and the robot stirred with a soft whir of servomotors. "Army surplus combat cyborg. Insurgency model with a synthetic plastene skin sheath . . . or at least what's left of one. Used in the last Oil War. He's not a particularly pretty boy, but he's as tough as a tank."

"Those people outside. They follow him . . . they seem to—?"

"Worship him?" Locke shrugged. "Yes. I think that about sums it up. The simple fools think of Rex as some sort of a God-sent instrument of justice meant to lead them in a war against their Norman overlords. They'll do anything he tells them."

"You mean, anything *you* tell them?"

He laughed. "Indeed. Rex is programmed to take my verbal commands only. They think 'The Hood' is leading them. And that works just fine for my purposes."

"And what are they, Mr. Locke?"

He tapped his nose. "We'll talk later." He got up from his stool and stooped down to exit the small hut. Liam could hear the crowd outside and Locke's voice explaining something about the "sheriff being a useful hostage."

Liam turned to look at the robot's face: half human, half rusting metal dappled with peeling army-green paint. And two small, faint pinpoints of blue light: LEDs that glowed dully, just like the powerup indicator on the displacement machine back home in 2001.

Liam nodded gingerly and waved. "Uh . . . so, um . . . hello."

It continued to stare at him, motionless and silent.

Chapter 54

1194, Nottingham Castle

Bob surveyed the recruits as they trained, standing in the middle of several dozen of them, paired and sparring with wooden baton swords and wicker shields. The sun had climbed high enough now that it shone down into the castle's main bailey, making the men perspire under the weight of their chain mail.

He observed their leaden and clumsy swordplay and evaluated their abilities as individual combat units.

[Evaluation: combat efficiency—insufficient]

There was no numerative score he could sensibly apply to them yet; they were that bad. Barely better than malnourished old men and young boys, struggling to remain standing under the weight of their armor, let alone able to sustain effective melee combat with properly weighted swords and heavy iron shields.

However, merely having columns of men tramping around the Nottingham countryside wearing the royal burgundy tunic and managing to approximate the look of soldiers seemed to have had the effect that Liam was after. The banditry, the raids, the lawlessness had receded from the town and the surrounding farming villages and disappeared deep into the woods.

Bob's AI took a moment to shuffle through a high-level menu of mission objectives. The current primary goal of subverting a peasant uprising originating from Nottingham *appeared* to have been met. But until he received a tachyon signal from the field office confirming that history had realigned itself, it remained a mission goal yet to be crossed off the list.

Liam O'Connor seemed content to leave the majority of the logistics of running the castle, leading the garrison, and overseeing the feeding of the people of Nottingham to him. The fleshy part of Bob's mind seemed to want to communicate something to him about that. An emotion of some sort. He tried to identify it, tried to find a human label for it, and finally came up with one.

Pride?

His silicon mind stepped in and decided to phrase that more concisely.

[Analysis: mission achievement verification bonus]

He tried out one of his library of smiles—one of the smaller ones that looked less like a horse flashing its gums. It matched that small buzz of satisfaction he was feeling. He decided the smile worked, and matched this mild emotion he was currently experiencing. He labeled it: **[Proud-Smile-001]**.

A voice calling down from the gatehouse disturbed his musing. He looked across at the gatehouse's entrance archway to see a wounded man being helped through the gates by several others.

"You may now rest," he instructed the drilling recruits, and stepped across the courtyard toward the new arrivals.

Drawing closer, he could see the burgundy and amber colors on the man and recognized the face as one of the dozen men assigned to escort Liam to Kirklees Priory. He was aware that Liam was a day late, but had assumed he had decided to stay with Cabot a second night. Bob's pace quickened until he stood beside the man being lowered gently to the ground by several townspeople.

"Sire," said one of them, "we found 'im collapsed in the marketplace."

Bob knelt down and inspected him. Blood soaked half his tunic, turning it almost black.

"He will not survive for very long. He has lost too much blood."

The soldier was one of the first intake of recruits; Bob retrieved the man's name from his database. "Henry Gardiner, you must tell me what has happened."

The man looked up at him. "Sire . . . they ambushed us! They . . ." He coughed, spluttering a dark spray of blood down his chest. "A . . . a drink . . . please."

Bob called for one of the water-bearers and then carefully helped the man to sip a ladle of water.

"Continue when ready," he said as the man finished and let the ladle go.

"Ambushed us . . . yesterday. The Hood's men . . ." He panted in short rattling breaths. "The sheriff . . ."

"What has happened to the sheriff?"

"Took . . . took him."

"He is alive?"

Henry Gardiner appeared to be waning fast, his eyelids fluttering, his face pinching from the pain.

"He is alive?" Bob repeated insistently.

"Aye . . . y-yes . . . they took . . . they took him."

Bob nodded. "Understood," his deep voice rumbled. He turned to one of the recruits standing nearby. "Fetch this man some mead from our storeroom." He estimated the dying man had another hour of life left in him. The alcohol would at least make it a comfortable one. Bob evaluated the man deserved at least that for dutifully struggling back to make his report. His gray eyes swiveled onto the townsfolk who'd helped him in. "You are good civilians. I am grateful for your assistance. You may also drink some mead."

The men tugged their forelocks with gratitude.

Bob rested a hand on Gardiner's shoulder and squeezed it gently. "You have functioned well, Henry Gardiner."

He stood up, his mind already shuffling through a decision-tree of actions he would need to take. There wasn't a great deal of calculative effort required to come up with the conclusion that retrieving Liam *alive* was the preferred course of action. It didn't conflict with the primary objective; what's more, Liam O'Connor's role as sheriff had proven to be effective among the local population. The people appeared to like him and would want their sheriff back.

Bob had already made the decision to find and rescue him. He was just waiting for his code to spit that out as a formal menu option.

But finding him, finding where exactly the Hood's men were encamped within the forests of Nottingham, could take days, weeks, perhaps even months. He didn't have that kind of time. He had just twenty-three days left until either he returned to 2001, or his silicon mind fused itself here in 1194.

Little time to waste.

If there'd been a skirmish in the forests—an ambush, logically—it would have occurred on the track running north-east between Nottingham and Kirklees Priory. There would be detectable signs of the fight still: bloodstains, scuff marks . . . perhaps a trail to follow. Perhaps the raiders were still in the vicinity.

He turned to look at the men in the guardhouse above. Several faces were peering down curiously. One of them he recognized as belonging to a member of the original guard that had escorted them here from Oxford nearly six months ago; like Eddie, a veteran with experience. He pulled the man's name from his database.

"Jethro Longstreet?"

"Sire?"

"Under the authority of the Sheriff of Nottingham, I am promoting you to garrison commander of this castle in my absence."

He could see the man's eyes widen with disbelief.

"You will continue the daily patrols of the farms outside." His voice echoed around the castle's walls. "You will continue supervising morning food distribution in the town marketplace. You will also maintain the training regime for these new recruits. I will be absent for several days. Are these instructions perfectly clear?"

"Aye . . . aye, Sire."

"Then proceed in this role."

He turned to the men standing nearby. "Bring me a horse immediately."

Chapter 55

1194, Oxford Castle

Becks detected noises of distress coming from the castle's outer walls: raised voices, high-pitched and signifying alarm. And one of those voices she identified as John's.

A few minutes later he staggered into the great hall, gasping, looking for her. His eyes found her standing beside an arched window, doing her best to look serene and ladylike. He came quickly over.

"'Tis true! I have j-just this minute heard!" he stammered.

"What is true?"

"R-Richard—he has s-set foot in England!" John's face was ashen with fear and damp with sweat. "The messenger . . . the messenger arrived this morning! He tells me he set foot in Dover yesterday!"

Becks consulted her database and a map of England. It was 118 miles from Dover to Oxford. A piece of data she didn't have was how many miles an army from this period could travel in a day. However, a determined man could cover that distance in two days. John had already told her his brother most likely would gather supporters along the way, with his growing army eventually catching up with him.

"Do you believe he will come to Oxford immediately?" she asked.

John nodded frantically. "He will come here directly, b-because he believes the Grail is here!" He swallowed nervously. "I will have to be the one to tell him—tell him that it's lost. It was on *my* instructions the Templars were taking it north to Scotland." John's nerves spilled out and became a manic laugh. "He's going to kill me!"

"I will protect you," she said calmly.

He wandered over to the balcony and looked out across the city. The heat of a mid-morning sun was baking the castle's stone walls, and the air shimmered above the crenellations, making the dark slate rooftops of Oxford's shacks and hovels dance and undulate beneath the cloudless blue sky. "Why has your colleague, Liam, not managed to find it yet? It does not sound like he has even *started* to look!"

There had been several couriers from Nottingham over the last few months, bearing a detailed account of matters up there. Most of Liam's reports had been on his efforts to win over the starving populace, to carefully rebuild some semblance of royal authority, law and order . . . all in John's name.

"He has been busy stabilizing the region," she replied. "Only when he has the support and sympathies of the people will he have a chance of locating this outlaw who has stolen your Grail." She was quoting Liam's words from the last report.

"I know! I know!" snapped John. "But we have no more time now for making friends of the peasants! Richard will be here *this very night* . . . maybe tomorrow." He turned to look at her, trembling as he spoke. "Do you understand? There will be blood when he discovers it is lost! *My* blood!"

Becks's eyes narrowed. She looked back out at the walls of the castle, the walls of Oxford. "You could hold out against him. Prevent him from entering the city."

John scratched at his beard, a nervous tic of his that Becks had noticed gradually become increasingly pronounced over the last six months. "The city would fall to him," he said. "The people here *love* him."

Becks nodded slowly. His evaluation was, of course, quite correct. She trawled through her database of history for this period and immediately hit upon the obvious solution. A solution that, as it happened, would also align with history as it was *supposed* to happen.

"You must retreat north to Nottingham," she said. "The castle has a better defensive configuration, and the city is sympathetic to you."

John licked his lips, breathing noisily through his nose as he gave her suggestion serious thought. "NO! No, that w-will anger him f-further!"

Becks's store of data on the *correct* timeline indicated a successful defense of the city and a siege by Richard that lasted several weeks. The siege concluded with John's surrender and Richard demonstrating uncharacteristic mercy for his brother, letting him live as long as he swore allegiance to him.

That was the history that *needed* to happen now to prevent an unacceptable level of temporal contamination.

"Nottingham is loyal to you," she said. "The city will hold. This may give the sheriff enough additional time to locate the Grail for you. The Grail could then be used as a bargaining tool, allowing you to negotiate an acceptable surrender."

He looked at her. "You think that is possible?"

"Of course it is. Liam may already have enough local intelligence from the people to successfully locate these outlaws. Winning their loyalty and support as he has been doing has been a necessary first step."

"Perhaps you are right." He cupped his chin in a shaking hand. "Yes . . . yes. Perhaps then, that's—yes, that's what I should do."

"The other alternative is to remain here," she added. "Which I calculate would be a tactically poor choice."

He reached out for her and grasped her arms suddenly. "What would I do without you?"

She flashed one of her carefully selected smiles at him.

John's face seemed to have reclaimed some of its color. "Behind such beauty, you have a mind just as cunning as any ambassador or general. I . . . I—"

Becks eased herself from his tight grip and pushed him gently back. "My lord, we should set forth immediately."

"Yes . . . yes, that would be advisable." His lovelorn puppy eyes cleared and focused on more practical matters. "Yes, we must assemble a caravan immediately."

Yet he stared at her in silence for a while longer, his blue eyes narrowing, marveling at her. "If only it were the way of things that I had been king. You would truly make a formidable queen."

A part of her mind calculated whether she should reveal his future to him; whether knowing what fate awaited him would strengthen his resolve to stand up to Richard. But a hard-coded protocol reminded her that knowledge of the future to any man was just as big a contaminant to history as any careless time traveler. There were other ways to ensure he found some backbone and stood firm against Richard when the time came.

"Be strong for me now," she said gently, teasingly. "And perhaps I will yet be your queen."

Chapter 56

1194, Sherwood Forest, Nottinghamshire

"What are you going to do with me?" asked Liam.

Locke looked up at him. "I don't really know," he replied. "My *merry* men," he said with a hint of sarcasm in his voice, "were rather eager to make an example of you. It's down to the fact that you're a rich Norman and they're all poor Saxons."

"But I'm Irish, not French!"

He shrugged. "All they see is a rich young man in expensive clothes." He pared a hunk of venison off the bone and handed it to Liam. "As it always was, it shall always be . . . rich overlords, a poor underclass, and a world of hatred between them."

Liam chewed on the meat, surprising himself at how hungry he was. "Mr. Locke, the things you've said about your time . . . it doesn't sound too good."

He smiled sadly. "No . . . No, it isn't." Locke held him with his eyes. "In my time things are going very badly, very quickly."

"How do you mean?"

"Where do I start? We've exhausted the world of its resources. The world ran out of oil in the late 2030s. It ran out of coal and natural gas in the 2050s. It ran out of many of the essential minerals and ores at the same time. We lost so much land to the advancing seas, land that contained fertile soils, mines, oilfields. And there were wars. Plenty of them. Regional wars, as billions of dispossessed people migrated from flooded lands to already crowded ones."

Locke shook his head sadly. "It's a mess all of our own making. Perhaps if we'd changed our ways at the beginning of the twenty-first century, if we'd managed to control our population, if we'd all been less greedy for shiny new things, then perhaps we wouldn't be in the mess we're in now. It's an exhausted world. It's a *dying* world."

Liam looked at the hunched form of the robot in the corner; just a dark outline and two pale blue eyes. "Mr. Locke, why *did* you come back here? It wasn't just to escape that world, was it?"

Locke sighed. A long silence followed, and outside they could hear the evening routine of camp: voices raised, several dogs barking hungrily. Liam had imagined the camp might have been alive with folk songs around a fire and the good-natured exchange of merry freedom-fighters. Instead there were the desperate sounds of a refugee camp—a hundred ragged half-starved outlaws living off what they could trap or steal.

"You're right. There *was* a mission." He picked at his teeth. "Of sorts. An objective." He frowned for a moment, as if trying to remember what it was. "In my time there are only a few of us left. No longer influential, no longer the silent power behind presidents and popes. We're just a small band of believers."

"Believers?"

"Templars."

Liam stopped chewing. "You're one of them knights? But you're . . . you're from the *future*, so you are! You saying they've got Templar Knights in the future?"

He laughed softly. "Well, not if you mean men running around in chain mail and waving big swords, Liam. But yes, there are Templars— men who believe. Men who still hope, even now at this late stage, that God will step in to save us from ourselves."

Locke's face reminded him a little of Cabot: a face etched with a lifetime of memories and set with a grim determination to see the right things done.

"We put our faith in technology. All of us. We saw we were running out of oil, but instead of using less of it, we assumed technology would eventually find us a miracle. Free energy, harmless energy for all. But there was no man-made miracle. We used up oil, and then there came the Oil Wars. The world became obsessed with fighting itself for dwindling resources, and the oceans and skies grew more polluted. The ecosystem began to collapse. There was a hope technology could engineer new forms of genetic life that could restore the balance, bacteria that would eat carbon out of the air and help to cool our world down again. But it was too little and too late. All we did was create bacteria that poisoned the sea with big toxic blooms. The more we tried to bail ourselves out with technology, the worse we seemed to make it."

Locke shook his head. "So all that's left now is blind faith that there's something else that can help us."

"God?"

He shrugged. "Who can say? God, or perhaps something God-like. Something greater than man."

Liam looked down at the candle. "I'm not a real believer, Mr. Locke, truth be told. If there is a God."

"I'm not sure what I believe either; but hope and belief are practically the last things we have left."

"That doesn't sound like much."

"And we have knowledge . . ."

Liam looked up. "Knowledge?"

Locke seemed reluctant to continue, as if debating with himself whether to say more. Finally he spoke in a voice little more than a whisper. "Knowledge of a prophecy."

"What?"

"A prediction, a prophecy. Something we've known about for over a thousand years."

"You say 'we.' You mean the Templar Knights?"

"Yes. The name has changed, of course, depending on which conspiracy nuts you listen to. Templars, Masons, the Illuminati . . . Priory of Sion, New World Order. There have been all sorts of imaginative and ridiculous names for us over the decades and centuries. But we started out simply as an order of soldier-monks in Jerusalem." He laughed drily. "No more, basically, than janitors, temple security guards—hence the name Templars."

Liam recalled Cabot's story. "But something happened, didn't it? Something was discovered by the security guards."

Locke nodded. "You know the story, then?"

"I suppose I know *some* of it. I know knights found a scroll and it became known as the Grail. Right?"

"Indeed. The Grail—a chalice, a cup: a symbol of containment. Containment, yes . . . but not of a liquid, not the blood of Christ. A secret."

"Secret? This prophecy?"

"Yes."

"What is it?"

Locke laughed. "Just like that? You ask and expect me to tell? Secrets that men like myself have been keeping and passing down from one brother to another? From grandfather to father to son?"

Liam thought about it for a moment, then nodded. "Why not? Who am I going to tell, sitting here?"

Locke laughed some more."Maybe I will trade secrets with you."

Liam nodded. "All right."

"So, then"—Locke hacked another chunk of meat off for Liam— "tell me, why exactly were you sent back here?"

Liam wondered whether to mention the Voynich Manuscript. It was what had started off this mission, the first bread crumb in a trail that ultimately had led him here, into this mud hut in the middle of Sherwood Forest. "The Grail," replied Liam.

"You wish to decode its secrets too?"

"Aye." A question suddenly occurred to Liam. "How did you know where to find it?"

Locke sat up. "The Grail disappeared from history at the beginning of the thirteenth century. It simply vanished. Became nothing but a myth from then on. But we've always known it existed. And we've always known it was never just a mere cup."

He began to carve another ragged hunk of meat from the bone. "We have Templar records. Letters of instruction, personal correspondence dating back to the brotherhood's inception and papal blessing in 1129. So we've always known King Richard got what he came for in the Holy Land. But it is there that the trail goes cold. Until, that is, the Second World War."

Liam's eyebrows lifted.

"A German bombing raid over Oxford in 1943 damaged some ancient castle buildings. Old crypts were disturbed, unearthed. And, as a result, documents that hadn't seen the light of day for over nine hundred years emerged. One such document was attributed to King John, written actually before he became king, while his brother Richard was still being held for ransom in Europe."

Locke passed another hunk of meat over the candle to Liam. "It was a letter of instruction to some knights to transfer King Richard's 'sacred possession' north to Scotland. John, we suspect, intended to hide it from his brother to use as a bargaining chip. Or maybe he really did think his brother's haul from Jerusalem would be far safer in Scotland. But history tells us it never arrived there. It became lost. John's letter of instruction was the very last mention of it."

Locke half-smiled. "There was a date on John's letter. So, we finally knew a pretty exact where-and-when for the Grail. And the brotherhood has, of course, known that since the letter finally surfaced, courtesy of a Luftwaffe bomb. The plan, therefore, Liam, was to retrieve the Grail and decode its secrets."

"But you can't, can you?"

"Ahh, I presume you know about the key?"

"The key to decoding it?"

"A *cardan grille*. A template with viewing slits, that one rests over the encoded text. Yes. And without that, the Grail is just a scroll full of meaningless words."

"And King Richard has it?"

"Indeed."

Liam frowned. "So, how were you planning on getting this grille off him?"

"To lure him here, of course. Stir an uprising in Nottingham that he'd insist on dealing with *himself* on his return. He does have a reputation for recklessly leading from the front. A taste for the blood-rush of battle." Locke glanced at the motionless squatting form of the robot. "And, if such an opportunity presented itself, my big friend here, in the heat of battle, might be able to get through to Richard . . ." Locke shrugged. "It's not much of a plan, but it's all I've got."

He turned to Liam and smiled, not unkindly. "But you've done such a good job of winning over the locals that my fledgling uprising looks like it's going nowhere. Six months ago I had nearly a thousand men out here in the woods. Most of them have returned to their homes now, what with your pardon. I presume the amnesty for outlaws was your idea?"

"I'm sorry," Liam replied. "Your uprising was causing waves in the future."

Locke's smile faded. "Well, I imagine it isn't any longer."

"But you have the Grail. That will still bring Richard to you, right?"

"Of course. He wants what I've got, and I want what he's got. Perhaps we'll make a deal."

Liam frowned, a question occurring to him. "You said your

brotherhood has known where the Grail might be intercepted for ages. Since, what? 1943? So when exactly have you come from, Mr. Locke?"

The last time Liam had asked Locke the question, he'd replied rather cryptically, "The end."

"Is it much farther into the future than me?"

Locke said nothing, the half smile frozen on his face, teasing Liam.

"One hundred years? Two hundred? . . . Five hundred?"

"The end," said Locke again, offering nothing more.

"The end?" Liam hunched his shoulders. "Ahh, come on, what is that supposed to mean? Do you mean the end of the century?"

The older man said nothing.

"The end of what? . . . End of the *world*?"

Locke relented. "It really boils down to how you interpret this world around us, Liam. In a scientific way, or in a spiritual way. Is it an ending, or a beginning?"

Liam ground his teeth with frustration. "That means nothing to me, so it does! That's just the kind of mumbo-jumbo I'd expect from a priest."

"The prophecy, Liam. We've always known the Grail contained a detailed prophecy. Something happens on a certain date, a certain year."

"Something?"

"Something." Locke spread his hands. "We don't know what. That's what I came back to find out."

"Something," muttered Liam again. "Something good or something bad?"

"I suppose if you have faith, Liam, if you can believe in a caring God, then it can only mean something wonderful will happen."

"And do you?"

Locke scratched the tip of his nose. "I suppose I'll make up my mind when I've managed to decode the thing."

Chapter 57

1194, Sherwood Forest, Nottinghamshire

Moonlight illuminated the forest track in front of Bob. It was just possible to see the dark stains of congealed blood in places, the scuff marks of boots, the glint of several twisted and broken loops of chain mail, and the pale feathered fletching of a few arrows deeply embedded in the dirt.

Bob reined in the horse and stepped down onto the track.

It was silent except for the hiss of a breeze through the endlessly stirring trees and the far-off hooting of an owl. He examined the signs of battle more closely.

Heavy boots close together had rucked the dirt, and many small gouges in the mud suggested arrows that had embedded themselves in the ground and been retrieved later. Bob nodded with calm certainty that this was the site of the ambush that had happened more than twenty-four hours earlier.

He wandered over to one side of the track, pushing aside the thick ferns and bracken that filled the forest floor between the stout oak trunks. He soon found the first body, hastily pulled out of sight and dumped amid a thick clump of nettles, stripped of anything of value and left as carrion. He picked his way along the edge of the track, finding several more bodies, all of them stripped of their mail and leather boots and left with nothing but their leggings and bloodstained tunics.

Half a dozen bodies in total. He flipped the last of them over; to his relief, none of them was Liam.

Relief.

Bob queried his mind for greater clarification. His onboard hardware looked dispassionately at the impulses coming in from the organic nub of flesh that barely deserved the term "brain." The tiny electrical impulses fired off by the rat-brain-sized organ conformed to a pattern that humans would call an emotion.

Yes. Relief.

He stood up and listened to the night, hoping that beyond the hiss of stirring branches he might hear the faint and distant cry of human voices raised in drunken celebration or calling for help. But he heard nothing. Just the owl.

Bob's decision-tree had been here before. On his very first mission he'd lost Liam in the aftermath of a battle for the White House; Liam had been taken away in one of a column of prison trucks. His AI then had been woefully unprepared for the decisions it had to make. But he'd managed to do it. He'd reprioritized the mission goals to put rescuing Liam at the very top. Technically a breach of his programming, but also something he'd been proud of.

This time around, it was a far easier decision. This mission's goals were so poorly defined and ambiguous that devoting what was left of the six-month mission envelope solely to finding his friend Liam was a nanosecond evaluation.

But how?

He could wait until dawn and attempt to identify a visual trail. A body of men moving through the thick undergrowth of Sherwood Forest would leave behind something that even an inexperienced tracker could follow.

He decided that was to be his plan of action, and settled down in a hunched-over squat amid some nettles to wait for the light of dawn. He wouldn't sleep. Instead his mind would do what it always did when the rest of the world was in slumber: a defrag. A chance to play through the endless terabytes of data stored on his hard drive.

Memories.

To replay it all, every single image, every sound, every sensation, every smell. To try to make connections, associations, to understand a little better what it would be like to have a real brain. To be a *real human*, instead of an engineered tool . . . a meat robot.

He'd just started unpacking and sorting through a slideshow of memories when he detected the faintest odor of woodsmoke. Not the ever-present odor ingrained into the tunic he was wearing, the smell of melted tallow mixed with stale sweat. This was on the air—a fire was burning somewhere out in the forest tonight, caught on the fresh breeze and carried for miles.

He sniffed loudly, his broad nostrils flaring like a horse's.

The faint smoke smell again.

He stood up quickly, scanning the woods in a steady 360-degree arc, hoping to detect even the tiniest flicker of light deep in the woods. He saw nothing. But he had the scent. Not just the smell of dry seasoned logs, but the vaguely minty odor of pine needles burning.

A campfire.

He decided to follow his nose.

Chapter 58

1194, Sherwood Forest, Nottinghamshire

It was morning, and a mist mingled with the white smoke of a dew-damp cooking fire, drifting up through the canopy of branches above.

Liam watched Locke's camp slowly stir to life; men in rags turning over under their damp capes, robes, and animal-skin covers. He heard the snotty rattle of someone clearing his nose and hawking it out onto the ground, and the distant *chup chup* of someone already up and cutting firewood.

Locke was trusting him not to run, allowing him the freedom to move around the camp. Liam felt the men's eyes on him, distrusting eyes, resentful eyes. If he *did* attempt to run from the camp's perimeter into the thick undergrowth, he was certain any number of them would gladly take the opportunity to hunt him down and put an arrow in his back. And he wasn't really going to get far barefoot. Locke had him remove his leather boots and donate them to one of his men, a gesture of humiliation that had proved popular: a Norman noble reduced to picking his way around the camp as barefoot as a common street beggar. The men clearly liked the idea of that.

Liam watched Locke emerge from his hut, stretch, and yawn. The robot came out behind him, swathed once more in robes, the top half of its metallic head lost in the shadows of its hood, the plastic-skin chin and jaw just barely visible.

"Listen! There is news!" announced Locke. All heads turned toward him; the various activities of stirring men came to a halt. "Our leader, the Hooded Man, has received news." Locke nodded respectfully up at the robot standing beside him, a foot taller. "News from Nottingham. It is said King Richard has returned to England! And, as I speak to you now, he is traveling northward, toward us!"

Voices sounded through the camp; Locke's men were unsure how to greet the information.

"Also, it is said his brother, John, has fled from his castle in Oxford and is on his way to Nottingham! There is talk in the town that a feud exists between the king and his brother. That John may choose to challenge Richard and make a stand at Nottingham!

"Our Lord Hood is considering this important matter. If there is to be a battle there in the coming days, then both sides will be looking for fighting men like ourselves to fill their ranks. We have a chance to air our grievances, to discuss the unjust taxes that have driven us all into these woods out of hunger. More than that, we have a chance to perhaps seek assurances from either Richard or John—whomever we choose to offer our support to—that we are all to be pardoned and our status as outlaws revoked."

Several of Locke's men cheered at that. Liam sensed that it was fear of being arrested and hung as criminals that was keeping the majority of them from returning to their families and homes.

"We have a chance to make ourselves heard. Our leader will be deciding over the next few days with whom we shall throw in our lot!" Locke grinned at the men. "And we can only pity the army that does not have the Hood fighting for them, eh?"

The men cheered.

"He is truly unstoppable!"

The men roared.

"Immortal!"

They roared support again.

"Because he has been sent by God to free poor Englishmen from slavery to these Norman lords! We will have God on our side, whichever side we choose—and that makes us formidable! So ready yourselves, lads. There will be a fight coming soon. Sharpen your swords, restring your bows, and be ready for it!"

Locke said something quietly to the robot, and it raised a sword and held it aloft. The forest filled with a cacophony of voices, every last man, young and old, on his feet and punching the air excitedly.

Liam looked around at them. None had the faintest idea they were pawns being used by Locke, additional battle-fodder for whichever Plantagenet—presumably Richard—Locke intended to make a deal with. If it was true, if both John and Richard were converging on Nottingham, then probably Locke was hoping to get an audience with Richard—and then what? Try to steal Richard's *cardan grille*? Or offer to share the Grail's secrets with him?

It occurred to Liam that *that* would be the worst possible outcome. Someone as crazy and as powerful as Richard, privy to whatever revelations or prophecies might be hidden in the Grail?

I really have to get out of here. I have to go back to Nottingham. More than anything, he wanted to find both Bob and Becks and return home to 2001. All of the things that Locke had told him about the future he needed to share with Maddy and Sal. Particularly Maddy— she would make more sense of it than he ever could. She'd have a far better idea of what they needed to do next.

He wondered what Bob was doing right now, whether the support unit had yet found out about the ambush and was in the middle of Sherwood Forest already searching for him, or whether he was waiting in Nottingham Castle, still expecting him to return.

What about Becks? Where's she? With John?

If she was, then presumably she'd also be able to make the rendezvous if John was traveling north to Nottingham. He had a horrible feeling both support units were going to turn up in that field in a week's time without him and would go home, leaving him here as Locke's prisoner.

Locke nodded at Liam and beckoned him over as the gathered men dispersed to their various morning tasks: foraging for food and firewood, boiling a meager pottage for breakfast.

"Liam," said Locke, "come inside and have some breakfast with me."

He ducked down through the entrance and followed Locke and the robot inside, back into the stuffy, smoky gloom of Locke's humble shack. Locke sat on his bench; the robot hunkered down by his side like a loyal dog.

"You heard?"

Liam nodded. "I heard what you said just now."

"Apparently the streets of Nottingham are buzzing with the news. The people favor John. They see Richard for what he is—an absentee ruler who's ruined the country."

"Mr. Locke, can I ask . . . do you have this Grail here? Is it somewhere in the camp?"

Locke eyed him cautiously. "That's for me to know and you to mind your own business."

"What do you intend to do with it?"

"I will do whatever it takes to unlock it."

"You'd make a deal with Richard?"

He shrugged. "I would. I'd betray all those gullible morons outside if that's what it takes."

"But you have no idea what's in there. Have you considered the prophecy you're hoping to find might just be a message from someone like me—another time traveler?"

Locke frowned. "And is it? Do you know?"

"No . . . I—no, I don't know. But that's my point: it could be *anything*! Surely it would be dangerous to give someone like King Richard that kind of knowledge. It could completely change the course of history—"

"And is that such a bad thing, Liam? From where I'm sitting—the time I come from—maybe giving King Richard a brand-new history, a new destiny, will give us an entirely different timeline and a different—a *better*—future. It certainly couldn't be any worse."

"But there could be a worse one, so."

Locke shook his head. "What? What's worse than an overheated, poisoned, dying Earth?"

"I don't know! All I *do* know is what we were told. That to mess with time like this, to change it, weakens the walls between us and . . . and chaos."

"Chaos?"

Liam didn't know enough to explain himself any better. Not for the first time he wished Foster had stayed around long enough to talk them through all the things they needed to know. "It's what we go through when we travel in time. A dimension . . . a place that is just . . . *chaos*. Perhaps even what some people call *Hell*."

Locke's eyes narrowed. "I recall only a falling sensation."

"It's more than that. Look, Mr. Locke, I've . . . I think I've seen things, so I have . . . things in there." Liam couldn't find any better way to say it than that. But in that milky nothingness, he'd seen them: *entities* swimming closer and closer to him each time he traveled, as if they were growing familiar with him. As if they sensed a regular traveler, someone who might offer them a way into the real world.

"Mr. Locke, the only thing I know for certain is you can't just mess with time. If this Holy Grail of yours was meant to be lost in the woods and end up nothing but a myth, if that's the history that's *meant* to be, then so be it. And maybe what you want to do, and what I came back to do—to find out what's in there . . . maybe that's a big mistake. Maybe it's best that no one finds out what's written."

"Liam, we've waited since the discovery of that scroll in Jerusalem—eleven hundred years of waiting to know. I'm not going to walk away from that now." He shook his head almost sadly. "I *can't* walk away from that."

Liam was about to reply that Locke had no choice, but then the pause in conversation was suddenly filled with a crack of snapping branches and the clatter of an avalanche of dislodged dry mud from the shaking wattle-and-daub wall. Another loud crack followed, and a ragged, uneven circle of daylight appeared.

Locke's jaw dropped. "What the—?"

A round head topped with dark shaggy hair pushed through the hole. "Liam O'Connor?"

Chapter 59

1194, Sherwood Forest, Nottinghamshire

Liam gasped. "Bob!"

Bob turned to look at him. In a flurry of noise, showers of cascading mud, and a cloud of dust and flying splinters, he burst through the wall. Liam was wiping grit out of his face when he felt big fists grab him roughly and pull him to his feet.

"STOP HIM!" he heard Locke scream in the confusion.

But suddenly they were outside in the blinding daylight. Liam grunted, the wind knocked out of his chest as Bob picked him up and flung him over his shoulder like a sack of cornmeal. He ran with heavy loping strides across the camp past wide-eyed men and boys, stunned into inaction at the sight.

"STOP HIM!" Locke's voice pealed across the camp. "HE HAS THE SHERIFF!"

Liam's face banged and bounced heavily against the rough chain mail draped over Bob's chest. He managed to twist his neck enough to glance around at a world upside down: men grasping for weapons, men scrambling out of Bob's way. A large man with a mane of ginger hair twisted into greasy rattails chose to remain in Bob's path. He held in two muscular arms a long-handled woodcutter's axe.

"Yield!" he challenged. But Bob's loping pace remained unchanged.

With a roundhouse swing he brought the axe's blade around on a trajectory that was going to end up smashing directly into Bob's chest—and Liam's face.

"Jay-zus! Bob, look out!"

Bob blocked the swinging axe with his forearm, but the weapon's blade bit deep through the chain mail. Sharp hot splinters of shattered iron rings stung Liam's face, and he screwed his eyes shut instinctively to protect them.

He felt Bob's body lurch beneath him and heard the thud, crack, and grunt of several exchanged blows landing home, then the agonized scream of someone—presumably the unfortunate ginger-haired man—suddenly cut short with the snapping of cartilage and bone.

Liam's head was bouncing and banging against chain mail again as Bob resumed running, and Liam dared open his eyes to the upside-down world once more, to see they were nearing the edge of the camp clearing. Bob bulldozed his way past several old women scrubbing clothes in a large wooden tub.

A moment later they were crashing through bracken, twigs, branches, and thorns slapping and tearing at Liam's face as Bob continued to bound through the woods like the world's clumsiest gazelle. Liam was still struggling to get his breath as each loping stride brought his ribs crashing down against the hard slope of Bob's shoulder and slammed his lungs empty of air like a blacksmith pumping vigorously at his bellows.

"Bob!" he managed to gasp after a while. "Stop!"

"Just a moment," Bob's voice rumbled back. "We are not safe yet."

Bob scrambled down a steep slope, almost losing his balance several times. At the bottom he waded knee-deep through a stream, sending showers of spray up into Liam's face. On the far side he scrambled up a slope, then, finally reaching the cover of a large fallen oak tree, he bounded over its thick trunk and hunkered down on the far side. He eased Liam off his shoulder and onto the ground, where his gray eyes quickly studied him.

"Are you hurt, Liam O'Connor?"

Liam struggled for air. "You mean . . . apart from a few cracked ribs?"

Bob scowled skeptically.

"I'm . . . fine. I'm fine," Liam gasped, waving the comment away. "Just joking."

From the far side of the stream echoed the sound of dozens of voices calling out to each other—a search party already beating the woods for them. Liam wondered how much effort they'd put into that. Having the Sheriff of Nottingham as a prisoner might have been a bargaining chip if Locke intended to deal with John. But clearly that wasn't his plan. The Grail was his true prize. Leverage that would work on Richard alone.

"Bob," Liam whispered.

Bob was still scanning the slope opposite.

"Bob! They have the Grail!"

The support unit turned to look down at him. "Are you sure?"

He nodded toward the slope and the camp back in that direction. "It's over there. The leader of those bandits—he *is* a time traveler, just like we thought! But he's not one of us. He's not, you know, a TimeRider."

"Who sent him?"

"I didn't really understand. But he's come back to get it! The Grail. I think it's back in that hut! Or, if not, Locke knows where it is."

"Locke?"

"The leader! James Locke," he hissed impatiently. "The leader!"

"I see. You wish to return to retrieve it?"

Actually no, he really didn't. Going back to the camp was the last thing he wanted to do. "Yes," he sighed. "I think we have to go back."

Just then he felt the fallen oak tree vibrate. He sat forward and looked along the trunk toward the splayed and unearthed roots at the end—and saw the dark, fluttering, wraith-like form of The Hood, crouched like a beady-eyed bird of prey looking for a morsel of food.

"Oh, come on," he muttered, "give us a break!"

Chapter 60

1194, Sherwood Forest, Nottinghamshire

The Hood jumped down, and the trunk, free of its burden, flexed with a woody creak that disturbed several crows nearby. The shrouded form slowly pulled itself from a squat on the ground to its full height.

Bob turned to face it, his arms and legs flexed, ready for action.

"Bob, be careful! It's a metal robotic thing!"

The Hood's head slowly turned toward Liam. In the shadows he thought he saw the faintest blue glimmer of its LED eyes.

"Warning!" boomed Bob. "You are not authorized to participate in events that will change history!"

The Hood's gaze smoothly panned toward Bob. There seemed to be an unspoken challenge in the way it silently regarded him. Then, without warning, its glove-covered hands pulled the cloak up over its body and tossed it aside.

Liam gasped at the sight, horrific in a way, yet also fascinating. Beneath the cape its form had looked so convincingly human. But now exposed, as he looked at the metal frame, speckled with blisters of rust and flecks of old combat-green paint, he wondered how anyone could ever have been fooled into thinking this thing a man. Flesh-colored plastic, in some places scorched black, in others melted and bubbled like toasted cheese, hung from its arms and shoulders and neck. In a few areas it was actually entirely unmarked and looked very much like real human skin, hanging in sagging loops like the putrefying flesh of some undead being.

"It's an old war robot," said Liam. "That's what Locke said."

"Affirmative," replied Bob. "Configuration matches Korean model, dating from the early 2040s."

"Right," nodded Liam. "Uh . . . does it—can it talk?"

"It can communicate using synthetic speech circuits. Not convincing. This functionality may have been disabled."

"Does it understand us?"

Bob's eyes remained on it, watching, waiting for the thing to make its first move. "Yes, it does."

"Could we . . . could we convince it, you know, to n-not hurt us? To be our friend?"

The robot's gaze swiveled smoothly toward Liam, its dented and corroded metal skull cocked to one side, blue lights regarding him with cold curiosity for a moment.

Bob watched the robot. His database included a catalog of AI variants—family trees of artificial intelligence code, from the first viable self-cognitive versions developed in the late 2020s right up to his version number, compiled in 2053. Bob identified this model robot as an old North Korean combat unit. Mass-produced in the mid-2040s and used to devastating effect in the first Pacific Oil War. His records indicated that hundreds of thousands of South Korean, Chinese, and Taiwanese, as well as their own North Korean civilians, were butchered by this model. They were unreliable, with friendly/hostile identification software that was prone to error. Understandable, given that the original AI was pirated code adapted to work with imported Chinese chip sets.

Bob decided to attempt a Bluetooth handshake. Beneath the Chinese or Korean language interface would be a common programming language.

[W.G. Systems AI V7.234c. Please identify]

The robot turned its gaze slowly to Bob.

[SolSun Inc.: V3.23—날짜: 29-06-45]

[Communication protocol. Please select: ASCII-English. Hexadecimal. Binary]

[Selecting ASCII-English]

"We have a communication channel open," said Bob.

Liam nodded. "All right. Well, could you ask it to be a good fella and leave us alone?"

"Negative. It will have mission parameters, just as I do." Bob decided that finding out what it thought its mission was would be the most useful line of inquiry.

[Specify mission parameters. Highest priority first]

[Mission Priorities—Primary: 순서 의정서 FOLLOW ORDERS IDENT J. LOCKE 순서 의정서—Secondary: Locate, identify hostile forces in target combat zone]

Bob turned to Liam. "Its code has been hacked."

[Identify "target combat zone"]

The robot's gaze shifted to the trees, the thick branches of oak leaves and acorns above them, then back to Bob.

[Target Combat Zone—35°43'56.27"N/127°47'19.17"E. Kumwon-San, South Korea]

"Bob! What's going on? Tell me. What's it saying?"

"It appears to be following mission instructions from a war that ended in 2049. It believes it is in a Korean jungle. It also believes the year is 2047. This unit was not properly decommissioned. Its mission program is still active, but has been crudely hacked to make it follow the verbal commands of J. Locke."

"Well, can't you just tell it that it's wrong?"

"Negative. It has no way of identifying the correct year."

Liam eased himself slowly back along the ground away from the Hood's unmoving form. "Is there not a way you can, you know . . . convince him to—"

"I will try."

[Information: current location is 53°9'56.49"N/1°51.43"W. Sherwood Forest, England]

[Negative]

[You are outside the target combat zone]

The robot's response took a moment to come back.

[Current location coordinate offset is within target combat zone]

Bob tried a different approach.

[Information: current date is 12 June 1194]

[Negative. Present time data is 11-03-2047, 07.45 hours]

[Transmitting correct time data]

The robot received the information, then cocked its head curiously.

[Transmitted data 순서 의정서. Data confirmed as valid. Please wait]

[You are beyond mission parameters. You are not in the target combat zone]

[순서 의정서. Data conflict]

[Deactivate combat status immediately]

The robot's blue LED eyes dimmed and flickered out, and its frame sagged and shuddered.

Liam clapped his hands together. "Bob! You did it!" He got up off the ground and took a cautious step toward the immobile statue of corroded metal and melted plastic. "Jay-zus-'n'-Mary, you made it turn itself off, so you did! You're a bleedin' genius!"

Bob shook his head. "It is not turned off. It is merely . . . considering."

Liam's eyebrows arched, and he stopped mid-stride. "Oh, in that case . . ." He took several steps back. "Couldn't we just hit it over the head? You know, while it's busy *considering* things?"

"An offensive action may activate its self-defense routine."

"Oh. How about we just run?"

Bob's mouth had just opened to reply when the statue stirred to life with the soft whirr of servomotors.

[Primary mission priority override]

The blue eyes glowed once more.

[Verbal command from J. LOCKE (password verified)]

[Command received 4 minutes, 34 seconds ago]

[Command status: active]

[Command = "kill them both"]

Bob eased his broadsword out of its sheath; the scrape of metal on leather seemed deafeningly loud in the stillness of the woods. The noise seemed to trigger a reaction from the robot. It pulled its own sword from its scabbard and, holding the weight of the long blade effortlessly in one hand, it advanced toward Bob.

"Liam O'Connor, you should run."

Chapter 61

1194, Sherwood Forest, Nottinghamshire

The robot's last step took it within striking range, and with a whiplash movement it swung its sword at Bob's head. Bob quickly raised his own, parrying the blow with the sharp, vibrating clatter and ring of metal on metal.

Bob's riposte was a lightning-fast lunge toward the robot's "armpit"— hydraulic fluid pipes momentarily exposed between plates of pitted metal armor. The lunge nipped at one of the pipes, causing a clear yellow liquid to spray out under pressure.

The robot swung its arm down, snapping Bob's sword like balsa wood. It reached out and grabbed Bob by his neck, lifting his feet off the ground and hurling him like a child's toy against the fallen oak. He bounced off the stout trunk. The tree shuddered under the heavy impact.

"You must run!" barked Bob as he struggled to get to his knees.

Liam shook his head. "I can help!"

"RUN!"

The robot reached down and grasped hold of Bob's right ear in an attempt to lift him up off the ground. But with a loud ripping sound it was torn from his head, spattering them both with a thick gout of blood. The robot tossed the ear aside and reached down again, this time picking up Bob by his neck, raising him above its head.

Liam could see a fine spray of the yellow liquid puffing out from the rubber pipe that Bob had managed to slash with his blade. It was pumping out in arterial pulses . . .

Like blood . . . just like robot blood.

The robot carried Bob, still aloft like some sort of trophy, toward the trunk, and then slammed him down across it. Liam thought he heard something snap as Bob grunted and rolled off the side, falling heavily to the ground.

Jay-zus. It's going to kill him!

The robot thrust the sword still held in its other hand through Bob's left upper arm, skewering him to the trunk like a butterfly pinned in a collector's cabinet.

"Bob!" Liam shrieked. Bob struggled to wrench the sword out of the wood, but its blade was buried at least a foot deep into the old dead oak.

With Bob pinned down, the robot now slowly turned around to focus on Liam, blue eyes softly glowing, evaluating its next target.

"Please!" Liam's voice quaked. "I'm not in your war!"

It advanced on him.

"Hey there! H-hey! James Locke said to go an' get me, right? Not . . . n-not *kill* me!"

Liam fell as he took a backward step, landing amid a cluster of nettles. The robot stood over him and then slowly squatted down, placing one glove-covered hand around Liam's throat.

"P-please! I can help Mr. Locke! I can h-help . . . h-him!"

Behind the robot, Liam thought he heard something crack and rip. Or maybe that was the sound of the tendons in his own throat. He felt the robot's fingers begin to compress his windpipe, firm and steady like someone winding a vise closed, feeling tender muscle, trachea, cartilage, and his Adam's apple pressing in on each other. His eyes saw white sparks, his ears roared with pulsing blood struggling to find a passage up to his brain through a dangerously compressed carotid artery.

Then, suddenly, hot, foul-smelling liquid was splashing into his face.

The hand around his neck twitched painfully as if attempting to snap it, but then released its grip like someone had suddenly decided to spin the vice's handle the other way. The hand dropped down onto his chest like the lifeless appendage of a paralyzed man.

His vision cleared again, and he saw the robot's left arm dangling by its side. From beneath its armpit the rubber pipe flapped like a serpent, gushing yellow liquid in hot spurts. The combat robot flopped to its knees, blue-light eyes looking down uncomprehendingly at its powerless arm.

Behind it he saw Bob standing triumphantly with the broken, jagged remnant of his sword in one hand. His other hand, his left arm, was a dangling tattered stump that ended with the fragments of an elbow and dangling loops of frayed tendons and muscles.

Bob thrust the sharp edge of his broken sword into a small gap between the robot's armor-plated shoulders and twisted. The robot lurched, and more of the clear yellow liquid spurted out under high pressure.

The robot's half metal, half plastic face seemed to express something. Surprise. Shock. Then finally, with a whirr of hidden motors working against hydraulic pressure that no longer existed, it collapsed onto its side.

"We were fortunate. It appears the combat unit's rear motion sensor panel was damaged in an earlier fight," said Bob matter-of-factly as he began to examine the ragged remains of his left arm. The arterial spurts of his own opened veins were already beginning to cease as the blood clogged into a thick sealing glue.

"Bob!" Liam managed to gulp. "Your . . . your arm!" He looked around Bob's wide frame to see the rest of it was still pinned to the tree.

"I will live," he said gruffly. He looked down at the robot. "It is still active, although motion on its combat chassis has been disabled."

Liam could see the blue-light eyes burning angrily still and its head turning frantically left and right with the loud whirr of a small over-worked motor, as if that alone was going to move its heavy, lifeless chassis across the forest floor.

"What—what did you do to it?" Liam struggled to talk. His throat was killing him.

"I severed a major hydraulic pipe. The liquid provides the pressure system that enables the servomotors to activate limb movements." He examined the disabled robot. "A design flaw of mechanical units," he said dismissively. "They cannot heal themselves. They are old technology."

"Right."

Bob started looking at the ground until he spotted what he was after. He stooped down and picked up a rock the size of a human head.

"What are you doing?" asked Liam.

"This unit is still active. It needs to be destroyed."

As Bob raised the rock over his head, Liam found himself looking away. Even though it was just a machine on the ground, the plastic skin from the nose down made at least half its head look too human for him to want to watch it being smashed in.

He heard several heavy thuds, followed by a clanking and the clattering whirr of some part of it still working frantically. Another final thud, and the noise stopped.

"Is it . . . *dead*?"

"It is dead," Bob replied.

Liam turned to see a flattened hump of crumpled metal and shredded flesh-colored plastic.

"Before this unit found us, you indicated we needed to return to the camp."

Liam looked at Bob. "We can't go back. You're in no condition to fight. Not like that."

"My combat proficiency has merely been reduced by fifty percent. I am still an effective combat platform."

Liam looked at him. Perhaps he was right. Even with one arm Bob was a threat to any poor man who decided to stand in his way. But, looking at the pitiful dangling shreds of his left arm, Liam didn't feel he had the heart to ask—no, to *order*—Bob to fight his way back into the camp.

Then his gaze rested on the robot's discarded dark cape and the tattered rags and woollen hose that still clad the dead machine's body.

"All right . . . All right, I've got an idea. I guess we should bury the robot first?"

"Correct. The metal will corrode in due course."

"Well, let's undress it first." He looked at Bob and cocked an eyebrow. "Guess who you're going to pretend to be . . ."

Chapter 62

1194, Sherwood Forest, Nottinghamshire

Liam eyed them cautiously as he stepped through the camp. There were expressions of hostility. Someone threw a handful of horse dung at him. It broke up in midair and rained down his chest as Liam covered his face behind bound hands in case there was any more coming his way.

Behind him, the tall hooded figure silently prodded him forward with the tip of his sword, and the crowd jeered as Liam stumbled and nearly fell. They made their way across the camp, the crowd parting reluctantly to let him through; he felt the soft tap of spittle on his shoulder and in his hair, and grimaced beneath his hands. The crowd was growing noisier.

"Bloody French scum!" a woman shouted, and Liam felt something hard and sharp bounce off his back.

"CEASE!" boomed Bob from behind him.

The effect that had on the press of gathered people was instantaneous. An utter silence. So quiet, in fact, that Liam could hear the gentle crack of burning kindling and the bubble of simmering water from a cooking pot nearby.

They've never heard the Hood talk before.

Perhaps that was a mistake. He wondered if the silence would be broken by someone claiming the hooded form was an impostor. But instead the respectful silence remained, and the crowd parted before them, all the way to Locke's hut.

Liam led the way, doing his best to continue to look cowed, beaten, and humiliated. With one last unnecessarily hard prod from behind that made him yelp, Liam stooped down through the low entrance and Bob followed behind.

The hut was lighter. Of course it was; Bob had casually demolished one side of the round wall.

He saw Locke standing, a gun aimed at them held in his shaking hands. "Stay where you are!" he snapped. He glanced at Bob. "Where is it? What have you done with my combat unit?"

Bob pulled the hood down. No point maintaining the ruse. "Your combat unit has been deactivated."

Locke's eyes narrowed. "Good God . . . you're a—you're a *genetic* model, aren't you?"

Bob nodded. "W.G. Systems combat prototype. Fetus batch WGS09-12-2056."

"My God!" he gasped, with a smile of admiration.

"Lower the weapon," said Bob.

Locke hesitated, staring at the tip of the blade and realizing his gun wasn't going to stop the giant standing in front of him. He slowly dropped his aim. "What now?" he asked quietly.

Liam flexed his wrists and wriggled out of the loose rag binding. "The Grail. It's here somewhere in the camp, isn't it?"

Locke was silent. His face offered nothing.

"Come on, Locke," said Liam. "We're here for the same reason you are. We need to know what's in it!"

"The prophecy?"

Liam shrugged. "If that's what it is. If that's the big secret in there, then yes."

Locke's eyes remained on the sword.

"Come on . . . Look, we've got the same goal, right? We can work together, so we can. There's something coming, right? And there's a warning about it in the Grail. Tell us where it is, and maybe we can work out how to read the thing together."

The man shook his head. "King Richard possesses the *only* way to decode the Grail."

Liam glanced at Bob for help. But the support unit had nothing to offer at that moment. "We could take it back to our field office. We've got a powerful computer. There has to be a way we can use that to help us decode the thing."

"You have a way back!?"

"Yes."

"A way back to the *future*?"

"Of course! We've got a rendezvous—time, place, and everything."

Locke shook his head. "You're lying! Apart from Waldstein, no one's ever managed to develop a reliable return system."

"We have."

"My God," he whispered. "Good God . . . then you people are for real. This agency of yours . . ."

"The agency is real," said Bob.

"Come on, what do you say, Mr. Locke?"

"We . . . we need what King Richard has in his possession. We would need the grille. There is no mathematical way to decode it."

Liam's brow locked. "There must be another way. But look—it seems to me the one thing we *can't* do is allow King Richard to have both, right?"

"Affirmative," said Bob.

"History as it is says the Grail is a myth," continued Liam. "That's how it goes. It gets lost. It becomes a myth, and that's all there is to it, no matter what secrets lie in there. It certainly *doesn't* end up being found by King Richard and . . . and *inspiring* him to run off again to conquer the world on some fourth crusade or something."

"Information: the correct history is that King Richard attempts no more crusades. The last five years of his reign are spent attempting to re-establish royal authority in England and reclaim his lost territories in France."

"Right. No Grails. No more crusades. He's all done with that."

Locke stroked his bearded chin thoughtfully.

"If we can work out how to decode it, we will, you and me. And if we can't, well . . ." Liam shrugged. "Then we make sure it stays lost. Mr. Locke? What do you say to that?"

He pressed his lips together. "Perhaps."

"There is little time to delay," said Bob. "If King Richard's forces are on the way to Nottingham—"

"The Grail would be safer in Nottingham Castle than out here in the woods," cut in Liam.

"Affirmative."

"And *then* we can decide our next step."

"All right." Locke finally nodded. He handed the gun to Liam. "All right. I . . . I suppose, yes. But I should speak to my people out there first."

"What will you tell them?"

He looked at Bob. "If you wear the hood as you just did, they will believe you are the Hooded Man." Locke again stroked his beard thoughtfully. "I will tell them we must offer our loyalty to John. That we should prepare to leave for Nottingham." He stepped toward the doorway and then turned to Liam. "If they return to Nottingham . . . you do still have the authority to pardon them all, correct?"

Liam nodded. "Yes. Until I hear otherwise from John, I suppose I'm the sheriff."

Locke smiled. "Thank you. They're not outlaws. They're not bad people; they're just hungry, desperate." He ducked and stepped out of the hut.

Liam let loose a breath and waited until the sound of Locke's footsteps was lost amid the babble of voices outside. "Well, that went better than I thought it would."

"Do you trust Locke?" asked Bob.

"He's after the truth, that's all. The same thing as us. And he came back here using a one-way time machine. That's a pretty brave thing to do. Not sure I'd have the guts to do that."

"But do you trust him?"

"Yes . . . yes, I think I do. I think we have to. It makes sense we should work together, right?"

Bob didn't look entirely convinced. Liam nodded at the torn remnants of Bob's arm. "How is it?"

"Gone," replied Bob flatly.

Liam winced. "Well, what I mean is, how's what's left of it—the upper bit?"

"The arteries are sealed. There is no additional blood loss. I will need to dress the wound to ensure no foreign matter gets into it and causes secondary infection."

"It will regrow, right? You're not going to be stuck as a one-armed support unit forever, are you, Bob?"

Bob shook his head. "It will not regrow on its own. I will need to return to a growth tube for healing."

"Right. Well . . ." He slapped Bob affectionately on the back. "That'll be first thing on the 'to-do' list when we get home." He grimaced. "Poor Bob. It always seems you have a tough time of it, both occasions we've gone back."

"That is my role."

"Aye, but . . . Ah well, I suppose I—"

They both heard a sudden commotion: voices calling out, the sound of horses' hooves thudding on soft ground.

"What's going on?" Liam ducked down and stuck his head outside to see Locke's people standing around bemused and motionless, watching the retreating rear of a baggage cart bounce across the lumpy ground of the camp and rattle onto a narrow track that curved and weaved into the forest and out of sight.

Liam cursed. He stuck his head back in. "That slippery sod!"

"What has happened?"

"Locke—he's bleedin' well run away!"

Chapter 63

1194, Sherwood Forest, Nottinghamshire

"He won't have left without it," said Liam. "Not without the Grail, I'm sure of it."

Bob nodded. "Then we must catch him."

Liam ducked back out the entrance and was pushing his way through the crowd when several pairs of hands grabbed him and wrestled him to the ground.

"An' where ye goin,' Frenchie?" snarled someone.

Liam heard the grate of a metal blade being unsheathed.

"RELEASE HIM!" Bob's voice boomed across the clearing once again. He strode forward, his face once more covered by the hood. "STAND BACK!" The crowd did so instantly, drawing away from Liam as if he carried the plague. Bob reached down with his one good hand and helped him back to his feet.

"We need horses," muttered Liam out of the side of his mouth. "We'll never catch him on foot."

"WHO HAS A HORSE?"

The crowd was silent.

"Bob, tell them you're taking me to Nottingham," he whispered. "Tell them you're going to force me to write a pardon for them all. They'll be free to go back to their homes."

Bob nodded and repeated Liam's words in his parade-ground voice. The people listened in stunned silence. As he announced they'd be free to return home, an uncertain cheer rippled through them. Uncertain, perhaps because to them it sounded too good to be true.

"Where has Locke gone?" asked someone.

"I'll tell them," uttered Liam to Bob. He cleared his throat. "Locke has gone to offer his services to King Richard!" Some of the men in the crowd cheered at mention of the king. "Oh, I wouldn't be so quick to cheer him," Liam continued. "I wouldn't be so sure Richard's here to save you from John! He'll come here first, I'd wager. Come here and deal with you all, before dealing with his brother!"

"You're lying!" someone shouted. "You are *John's* man!"

Others in the crowd murmured their agreement. Liam could see none of them was going to believe a single word he uttered. "You better tell them," he whispered to Bob.

"HE IS TELLING THE TRUTH!" barked Bob. "RECOM-MENDATION: LEAVE THIS CAMP IMMEDIATELY AND RETURN TO YOUR HOMES! KING RICHARD IS COMING AND WILL KILL YOU ALL!"

The wood was suddenly filled with raised voices, all speaking at once.

Through the crowd, on one side of the clearing, Liam spotted a solitary malnourished horse, tied to a tree and staring listlessly out at the noise and commotion in front of it. He nudged Bob gently. "Over there. Do you see it?"

"Affirmative."

"I WILL NOW LEAVE WITH THE SHERIFF. YOU WILL ALL BE PARDONED!"

Bob led the way, dragging Liam with him by the arm. The crowd was beginning to break up into knots of people arguing with each other—some determined to stay here, some wanting to go home. An old man reached out for Bob, his hands grasping at his cape. "Please don't leave! We follow you! We came here to follow you!"

Liam glanced up at Bob. He couldn't see Bob's eyes beneath the shadow of the hood, but a gentle tip of his head assured Liam he had an answer. "It is over, old man! There will be no uprising now. You must go home!"

With that he grabbed Liam by the arm again and pulled him forward through the milling crowd.

But the old man was not to be shaken off so easily. "You cannot leave us now! We have nothing! We have"—he grasped at the cape again, but this time the old man's frail hand grabbed at material farther up and as Bob stepped away, the hood pulled back off his face and flapped down onto his shoulders.

The effect was instant. A silence once more; arguments momentarily forgotten, voices hushed, and eyes growing ever wider as they stared at his face.

"'Tis the man who was here earlier!"

"A trick!" someone else cried out. "To rescue the sheriff!"

Liam jabbed Bob in the ribs. "Run!"

Bob's one good arm stretched out and snatched a longbow from the hands of a young man standing nearby. He swiped it around, smacking the heads of half a dozen of those too slow to duck. And then the pair of them were running for the horse.

Liam's bare feet stumbled through the embers of a fire, kicking up a shower of sparks. He yelped and hopped as those nearby frantically brushed off and patted down embers on their dry rags and lank hair. Liam was still hopping and yelping as Bob tossed the longbow aside, scooped him up under his arm, and a moment later hurled him over the rear of the horse. The animal bucked and complained at the sudden load deposited on its back.

Bob snapped the horse's tether from the tree with a savage jerk and then swung a leg over. With a brutal kick of his heels into its flank he startled the horse forward into the crowd, knocking aside hands reaching out to grasp the reins and wrest the horse from their control.

They clattered through the rest of the camp, the horse's hooves kicking aside the frail wooden frames of tents and hovels, people lurching back out of the way at the last moment, curses and stones whistling through the air at them. And then they were on the narrow forest track.

Chapter 64

1194, Nottingham

John stared with utter bemusement at the people in the marketplace. They respectfully made a pathway for his escort of soldiers and the two dozen carts and wagons containing his baggage and essential royal staff of servants.

"I do believe they're . . . uhh . . . they're *cheering* for *me*," he muttered to Becks.

She rode on horseback beside him, sidesaddle rather than astride, dressed in fine linens that fluttered lightly and gracefully. "Yes, my lord, it appears they are."

"That makes a rather pleasant change," he murmured, self-consciously waggling a limp hand back at the people. They roared approval at the simple gesture.

Leaving Oxford hadn't been quite so pleasant. John had felt compelled, for his own safety, to hide in one of the wagons while his escort of soldiers had had to push and shove the angry crowd aside to allow the column through the main gate. He'd heard jeering and cursing, swords being unsheathed, and the thumps and bangs of fists and booted feet against the wooden trap of his wagon.

"It seems your friend has won them over for me."

Becks nodded. "Yes. He has been very effective."

He smiled and nodded at the people. "And they are staying put . . . even though they must have heard by now that Richard's army approaches."

Becks nodded as she rode in silence. She offered him a faint smile, the slightest curl of her lips.

John felt his heavy heart lift. For the first time in years, he actually felt . . . *liked.* These people could have abandoned Nottingham to its fate. They could surely leave and find shelter elsewhere, in other towns, other villages. But they'd decided to stay, prepared to show the king that they actually approved of *John's* stewardship while Richard had been away on his foolish crusading, bankrupting them all.

He noticed the market stalls were well stocked. A good summer's crop that had managed to be harvested without the disruption of roving gangs of bandits and villains, leaving smoldering fields and dead farm workers in their wake. The people certainly looked better fed than those in Oxford—not all pallid skin drawn up against hard-edged bones and dressed in rags, but people who looked well. People from better, happier times.

That at least was some comfort.

If Richard wanted to besiege this town, then he was going to have a hard time of it. The walls were good, the town's position a strong one. There appeared to be supplies of food within and a population that was willing to make a stand for him.

But the Grail?

Has he found it yet?

John's heart skipped anxiously at the thought. There would be no need for any kind of a stand, a battle, a siege, no need for any of that nonsense if that curious young man, *Liam de Connor*, had managed to successfully track down the bandits and get back what they'd taken.

He could hand it over to his brother and then beg his forgiveness for losing the Grail. Beg his forgiveness for failing to find that ransom money for two long years. He could beg, and publicly stoop to kiss his brother's hand, and, perhaps, that and the safe return of the Grail would be enough to appease him. There would be a beating with a cane later, of course. Away from public eyes.

Royalty can never afford to be seen as frail . . . just as mortal as any common man.

Richard would delight at that: stripping him, beating him, having him beg and plead like a pitiful dog. It wouldn't be the first time he'd done that to him. But Richard would have his precious Grail with all its priceless Templar secrets and be in a good mood. He'd be distracted into thinking about future insane campaigns in faraway lands, now that he had his holy relic.

And John would get to keep a head on his shoulders.

He glanced up at the sturdy keep in front of them, in the center of Nottingham, hoping to catch sight of his new sheriff riding out to greet them on horseback. Hoping to see a sign, a smile and a small nod—a gesture to assure him that all was well, that he could relax once again.

That he has the Grail.

"No welcome," muttered John. "Is no one at home?"

He could see the bobbing of helmeted heads between crenellations. The castle appeared to be garrisoned still. But a greeting party on horseback should have emerged by now, out of mere courtesy.

"I wonder where the sheriff is?"

🕐

"Up ahead!" Liam shouted. Sitting across the bouncing rump of the horse, his voice warbled like a songbird. "That's him!"

The cart ahead of them was rattling along the narrow track, wheels wobbling and straining as they careered over the humps of tree roots. In the back of the cart, tethered bundles of firewood and several sacks of apples rattled and rolled around as Locke kicked and cajoled his horse to pick up the pace.

They closed on him quickly. Even their weary-looking old horse, all bones and hide and ready for the butcher's cleaver, was making better progress than the wide-axled cart down what was barely more than a winding footpath.

Locke must have heard them approaching, since he turned to look over his shoulder. It took him all of a second to realize the cart was too slow. He reined in the horse, reached around into the back of the cart, grabbed a small, dark wooden box no bigger than a hatbox, and leapt off the seat onto the track.

"He's bolting!"

Bob nodded. "Get off here," he grunted. "I will pursue him."

Liam slid clumsily off the back of the horse, the still-raw soles of his feet jabbing him painfully as they settled on sharp stones. Bob kicked his heels and clattered off down the footpath, turning the horse left into the trees where Locke had disappeared moments before. Liam listened to the receding thud of hooves and the occasional crack of a dried branch echoing through the wood as Bob gave chase.

He made his way slowly down the path toward the abandoned cart, yelping and grimacing at each sharp stone, each fir cone he stepped on. Finally he drew up beside it. The horse eyed him irritably, as if even he knew this was no track for a cart. It snorted, flaring its nostrils.

"Easy there," said Liam. He pulled himself onto the back of the cart and allowed himself to collapse, exhausted, among the apples that had spilled out across the flatbed.

Chapter 65

1194, Sherwood Forest, Nottinghamshire

Bob steered the horse through the woods, deftly ducking the low swoop of branches. Up ahead he could hear Locke scrambling his way over fallen branches that cracked noisily under his feet, making far too much noise to hope to evade him.

He caught a glimpse of Locke. The man was making pitifully slow progress, the wooden box tucked under one tired arm, pushing his way through a tight bush of brambles with the other.

"Cease running!" Bob called out. "You will not escape!"

Locke stopped and turned. His eyes widened at the sight of Bob calmly steering the horse as it picked its way through the undergrowth toward him.

Locke seemed to realize he was wasting his time. He slumped down onto a small boulder, winded and spent. Bob swung his leg over the horse, dropped heavily down to the ground, and approached him.

"I presume you want this?" said Locke, holding out the box.

Bob reached out his one hand for the box. He placed it on the ground, lifted a small metal clasp, and opened the lid. He stared at the contents in silence for a moment before closing it.

"Who are you people really?" asked Locke between labored gasps.

Bob's gray eyes studied him silently.

"You're just a dumb robot, aren't you? Inside all that skin, blood, and bones, a dumb robot. Just like my war-surplus mech—a machine under orders."

"I have mission priorities," said Bob drily.

"And what do you know about what's in there?" Locke said, nodding at the box.

·Bob was silent.

"Right." Locke nodded. "Not much, huh?"

"The item known as the Holy Grail may contain sensitive information about the agency. That is why we seek to obtain it and decode its contents."

Locke laughed, a wheezy, dry cackle. "Is that it? Is that *all* you think might be in there? Something that could expose your little agency?" He shook his head and laughed some more. "You really have no goddamn idea, do you?"

Bob's eyes narrowed. "Explain."

"That," he said, nodding at the box, still struggling for breath, "that contains something far more important. Your secret agency is nothing compared to this. It's a speck of dust compared to this!"

"Explain."

"It's our future . . . it's *everyone's* future. Don't you know this? There's a door that opens in 2070. A door that opens on something that—"

"What?"

Locke shook his head. "That's just it—we don't know. *No one* knows! That's why I was sent back. To find out—to decode it. To get a warning through to everyone in my time. So that they can *prepare* themselves!" Locke spat phlegm onto the forest floor. "Good God, you have to help me! You have to help me get the key from King Richard and—"

"Your mission priorities are in conflict with mine," replied Bob.

"What? What the hell kind of priorities are more important than knowing what's going to happen?"

"Mission priorities: Retrieve the Grail. Decode the Grail. Correct contaminated history. Locate and terminate potential contaminants."

Locke looked up at him. "'Terminate potential contaminants?' Oh, I see. I get it . . . You have to kill me?"

"Correct," said Bob, pulling his sword out of its scabbard. "Your presence in this time represents too much of a risk to the timeline."

Locke's eyes followed the dull glint of the sword's edge. "Look, I have no modern technological artifacts on me. I'm just one man on my own. You *could* let me go. You *could* let me just walk out of here. You see, I *don't want* to go back to 2070! I really don't!"

Bob silently appraised him.

"Please! Just let me go. What could I say that anyone would believe anyway? I'd just be considered a madman! A village fool!"

Some small part of Bob's brain registered the growing desperation in Locke's voice . . . a desperate desire not to die—to live longer. The small part of his brain could understand that animal instinct. Even sympathize with it.

"Get up," said Bob.

Locke clambered slowly to his feet.

Bob raised his one good arm and pointed into the woods with the tip of the blade. "You must run in that direction."

Locke looked confused.

"Run in that direction. You must leave the county of Nottingham immediately. Any attempt to influence historical events will be picked up by us, and we will return to kill you. Is this clear?"

Locke nodded. "Yes . . . yes, of course."

"Then proceed."

"Go? Now?"

"Immediately."

Locke stepped away from Bob, cautious backward steps at first, then, a few yards from him, he turned tail and began to run.

Bob silently watched him pick up the pace as he ducked and scrambled through the undergrowth. Certain now that the man wasn't going to dare to look back again, he pulled the sword back over his shoulder, poised for the briefest moment as he calculated speed and trajectory, then flung the blade forward.

It whistled through the air, one complete cartwheel hilt over tip, ending with the tip facing forward once more just as it made contact with the soft fleshy space between Locke's shoulder blades. He tumbled forward, and kicked once on the ground.

A moment later Bob stood over the man's body and retrieved his sword, wiping the blood off on Locke's clothing. His silicon mind quietly crossed off the lowest entry on his list of mission priorities. His animal mind begrudgingly murmured approval of the small mercy he'd given to Locke, letting him believe he was going to live. Death came without any warning . . . and quickly.

A small mercy, at least.

Chapter 66

1194, Nottingham

He wasn't sure if he'd actually fallen asleep. He must have, because all of a sudden he was looking up at an evening sky, free of overlapping branches and leaves, and the cart's wheels were creaking easily along a rutted track. He sat up and turned to see Bob's wide shoulders swaying in the driver's seat.

"Did you get him?"

Bob turned and looked at Liam. "Locke is no longer a contamination issue."

"What? You mean he—?"

"I managed to acquire what we were after," Bob interrupted. He pulled some sackcloth aside to reveal a small, dark wooden box. The lid was decorated with the faint lines of a geometric pattern carved a long time ago and attached by old iron hinges.

"Bob! Is this really it? Is this the Holy Grail? Did you open it?"

Bob gave his best grin, the one that would give small children nightmares. "I believe it contains what we have been looking for."

Liam reached out for the box, touching the wooden grain lightly with his fingertips, the faint lines of the carving on the lid. The oddest sensation. He felt a tingle of energy course through his hands, the fine downy hairs on his arms raise, and a shudder of something—fear? excitement?—ripple through his body.

Inside this is the Holy Grail. The Holy Grail, *Liam.*

The very thing sought by figures of legend, King Arthur and his Knights of the Round Table. A relic thought to be the cup of Christ, a chalice . . . or just a myth, a metaphor. But here it was, in the back of a bouncing cart full of rolling apples.

Carefully, reverentially, he eased the lid slowly up, half-expecting the sky above to crack open and reveal a God ready to smite him with a bolt of lightning for daring to consider himself worthy enough to look upon his very words.

Inside the small box he saw a threadbare canvas bag, a drawstring at the top pulling it tightly closed. The canvas bag rested on a shallow bed of coins, stamped with the face of King Henry II, Richard and John's father. Liam guessed that was some of the money Locke's bandits had managed to rob from tax collectors and merchants foolish enough to travel the forest tracks of Nottingham during the last two years.

Carefully, he lifted out the canvas bag and loosened the drawstring to look down inside.

He could see the handle of a wooden scroll spindle and the frayed edges of yellowing parchment wrapped tightly around it. He felt an almost overpowering urge to pull it out of the bag and unroll the parchment, but the cart was rolling and bucking as the wheels rode up and down ruts in the track. One bump, and it could tear in his hands.

He stared at the frayed edges curled around the spindle. Somewhere on those pages of parchment, the word "Pandora" was written. A message, a warning that—if Maddy was right—someone wanted them, specifically them, to know about.

He felt that shudder down his spine again, as if simply by holding this roll of parchment, looking at it, he was waking something up from a deep slumber, disturbing it . . . foolishly prodding it.

He pulled the drawstring tight again and gently laid the canvas bag back on its bed of coins and closed the lid.

He shuffled forward and tapped Bob on the shoulder. Bob turned his head, and Liam found himself looking at the frayed and bloody edges of what remained of the top rim of Bob's right ear. A line of dark dried blood ran down the side of his neck and disappeared beneath the folds of his dark cape.

"Bob . . . that's really it, isn't it? We've got . . ."

He looked down again at the box. *We've got, quite possibly, the most important piece of rolled-up paper that has ever existed.*

He was wondering whether to voice that out loud, or whether saying it was somehow pushing their luck, inviting some sort of lightning bolt.

"Caution!" said Bob suddenly.

Liam looked up from the box. The dusty track had just brought them over the brow of a hill. There below them like a child's play set, shimmering amid the midday warmth, was the walled town of Nottingham, busy with activity. A welcome sight for Liam. Or at least it would have been, had it not been for the spreading dark line of figures casually crossing and flattening the patchwork of furrowed fields outside the walls.

Thousands of them.

He saw the flickering glint of chain mail armor among them: a forest of multicolored pennants fluttering above columns of men, trudging off the road leading up from the south and fanning out into the fields. He could see swarms of dark figures pulling equipment from baggage trains of carts, tents already being erected on beds of trampled crops, and long beams of wood being worked upon by teams of carpenters with the percussive *rattle-tap* of dozens of hand axes and hammers.

"It appears King Richard has arrived," said Bob.

Down the sloping track leading to the town's main entrance, Liam could see a river of traffic emerging. King Richard's soldiers seemed to be permitting those who wanted no part in the siege to leave. Mostly merchants, visiting tradesmen driving out empty carts: people with no special allegiance to the place and no wish to die for a cause.

"Letting people out. But no one in," Liam commented.

"Affirmative."

He looked down at the milling chaos outside the opened gates to Nottingham. Perhaps, if they could get down there among all that confusion, they could find a way to sneak in.

"Bob, let's see how close we can get before someone stops us."

"Affirmative."

"And you better pull up your hood . . . your ear's going to attract attention."

Bob did as he was told, working the hood over his shaggy head. Then with his one good hand, he grabbed the reins and kicked the horse's rump. It staggered wearily forward, and the cart's wheels creaked once more as they descended toward the scene below.

A couple minutes later they were passing the first of the merchants streaming out, many of them irritably shouting that they were heading the wrong way and should either turn around or get off the track; otherwise, they met with no interference—until a picket of soldiers thirty yards ahead of them, wearing olive-green sashes over leather jerkins, began waving them down to stop.

Liam cursed. "What're we gonna do?" he hissed from the back.

Bob shrugged casually. "I am evaluating."

"Well, we don't have time to evaluate, dammit!" Liam gritted his teeth. They were a hundred yards from the main entrance, and all of that distance was a confusion of people. Surely, if they could just lose themselves in that . . .

The soldiers ahead of them were now stepping on to the track and into their way.

And what if they decide to search the cart? What if one of them decides this little box looks rather nice?

"Bob, I think we're going to have to go for it."

"Clarify 'go for it.'"

"Don't stop. Just go. Go very fast!"

Bob nodded. "Agreed."

He whipped the reins across the horse's shoulders, and for good measure swung a hard kick once more at its rear. The horse bellowed a complaint, but all the same broke into a begrudging canter.

The soldiers ahead of them called out warnings to stop but, at the very last moment, stepped aside to avoid being run over.

As they swept by the men, angry voices rippled orders, and another party of soldiers farther up, overseeing the merchants' exodus, readied themselves to stop the cart. Liam could see these ones were better equipped for the job, armed as they were with pikes. Just one of those braced firmly against the ground would be enough to run their horse's chest through and bring it down in an untidy heap.

What they needed was a stampede. A distraction. Chaos. What they needed was . . .

He reached for the box, yanked the lid open, and carefully tucked the drawstring canvas bag into the folds of his cloak. What was left inside, a small mound of gold coins, he scooped up into his hands.

"Bob!" he bellowed over his shoulder. "Shout 'free money'! Shout something like 'free money,' really, really loud!"

Bob craned his hooded neck to look at Liam and saw him holding the handfuls of coins. He seemed to understand what Liam was up to. "MONEY!" his voice boomed above the pounding hooves and the labored creak of their spinning cart wheels. "HAVE FREE MONEY!"

Liam tossed a handful of the glinting coins over the left side of the cart and into the tall grass beside the track. The result was almost instantaneous—like tossing a handful of bread crumbs into a courtyard full of pigeons. Merchants' wives walking beside their husbands' carts, the foot traffic, tradesmen's helpers old and young, children, all swarmed off the dusty track and began scrabbling in the tall grass.

Bob steered their horse, cutting in between two carts and putting them on the right side of the traffic emerging through the arch of the gatehouse as Liam tossed another handful into the crowd around them.

"FREE MONEY FOR EVERYONE!" bellowed Bob again.

Hands snatched and grabbed for the coins tumbling through the air. They were now level with the pikemen—the soldiers on the left of the surging river of people, Liam and Bob on the right, separated by a roiling sea of grasping hands fighting each other to get within reach of the last shower of coins.

The soldiers pushed their way angrily through people bent over double and scrabbling in the dust to get to them, but then Liam tossed a handful right at them. Coins clanged like shrapnel off their helmets. It did the trick, stopping them dead, as they too dropped to their hands and knees to grab for what they could.

The large arched entrance to the town loomed above them, and Bob savagely kicked their poor beast one last time, raising their canter to a reckless gallop. Its hooves clattered and scraped noisily off dried mud onto cobbles and flagstones, and the tail end of the evacuating merchants ahead of them swiftly parted on either side to avoid being flattened as they passed beneath the archway and into the market square inside the wall.

"FREE MONEY FOR EVERYONE!" Bob's deep voice echoed across the market, bouncing off the inside of the stone walls like the blast of a ship's foghorn. Liam tossed out another fistful in their wake, ensuring none of King Richard's soldiers were going to be able to push through the entrance after them, plugged as it was with people doubled over searching for coins.

"We're in!" Liam shouted. "We did it!"

Bob reined the horse back and it slowed down to a blown, wheezing trot.

People around them, soldiers too—this time wearing the burgundy and orange colors of the town's garrison—flocked around the back of the cart, looking in at the remaining coins scattered across the flatbed.

Why not? Liam grinned.

He scraped up the last of the coins and threw them out into the crowd.

"Money for the poor!" he shouted.

Chapter 67

1194, Nottingham Castle, Nottingham

The first thing Liam registered as he and Bob stepped through the velvet drapes into the keep's main hall was Becks. She was standing by the arch that led out onto a wooden balcony, poised in a ridiculously-not-her demure and ladylike pose, long embroidered linens and lace fluttering glamorously from her in the breeze.

"*Salutations, Liam. J'espère que vous allez bien?*"

Liam bit his lip, resisting an inappropriate urge to giggle. Instead he tipped a polite nod at her. "Greetings, Lady Rebecca."

She switched to English. "Greetings to you also."

John stepped into view from the balcony. He smiled, genuinely pleased to see Liam. "Ahhh! My sheriff! 'Tis the man of the hour!" He stepped forward to greet him. "I am indebted to you. I truly am! I arrived here earlier today to, would you believe, cheers—actual *cheers* from the peasants!"

Liam bowed. "They are loyal to you, Sire."

"Indeed, but I suspect it has been your common touch as sheriff that has earned me their affection, hmm?" John's face adopted a mock-serious expression. His thick brows knotted. "I noticed your rather *flamboyant* entry to the marketplace just now. Congratulations for making your way through Richard's lines outside . . . but, I must ask, is it customary now to hurl handfuls of royal revenue at the people to gain entry?"

"Ahh, yes, that. Well, er . . . I—we, umm—"

John's frown faded and he waved the question away. "It matters not to me any more. Now he is back home, it is Richard's money you were throwing anyway. Not mine." He stepped closer to Liam. He could see there was something far more pressing on John's mind than mere coin. "Now . . . Please, please, you must tell me," he said more quietly. "I . . . I need to know—"

Liam quickly nodded, saving the man any more anguish. "'Yes' is the answer, Sire. I have it. We have the Grail."

John sagged with relief, his breath puffing out in a barely suppressed gasp. "Oh, thank the Lord! Thank the Lord!" He settled down heavily into a wooden chair, robbed of the strength to remain standing. "I cannot tell you how . . . how *vexed*—how so very worried I have been!"

Becks stepped into the room and stood beside him. Liam noticed the graceful way she moved and the way she gently caressed his brow. No longer did she have the swagger of a tomboy, no longer was she another Bob in a girl-suit. She was all grace and elegance.

Now that's very weird, so it is.

He smiled, proud of what she seemed to have learned over the last few months, of her ability to adapt so convincingly. Not so long ago she'd barely managed to pass herself off as an American high-school student. Now here she was, quite believable as a medieval lady of noble blood.

"Calm yourself, my lord," she cooed softly. "Did I not say my friend Liam would retrieve it for you?"

John nodded and smiled. "Yes, my dear . . . yes, so you did. I should never have doubted you."

"Bob helped, of course," said Liam, shrugging. "Actually, he did most of the hard work."

Bob emerged from behind the drapes and nodded politely at John and Becks.

"Good God!" said John, his eyes suddenly as round as pickled eggs. "This man needs a physician!"

Bob looked down at the ragged, shredded stump of his left arm, dangling shreds of tattered skin and the rounded white nub of a bone. "The wound is no longer bleeding. It is not life-threatening."

"Your arm is GONE, man! You should be attended to *immediately*!" gasped John. He got up from his chair and led Bob back toward the drapes. He called out for one of the guards standing outside to take Bob to the garrison's apothecary. "And be double quick about it, fool! The man needs it bound!"

He returned, pale-faced and shuddering. "Ughh! I . . . have a poor stomach for such things." He puffed his cheeks queasily. "Oh, quite horrible. All that . . . gristle and—and . . ." He reached for a cup of wine and drained it, then wiped his mouth. "Now, to matters of importance." He pointed to the balcony. "I should waste not another moment. We must surrender the town immediately!"

"What?"

John nodded his head vigorously. "Indeed, yes! I have what he wants." John looked at Liam. "Where is it, by the way?"

Liam nodded down at the box in his arms. "Right here."

John glanced at it. "And it is safe? Complete? Undamaged?" He had little interest in opening the box and inspecting the parchment itself. Holy relics and Templar superstitions were his brother's obsession, not his.

"It is fine."

"Good. Then there's no need for this battle to take place. No need for bloodshed today. I shall arrange a parlay with him at once!"

Becks leaned down, speaking in soft, soothing tones to him and gently stroking his forehead. "That is a bad idea. The Grail is *all* that you have to bargain with. You must hold on to it. *Tu dois être courageaux et fort, mon cher.*"

Liam was again impressed with how much her AI had picked up, how convincing she sounded and looked.

"I am tired, my dear lady," muttered John, closing his eyes. "Tired of fearing him. Fearing his return. I want this to be over with, so I can rest—"

"And it will be. Soon," she cooed, "soon. But you must be strong. Be strong for me."

He opened his eyes. "For you?"

She nodded. "You must be strong and make your brother wait." Becks glanced toward the archway and the balcony. From afar, the sound of carpenters at work echoed across the walls of Nottingham. "Let him build his siege weapons, let him waste time; then you should parlay."

John closed his eyes as she caressed his forehead.

"You should rest, my lord. There's time for that, and you have slept little."

John nodded. "I am so very tired."

Becks glanced up at Liam. "Rest now, my dear. Take some more wine. And I shall go and arrange supper for you and the sheriff."

She stood up and discreetly beckoned Liam to follow her out of the hall.

Chapter 68

1194, Nottingham Castle, Nottingham

"Jay-zus, Becks!" whispered Liam. "You were completely convincing back there. Does John . . . is he in *love* with you or something?"

She shrugged. "He has developed an infatuation for me. I have attempted to analyze why this is so, and have no valid conclusions to make. He has said he finds 'my unladylike fortitude bewitching.' The important factor is that this is useful leverage, which can be applied if needed."

She hushed as a castle servant passed them in the small, dark hallway. She beckoned Liam to follow her until she found a low wooden door on their left and stepped inside. They were in a small pantry; it was empty, save for several shelves laden with clay pots of preserves.

Liam reached out and grabbed her arms. "It's good to see you again, Becks! Bob and I were becoming worried about you, so we were."

"I have been in no danger," she replied calmly, with a hint of a smile for him. But then it was gone. More pressing matters to attend to. "John does not have the will or the courage to stand up to Richard. But my history database shows this siege *does* take place. That John does make a stand against him. Nottingham holds out for a week."

"That needs to happen, then, right? To ensure history is back to where it was?"

She nodded.

"What about the Grail?" said Liam. "Richard isn't meant to get his hands on it, is he?"

"There is no information on that in my files. This would indicate—"

"That the Grail vanished. Ended up getting lost."

"Affirmative." She cocked her head, considering a suggestion. "We could destroy it."

Liam shook his head. "No—no, I think there's much more than we thought in there. Not just this word 'Pandora' . . . there's some sort of prophecy about the future."

"Prophecy?"

Liam shared with her everything he could remember Locke telling him. He told her about the robot he came back with, about the Templars who'd sent him. He talked uninterrupted for what seemed like ages. Finally, he described Bob chasing Locke off into the woods and retrieving the box. She now knew everything he did.

"Then there may be strategically important information we can retrieve by decoding this document," she said calmly, gazing at the wooden box in Liam's hands.

"Exactly. And the only way to do it is to use this grille thing out there, in King Richard's possession."

She shook her head.

"What?"

"I believe there is another factor involved."

Liam frowned. This was already confusing enough for him. "What are you talking about?"

She reached under the layers of her gown, fumbling awkwardly for a few moments before pulling out a scroll of parchment. It was flattened and creased. He didn't dare ask where it had been wedged.

"This is a document known as the Treyarch Confession," she said. "It is an account of the discovery of a scroll dating back to—"

"Bible times?" cut in Liam. He remembered Cabot's description of it months ago.

"Affirmative."

"Where did you get it?"

"That is irrelevant information. I have scanned the text of this and analyzed the content."

"And?"

"I calculate a fifty-seven percent probability that the Treyarch Confession is the *correct* key for decoding the Grail."

"What?" He looked at the creased and tattered parchment in her hands. "*That's* the key?"

"Fifty-seven percent probability that it is. Correct."

"So what's King Richard got, then?"

"A piece of worn leather with holes cut into it."

"Why? What makes you think that this is the real thing?"

She carefully unrolled the parchment until it was spread almost two yards along the stone floor. She pointed to illustrations in the margins on both sides of the text. "These decorative illustrations are common for the time. Typically they mirror the theme or message of the text. Observe," she said, moving her finger down one margin. "These illustrations are just simple geometric patterns. They have no discernible symbolism or meaning."

"They're there just to make it look nice?"

"Correct."

Liam noted the patterns were intermittent; a dense, intricate block of cross-hatching and swirls about two inches square, located every ten or eleven inches down the margin on either side.

"The patterns are identical," Becks said. Liam looked more closely. Yes, they were. Line for line, curl for curl—the same ornate pattern.

Becks's finger moved down the scroll and finally stopped. "Except these four." She pointed them out, two on each side. Liam struggled to see the difference by the guttering candlelight. His eyes strained as he studied them, again comparing lines and curves.

"Look very closely," said Becks, pointing to a faint pen stroke in the pattern—the slightest hint of a minute cruciform, easily lost amid the confusion of elaborate ink swirls. She pointed to another of the four. Again, the hint of a cross, but in a different location within the pattern. And then the other two. "The cross appears *only* in these four blocks of pattern."

He looked at her. "So?"

Her brows knotted momentarily, perhaps a learned gesture of impatience. "Each cross could indicate a corner."

He looked back down at the parchment. She was, of course, right. "Four corners . . . ?"

"Four corners of a box."

He looked back down again.

She continued. "I calculate with reasonable probability that this is an instruction on how to build a *cardan grille* to decode the Grail. The corners of the template would line up with the four crosses." She pointed at the handwritten text that would be framed by all four markers. "And some of the letters of the text within the template area should be identifiable as 'window candidates.'"

"What do you mean?"

"You would mark where the letter was on the template, and cut out a small square of the template around it, thus creating a window."

"Ahh! I see." Liam grinned. "And you cut out all these little windows, and then you lay this template on the rolled-out Grail, and . . ."

"Correct." She nodded. "Making sure you line up the template with similar corner markers. And the letters you see through the windows that you have cut out spell the hidden message."

"That's—that's genius, that is! You could be right!" He got up off his haunches and started to look around for something they could use. "We could make our own grille right here! Right now!"

"No," she replied. "We can't."

"Why not?"

"We do not know which letters are the window candidates."

Liam's excitement vanished with a sigh. He'd assumed she'd already identified which were the ones.

"On several occasions this document switches from Old English to another language. As you can see, it does so within the area marked by the crosses." She pointed out the change of language to him. "I do not have this language file in my database. We have to presume there would be clues within this text to identify which letters are the window candidates."

Liam scratched at his chin. "Would Bob know this language?"

"No. We had the same files downloaded before the mission."

Liam looked at it; he recognized some of the letters from the alphabet, but there were others that were totally alien to him. "Well, this is no good." He slumped back down again on the cold stone floor.

"Suggestion."

"What?"

She began to carefully roll up the Treyarch Confession. Finally it disappeared again under the folds of her long dress.

"Oh, hang on," said Liam, realizing what she was thinking. "You can't take it to Kirklees, Becks! We're surrounded by Richard's army. It could end up falling into Richard's hands."

Becks reached for the candle flickering on the floor between them. "Then the alternative is that we burn both documents before Nottingham falls to King Richard. What is your decision, Liam O'Connor?"

Chapter 69

1194, Nottingham

Becks managed to make her way through the picket lines of soldiers. Not too difficult. The few men on guard duty were too busy discussing how they were going to spend their share of the spoils once Nottingham had fallen. Rumor was, King Richard was going to turn a blind eye to any looting or pillaging in the immediate aftermath, just as if this was a siege taking place in the corner of some foreign country.

Toward the rear of the camp she found the assembled carts of the baggage train and, tethered nearby in a temporarily erected corral, the horses. She picked one, untied it, led it quietly out, and was cantering away up the track toward the nearby forests before the mead-soaked old man dozing instead of watching over the animals registered they'd become restless and that one of them had in fact gone missing.

The canter became a carefree gallop along the dirt track leading to the brow of the hill overlooking Nottingham. She took the northeast route through the forest, partially following Liam's directions, partially relying on the precise coordinates in her head.

Liam had warned her to be wary of bandits, but the forest presented no threats to her; the shabby band of villains Liam had mentioned, Locke's people, had either disbanded and gone home or disappeared deeper into the woods in an attempt to evade any punitive raids Richard might decide to unleash.

Through several hours of night she covered winding miles of nothing more than the hissing of trees stirred by a lively breeze and hooting birds, until finally, just as her silicon mind indicated she would, she caught sight of the dark, low forms of the outbuildings of the priory.

🕐

Sébastien Cabot was awake in an instant. His soldier's instinct to reach for the dagger hidden under his straw mattress kicked in, only to be stopped by the lightning-quick grasp of a firm hand around his wrist.

From the slither of moonlight stealing through the narrow window into his bare room, he could see just the dark outline of someone leaning over him. "Who—who is . . . ?" he blustered, his voice still thick with sleep.

"This is Lady Rebecca," she whispered.

Cabot struggled to sit up. The wooden frame beneath his mattress creaked. "Good grief! What are ye doing here? The other monks—"

Her hand smothered his mouth and pushed his head down heavily against the mattress with a soft thud. "Be quiet and listen!" Her hand remained clamped over his lips until he finally nodded. She lifted her hand, and he sucked in a much-needed breath.

"I have obtained the Grail document," she said without any preamble.

"WHAT? MY GO—!" His voice bounced off the stone walls of his room.

Her hand clamped his mouth firmly again. Above the bulbous end of his florid, pockmarked nose she noted the wide rolling whites of his eyes. For a moment she considered how expressive human eyes could be; just those alone seemed to be able to communicate a whole language of emotions. Cabot, for example, right now appeared to be communicating an emotion akin to profound shock. She made a note to try rolling her eyes like that sometime.

"I also have the Treyarch Confession," she added, her hand remaining over his mouth as he grunted and struggled. "I will need your assistance in translating a section of it." She waited a few moments for that request to settle in and for Cabot to stop making that muffled mewling noise beneath her firmly clamped palm. When she was sure he wasn't going to blurt out loudly again, she slowly lifted her hand. "Will you assist?"

Cabot gasped for air, sucking in breath through his mouth. After a few seconds he managed to talk in a hoarse whisper. "Ye . . . ye have them *both*?"

She nodded.

"Here? Right here with ye?"

"Yes. Will you assist me?"

"Good Lord! I—I . . ." Cabot struggled to frame an answer. Becks once more hushed him, this time with a finger pressed against his whisker-lined lips.

"We will discuss this further in your graveyard," she said. "Put clothes on now. I will see you there in five minutes." She let go of his wrist and got up. "And bring a candle."

He picked his way through weeds and brambles that scratched at the bare ankles below the coarse hem of his robe. By the scudding light of the moon he spotted the dark outline of Lady Rebecca standing perfectly still beside a gravestone.

"My lady?" he called softly.

"Here," she replied.

He joined her. "Ye . . . Last I heard, ye were in Oxford."

"John has relocated to Nottingham. King Richard has come north with an army."

"Yes . . . yes, the county is full of this news. But—the Grail? How did ye find—where was—?"

"The Grail was recovered from the bandit known as 'The Hood' earlier today," she replied quickly, as if answering the question was valuable time wasted.

"How did they manage to find him?"

"That is unimportant. The Grail document can only be decoded with the correct *cardan grille*," she said, reaching into the folds of her dark robe.

She saw the whites of Cabot's wide, round eyes again. "Ye have it?" he asked. "Don't tell me ye have stolen it from King Richard?"

She ignored his question and calmly pulled out the Treyarch. "This document is written in Latin and Norman French," she began, "but there is one passage written in a language I have no data on. Your assistance is required to identify the language."

She carefully started to unroll the parchment. "You may light your candle now if there is inadequate light for you to see."

Cabot shook his head impatiently. "'Tis not necessary. The moon is enough. Please continue."

She resumed, turning the wooden spindle and spreading out the long curled sheet of parchment on the ground. By the moon's wan light, the pale paper seemed to almost glow, the dark spider-lines of ink across it every bit as clear and legible as they needed to be.

"The unidentifiable language is located here," said Becks, pointing to a passage three-quarters of the way down the scroll. She put rocks out along the edge of the parchment to stop it from curling up again and then leaned back so that her shadow didn't fall across it.

Cabot squatted down and inspected the writing closely. "This here," he said, running his fingers along the curls of writing. "'Tis a form of Gaelic, I believe."

"You know this language?"

He grimaced. "I know *some* words of it. And there are many forms of this language. I could perhaps translate this for ye if I had some time—and a library of other Gaelic works to compare it to."

She cocked her head, and her eyebrows locked in concentration for a moment. After a minute of silent consideration, she nodded slowly, a decision made. "The contamination risk is acceptable for the moment," she muttered.

"What is that, my lady?"

Again she ignored him. "You will come with me, please," she said.

"Where?"

She got to her feet and began foraging among the tall weeds around the gravestone until she finally found what she was after: a long lumber nail. She crouched down in front of the gravestone and began scratching deep lines into the granite.

"What are ye doing?"

"Communicating."

She carried on in silence, nothing but the sound of scraping and scratching and stone grit tumbling to the ground. "I am requesting an immediate portal."

"What is this? What are ye up to?" asked Cabot once again.

She turned to look at him impatiently. "You are coming with me."

"Coming with ye? Where to?"

"The future."

Chapter 70

2001, New York

Sal looked at them both. "*Jahulla!* That was one," she said. "Did you feel it?" The other two looked at each other. Maddy quickly got up from the table and went over toward the bank of computer monitors.

She sat down at the desk and downloaded the image again from the still-connected drive outside. As it flickered open on the screen, Sal leaned over and traced a finger along the faint new lines on the photograph. "There's another message on your gravestone."

Adam scribbled down the pigpen glyphs onto a pad of paper.

The girls watched him impatiently as he checked each symbol against the table he'd drawn up on the page of writing paper earlier. "Well?"

"Just hang on!" His eyes narrowed as he double-checked some of the symbols on the new row that had appeared on his photograph. There were faint lines there, lines that might not have been part of the original carving, and lines lost to nearly a millennium of weathering. He looked down at the page of letters he'd deciphered and realized there were mistakes in there.

"First word is 'extraction,'" said Sal.

Maddy nodded. "The rest is a time-stamp. Twelve numbers, the first four a time, the last eight a date."

Sal grabbed a pen and quickly scribbled the near-words as numbers: 0445 13061194.

Maddy checked her numbers against what Adam had decoded. "Yes . . . yes, okay. Quarter to five in the morning, June 13th, 1194. Right?" She looked at the webcam. "You get that, Bob?"

> **Affirmative. I have been listening. Date stamp: 04:45, June 13, 1194.**

"There are no geo-coordinates, though," said Maddy.

"Same coordinates as last time, then," said Sal.

Maddy tapped a pen against her lips. "Yeah. You get that, Bob?"

> **Affirmative. Same geo-placement coordinates.**

She leaned back in her chair and glanced around Adam at the rack of equipment beside the empty plexiglass tube. The charge display showed a full line of green LEDs. "All right, we've got enough juice on the board to open it up, Bob."

> **Affirmative. Activating density probe.**

1194, Kirklees Priory, Yorkshire

Cabot looked around the field. Although the sun had yet to climb into view, the peach-stained sky was light now, a sky that would soon be a deep blue and cloudless—another hot summer's day.

"Why, pray, are we standing in this field?"

Becks raised a finger. "Just a moment."

Cabot looked around at the softly stirring ears of barley. They rustled and whispered among themselves as they waited in silence for . . . for what? Lady Rebecca had said "the future."

Days yet to be.

To visit one of those . . . it was a concept he could barely get his mind around. A day simply *is*. And then after the day has ended, it merely *was*, complete with whatever one remembered. To walk into what was *yet to be* . . .

He shook his head at the impossibility of it. Perhaps this lady and her friends were afflicted by some madness. He'd come across holy men in Jerusalem who made claim of things just as impossible and nonsensical as this.

"My lady, perhaps it would be best if we return to the grounds of the priory?"

She shook her head. "I am detecting tachyons, Cabot. It appears the message has already been received."

Tack-ee-ons? Another one of their strange words that he could only ponder the meaning of. He looked around the field, not sure what a "tack-ee-on" was, or what he should do if one were to approach him.

A fresh breeze stirred the barley, sending a gentle wave across the ears of grain.

"The portal is coming," said Becks.

Cabot's gaze flitted from one direction to the next. All he could see was the field they were standing in, the edge of the nearby woods, and a thin smudge of smoke rising from the priory just over the brow of the hillside. Then all of a sudden he felt a strong buffeting wind, cool against his cheek.

A dozen yards ahead, above the chest-high sea of swaying barley, he could just barely see the outline of a shimmering, undulating dome. Within it, he saw swirling dark details that flickered and twisted like the reflection in a disturbed pool of water. "What devilry is this!" his voice croaked hoarsely.

"It is a time portal," said Becks matter-of-factly. She started toward it. "Follow me, please."

But Cabot remained rooted to the spot, suddenly terrified of this thing that had no place being here in their field. He saw darkness in the middle of it, shapes he couldn't understand, demon-like shapes that seemed to be waving malevolently to him, beckoning him on.

This can be of no good, he cautioned himself. He glanced at Lady Rebecca and for a moment wondered if his more devout brothers in

the priory had been right all along, that there were demons and devils
and a dark place beneath the earth they stood on whither tainted souls
were taken and doomed to burn in torment for an eternity.

Becks turned and saw he hadn't yet moved. "Now!" she barked at
him.

Cabot shook his head. "'Tis . . . 'tis an evil work!"

She pushed her way impatiently through the stalks and grabbed his
arm roughly. "We are wasting time. The portal can only remain open
for a limited period on one charge."

"No!" He tried to wriggle free of her grasp. "No! Please!" But her
hand had closed around his lower arm like a vise. She began to wrestle
him forward toward the churning darkness.

"Oh, Lord, forgive my sins!" Cabot began to bellow, trying his best
to dig his heels into the soft dry soil. "I renounce all evil! I renounce
the Devil and his minions!"

Cabot threw a punch at her face. It landed firmly on her cheek,
leaving a graze and a welt that was sure to turn into a dark purple
bruise within the hour. Her eyebrows knitted disapprovingly.

"Please do not do that again." With both hands she grasped his
monk's habit and lifted him up off the ground. His arms and legs began
to flail frantically.

"Ye are a demon!" he screamed down at her face, his sandaled feet
kicking her stomach, her thighs. "I knew it!"

She staggered forward, just about managing to keep her balance as
he squirmed, kicked, and punched in her grasp.

"*No! Please! Have mercy on—!*"

Chapter 71

1194, Nottingham Castle, Nottingham

"WHAT!" roared John.

Liam looked at Bob standing beside him, a quick warning glance to him to be ready for anything. There was no knowing how John was going to react to the news.

"I said it's gone, Sire. Lady Rebecca took it last night."

The skin on John's face raced through several shades of crimson anger, then it drained to a pallid gray. "Good God! She was a traitor! She was a spy of Richard's! She was—"

"No," Liam interrupted him. "No, she has nothing to do with Richard, Sire."

John's anger was already spent, gone in a moment, leaving him quivering and looking lost.

"She . . ." John's jaw worked silently. "She . . . But I thought we were . . . in love." He looked slowly up at Liam, and Liam could see tears filling the man's hooded eyes. "But, do you say she was taking me for a . . . for a fool?"

Liam couldn't deny that. Yes, she had been using him.

"Lady Rebecca has taken it to a safe place," said Liam. The fluttering of nerves in his own voice had gone. John didn't look like a tyrant about to order his head be cut off. Liam had expected a torrent of abuse, a face full of royal spittle. Instead, John looked like a child all of a sudden, abandoned, frightened, and lonely.

"She told me to . . . to be *strong*," he said quietly, a tear rolling down his cheek into the wispy bristles of his beard. "For her, you know? I would have been." He swiped at his cheek with a sleeve. "For her, you understand? For her . . . I would have stood up to Richard."

Liam looked over John's slumped shoulders at the arched alcove and the balcony beyond. In the heat-shimmering distance beyond the walls of Nottingham, he could see the endless rows of multicolored tents and marquees of Richard's assembled army, the sturdy lumber A-frames of half a dozen catapults being swarmed around and finished by carpenters. They looked like ants at this distance.

"I have to surrender to him," whispered John. "I have to capitulate. The longer I leave it, the angrier he will get! He will—"

"No!" said Liam.

John looked up at him sharply, a flash of irritation in his eyes at Liam's insubordinate interruption.

"Listen, Sire . . . if you *do* surrender while you have no Grail, you have *nothing* to bargain with!" Liam didn't need to finish that thought for John. By the look in John's red-rimmed eyes, he knew exactly what *that* meant for him.

"But, if you stall . . . ," Liam continued.

"'Stall'?" A word John was unfamiliar with.

"If you wait. Let Richard think you have it. Maybe even threaten to destroy it if he attempts to attack—"

"*Destroy it?*" John's eyes looked like they'd glimpsed the very bowels of Hell. "Can you imagine, Sheriff—can you imagine what he would do to me? If I . . . If I were to . . ."

"Would he dare risk that, though?" Liam cocked an eyebrow. "Really? After all he's done to get hold of it, would he risk you putting a candle to it?"

John swallowed nervously. "He . . . he would know I *daren't*."

Liam looked at the man, trembling and pale. *Perhaps he would at that.*

"You still have to be strong, Sire. You need to arrange a meeting with him, to tell him we have it here—and, unless his army disbands, you will burn it yourself."

Bob opened his mouth to say something. Liam knew what it was: a warning about time contamination. The way history was *supposed* to go, Richard's siege was successful and John surrendered to his older brother. Liam patted his good arm to hush him. John didn't need to hear that right now, that he was destined to surrender.

"Buy us a little time, Sire," said Liam. "Meet with him . . . *convince* him that you will destroy it if he attempts to attack us."

John stroked his chin obsessively, the faint tremor of a nervous tic in his quivering jaw. Liam wondered if the poor man could convince anyone of anything right now.

"Lady Rebecca will be back, I assure you. She'll be back with the Grail."

I hope.

"And then you can arrange a truce, Sire. You'll have something you can use to bargain with."

Chapter 72

2001, New York

Sébastien Cabot kept his eyes firmly clenched shut, not daring to get his first glimpse of the underworld and the Devil's workings. Through his closed lids he could sense it was a dark place. His ears picked out sounds he'd never heard before, soft beeps and hums that could only be the devices of evil stirring, ready to tear his mortal soul apart.

"And who's *this*?" a female voice sounded. He sensed they were standing in some cave, perhaps on a ledge that overlooked an infinite cavern filled with a squirming sea of tormented souls below, burning in agony, prodded, stabbed, and tortured by demons wandering among them.

"Cabot." He recognized Lady Rebecca's voice in reply.

"Cabot? Like—like in the message? The same guy?"

"Affirmative. He is here to help."

Cabot slowly opened his clenched-shut eyes. He first saw his sandaled feet on a hard, pockmarked, and stained stone floor. And as he looked up he saw Lady Rebecca and three other strangely dressed people staring at him with curiosity. No demons. No fire. No tormented souls.

One of them stepped forward. A young woman. She had long frizzy hair and pale freckled skin. On her face were two ovals of glass that glinted reflection from a bright bar of light above him that buzzed and flickered slightly.

"Hey, pleased to meet you," she said, extending a hand toward him. "I'm Maddy."

Cabot's dry mouth opened and closed without producing anything. Finally, he managed to say something. "This . . . this place? 'Tis *not* Hell?"

The frizzy-haired girl shrugged and smiled in a friendly way. "Guess that's a matter of opinion, really."

Some time later—Cabot, still lost in a state of numb shock, had no idea how long: perhaps an hour, a day, perhaps only a few minutes—he found himself and these curious strangers sitting around a long wooden table on padded chairs. He held a cup full of a warm and bitter brown drink. The other girl in this place, dark-skinned like a Turk and wearing black clothes splashed with a lurid orange and pink design of some sort—she'd been introduced as "Sal"—had told him the drink was called *Koff-eeee* as she'd pressed it into his hands.

". . . has a section in it that is marked by four corner markers," Lady Rebecca was saying. "In these margin illuminations. Here, here, here, and here."

The man with them—named Adam—hunkered over the table beside Lady Rebecca and examined the Treyarch Confession more closely.

"My God, I think she may be right!" he said. "They've got to be grille markers."

Maddy joined them over the table. "Show me."

"See?" said Adam. "Like corners, embedded subtly into the illustration's pattern."

"Yeah—oh man, yeah, I see it!"

Adam looked at them. "Basically this is the blueprint . . . instructions on how to make a *cardan grille* to decode that," he said, pointing to the small wooden box containing the Grail.

"It is this passage of text," continued Becks, spreading her hands across the Treyarch, "that is being indicated. But it is in a language we do not have data for. An extinct form of Gaelic. Cabot," she said, pointing at him, "has knowledge of this language."

All eyes suddenly rested on him. He put down the mug of hot liquid on the table and spread his hands apologetically. "I . . . uh . . . I know but a *little* of it," he said. "I served the order alongside another Templar, Irish, a man who came from *Dún Garbháin*."

Maddy cocked a finger, inviting him to lean over. "Well, come on and take a closer look, Mr. Cabot. See what you can figure out."

Cabot pulled himself up out of his chair and joined them over the document, rolled out and spread flat on the table and almost as long. A steadily burning light in a small wire cage dangled from the arched brick roof just above them. He wondered what made it glow so steadily. It was certainly no flame.

He turned his attention to the elaborate curls and flourishes of handwriting before him. By contrast to the feeble flickering candlelight the priory's monks worked to after dark, this steady light let him see as if the table was standing outside in a field in the middle of a bright summer day.

"This," he began, moving a leathery old finger along the first lines of text, "this I believe is a form of Irish Gaelic." His finger traced the words, his lips moving in silence for a while.

"I tell ye, 'tis hard to read, but . . . I think this first line is a prayer of silence. *Be thy true a servant*, or perchance that reads *to help?*" Cabot growled with frustration. "*Seek ye not in . . . matters of truth of . . .* or 'tis some other meaning. *Take not matters of light . . .* Achh! My Gaelic is too poor to read this."

"What do you think that's supposed to mean?" asked Sal. "'Matters of truth?'"

Maddy shrugged. "Just a bunch of weird voodoo crock." She looked at Cabot. "Is there some hidden meaning in there that we're supposed to get? Like, is it cryptic or something?"

He shook his head. "'Tis as close as I can understand it. The rest is beyond me."

They stared at the swirls and strokes of writing, a meaningless jumble of accented and contorted Latin letters.

"Maybe it's not actually meant to *mean* anything," said Adam. The others looked at him. "Maybe it's not the words themselves that are the clue, but *how* they're written. Cabot?"

The old man shrugged. He studied it in silence for a while. "My knowledge is poor, ye understand? 'Tis been a long while . . ." He hesitated a moment.

"What?" asked Maddy. "What is it?"

He shook his head. "'Tis poorly written. This man, Treyarch, was clearly no scribe."

"What do you mean?"

Cabot pointed to one of the words in the sentence he'd loosely translated. "This letter is wrong. 'Tis written upside down."

Adam hunched closer to it, his nose almost touching the yellowed parchment. "I wonder . . . ," he whispered to himself.

"Wonder what, Adam?"

He looked up at them. "You got a decent digital camera?"

"I've got my iPhone," replied Maddy.

"What's that?"

Of course. She smiled. *2001 . . . iPhones are still a twinkle in the eye of some Apple designer.*

"It's just my cell, but it's got a built-in camera." She went over to the computer desk and returned with it a moment later.

"Get a decent image of all of the text between these corner markers," said Adam.

She climbed up onto one of the armchairs to get a bird's-eye view of the scroll, then snapped several images. "What now?"

"Photoshop," said Adam, pointing back toward the bank of computer monitors.

A minute later, Maddy had downloaded the four images she'd taken of the Confession onto one of the computers, and they were looking at them within the image-editing software. Cabot's eyes were comically round with wonder as he stared at the dozen glowing monitors.

"So," said Adam, clicking on a dropdown menu. "I'm going to

lighten these images up a little." He selected the clearest of the four images and tweaked its brightness. The rich yellow of the parchment became a lighter vanilla, and the black ink became a deep blue.

"Thing is," continued Adam, "when using a grille, you place it down on the blank parchment with the windows already cut out, and then you write each letter of your message on the little windows of parchment you can see. Then, when you're done, you let the ink dry first before removing the grille, so you don't smudge it. That would give the game away, right? Only *certain* letters being smudged?"

The others nodded. Made sense.

"So, what you have then is a page of isolated letters. Then you write the rest of some meaningless or innocent-sounding message that incorporates those letters."

He clicked on a menu and pulled down another batch of editing options. "But quite often, in between these two stages, you might be writing with a different well of ink."

"It's the same color," said Maddy, pointing at the image on-screen. "It's black . . . well, dark blue, now that you've lightened it."

"Every well of ink is slightly different. You made your own ink back then."

Cabot nodded. "This is right."

"It's homemade ink, not factory made. Every time you make it, it's slightly different. To our eyes, yes, it's all black ink, but in Photoshop, just one variation of the RGB value . . ."

"RGB?"

"Red, Green, Blue—essentially, tone . . . hue," said Adam, "and we can separate it out. Exaggerate it enough to see." Adam zoomed in close on the writing, then selected another menu option, producing a slide bar. The mouse cursor dragged the marker and moved it slowly along the horizontal bar. The image started shifting tone, the paper easing from vanilla to amber to pink, and the ink sliding from a deep blue to a deep green to a deep ochre.

"Oh my God," whispered Maddy.

The upside-down letter that Cabot had identified was a slightly yellower ochre than the rest.

"Zoom out," she said quickly. Adam did so, pulling away until the whole of the captured section of text was on the screen. Among the page, several hundred characters stood out from the rest—as distinct as minstrels at a banquet.

"Only him," one of them growled insolently. No reference to John's titles, no honorifics.

John gently tapped the sheriff and his large one-armed man to indicate they should stay where they were and stepped forward toward the tent's entrance.

He pushed aside a drape of heavy velvet and entered the cool dim interior of the tent.

He saw a small wooden table with a flagon and cups on it and two collapsible campaign chairs of oak and leather, with Richard sprawled casually in one of them.

"So, my little brother, you dared to come out to see me yourself, instead of sending a lackey."

John nodded. "Y-yes." He hated the strangled warbling in his voice. He sounded like a woman beside the deep masculine growl of Richard's drawl.

Richard snorted laughter. "You better sit before you collapse."

John obediently settled into the other of the two chairs.

Richard sat forward, the chair creaking under the weight of the man in his chain mail and armor plating. "I'm ready for a fight, little brother. Are you?"

"I—yes—I'm—"

Richard laughed again. "Ha! You little runt. You couldn't fight your way off a nursemaid's teat!" He picked up the flagon and poured some watered-down wine into his cup. "But I am not here to punish you this day." He emptied the cup with one swig, spilling wine down his thick blond beard.

"Now, I've been hearing rumors, since landing on these godforsaken shores, that something very precious to me has been lost by you. You know what I'm talking of, don't you?"

John nodded. Although whether it stood out as a nod instead of another involuntary tic, he wasn't sure.

"I know you are a fool, dear brother, but not *that* much of a fool

Chapter 73

1194, Nottingham

John struggled with great difficulty to keep the trembling to a minimum. He knew his nervous tic must be showing: that slight jerk of his head now and then, the impulsive stroking of his chin. No way to hide that. But the rest of him was hidden beneath flowing robes. Richard would know he was terrified of him, but the other barons, earls, and dukes were only going to see him from afar.

His sheriff, the very strange Liam of Connor, and his even stranger squire, Bob, walked with him along the dusty track leading out through the gates of Nottingham toward the small burgundy-colored tent erected on its own in the middle of no man's land.

He waits in there.

Beyond the tent, Richard's army stood in battle lines, a row of six gigantic catapults behind earthworks, ready to bombard the walls of the city. An endless sea of glinting helmets and chain mail, pikes and pennants watched silently as they approached.

"Relax, Sire," whispered his sheriff. "Remember, you have in your possession the thing that this is all about. Right?"

John's head nodded quickly. A good man, this sheriff. He offered Liam a faint smile as they came to a halt outside the tent's portico. Two soldiers were standing guard outside.

to lose it. So . . . I can only presume this is a fiction." Richard smiled for the first time, a cold smile that meant absolutely nothing. "It seems you have grown a backbone after all. This is your attempt to bargain with me, eh?"

John could see that smile wavering. He could see it turn into a snarl in a heartbeat, followed by a sudden whiplash of movement and a blade sunk deep into his throat. Richard could do that and not think twice of the consequences.

Be very careful.

"I . . . I have it, brother."

"Excellent! Of course you do. And now, I thank you for keeping it safe these last two years. You will hand it over to me and perhaps—*perhaps*—I will overlook your reluctance to pay my ransom. I will overlook your many attempts to undermine my authority while I have been away fighting for Christendom."

John felt his legs trembling beneath his robes, his bladder loosen, his stomach flip and churn.

Be strong.

"It is safe, Richard. I—I shall . . ."

"You shall what?"

John swallowed drily. "I shall h-hold on to it for n-now."

The smile froze on Richard's face. He reached for the flagon and topped his cup up again. "Your pitiful attempt at defiance is almost amusing. But I have no time for that now."

"I am s-serious, brother," John uttered, the words stumbling out of his mouth like a drunkard from an inn at closing time.

Richard's eyes narrowed. "'I . . . I . . . I am s-s-serious, b-b-brother,'" he mimicked cruelly in a shrill, high pitch. "I will not be *bargained with* by you, you pitiful woman!" He shook his head at the very thought of that. "You are a child, a baby. You always have been. You play at being king while I have been away. And now you dare—you *dare* to play with *this*?"

"It is just a scroll of words," said John. "It means nothing." But almost the moment he said it, he regretted it. He expected his brother to leap off the chair, to slap his face with the hard back of his hand. But instead Richard's response was measured, calm.

"It is God's instructions . . . instructions meant for me and me alone."

John looked at his eyes. They glistened with a frightening sense of glee, of purpose.

"You stand in the way of the Lord's intentions, brother. A very dangerous place to be."

John took a deep breath, steadying the churning in his stomach, hopefully steadying the unfortunate tremor in his voice. "Disband your nobles and their men, leave Nottingham, and I shall g-give you the Grail."

"No." Richard looked down at the ground. "These are the choices *I* present to *you*. Surrender the Grail immediately, and I shall consider some leniency. I am, after all, known for my mercy. If I have to take Nottingham to obtain it, I *will* have your head."

"Attack the city and—and I shall burn it before you get to m-me."

Dark hooded eyes settled on him for a long while. "Then, dear brother, you will know the agony of a witch's fire before I have you opened up and quartered. You will see your own heart in my hand before your head comes off."

God help me.

John stood up. "I am leaving. We are done!"

Richard remained seated. "Then you will die very badly, brother."

John pushed his way past the velvet drapes, cursing as his robes tangled with them and he stumbled awkwardly out into the open, Richard's raised voice following him.

"If you burn it, you fool, you will die badly!"

Chapter 74

2001, New York

"But those letters, they don't spell anything!" said Maddy. "They're just a bunch of weird Celtic squiggles."

Adam was looking around her messy desk for something. "It's not the letters we want—just where they are on the page. Have you got any cardboard?"

Normally there were half a dozen pizza boxes lying around, but she'd thrown away a whole bunch of them the other day. "Huh? What do you want cardboard for?"

Sal looked around at the filing cabinet to the right of the computer table. Liam had left a breakfast bowl up there and, being the scruffy *shadd-yah* he was, the box of Rice Krispies. She reached for it.

"This any good?"

Adam grabbed it. "Yeah. Scissors?"

Both girls shook their heads.

"This isn't a freakin' craft store," said Maddy.

"I need to cut out windows," said Adam. "Have you got *anything*? A pocketknife?"

Cabot reached into the folds of his monk's habit and pulled out a small knife. "Would this do?"

"Perfect."

Adam grabbed the knife from him. He pulled the bag of Krispies out and then began to hack at the cereal box. Maddy frowned. "You gonna make something you saw on *Sesame Street*?"

Adam ignored the jibe and pointed at the computer screen. "Make a note of those stand-out letters." He took his cardboard box and Cabot's knife across to the kitchen table where the Treyarch was still stretched out under the glare of the overhead light.

He finished cutting one side of the cereal box and laid it print-side down on the parchment, carefully lining up the ragged corners of the cardboard with the corners of the margin illuminations.

"Too big," he muttered. He began trimming one side, cursing as Cabot's serrated blade chewed at the flimsy cardboard, leaving a rough, uneven, shredded edge.

Sal, Cabot, and Becks joined him.

"This'll be no good for cutting out the windows," he said. "I need an X-Acto knife or something. The cardboard's just shredding."

Sal looked down at the parchment. "Why not just cut the letters out of this Treyarch thing?"

Adam looked at the ragged, wobbling scrap of cardboard in his hand, then down at the unraveled scroll. "Yeah, why not?"

Cabot's eyes grew round. "But—but 'tis a valuable account from the First Crusade!"

"No," said Adam, "it's a *cardan grille* in disguise. That's all it is. That's why it was written. It's the real key to that," he said, gesturing at the wooden box perched on the end of the table.

Maddy rushed over with a sheet of paper in her hand. "I printed it out." She laid it down on the table, the highlighted characters still just about discernible from the rest of the text. "Okay," she said, "this first line, it's this character that's highlighted," she said, pointing to the upside-down Gaelic symbol Cabot had noted minutes earlier.

Adam took the knife and carefully dug its sharp tip into the parchment and the wooden table beneath.

"What if we're wrong?" said Maddy. "What if it's something else? You're about to cut holes in this thing, and, like, there's only this one copy!"

Adam hesitated a moment. "Ahh . . . true." He blew air through his teeth.

She looked down at the printout. "But looking at that . . ."

He nodded. "Exactly. Those letters are different ink. There's only one reason you'd write certain letters out of order like that."

"Yeah . . ." She shrugged. "Ahh, heck—go for it."

As Adam began cautiously cutting the first character out of the stiff parchment, Cabot absentmindedly crossed himself with the tips of his fingers and muttered an apology in Latin to God above.

Chapter 75

1194, Nottingham

Liam and the soldiers standing alongside him ducked again at the warning shout from the gatehouse. Half a dozen rounded boulders the size of mead barrels came hurtling over the top of the city wall, and with a clearly audible whistle arced downward into the market square.

One landed with a heavy thud that he felt vibrate through the ground. It sent up a mushroom cloud of dust and soil and chicken droppings. The others found market stalls and the wooden shacks that surrounded the thoroughfare, shattering them like eggshells.

"Jay-zus-'n'-Mother-Mary!"

Bob stood beside him, calmly evaluating the paths the boulders had taken. "Information: they are adjusting their angles of trajectory." He pointed toward a section of wall twenty yards to the right of the city's main gatehouse. "They are aiming for that. The wall there is weak."

Liam could see a faint discoloration to the section of wall, as if different stone had been used there to patch up an age-old breach.

The first few volleys had overshot the wall and disappeared among the jumble of slate and wood rooftops in the middle of Nottingham, sending up plumes of dust and smoke into the cloudless blue sky. A fire had been started in among the houses somewhere; and the darker column of smoke, growing thicker, suggested it was beginning to take hold and spread.

Liam could feel the nervous darting eyes of hundreds of the town's people on him; looking to their young sheriff to issue his orders.

Oh, just great. Fantastic. I've never commanded the defense of a siege before.

"Suggestion."

Liam leaned closer to Bob. "Yes, please—I've got no idea what to do, so help me."

"The wall will fail there," he said, pointing toward the discolored section. "We will need to concentrate the garrison where the breach will be."

"Right."

Bob pointed up to the top of the city wall and the gatehouse. Nottingham's meager garrison of troops were mostly dotted along the front wall, firing sporadic, unaimed arrows toward the metallic, shimmering, glinting mass of Richard's assembled army. "These soldiers, also the ones held in reserve to defend the keep, are not efficiently deployed," rumbled Bob.

Liam watched them cowering behind the crenellations as arrows flickered over the wall, occasionally sticking their heads out to return the odd shot. Bob was right. It appeared Richard had not bothered with taking more time to build siege towers. He'd efficiently evaluated the city's wall and decided the obvious weak section was his way in. Half a dozen trebuchets working over that part of the wall was all that was needed. The fight wasn't going to focus around the gatehouse, nor be for control of the wall tops. The fight was going to be concentrated around the breach, just as soon as the masonry had finished tumbling down and the dust settled.

Liam looked at the wall section at the same moment that voices from the gatehouse called out another warning. Several boulders arced languidly over the top, their shadows racing across the cobbles and dirt of the market square as they came to earth much closer, and thudded with impacts that shook the ground again beneath Liam's feet.

But one shot landed on target. He heard the deep crash and boom of the projectile rock against masonry, and saw a spider's web of cracks suddenly appear on their side of the wall. Dirt, dust, and shards of dislodged flint and rock cascaded down in a clattering shower onto the market stalls standing near the base of the wall.

Liam turned to Bob. "We're going to need everyone right here, aren't we?"

Bob nodded. "Correct."

Liam nodded and spat grit from his mouth. He really could have done with John being out here; for him to be seen by his people standing shoulder to shoulder with them, with his appointed sheriff, instead of cowering in the keep.

Time to lead, Liam. Come on, Mr. O'Connor . . . we've been here before.

True, but it was just a class of kids last time. Not a whole damn city.

Come on, they're all looking at you! Waiting for you. Do something!

He cupped his mouth and waited for a lull in the noise: the distant sound of Richard's men chanting taunts, the frightened mewling of womenfolk and children, the braying of donkeys, the squeal of a pig nearby, dragging itself in panicked circles, both back legs and rear end crushed to a bloody, bone-splintered pulp by the fallen masonry of the wall.

"ALL MEN-AT-ARMS TO ASSEMBLE HERE!" he bellowed at the soldiers standing nearby and those men up on the wall achieving nothing useful. He then turned to the townsfolk. He guessed there had to be over a thousand of them huddled in the open ground of the market square and clogging the narrow streets that led to it.

"EVERY MAN WHO CAN FIGHT, ASSEMBLE HERE!" He gestured at the already cracked wall, through a slowly clearing pall of dust. "THIS IS WHERE THEY WILL COME THROUGH! WE WILL HOLD THEM HERE!"

For a moment he wondered if they'd heard him. For an absurd moment he thought everyone was going to laugh at him—*Look at the boy playing at being a general.*

But voices carried his command onward across the market square and through the crowd, along the wall, one soldier to the next. He saw a flurry of movement, the backs of men, young and old, turning for their shanty homes to retrieve old weapons and farming tools.

Liam let out a gasp of relief, hiding it behind one gauntlet-covered hand. He hoped that to anyone watching him it looked like a casual yawn.

"That sound all right?" he muttered out of the side of his mouth.

Bob nodded, a dark brow lifted and the corner of his horse-lips stretched with a hint of pride. "Affirmative."

Chapter 76

2001, New York

They studied the rectangle of yellow parchment cut from the Treyarch Confession. Adam held it up carefully by two corners and looked at them through the patchwork of little square windows he'd cut out of it.

"It's so very fragile," he said. "I'm scared of tearing the thing."

"Let's get the Grail out," said Maddy. She reached for the Treyarch, now missing a rectangle four feet long by eighteen inches wide, and hurriedly wound it around its wooden spindle. Rolled up, she casually tossed it onto one of the armchairs and reached for the wooden box.

Cabot rested a hand on its lid. His eyes locked on Maddy's. "Ye understand what lies within?"

She nodded impatiently.

He glanced at the Treyarch tossed on the chair, already forgotten. "I trust ye will treat what lies within this box with more respect than ye did the Confession." His hand remained firmly on the lid. "In here are precious words many men have died for . . . and killed for."

"The Holy Grail, right."

His eyes narrowed. "Ye say that, young girl, like a . . . like 'tis just a flavor of preserve." He looked down at the box. "If 'tis what King Richard believes it to be, if it be what the Templars believe it to be, then this contains the hidden words of God. Ye understand this?"

Maddy pursed her lips and sighed. "Yes . . . yes, of course, I'll be very careful with it. Okay?"

Cabot shook his head with frustration. "'Tis not the scroll—the parchment and ink—I am talking about. That is merely the work of a man with a quill." He glanced at the parchment grille Adam was holding up carefully. "If *that* really be the key . . . By laying that atop the Grail and looking through the holes, we are looking upon the true Word of God. Is it truly for *us* to see?"

Maddy's first instinct was to brush the old fool aside. She didn't have the patience for this kind of superstitious nonsense. She didn't believe in some fluffy-haired Santa Claus–like guy sitting up on some heavenly throne and handing down sound bites of wisdom once every few millennia. She was about to dismiss his medieval superstition with a sarcastic comment, but then a solitary word pushed itself to the forefront of her mind and silenced her.

Pandora.

Her eyes dropped down to the box.

What's in there—the message hiding inside—includes the word Pandora.

There was no knowing what was about to be revealed. She looked around at Adam, Sal, Becks, Cabot . . . and wondered if this really should be for all of their eyes.

For your eyes only, Maddy.

"Uhh . . . yes, Cabot, perhaps you're right." She looked at Sal, then Adam. "I'm sorry, guys, this is something that I have to do alone."

"Why?" asked Sal. She sounded hurt. In truth, she probably was. After all, Sal, Liam, and herself were supposed to be a team: a shared bond, a shared trust in each other. Shared secrets.

But not this one. Not yet.

"Sal, I—I don't know why. Not yet. I just know somebody, some-where, in some time, has tried to warn me about *something* with the word 'Pandora.' That's all I've got. That's all I know. If this is the answer," she said, nodding at the box, "then I have to find out what it is first. Then we'll talk." She looked at Adam. "And I'm sorry, Adam . . . this is meant for Sal, me, and Liam, when we get him back. Team first—that's how it works."

"What? You can't cut me out now. I mean, I've been helping you. Maddy, I worked out—"

Becks stepped forward. "Team strategist Madelaine Carter has authority on this matter," she said in a firm voice that hushed Adam. He'd nearly lost a finger from the casual twist of her hand once before. He didn't look like he was ready to try his luck again now.

"Sure, all right," he said, "if that's how you want this to go."

"Sorry, Adam," said Maddy. "Let me do what needs to be done first, and maybe there'll be more I can tell you in a little while. Okay?"

He nodded, putting the grille down gently on the table.

Maddy turned to Cabot. "I may not share your faith, and I'm sorry about that, but whatever truth is in here, I believe, is profoundly important. It's the *Holy Grail*, I know. I'll treat it with respect. I promise you that."

He lifted his hand slowly. "You may regret the truth you are about to discover."

She sighed. "Well, we'll see, won't we?"

She turned to Sal. "Will you take Adam and Mr. Cabot outside?"

Sal glanced at the support unit. "What about Becks?"

"She's staying."

A flash of resentment seemed to cross Sal's face. She looked like she wanted to say something. Maddy could guess what she was thinking.

You're trusting a robot over me?

But Sal merely nodded, then beckoned both men to follow her toward the shutter door. She cranked the doorway up until it was high enough for them to duck under into the night.

Maddy could hear their disgruntled murmuring as they walked together down to the muddy shingle of the river to watch the fishing boats in the harbor opposite.

"Becks," she said.

"Yes?"

"I'm going to open a locked partition on your hard drive."

Maddy trawled her mind for those three words. And then realized they were there in her head, ready and waiting.

"Okay, listen to me: iPad—caveman—breakfast."

Becks's eyes lost their focus for a moment; then almost immediately, her body posture changed, reset. No longer did she have the acquired modest stance of a noble lady, but instead she stood legs planted, hands by her side, like a marine on parade. Then she smiled faintly. "Acknowledged. The locked partition is now accessible."

"Good." She looked down at the wooden box on the end of the table and carefully lifted the hinged lid. Inside she saw the roll of parchment and the wooden tip of its spindle. She felt her heart quicken, her breath catch.

"This is the Holy Grail," she found herself almost whispering as she lifted it carefully out and rested it on the table. "Do you understand how to decode it?"

Becks nodded. "Of course. I have access to the rest of the data on my hard drive." Her left eyebrow cocked. "*Jay-zus*, I'm not stupid."

Maddy laughed. No need to guess who she'd been spending too much time with.

Carefully she turned the scroll's spindle and gently pulled the brittle parchment down the table, until finally, almost long enough to hang over the end, it was entirely unraveled.

Just like the Treyarch, there were margin illuminations down both sides, but this time much less elaborate. Simple crosses: the cross-swipe of a nib in dark ink, there to mark the beginnings and endings of different, meaningless passages.

She spotted what looked like sections of Latin—at least, she recognized letters from the Latin alphabet. She looked again at the margin markings: crosses, every now and then on both sides. She reached across the table for the template they'd cut from the Treyarch and lined up the top right corner of it with the first cross in the right-hand margin.

The top left-hand corner of their grille lined up with a cross on the left margin, but it was several inches too short for the bottom corners to line up with the next margin crosses. She looked down at the hundreds of squares cut in the parchment, seeing the slanted strokes of the Grail writing through the windows. One or two letters seemed to line up, to be perfectly framed, but the majority of windows showed letters half in, half out.

"Not here, then," said Maddy.

Becks's eyes ran systematically down the cross markings in the left margin. She stepped slowly down the length of the kitchen table, comparing measurements by eye.

"It should be placed here," she said finally, pointing toward two crosses. "The gap between these is precisely twenty-seven inches. The grille is also twenty-seven inches in length." Becks quickly examined the next cross mark down the left margin. "This is also spaced by twenty-seven inches."

Maddy stepped down her side of the table with the grille in hand and carefully lined up the top right and top left corners. She spread her hand across the parchment, holding down the corners at the bottom that desperately wanted to curl up again.

Oh my God.

"It lines up," she said quietly. She looked across the grille, and found herself holding her breath. Every small rectangular cutout in their grille perfectly framed a single letter. She lifted the grille away, looked again at the Grail document, and saw endless spidery lines of handwriting—none of the letters seeming to stand out, none asking for specific attention, and all of it unintelligible. She rested the grille back down again, carefully lining the corners up once more.

You ready to know, Maddy? Ready to find out what "Pandora" is supposed to mean?

The question frightened her. No—she wasn't ready. She knew the story of Pandora's Box. The young woman who wanted to know the secrets within a box—perhaps little different to the one sitting open on the end of their table—but, once the box was opened, all manner of evil spilled out that she could never put back inside again.

There's a reason this code word is "Pandora," right?

Maybe it was something that would be harmful to know. Something that could hurt her. Destroy her—or hurt the others? She looked at Becks, who watched her silently, waiting for instructions.

"I . . . I'm not sure I want to read this," said Maddy.

"Why?"

"I'm scared."

Becks looked confused. "It is just data, just knowledge. All information is tactically useful."

"Well, I'm not so sure. Sometimes knowing something isn't so good. You know?"

Becks said nothing.

"Look . . . I . . ."

God, I wish Foster was here. Or even Liam, she decided. After all, they were one and the same, weren't they? No. Not the same. Foster was Liam, but with a lifetime of knowledge, a lifetime of experience. One day, Liam was going to become that old man. But he wasn't there yet. She could imagine Liam standing here, impatiently fidgeting with frustration while she dithered like this.

"I want *you* to read it," she said finally. "Decode the whole thing."

Becks nodded.

"When you're done, I want you to come and get me and I'll password-lock your hard drive again. Understood?"

"Yes, of course, Maddy."

"And when you come for me, Becks, do NOT tell me *anything* about the message. Is that perfectly clear? I don't . . . I don't want to know yet."

"This is perfectly clear."

Maddy sighed. Whatever message was on this table would be safe on Becks's hard-drive mind for now. She decided she needed Foster's advice before she opened that mind. Better still, she could bring Becks with her to the park to find Foster sitting beside that hotdog stand, feeding the pigeons. Then they could both listen to it together.

That was *it*. She realized she didn't want the burden of knowledge to be sitting on her shoulders alone. She'd already done enough of that.

"You know what to do?"

Becks nodded.

"I'll be outside, then, with the others."

Chapter 77

1194, Nottingham

Oh, Jeeezz . . . this is it. This is it.

Liam felt bile roll up his throat as his stomach did its best to jettison the last meal he'd had. He spat it out along with the mouthful of grit he'd breathed in.

"They are coming," said Bob, standing beside him. He had a shield strapped tightly to the stump of his upper left arm. He flexed it. It functioned almost as well as if he'd had a whole arm to use. He flourished the long blade of a broadsword in his right hand as he took several steps up the mound of loose rubble and fallen stone, into the swirling eddies of dust.

Liam could hear the excited roar of Richard's army, racing heavily across the arrow-strewn ground outside toward the breached wall. It sounded like a locomotive coming down a track: the jangle of hundreds of harnesses swinging, the clatter of chain mail; men jogging as best they could under their body-weight in armor.

The inexperienced men of Nottingham's garrison standing on either side of him looked anxiously at Liam. Young boys and old men who'd done little more than drill with wooden swords.

Come on. Don't chicken out on me now, he commanded his quivering legs.

Liam raised his heavy blade above his head. "FORWARD!"

He picked his way up jagged boulders of shattered and sharp-edged flint to join Bob standing at the very top of the recently formed mound of masonry, and in that moment the roiling dust finally blew aside.

Before them, closing the distance of several dozen yards of already flattened grass, the front rank of Richard's army thundered toward them, a sea of different colors—the coats of arms and livery of a dozen or more noble families. An undulating line of sunburned and bearded faces split uniformly by open mouths, stretched wide and roaring as the arid, tufted ground between them narrowed all too quickly.

Here's all that history Foster promised you'd get to see, Liam. Right up close.

He braced his shield arm in front of him and looked to his right. Bob was standing protectively beside him, a three-foot-wide immovable wall of chain mail and muscle.

"Bob, I'm scared," he muttered, hoping his voice carried no farther than his support unit.

"Remain close," rumbled Bob. He looked down at Liam, his round, tufted, coconut head lost inside a coif of chain mail, gray eyes and thick-bridged nose lost in the shadow of his helmet.

"Remain close to me, and you will be fine, Liam O'Connor."

The front rank was clambering up the clattering mound of stone, arrows from civilian archers posted on the walls on either side of the breach finding targets amid the solid mass of men.

Liam had enough time to draw in one last ragged puff of air before he felt the terrific jarring impact of something against the edge of his shield, the vibration running painfully up his arm and almost knocking the breath from him. He instinctively ducked his head below the crinkled rim of his shield, and blindly swung his sword downward. It bounced with a heavy ring off something.

To his left, one of his men, one of his recruited garrison, a man perhaps only five years older, grinned at him, showing no more than a handful of yellowing teeth framed by a blond beard. He swung his sword down onto the man in front of him, its edge biting the curve between shoulder and neck. Dark blood arced into the air as he yanked his sword free.

Liam felt his shield suddenly lurch downward. He saw the fingers of a hand clad in a thick leather glove on the rim, yanking it roughly down and outward. Caught unawares, Liam found his left hand losing its grip on the shield's handle.

Jay-zus, no!

His shield clattered onto the rubble at his feet, and he had only the briefest moment to register the florid, hot face of the man in front of him, a face he was never going to forget. He was sure, as long as he lived, that this man was destined to live on in his nightmares.

Liam's response was ungainly and entirely reflexive, a lunge of desperate panic now that his shield had been ripped away and he felt naked and exposed, despite his thick quilted leather underlay and the heavy mail on top of it.

In the terrible slow-motion of heightened awareness, he saw the heavy blade of his sword swing down and bite deep into the side of the man's neck.

Time seemed to slow to almost a complete stop as their eyes met, the mercenary's cornflower blue, wide with surprise—slowly realizing that the blade lodged in his neck signaled the moment his life had come to an end.

The noise of battle going on around them seemed to be a hundred miles away. All Liam could hear was the roaring of blood through his veins, the hammer thump of his heart, the sound of his panting breath in his ears . . . and this man before him, now spitting dark gouts of crimson from his mouth and gurgling something—a defiant curse, a last prayer?

Liam found himself mouthing *I'm so sorry* to him, as if the dying man would actually understand, might even forgive him.

Then the moment was gone: slow-motion went back to normal speed, and Liam's ears once again filled with the sound of grunts and cries, the scraping and battering clang of metal on metal. The man with cornflower-blue eyes grabbed a firm hold of the blade with both hands, as if he was attempting to pull it out of him. But his strength was fast bleeding out, and Liam watched . . .

the man I just killed

. . . slowly collapse to his knees in front of him, then fall backward, disappearing amid the churning quagmire of struggling bodies, taking Liam's sword with him.

Liam found himself empty-handed as another thickset and red-faced man, sweating under forty pounds of mail armor, took his place. Liam cursed as the man grinned at his good fortune and pulled back to skewer him on the tip of his halberd.

Liam's face screwed up with anticipation, his arms held out in front of him in a vain attempt to fend off the point. But then all of sudden he felt himself being lifted off the ground by the scruff of his mail vest and tossed backward down the clattering pile of rubble toward the marketplace.

He cracked the side of his head on the sharp rim of a jagged piece of masonry.

It left him stunned, his ears ringing. He watched dark shapes stepping over him, clambering up the slope to join the press of men in the breach; farther above, the darting flicker of arrows heading into and out of the city; and high up in the rich blue sky, a pair of swallows chasing each other in slow playful circles, oblivious to the carnage beneath them.

A face full of bristles and a mouth containing a solitary tooth leaned over him. "Ye alroight down there, Sire?" Liam vaguely recognized the face as one of Nottingham's blacksmiths.

He nodded. A rough hand grasped his and pulled him up onto legs that wobbled uncertainly.

"I—I lost my weapon and my shield," he said.

"Not to worry." The man grinned. "There'll be plenty more to pick up soon enough, Sire," he said, then turned away, scrambling up the gravel to join the thick scrum of men fighting to hold the breach.

At the top, Liam thought he caught sight of Bob: the back of his head, his broad shoulders; one arm swinging a long-handled axe to and fro like a scythe.

His head was swimming with pain, a sharp stabbing agony that almost made it impossible to gather together a single coherent thought.

But he just about managed one.

When the hell's Becks coming back?

John watched the distant struggle from the balcony of the keep's Great Hall. From this far away, the squirming press of men looked like insects fighting over a dung hill.

Every last man of the garrison was over there, and a good proportion of the town's menfolk, all fighting for their town.

And fighting for me.

He felt sick of his weakness, his cowardice. The sight of blood had always left him in a cold dread.

You have not the heart of a king—that's why you shall never be one; something Richard had once said to him back when their father had been alive.

"Perhaps you are right," John whispered miserably. And yet . . . he thought he'd caught a glimpse of something inside himself. Perhaps "courage" was too grand a word for it, but it was a firmness of resolve, perhaps even a hint of defiance as he'd parlayed with Richard earlier.

I was strong then, was I not?

Strong?

He stroked his beard absently with a hand that trembled like an autumn leaf ready to take flight on a fresh breeze. "No . . . you are just a weak fool," he answered himself.

"Sire?"

John looked over his shoulder to see one of the keep's squires standing beside the drapes, a pale-faced, effeminate man in expensive linens. "Sire? Should we—should we not close the castle's gates? Should they break through, we would be safe in the castle a while longer!"

John felt something deep inside him turn away in disgust.

"No," he said finally. "Have you a sword and mail?"

The squire's eyes rounded. "Sire?"

"You heard."

"I—I suppose I have . . . somewhere . . ."

"Then fetch it."

"F-fetch it, S-sire?"

"Yes." John took a deep breath to steady the timbre of his voice. "We shall be joining them."

Chapter 78

2001, New York

Maddy leaned against the crumbling brick wall of their transplanted archway, watching the others standing over on the grass-tufted hummocks of silt along the East River.

"Madelaine?"

She turned around to see Becks standing in the opening beneath the fully raised shutter.

"You all done?"

Becks nodded an affirmative.

"If I lock your hard-drive partition again, what you know—what you've just read—it's all gonna be safe in there, right?"

"That is correct."

Maddy nodded thoughtfully. No one else would know what secret message was hidden in the Grail, not even Becks herself.

She'd already made up her mind on the matter: she was going to unlock Becks's partition with Foster present, and they'd both hear what she had to say. And then together figure out what it meant, what they'd have to do about it, if anything.

"Ready to lock away that information?"

"Affirmative."

She uttered the three words quietly. Becks blinked several times, then cocked her head. Her voice immediately returned to its softer, more feminine tone. "I register thirty-seven minutes of absent data . . ."

Maddy raised her hand. "It's okay, I've been talking with your alter ego."

Becks consulted something inside her mind. "My code-word-locked partition?"

"Yup." Maddy looked at the others. "You decoded the Holy Grail successfully. It's now safely locked away in your head." Maddy laughed. "Not even *you* can get in there."

Becks nodded approvingly. "A sensible precaution, Maddy."

She was about to say a thank-you when she heard Sal's voice calling her. She could just make out her small outline in the twilight, turning away from the river toward her.

"What's up?" she yelled back.

She replied something, but a sudden freshening breeze carried it away; ripples of cats' paws danced across the mirror-smooth water toward them as a fresh breeze stirred the millpond calm.

Something's coming our way.

Maddy looked at the sky and saw it: what looked like a rolling stormfront rushing toward them from out of the Atlantic Ocean.

"Hurry!" she shouted at Sal. Sal in turn beckoned the other two men to hasten after her up the shingle to their jagged brick bunker perched among the sandy dunes.

Their feet clattered off soft sand onto the broken fragments of sidewalk and alleyway that had transported to this reality along with the archway, just as the black stormcloud rolled over Manhattan Island.

"'Tis the Lord's coming," gasped Cabot somberly.

"No," said Sal. "Just a time wave."

Among the churning black clouds crossing the river toward them, Maddy thought she saw a dozen different city skylines flicker over Manhattan: one moment, towering pointed church steeples topped with cruciforms that reached for the sky, then the next they formed into the rounded bulge of mosques and onion-shaped minarets topped with crescents.

"My God . . . *Do you see that?*" said Adam, his voice competing with a growing thundering boom.

Wind danced around them, stinging their cheeks with whipped-up sand as they stood in the opening to the archway watching the world in flux. And then, the wall of undulating reality was upon them.

There was a moment of pitch-black as the tidal wave swept over. And then it was gone.

The archway was entirely dark and lifeless, then a moment later a light winked on inside and they heard the soft chug of the generator starting up in the back room.

Outside, it was a calm evening once more; the gentle lapping of low tide punctuated by the lonely plaintive call of a solitary seagull.

On either side of her, Maddy heard both Adam and Cabot gasping, Cabot the worst of the two. "God help me," he gasped, "did I just witness the Devil's work?"

"A reality shift," said Becks. "Events in the past have changed the present."

Maddy looked at the island of Manhattan. The lights of the fishing boats had gone. The lights of the town beyond were also gone. Instead she could only make out a thick, dark treeline descending down to the water's edge. "There's nothing there now!"

"Just woods," said Sal.

Maddy bit her lip. "Becks?"

"Yes?"

"What on earth was going on when you left the twelfth century?"

"King Richard was preparing to take the town of Nottingham from his brother."

"Oh great!" snapped Maddy. "Is that, like, *our* fault?"

"No," said Adam, "that actually happened."

"Well, something's still wrong back then!"

"The holy scroll thing?" Sal pointed toward the table. "Maybe we hung on to it too long?"

"Yes." Maddy nodded. "Yeah, you're probably right. We should get it back, ASAP."

"But . . . is that right?" said Adam. "Does Richard get his hands on the Holy Grail, you know, in *correct* history?"

Maddy shook her head. "I don't know! But it sure shouldn't be here in the twenty-first century."

"It goes missing. It gets lost!" Adam stepped back toward the table. "That's how this becomes the stuff of myth and legends. That's why people ended up thinking it was the cup of Christ! It gets lost, right?"

"Maybe we should just, you know, rip it up?" offered Sal.

They all stared in a prolonged silence at the unrolled parchment beneath the glare of the light above it.

"King Richard would kill his brother," said Cabot finally. "If he does not get what he's come for." The old man shook his head. "His anger . . . he would kill everyone in Nottingham."

"That doesn't happen," said Adam. "Not in real history. The siege of Nottingham lasts just a few days, John surrenders, and Richard forgives him."

Cabot looked at him. "Ye are certain?"

"Oh yeah. John's forgiven. In fact, he becomes king when Richard dies several years later."

"Then Richard must get what he wanted," said Maddy. "The Grail. Right? He gets it, he's a happy boy. John is forgiven."

"But . . ." Sal glanced at the table. "Isn't there some *big* secret in there? Some secret that makes him go on another one of those crusades, which—"

"Which results in England's complete financial ruin," cut in Adam, "and the invasion of the French king, Philip II."

Maddy bit her lip with frustration. *What do we do? Give it to him? Or not?*

Another long silence, all eyes on her, waiting for her to make the call.

"No." It was Becks who spoke finally. "No," she said again.

"No, what?" said Maddy impatiently.

"King Richard will find *nothing* in the Grail."

Adam suddenly grinned. "She's right! Maybe it's a—maybe it turns out to be a . . . a complete *disappointment* for him. Maybe what he ends up with is a useless scroll that he can't decode because—"

"Because the *real* grille was always the Treyarch Confession?" said Maddy.

Adam nodded. "And perhaps what he has, that grille guarded by the knights in Acre, that was just a red herring. A fake."

Maddy gave it a moment's thought. "Yes! Why would there be *another* key? The one Richard has is no good!"

"We should return it immediately," said Becks. "Reality is fluctuating."

Sal nodded. "That last wave was really weird . . . like it couldn't decide which way it wanted to go."

"Perchance the battle for Nottingham has begun?" said Cabot. "And 'tis that the outcome of this battle hangs in the balance?"

Maddy wasn't sure if this last time wave actually meant that. In fact, she wasn't sure what it meant, other than history was still somehow derailed. But then again . . . maybe the old monk was right. After all, the correct-history version of the siege of Nottingham hadn't featured a lethal killing machine like Bob back there fighting on the side of John.

"Okay. My mind's made up," she said. "Becks, and you too, Mr. Cabot—you're taking the Grail back, and you've got to get it to John to give to King Richard somehow. Make him a happy boy—happy enough to let his brother live."

She bit her lip.

Oh crud. Is this the right call?

Chapter 79

1194, Nottingham

Liam had managed to work his way up beside Bob again, armed with another shield and this time an axe; both homemade by some artisan blacksmith. In between ferocious swings, he'd tapped Bob on the shoulder and let him know he was right there and watching his flank.

In front of Bob the descending slope of rubble of the collapsed section of wall was covered in a thick carpet of mangled bodies, bludgeoned and cleaved by his swooping axe blade. On either side of them stood the defenders, now mostly the citizens of Nottingham, dotted with one or two dozen remaining men of the garrison, in their burgundy and amber tunics.

The attackers' momentum seemed to have been stalled for the moment; the front rank of men decorated with the colors of a dozen different coats of arms began to slowly recede down the ever more cumbersome and slippery mound that led up to the breach.

Liam allowed himself a hope that the attack had faltered, that the men of Richard's gathered army had lost heart already. But it was soon obvious that the men had been summoned by the distant call of a horn. They were retreating to take a water break.

He found himself laughing, almost hysterically.

Bob glanced at him over his shoulder. "What is funny?"

"It's like halftime at a *peil Ghaelach* match," snorted Liam. The flitting of arrows overhead ceased as if archers on both sides had agreed to a temporary truce.

He could see women and children with buckets slung on yokes over their shoulders moving swiftly among the ranks of Richard's men as they dipped their helmets and grubby hands in and scooped and sloshed much-needed water into their mouths and onto their faces.

From behind Liam women also emerged from the market square with buckets and hides full of water, which the fighting men eagerly sipped and poured over their heads.

Of course it made sense to him. He realized how desperately hot he was under the leather and mail and, of course, he'd only fought briefly. Water, and an agreed break in the hostilities during which it could be distributed, was as much a part of the twelfth-century battle-field as anything else.

"Bob," he said, rapping his knuckles on his back, "there's water. You should get some while you can."

Bob turned around. For the first time Liam saw the front of the shield strapped to the stump of his left arm. "Jay-zus, Bob—you seen that?" The shield bristled with arrows like a hairbrush. The enemy archers had been deliberately targeting him.

Several other arrows protruded from the front of his chest.

"Oh boy . . . you need to get some of this seen to."

"The damage at this stage is acceptable, Liam," grunted Bob. "I am still at fifty-five percent functioning capacity." His fat lips spread. "But you are correct . . . I could drink some water."

Along with the other men, they took their turn scooping cooling handfuls of water out of the buckets being passed up to them, and it was as Bob was glugging water like a thirsty dog after a long walk that Liam heard a muted cheer rippling through the crowd gathered in the market square.

He saw bodies part respectfully, and then finally, stepping onto the bottom of the mound of broken masonry, he recognized John, in heavy mail, holding a shield bearing the royal crest.

"Sire!" he called out.

John slowly picked his way up toward him. "Sheriff," he finally replied, winded from the exertion. He gathered his breath before speaking again. "'Tis hard enough walking in this, let alone climbing."

The men of the garrison standing nearby respectfully dropped to their knees.

"Oh, stop that!" barked John with his best try at heroic bravado. "Save what you have left for the fighting, men."

"Sire," said Liam, "you'll be a target, so you will."

He could see how pale John looked, trembling inside his mail.

"Then," said John, running a tongue along his dry lips, "I shall just have to keep moving, won't I?"

A distant horn sounded again, and Liam saw the women and children moving among Richard's men scramble at double speed away from the front line toward the tents and marquees on the hillside in front of them. Almost immediately the flitting of dark arrows resumed, peppering the clear sky, and the men fifty yards away reformed their lines in preparation for the renewed assault on Nottingham.

Maddy turned around toward the water tube. Becks was just about to climb the stepladder to get into the water.

"Becks! What happened seven hours before you left 1194?"

Becks stopped, consulting her memory. "Precisely seven hours? I was walking along a stone passage."

Maddy flapped her hands impatiently. "Or thereabouts. Anything *significant?*"

"Six hours and forty-three minutes prior to the time-stamp, I scaled the outer wall of the city of Nottingham."

"Go back a bit."

Becks tilted her head. "Seven hours and three minutes prior to the time-stamp, I was saying to Liam and Bob that 'I would be fine.'"

"Oh come on! Go back more. Something *significant!*"

Becks spooled memories silently for a moment, then finally her eyes locked on Maddy's. "At eight hours and fifty-six minutes prior to the time-stamp, I was speaking with John."

"What the hell did you say to him? *Exactly!*"

Her eyelids fluttered. ". . . A man must find at least one moment in time to make a stand for himself . . . or live a life burning in the flames of regret."

Maddy looked to Adam.

He shrugged. "It's very poetic."

> Checking quotation database. Just a moment . . .

She turned back to Becks. "You think that's, like, changed history somehow?"

"I believe it may have *inspired* him," Becks replied. "John was considering immediate surrender to his brother. However, correct history shows he held out for five days. I decided he needed . . . *encouragement.*"

Maddy sighed. "Well, guess what? Looks like it worked."

> Quotation source: Rock band—EssZed. Lyrics to song.

"Yeah, thanks, Bob. So"—she turned back to Becks—"you think maybe saying that quote to—"

Chapter 80

2001, New York

Maddy and Adam stared at the monitor while Sal helped Becks and Cabot ready themselves for transport back to 1194.

"What do you mean, you can't use Becks's time-stamp?" asked Maddy.

> There appears to be too much instability to lock on to a reliable window.

"What does that mean?"

> Reality is fluctuating unreliably between two preferred states.

"It can't make up its mind," said Adam.

> That is a fair analogy.

"Well . . . what? Do we wait? Do we risk it?"

> We can risk sending them back using Becks's time-stamp, but I cannot anticipate the result of that.

Maddy balled her fist on the desk. "Okay, then . . . how big is this instability?"

> Please restate the question.

"How . . . far, how much time is affected by it? What I mean is . . . is it regionalized? Like a storm or something?"

> The fluctuating timelines appear to branch from between seven and nine hours before Becks's return time-stamp.

"I also offered myself to him."

Sal's jaw dropped. "You mean . . . ?"

Becks looked down at her. "Marriage."

"If he . . . what? Showed you he was a big tough man?" said Maddy. "If he stood up to his brother?"

"Affirmative."

Maddy shook her head. "Oh well, looks like you really *encouraged* him all right." She turned back to the monitor. "Bob . . . what competing histories are we getting out of this?"

> No information. The fluctuation is too rapid to generate timelines.

"That's why we're not getting time waves?" said Adam.

> Correct. However, this oscillating status is unstable and dangerous.

"Dangerous?" Maddy pushed up her glasses. "What's that mean exactly?"

> It is a stress factor on the reality wall.

Adam looked at her. "The reality wall?"

"What separates us from chaos space," she replied quickly. "Bob, what are we supposed to do?"

> The instability may settle itself. Or it may increase in severity.

"And if it does do that—if it gets worse?"

> No information.

"*No information?*" she howled, exasperated. "But look, it's not a good thing, right?"

> Not a good thing. There are several essays on chaos space written by R. Waldstein and E. Chan in my database.

"Can you sum them up?"

> Chaos space is a dimension where the laws of quantum physics are contradicted. Theoretically, the effect on normal dimensions would be their complete destruction.

"What does that mean? Like, all of Earth . . . destroyed?"

> **Negative. Everything.**

"Ev—everything?"

> **The entire universe.**

Maddy suddenly felt light-headed and short of breath. "Oh crap. Oh my God! We've . . . we've really messed up." Her hands scrambled across the clutter on the desk for her inhaler. "We've—"

"Maddy." Adam put a hand on her shoulder. "Maddy, come on, calm down . . . don't lose it."

She found the inhaler and pulled hard on it several times. She doubled over on her seat, her head between her knees, the wheezing rasp of her contracting throat sounding like a blacksmith's bellows.

Sal was over beside her, an arm across her shoulders. "Maddy? You okay?"

She shook her head. "Second . . . ," she wheezed. "Gimme . . . a . . . second . . ."

Adam looked down at her. "This is all going wrong, isn't it? This organization of yours, it's—"

"*We're still learning*," Sal snapped defensively. "We've been in worse situations." She bent down and stroked the hair out of Maddy's face. "Right, Maddy? We've gotten out of worse things."

Maddy pulled again on her inhaler, then lifted her face. "Yeah . . ." Still wheezing. "Yeah," she said again. "Bob?"

> **Yes, Maddy.**

"Becks and Cabot *have* to go back with the Grail, like *right now*! Find us the best window you can—as close to the castle as possible."

> **Affirmative. Searching.**

"But it's unstable, isn't it?" said Adam. "Your computer was saying there's a risk of sending them—"

"There's always a freakin' risk," Maddy muttered wearily. She pulled herself up off her elbows and faced the desk again. "Bob? Come on, give me something!"

> **Just a moment . . . Searching.**

She checked whether their displacement machine had enough

charge. It looked good. She turned to Sal. "Get them in the water, Sal. Go get them ready!"

Sal nodded and rushed over to the plexiglass tube.

"If it's unstable, what could happen to them?" asked Adam.

"They could end up turned inside out and looking like a plate of lasagne," she replied.

"I wish I hadn't asked."

"Or worse."

Adam made a face. "Worse! How could you get worse than that?"

She lowered her voice. "They could end up stuck in chaos." She turned to look at him. "Tell me, do you believe in Hell?"

He shook his head. "You kidding? I—no . . . of course not. It's an invention of the Catholic Church. Just a bunch of old religious mumbo-jumbo."

"That's what I used to think. But, you know, I wonder. Is it?"

The dark dialogue box on the screen in front of them suddenly flickered with the movement of computer-Bob's cursor.

> **I have a candidate time-stamp that is currently holding a solid state.**

"How long will it last?"

> **There is no information how long it will last. Perhaps only seconds.**

"Activate a ten-second countdown. NOW!"

> **Affirmative.**

She turned to see Becks *splosh* into the water, the Grail once more in its box, the box sealed in a plastic bag. Cabot was standing at the top of the stepladder, regarding the chilled water at his toes. "But, please, young lady, why do we have to get into . . . ?"

"JUST GET HIM IN!" shouted Maddy above the growing hum of energy building for a release.

Sal climbed up the steps of the ladder. "Mr. Cabot, you have to get in the water. Please!"

She spun around to see the countdown on the screen.

Four . . . three . . . two . . .

"PUSH HIM IN!"

Sal nodded and threw her weight into a hard shove against the monk's thighs. He teetered for a moment, arms cartwheeling for balance, before he toppled forward into the tube, sending a small tidal wave of water splashing over the side and onto the floor. The stepladder wobbled under Sal's sudden lurching movement and tipped back against the brick wall, the legs sliding along the concrete floor, dumping her onto a storage shelf full of cables and toolboxes that cascaded down and clattered to the ground along with her just as the displacement machine discharged its energy. The plexiglass tube flexed violently and thudded with a boom as the water, Cabot, and Becks vanished back into the twelfth century.

As Sal rolled on the floor among spools of cable, yelping with a sprained wrist, and the echo of the flexing boom bouncing around their archway slowly faded, Maddy could only wonder how it was that mankind—perhaps even the whole universe—had ended up resting its fate in the hands of an amateur little outfit like theirs.

Chapter 81

1194, Nottingham

They landed within the keep's outer bailey, the splash of thirty gallons of water echoing off the tall stone walls. Cabot landed heavily on his side, grunting at the impact on hard cobblestone. Becks landed on her feet, poised and ready for action.

The keep itself was devoid of any activity. A pair of soldiers manning the gatehouse emerged from the cool shadow of the archway to find out what the noise was all about. They gazed in bemusement at the old monk and the woman in the leather corset and dark woolen tights.

"Where is the Earl of Cornwall?"

"Not 'ere, love, 'e's fightin'," one of them answered, and then suddenly it occurred to him they might not have the Earl's best interests in mind. "'Ere! Ye be spies?" he barked at them. "Ye stop roight there!"

Becks calmly handed Cabot the box and approached the soldiers open-handed and with the most alluring smile she could conjure up.

"Let me explain," she started to say.

Ten seconds later, both men were on their backs, one of them out cold, the other with a broken wrist. Becks tossed Cabot one of their swords as they jogged out of the keep through the open gatehouse, crossing the bridge over the river and following the main track through the center of Nottingham toward the marketplace, toward the noise of a raging battle in progress.

The marketplace was filled with the squirming, howling wounded: men and boys missing limbs, heads and faces split open, puckered and purple wounds that were clearly mortal. Children with water and bloodstained rags moved among them providing what comfort they could, ignoring the occasional arrows that dropped down into the square and clattered on stone slabs or thudded and embedded themselves into the earth.

Up ahead, to the right of the city's gatehouse, a seventy-five-foot-wide breach in the wall was plugged with a rising sea of struggling humanity. Soldiers and civilians, men old and young, even some women, pressed into one enormous writhing scrum. On the walls to either side, she saw soldiers and citizens firing arrows, children hurling stones down at the attackers outside—a city-wide attempt to defend themselves. And a convincing job they seemed to be doing of it thus far. The sun was well past midday in the sky and halfway into the afternoon.

She realized the fluctuating timelines were stemming from this struggle that could go either way. Even though Richard's army was far greater than the number of people in Nottingham, its motivation to fight would be entirely mercenary.

On the other hand, the people of Nottingham were fighting for their very lives. If they could hold those soldiers in the breach long enough, if the battle were to spill into another day, and another day . . . quite possibly the assembled nobles with their men-at-arms might begin to stand down, their selfish allegiances to the king softening.

She scanned the front line of the fighting and quickly spotted the silhouette of Bob, head and shoulders above everyone else.

She took the wooden box from Cabot and tucked it under one arm. "Stay close to me," she commanded him, before picking her way through the marketplace carpeted with the dead and dying, arrow stems sprouting from the dirt like freshly grown weeds.

She clambered up the incline of rubble, forcefully barging aside tired men from her path, scanning faces on both sides: looking for Liam, looking for John. She collared a garrison soldier clambering downhill, blood-soaked and exhausted. "Where is the Earl of Cornwall?"

He shook his head, and she realized that over the din of roaring voices and the clatter and ring of blades on shields he could not hear her.

"WHERE IS JOHN?" she bellowed directly into his ear.

The man pointed a shaking finger uphill. "He fights alongside us!"

Becks pushed past him, her feet finding a soft carpet of bodies now that shuddered and twisted underfoot. Above the din she could hear the bass notes of Bob's voice, a deep roaring anger that seemed to fill the entire space of the breach, like an echo of whale song or the trumpeting of some enraged elephant.

She picked out his head and shoulders again—slow, shuddering, sweeping movements that told her he was fast on his way to becoming a spent force now, exhausted from exertion or loss of blood—quite probably both.

She was nearly at the crest of the small hill of debris and bodies when she heard the sharp peal of a distant horn above the cacophony.

The clatter and ring of blades almost immediately ceased as both sides of the struggle on the mound halted their melee and disengaged, weary catcalls and taunts being exchanged as the men of Richard's army withdrew to take another water break.

Becks took advantage of the lull in the fight to push her way up the last few yards.

"Bob!" she said.

He turned slowly. His eyes flickered recognition, perhaps even relief. "Becks."

"I need to locate John and Liam."

Before Bob could point them out, Liam's voice rang out. "Becks!"

She turned to see him squeeze past some bloody and grimy men descending the slope to get to the water-bearers. He stepped awkwardly over several entangled bodies and then, with a careless relief, swung his arms around her.

"I thought we'd lost you, so I did!" He lowered his voice. "We thought you'd open a window directly after you left!"

She nodded. "There were difficulties. This battle is causing instability." She regarded the thick carpet of bodies beyond the city wall. "You are doing *too* well."

Liam snorted humorlessly. "*Too well?* You've got to be joking. One more push and they'll be through for sure."

She shrugged. "Perhaps not. The light is failing, and fighting will cease for the day. Another day will weaken the attackers' resolve and strengthen the defenders' morale." She caught a glimpse of John, looking exhausted and drenched with sweat beneath the weight of his mail and helmet, and smeared with drying blood. He was talking animatedly with some of the other defenders, high on the adrenaline rush, sharing the water with them.

John is in danger of becoming an inspiring leader.

She tipped her head his way. "He is becoming strong."

Liam followed her gaze and understood what she was saying. "This—this fight; it's changing him, isn't it? Changing his destiny."

She nodded. "It is causing contamination."

He noticed the box clasped under her arm. "You've brought it back. Does that mean . . . ?"

She finished his thought. "Yes. It is safe to pass on to Richard. He will get nothing from it."

Liam could hear Cabot talking to John now, the old friends embracing. Then the monk gestured up to the top of the mound toward Becks. Liam saw John's face suddenly crease with relief and joy. They made their way up to join them.

"My lady," gasped John, breathless.

Liam and Bob silently looked on in admiration as Becks swiftly changed her manner. "Sire," she replied softly, with a tender, restrained smile that lingered just for him.

"Sire," cut in Cabot, "Lady Rebecca has it right there." He was careful not to say "Grail" in case the word carried down the slope to the others. "You can now make terms with King Richard."

John sneered. "I shall not bow down to him . . . to that *animal*. Never again!"

Becks reached a hand to his face and stroked his cheek. "My dear, you have shown your honor today, shown courage. You have been strong."

"The king will respect that," said Cabot. "Ye gave him a good fight, Sire."

John spat a mouthful of thick phlegm at the ground. "I would sooner cut off his hand than kiss his royal ring!"

"You have done what was necessary," whispered Becks. "Now you should make peace with your brother—"

"Or you'll risk dividing this country with a war, Sire!" said Cabot.

John's eyes studied them both, then he nodded at Liam. "What do you say, Sheriff? You have led well here; I would trust your counsel as well."

Liam wiped grime and sweat from his forehead. "I think they're right, Sire." He pressed his lips together. "Nobody else needs to die here today." He glanced at the box. "And you can parlay reasonable terms now, Sire."

John stroked his chin thoughtfully for a while. "But that brother of mine is a danger to this country. His endless wars— his crusades— his obsession with *this*—"

"My lord?" Becks leaned toward him and whispered something in his ear. The expression on John's face slowly changed as her lips moved.

"How would you know of such things?" John quietly replied a moment later.

She smiled at him. "You must trust me on this."

He regarded her in silence for a long while. "Lady Rebecca, I have never before encountered someone quite so . . ." He shook his head, struggling to find the right word.

"Trust me," she whispered again. "Your time will come."

He clamped his jaw and then finally, slowly, nodded. "I will speak with him, then."

Chapter 82

1194, Nottingham

John noted the look of surprise on his older brother's face as he entered the dark gloom of the tent.

"Little brother," Richard's deep voice growled with amusement, "you look like you have finally got your hands bloodied in battle."

John stepped forward. He said nothing.

"You surprise me." Richard laughed. "Finally, you seem to have outgrown your wet-nurse. I suppose, because you have at last managed to wield a sword in battle, that you consider yourself a man, huh?" Richard's smile turned to a sneer. "Hardly. You are still a snot-nosed whelp. But I will credit you with taking a first step."

John met his stern gaze. "Thank you," he said flatly.

"Now," Richard stood up. "The matter at hand. You have the Grail with you?"

John pulled the scroll from a fold in his tunic.

Richard slowly nodded. John could see the stretching pink of his lips among the thatch of blond bristles. "Oh yes," he whispered. "You have no idea, do you, little brother? No idea of the power this . . . this yard of parchment conveys?"

"It is just words."

Richard's deep laugh filled the tent. "Just words, he says. Just *words*!"

Richard shook his head. "You are an imbecile. This is a message from God. A message given a thousand years ago—a message that was always intended for *me*. Do you not see? The wars I have fought, my crusade against the infidels, it was at the Lord's bidding. He spoke to me, told me where to find this message. And you thought to steal it? To use this to *bargain* with me?"

His face darkened. "I would happily cut out your tongue, little brother, pluck your eyes from their sockets and hurl your head into a field for the crows to dine on, for your daring to play with my destiny. But . . ." He smiled. "But you have shown some spirit in fighting me today. I like that." He held his hand out to John. "Now, give me the Grail, and I will consider leniency for you."

"And what of the people of Nottingham?"

Richard's thick eyebrows arched. "You actually *care* for those peasants?"

"They fought with courage."

"They are no more than farm animals, little brother, beasts of burden. They fight because they are commanded to fight. No more brave than a horse that charges because its rider has kicked its flanks."

"I am asking for leniency for them."

"Their king has returned!" Richard snapped irritably. "Those . . . those *vermin* dared to challenge my authority! A few hundred of their heads on spikes lining the road into Nottingham will ensure I have no more nonsense like this to deal with!"

John felt his resolve weaken. "But they were merely defending their homes."

"Give me the Grail."

Push him not too far . . . he might still decide to have your head!

Richard's outstretched fingers wriggled. "The Grail. Now!"

John clasped it more tightly. "Give me—"

"Give me?" Richard's eyes widened. "Give me? You say 'give me'? I will give you exactly what I decide to give you! And *if* it is your life,

then it is only because it is—because it is not *wise* for the common folk to see royal blood spilled!"

John could see his brother struggling to control a burning rage, a pinkness in his cheeks, a throbbing vein across his forehead.

"I . . . I insist I have your word there will be no example made of them."

Richard's eyes narrowed. "Do not anger me further, little brother," he said quietly. "I have been patient enough with you."

John quickly held the scroll toward the candle burning on the table in the center of the tent.

"STOP!" yelled Richard.

"I will burn it, brother—I will!"

Richard's wide-eyed stare flickered from the candle to the edge of the parchment, mere inches away. His face darkened with rage, his lips twitched, his hands slowly reached for the sword beneath his cape. Then, like sun piercing through scudding gray clouds, his demeanor changed. He suddenly laughed.

"Good God, you've grown some fighting spirit!"

John held the scroll where it was.

"So be it! You will have my word."

"Nottingham will not be punished?"

Richard slowly shook his head. "They will not."

John felt his guts loosen. He struggled to keep a gasp of relief inside him.

"Then you can have your piece of parchment," he said as calmly as he could manage. He held it out toward King Richard. Richard took it from him and unraveled several inches of it to be sure it was the Grail. He examined it in silence for a moment before carefully rolling it up again.

"As king, my word is, of course, law," said Richard.

"You will honor that?"

He nodded. "I will. Now . . . kneel and kiss my hand."

John steadied himself with a deep breath, then stooped to hold Richard's proffered hand.

"You are going to see, little brother, the making of one kingdom stretching from this miserable wet island of England to Jerusalem. One kingdom under God . . . under me."

John struggled to suppress a wry smile on his own face as he pursed his lips. There had been something about Lady Rebecca's whispered assurance—an assurance about things yet to be—something in the way she said it that made him actually believe it to be true.

The Grail will give him nothing, John. And you will be king in less than five years.

"Kiss my hand!" commanded Richard.

"Yes . . . yes, of course," muttered John.

Chapter 83

2001, New York

Adam stood beside Sal and gazed out at the darkness. America, or at least what they could see of it, was a dark wilderness of tall cedar trees beneath a clear night sky and a crescent moon that gazed down at its own shimmering reflection on the gently rippling surface of the East River.

"It's like . . . It's just how I imagine America must have looked before Columbus first landed," Adam whispered. "Out there somewhere, there must be tribes of Native Americans running around, free and living just as they were back in the fifteenth century."

Sal nodded. "I like it like this. No people."

"So . . . Maddy said you came from 2026?"

"Yeah."

"Tell me, what's it like?"

She shrugged. "Crowded. Busy. Noisy. At least where we lived."

"Is there any really cool, you know, technology?"

"Like?"

"I don't know—flying cars or something?"

Sal snorted. "No. It's all rickshaws and battered old Nanos. The air's thick with toxins and stuff. And there were the troubles in the north."

"Troubles?"

"Terrorists, bombs. Things weren't so good with Taliban-Pakistan. My father worried about what was going to happen in India, what with that and the flooding areas and the migrants."

They listened to the woods, the call of a heron, the lapping of the river up the shingle nearby.

"The future doesn't sound so great," said Adam.

"Uh-uh. I remember . . . everything felt so . . . so"—she struggled to find a word that worked—"so *temporary*. Like you couldn't really get used to anything, because you knew it wasn't going to last forever."

"Sheesh, that's *my* future too, then. Twenty-five years from now." He did a quick calculation. "I'll be fifty-two or fifty-three then. I wonder if I'll still be in New York."

"New York's not so good," she replied. "They started evacuating parts of it."

"Flooding?"

"Uh-huh. And growing crime and food riots and stuff. Like we were having in Mumbai."

"Jesus." Adam sighed. "You make the future sound depressing."

"Sorry," she replied softly.

"No—it's not your fault, Sal. Thanks for, you know, being honest about it." He pursed his lips. "Makes you wonder why you bother doing anything if that's how it all goes. Like, why am I bothering with my consulting job? Saving up for a retirement that sounds like, well . . . a nightmare."

"It's only a nightmare for the poor," she replied. "For those with lots of money it's just—" Sal hesitated.

"Sal? What is it?"

She looked at him. "I think there's a big wave coming." She leaned around and ducked her head under the shutter. "Maddy! Time wave! Big one!"

Maddy pulled herself off the bunk and staggered bleary-eyed to join them in the doorway.

"There it is!" said Sal, pointing east.

A dark wall approached; like last time, rolling in from the Atlantic, looking like a mountain range advancing rapidly toward them.

"Better come inside, so you're not right on the edge of the concrete," Maddy said, pointing at the crumbling boundary of the office's force-field effect. Adam and Sal shuffled quickly inside and crouched on the floor just inside the archway.

"Here it comes," muttered Maddy. "I just hope this one gets us back."

Adam watched the churning black wall approach like a tsunami, blotting out the sky, the stars, the crescent moon. "I wonder whether we'd be better off hanging on to this," he said, nodding at the wilderness. "Given how it all goes in the future."

"Too late," said Sal.

The time wave rolled over Manhattan, and the distant tall trees quivered and shook and swirled into a maelstrom of flickering possibilities. As the wave swept across the broad river, Adam thought he saw the ghostly outline of skyscrapers forming. Then, with a fresh gust of wind pushed before it, the wave was over them; a destructive tornado passing momentarily overhead, eating up a reality that shouldn't be and laying down, in its wake, a reality that should.

And then, as soon as it had arrived, it was gone.

Outside was a cobbled street littered with plastic bags and several wheeled trash cans, and the ambient noises of New York.

Sal was the first to step out. She looked to her left, toward the river, and nodded. "Yeah," she said, "looks like we're back home."

Adam and Maddy joined her. Manhattan glistened and shimmered in the night; the sky was punctuated with the far-off winking lights of commercial airliners coming in to JFK and LaGuardia. A distant police siren, the booming of someone's sound system.

A Monday night in New York, still very much alive, noisy and busy, even approaching midnight.

"I better go check our database and see if history's fully back," said Maddy.

Sal and Adam watched the night in silence for a while.

"I kind of liked Manhattan the way it just was," said Adam.

"Uh-huh," said Sal sadly. "Me too."

Chapter 84

1194, Kirklees Priory, Yorkshire

It was a cool morning, for a change. The clear blue sky with its relentlessly hot sun was tucked away behind a skein of combed-out clouds that grew thicker to the west.

Cabot looked out of the stable across the priory's parched vegetable gardens. "Looks like rain is coming. That is good."

Liam admired the old man's calming air of common sense. Amid all the things that had gone on, he was so very easily able to come back to his priory, to resume a role of quiet contemplation and address the practical matters of their small order.

"When will ye leave?" asked Cabot.

"Soon," replied Liam. "Bob and Becks have a device in their heads that sort of does them in if they stay in a place for too long. Time's nearly up, isn't it?"

Bob nodded. "Remaining mission time: thirty-seven hours, forty-three minutes."

"A window will open just before that time runs out," said Liam. "Unless we signal the field office to open one up sooner."

"Suggestion," said Becks. "It is not necessary to communicate again. The window in thirty-seven hours will be adequate."

"Agreed," said Bob.

Liam nodded. "Fine, then we're in no hurry."

The siege at Nottingham had ended peaceably. Although the citizens of the town had been quaking in fear at what King Richard would do to them, he had surprised them all with his unexpected leniency. There had been some grumbling among the assembled army and their controlling barons, earls, and dukes, who'd all been assuming they'd get a share of the town's loot.

John had been sent with an escort of soldiers to London, officially "pardoned" by Richard but perhaps not entirely trusted by him. Rumor was, John was going to be kept in the Tower for an undefined period as a punishment.

Becks had been allowed to visit him one last time before he was dispatched south. She said he appeared to be relieved to still have his head on his shoulders.

"He also appears to be exhibiting a different behavioral pattern," she'd reported after seeing him. Liam had asked her to describe it. "He no longer shakes. His at-rest heart rate is within normal parameters," she replied coolly. Liam had laughed at that. She'd managed to take his pulse as they'd embraced one last time.

"I believe he'd make a good king," Cabot had said. "He may not ever be a great commander of soldiers, but he has other qualities worth speaking of. Prudence. Caution. Compassion."

Compassion? Liam wondered now.

Perhaps. History was going to judge John harshly; he was destined to be known as England's worst king. The king unable to maintain control of the French territories his much "braver" older brother fought so hard to keep hold of. The king who signed the Magna Carta, granting legal rights to his subjects, but only because of the pressures put on him by England's "valiant" nobles.

There was a correct history, and it seemed like they'd managed to restore it. But Liam couldn't help wondering if this "correct" history, as it was recorded in history books and encyclopedias, was a *true* reflection of the past. A part of him was always going to wonder if the signing of the Magna Carta—signing away the most powerful privileges of the monarch—was *really* the result of nobles fighting for the rights of their peasants . . . or whether it was, in fact, King John's idea, a gratitude to the common people of Nottingham for fighting for him.

"Liam." Becks's voice cut through his musings.

"Huh?"

"Liam, Bob and I have one remaining mission task."

Liam looked at her, then at Bob. "What now?"

Bob answered. "The Voynich Manuscript dates from this time. It has yet to be written."

"We have to write it," said Becks.

His jaw sagged open. "Hold on! Are you—you're saying this Voynich thing was . . . ?"

"Was originally written by us?" Becks nodded. "Yes. It was written by us to ensure we visited this time, this place."

Liam frowned, trying to put the circular logic together. "But does that mean we've been here *before*?" He scratched at the place on his temple where a thin plume of gray hair grew.

"It could mean that at some point in time one or more of us has been here to seed the Voynich Manuscript," said Bob.

"You mean one of us *will* come here?"

"Correct. Since we have no knowledge of it, this has yet to happen."

"But . . . but that means deliberately altering history, right? The very thing we're supposed to be *preventing*?" His brows knitted with confusion. "Hold on! Does that mean those clues that the Adam fella spotted . . . ?"

"Those are clues that were deliberately seeded to ensure *Adam Lewis alone* was able to identify and decode a specific portion of the Voynich Manuscript, in order to flag our attention," said Bob.

"That is now no longer required," Becks continued. "The Voynich Manuscript must be written without those coded flags."

"But . . . ?"

"We no longer need to be alerted and brought to this place," said Bob. He turned to Becks. "This is also your conclusion?"

She nodded. "I concur. History is corrected. It is now an unacceptable historical contaminant for *any* of the Voynich to be translated."

"So, what're you going to write?" asked Liam.

"I have detailed visual records of the document. I can duplicate it as it was, but without the South American characters that originally flagged Adam Lewis's attention."

"So that means"—Liam frowned as he worked through the logic—"he'll have never known about us?'

"Affirmative. And, of course, he'll never have tracked us down in New York."

"Right." He glanced across at Cabot, sitting on a wooden bucket, looking almost as bemused at the exchange as Liam felt. "And what about our good friend here, Mr. Cabot?"

Cabot smiled. "Aye. I was wondering when ye would be considering me."

Both Becks and Bob looked at him dispassionately.

"No!" said Liam. "You're not going to kill him, so help me! We couldn't have fixed this all up without the fella's help. You're not going to hurt him—and that's an order to both of you!"

The support units calmly nodded. "Termination in this instance will not be necessary," said Bob. "Cabot is required to ensure the safekeeping of the document."

"Agreed," said Becks. "So long as you do not speak of all the things you have seen," she said, looking at Cabot pointedly. Liam realized she was right. The old man had gone through with her to the twenty-first century. God knows what he must have witnessed. But then Liam imagined little of what he saw must have made sense, so little could be of any use to him.

Cabot scratched his beard. "And who would believe what I have seen? They will call me a fool."

"She's right," said Liam. "We still need you to safeguard the Voynich Manuscript. It has to stay with you alone. You can't tell anyone about *any* of this."

"Fear not, Liam." He laughed gently. "I have no desire to be burned as a heretic. I will not talk of round worlds, or days yet to be, or a place called 'New' York. Ye can trust in that."

Liam smiled and offered his hand. "It's a deal, then, Mr. Cabot."

He grasped it. "A *deal*, Liam of Connor."

Becks and Bob both stood up at the same time. Liam guessed they must have been quietly exchanging data. "You two all right?"

"We should proceed with creating the Voynich Manuscript," said Becks. "It is two hundred thirty-four pages of manuscript, and will take approximately seven hours to duplicate." She turned to Cabot. "I will require parchment and ink. Do you have these things?"

Cabot nodded. "We have. The priory's librarian will not be a happy man, but I shall see to it."

"Thanks," said Liam. The three of them watched the old man go. "We can trust him," he said.

"We know where to locate him if a contamination originates from this point," said Bob.

"He is an acceptable risk," said Becks. "And terminating him would be simple."

Liam shook his head at them. "You really do make a charming couple, so you do."

They both looked at each other, then back at him. "Please explain."

Liam waved that away. "Never mind."

Chapter 85

2001, New York

"Yeah, the movie poster's gone," said Sal, standing outside the Golden Screen theater and studying the billboards. "What's that?" she said into her cell phone. Several yellow taxis lined up on the far side of 7th Avenue were honking at a delivery truck backing into a side road.

"Yeah, I'm positive! No sign of it. Nothing on the 'coming soon' list. It's gone."

She nodded several times at Maddy's instructions, then hung up. She looked around. This was Tuesday morning as she knew it; she was out and about a little earlier than usual, but it all looked as she expected it to.

Times Square hummed with life, the sky a deep welcoming blue, and there was no sign of the movie *The Manuscript*. It was gone. The tiny ripple they'd felt just half an hour ago had been Adam Lewis's claim to fame being subtly erased from history.

There would be no film starring Leonardo DiCaprio on the run from sinister agents and clutching an ancient-looking scroll in one fist.

She suddenly felt a rumble in her stomach and realized she hadn't eaten a thing since lunchtime yesterday. She checked her watch. It was 7:23 a.m. An hour and twenty-two minutes to go until Tuesday turned into its regularly scheduled horror show. Time enough to go for a bottle of soda and a bagel with cream cheese.

Maddy tapped her phone and put it down on the desk. "It's gone, Adam," she said. "The movie about you and the Voynich, well . . . it never happened."

He ran a hand through his hair. "What does that mean, though? Have I been *deleted* from the world or something?" His eyes widened with a horrible thought. "Oh God, is there another, different me out there somewhere?"

"No." She shook her head. "No, it's okay. There's just the one you. But your life's different now, that's all. If the wave had come while you'd been standing outside, you wouldn't know any different. You'd be off living that life, wherever it is. But because you were inside our field, it means you've got to go out and track your new life down, find out what it is . . . *where* it is."

"I—that's—are you telling me I might not be living in New York any more?"

Maddy shrugged. "You could be. You might be living back in England. Who knows?"

He pulled his apartment key out of his jacket pocket. "You're saying if I go back to my apartment, it might not be mine?"

"I have no idea. Probably not."

He looked like he was struggling with the idea of that.

"Your life is probably going to be *very* different, Adam. You should go find out what it is. Maybe call your mom and dad—you've got parents, right?"

He shrugged. "I did. God knows if I do now."

"Call them. Talk to them, find out who you are." She laughed softly, not unkindly. "They'll probably think you've gone crazy, though."

"You can say that again."

Adam stood up uncertainly and grabbed his expensive suit jacket, draped over the back of an armchair. "It's been a weird twenty-four hours, hasn't it?"

She nodded. "Very weird."

"I feel . . . I feel like I've known you, and Sal and the others, forever. But I knocked on that shutter just a day ago."

She smiled sadly. "That's time travel. Messes with your head."

He looked at her. "Could I not stay?"

The question caught her unawares. A part of her longed to say *yes*. To have someone she could share the leadership role with; to have someone she could offload onto . . . to confide in. To . . .

He can't stay, Maddy. You know that.

"Adam . . . I, uh, I don't think so. I'm not sure I have the authority, the *right*, to recruit people."

"But," he said coyly, "surely I know too much now? I've got to be some kind of a security risk. Better for me to join you guys, right? Than be out there—you know, blabbing about all the stuff I've seen?"

"I don't think you'll blab, Adam . . . I trust you. Anyway, if you come back here on Wednesday with a film crew in tow, you'll simply find us gone."

He hesitated, staring at her as a long, drawn-out, uncomfortable silence filled the space between them. "All right." He nodded finally, awkward, a little embarrassed. "Okay, well . . . I thought I'd ask, you know? If you don't ask, you don't get, right?"

She felt she owed him something of an explanation. "I'm sorry. The three of us are still new here. We're just trying to figure out whether we're doing our jobs right. And I . . . just don't think I'm meant—I'm *allowed*—to sign anyone else up for the cause."

"No, that's fine. Sorry I, uh . . . I asked." He stepped across to the computer table to collect his hard drive. "Is it okay for me to take this back?"

She considered that for a moment. His work on decoding the Voynich was on there; his photographs of gravestones in the Kirklees Priory cemetery were on there. But then, none of it would mean much to anyone now.

She nodded. "Sure."

He picked it up and tucked it into the pocket of his jacket. "I suppose this is good-bye, then?"

She pressed her lips together, holding back an urge to change her mind, to tell him he could stay. "Yes. It's good-bye, Adam," she said eventually.

His feet clacked across the concrete toward the door, and he pressed the green button. The shutter rattled up, letting daylight creep in across the archway.

He turned around. "Maybe one day I can write a book about it?"

"As long as you call it fiction." She smiled. "Become an author? Why not? Sounds like a great idea."

He ducked down to go under and looked outside. "Lovely day out there."

He was about to step out when she called out to him. "Adam!"

"Yes?"

"Your new life . . . I'm pretty sure it won't involve you working at the World Trade Center." She looked briefly down at her watch. "Just . . . listen, you don't need to go looking *there* this morning, okay? Go call your folks first thing. Forget about going to work."

"Will do."

"Promise me."

He looked back at her and made a face, confused. "All right . . . I promise."

"Go on," said Maddy. She found her voice catching. She didn't need him to hear that—to see that there was a struggle going on inside her head. "Go on and find what your new life is."

"Say good-bye to Sal for me," he said. Then he ducked outside, and she watched the gray flannel of his work pants walk up the cobbled backstreet and out of sight.

"Take care, Adam," she whispered.

Chapter 86

1194, Kirklees Priory, Yorkshire

They stood in the waist-high field listening to the hiss of a thousand ears of barley swaying in the gentle breeze. Becks handed Cabot an armful of sheets of parchment. "This is the complete duplication, with several minor alterations. You must look after it, keep it safe."

Sébastien Cabot nodded dutifully. "I will. We have a crypt below the priory. I will see to it that it is stored there."

"That is good."

Liam stepped forward. "Mr. Cabot, we owe you our thanks."

The old man grinned. "Aye, 'tis been a . . . a truly fascinating few months."

"That much is for sure."

He held a hand out to Liam. "I have learned so very much. Perhaps too much. My . . . my faith has been troubled."

"Well"—Liam grasped his hand—"if it's any help, despite all the things I know and all the things I've seen, I still pray to the fella upstairs—when I'm in a tight spot, that is."

Cabot nodded. "There is comfort in that, Liam. Thank ye."

"Information: tachyon particles detected," said Becks. The soft tones of a court maiden she'd used just for John had been dispensed with for now. She turned to regard the circle of low stalks in the field, clipped down close to the ground from the last time the portal had opened here. "Stand back," she cautioned.

A moment later their loose robes fluttered in the gentle gust of displaced air, and they were staring at the undulating sphere of the portal.

"I'm sorry, Mr. Cabot. I would invite you to come along with us, but . . ."

Cabot shook his head. "'Tis a world, I think, that would send me mad. Anyway"—he held out the parchment—"I have a duty here, do I not?"

Liam nodded. "Aye, that's true."

"We must go now," said Bob. He stepped toward the portal, then stopped, turned, and offered his one good hand to Cabot. "A pleasure working with you, Mr. Cabot."

Cabot grasped his large palm. "And ye. Truly, I have never seen a man as indestructible as ye. I would not be surprised if the superstitious folk in these parts tell fireside stories about ye, Bob, long after ye've gone."

Bob worked on a smile and let Cabot's hand go.

Becks was the last to bid him farewell. "If you ever see John again, tell him . . ." She hesitated, unsure how to complete the sentence.

"Shall I tell him that ye think fondly of him? That ye have returned to France?"

She nodded. "Affirmative. That would be an appropriate message to convey."

The portal still shimmered, impatiently inviting them through.

"We should go," said Bob. "It is unwise to open non-dimensional space longer than necessary."

Becks released the old man's hand and joined Bob and Liam at the edge of the sphere.

"Take good care of it!" said Liam.

Cabot nodded and watched as the three of them stepped into the churning perimeter, their solid outlines becoming wavering phantoms lost in a swirling dim world. Then, with a soft puff, the portal closed, leaving him alone once more in the swaying field of barley.

He looked up at some crows circling above the trees, now beginning to turn from their rich summer green to the golden hues that heralded harvest time. The stifling warmth of summer was soon going to give way to fresher winds.

He sniffed the summer scent with his florid nose and found himself considering an idea.

So, the world is round now, is it?

The thought placed the hint of a smile on his craggy face. A vaguely reassuring notion, that. He looked up at the sun in the sky.

And ye stay put, do ye? It's us *that wanders around* ye?

Again, a strangely comforting idea, that God's works might be far larger, far greater than this one little world full of greedy and insane barons, princes, kings, and popes.

Chapter 87

2001, New York

Sal watched the twisting, coiling outline of several figures embracing one another. She thought she could make out a swaying field of yellow wheat or maize and a blue sky.

Then the figures, three of them, stepped closer and emerged a moment later into the archway.

She almost didn't recognize two of them.

Bob's fast-growing coconut hair was a shaggy, coarse, dark, wild mess. The other thing she immediately noticed was that his left arm was missing at the elbow and one ear was gone.

"*Shadd-yah!* Bob!"

But Liam . . . it was Liam, though she almost could have passed by in a street and not have recognized him. His dark hair had grown. Uncut for six months, it hung down onto his shoulders; parted scruffily in the middle, it draped down on either side of his face like dark theater curtains. It was his wispy beard, however, that shocked her: a jaw lined with bristles, across his top lip a downy mustache, his mouth framed by a goatee.

"Liam!"

Maddy balled a fist in her mouth. "Oh my God, Liam. You look . . ." She didn't know what to say.

"Scruffy?" He arched his thick eyebrows. "That the word you're lookin' for?"

He grinned and stepped over, wrapping one arm around each of them, pulling the group all together in a clumsy bear hug. "Ahh, 'tis good to see ye, so it is!"

Maddy laughed. "You sound all funny."

He let them both go and stood back. "Aye . . . 'tis the Old Anglish, so. I'll be back to meself soon enough."

"*Love* your outfit!" said Sal, admiring his studded leather jerkin, cotton hose, and boots.

"Aye, they are well made."

Maddy looked Bob over. "Bob, the arm . . . Can you be fixed up like Becks was?"

"Affirmative. I will need the growth tube."

She turned to the monitors. "Bob, can you set that up?"

> **Affirmative, Maddy.**

The cursor blinked for a moment, then skittered along.

> **Welcome back, Bob and Becks.**

Both support units silently acknowledged that with a Wi-fi handshake.

"Where's that English fella, Adam?" asked Liam.

"He's gone," said Maddy. "Back to his life."

"Was Adam Lewis realigned?" asked Becks.

Maddy knew what she was asking: had he been outside when the last minor time wave came through? Was his memory wiped clean—was he living a very different life? She decided to keep matters simple for now. After all, she trusted him . . . sort of. And even if he did decide to rush to the nearest newspaper with his fantastic story, who was going to believe him anyway? If he led a curious journalist back to the archway this time tomorrow, there'd be nothing to see, just a vacant archway beneath the Williamsburg Bridge.

"Yeah . . . don't worry, he's *aligned*."

Becks nodded, satisfied with the answer.

Liam clasped his hands together. "So, it's been a long while since I had a nice hot shower."

Maddy wrinkled her nose. "Uh-huh, we noticed. Why don't you and Becks get changed into something less fancy and head over to the homeless shelter showers."

Liam nodded. "Aye, sounds like a plan."

"And when you're done, we'll go out and get something to eat." She looked at Bob. "You too. We can growth-tube you afterward if you'd like."

Bob's thick lips slowly stretched with what looked like something approaching a mischievous grin. "Aye, sounds like a plan."

Maddy rolled her eyes and looked at Liam. "I see he's growing a funny bone too."

Liam shrugged. "Right pair of jesters, so they are."

Adam stood at the intersection of the Bowery and Delancey Street, busy with morning rush-hour traffic.

A new life . . . and he hadn't the first clue what it was yet. His cell phone was in his jacket pocket. Maybe Maddy was right. Maybe he should dial up Mum. Whatever new course his professional life had taken, she and Dad were still likely living in their old bungalow in Chelmsford.

And what do I say, exactly? Hey, Mum, I've just come from another timeline . . . where am I living right now? Am I married? What job do I have? He chuckled at the thought of it.

But then he realized the cell probably wouldn't work. Its contract would never have existed; the SIM card's code number would be invalid.

A new life. And yet New York looked exactly the same as it did this time yesterday. He couldn't quite believe his apartment would no longer be his, that Jerry, the security guard, wouldn't have a clue who he was.

He looked to his left at the tall skyscrapers along Wall Street, the

Twin Towers standing proud, thrusting into the cloudless sky. He pulled his Trade Center security pass out of his breast pocket and gazed at his passport photo: a ridiculous grinning face above a crisp shirt and tie. If Maddy was right, this pass wasn't even going to get him past Reception on his floor, let alone allow him to enter the IT room and his personal office.

And his apartment keys? He pulled them out and jangled them in one hand.

Somebody else's home now.

He shook his head. It was too damned strange. Too weird. Standing here in a wholly unchanged world, unchanged except that Adam Lewis was living a very different life in it.

Mission Control to Adam: what if she made that up?

He didn't believe Maddy Carter would. She seemed the genuine type.

Okay, then, Adam. How about this: what if you just dreamed this all up? Huh? What if this has all been a hallucination? What if you've turned into a nutcase?

The thought of that sent a chill down his spine. "It happened," he told himself. "All that time-travel stuff happened. I'm not a damn nutcase."

Only one way to find out then, old pal. Hmm?

He looked at the Twin Towers, then glanced at his watch. It was just after eight in the morning. Maybe he should at least check: walk in and swipe his card at the reception desk, then see what happened. If it let him through, then it meant his old life was still there—the well-paid consultancy job, the fancy riverside apartment, the exclusive gym membership. It just meant he'd had one hell of a hallucination.

And, of course, it means you might need to go see a shrink.

He laughed at that. A therapist. Crazy. Maybe this whole thing had been some sort of trip. Maybe he'd had a little too much to drink last night? Maybe someone had slipped something funny in his beer?

Only one way to find out, Mission Control said again.

He tucked his keys back into his pocket and turned left, heading down the Bowery toward the World Trade Center. He figured half an hour from now he was going to be behind his desk again, wondering where the hell he'd gotten the fanciful idea that he'd actually spent the night in a dingy brick archway with a team of time-traveling kids.

Crazy.

Chapter 88

2001, New York

<u>*Monday (time cycle 59)*</u>
*I know Maddy wanted Adam to stay. I think she really liked him,
maybe fancied him or something. He could have stayed, though. We
could have fit him in somehow. At least he's got his life back now.
Lucky him. I wonder what he's doing. Where he is. Probably back
in England.*

    *Anyway, Bob's busy growing an arm, and Liam's shaved his hair
short. I don't like it. He looks more like a coconut than Bob does!
Oh, and the beard's gone. Liam used an electric shaver for the first
time in his life. Said the thing scared him half to death. He thought
it was going to eat his face off. I'm glad he's lost the beard. It made
him look so much older—that and his shock of white hair. He was
looking like an oldie.*

    At least now he looks more like himself.

    But, jahulla, *he is definitely older. He doesn't look like the boy I
saw when I first woke up. He's changed somehow. The eyes, maybe—
old before they should be.*

Sal put down the pen and took in the quiet archway. On Liam's bunk
was a small stack of history books that he was working his way through.

The one on top looked like it had something to do with the American Civil War; the cover was all flags and crossed swords and bearded generals. Right now he was downtown; he'd said he wanted to take a walk and clear his head. Sal got the distinct feeling he wasn't happy to be back as he let on. That maybe he could have been quite happy living in the year 1194.

"I was actually the Sheriff of Nottingham for a while," he'd told her rather proudly, and, she suspected, a little wistfully. Sal knew something was also troubling him. She'd heard him murmuring in his sleep last night . . . telling someone over and over that he was "so very sorry."

His eyes. Old before they should be.

Eyes. That word suddenly stirred a memory.

I saw something a couple of days ago; a bear, a child's teddy bear. I can't explain why it's playing on my mind. I know I've seen that bear before. I mean "before," like before me being a TimeRider. I just can't quite remember where or when. It's totally dullah. *Weirding me out!*

Through the open door into the back room she could see Bob's form floating in the nutrient-rich amber soup, gently kicking in his sleep as something close to a dream must be running through his head. His lower arm had grown bone first, and now was at the stage of sprouting ribbons of feathery pink muscle tissue.

It was quiet in the archway.

Becks and Maddy were out together to give Foster an update. Sal wanted to go along and say hi. But Maddy had said, "Not this time."

She's always doing that. Treating me like a child.

She sighed irritably.

"Just me," she said aloud, her voice echoing around the brick walls and coming back to her. She got down off her bunk bed with a squeak of springs, sauntered over to the computer desk, and sat down.

"Bob?"

> **Hello, Sal.**

"Wanna play a game or something?"

> **Certainly. What would you like to play?**

"Do you have any Pikodu puzzles on your system?"

> **Affirmative. Would you like to do a two-player one?**

"Yes."

One of the monitors flickered to life with a complicated mosaic of icons.

"And put some music on. Something really heavy."

> **What would you like?**

She clucked her tongue. "What about that band Maddy took us to see? What were they called again?"

> **EssZed.**

"Yeah, some of their stuff."

The faint rumble of a train passing overhead was lost behind the opening power chord of a distorted guitar and the rasping, deep drawl of the vocals. She sat back in her chair and nodded along to the beat. "Go on, then," she said, nodding at the webcam. "You go first."

Chapter 89

2001, New York

Foster was sitting on the park bench, just like the last time she saw him, pulling nuggets of bread from a hot dog bun and throwing them to a strutting pack of impatient pigeons.

"Hey," said Maddy.

He looked up at her and smiled. "You found me, then." He studied the girl standing beside Maddy. "And who's this?"

"Oh, yeah, this is Becks. We grew her."

Foster's eyes narrowed for a moment, then flickered with recognition. "Yes . . . of course! That's the female model. You know about the San Francisco drop point, I take it?"

"Yup."

His eyes were drawn to the swirling ridges of scarred skin running up her left arm. "Looks like she's seen action already."

Maddy sat down next to him. "A prehistoric monster bit her arm off. That's regrowth there."

His eyes widened. "*Prehistoric?*"

Maddy nodded. "That's a whole *other* story, Foster. I told you about it last time."

"Oh. This is not the first time you've come to me? I must seem like some senile old fart."

"Relax," she said, laughing, "it's only the second."

"Ahhh . . . So, how are you coping?"

She sighed. "Okay so far, I think. History's still in one piece." She looked around the park. A toddler was tormenting the pigeons, his parents a few dozen yards away watching him. No one close enough to eavesdrop. "Foster, I really need to talk to you about something."

He threw the rest of the bun at the pigeons and dusted the crumbs off his hands. "Go on."

"Does the word 'Pandora' mean anything at all to you?"

He tilted his head in thought. "Do you mean apart from the Greek legend?"

Maddy nodded.

"No . . ." He shook his head. "Nothing especially."

"When we were getting the spare fetuses from the San Francisco drop point, I discovered a handwritten note addressed to me, telling me to look out for it."

He frowned. "Odd."

"There's more." Maddy proceeded to spend the next ten minutes talking, explaining all about the Voynich Manuscript, Adam Lewis, the Holy Grail, and freemasons from the future. Finally she explained that some sort of prophecy, some Big Secret supposedly penned nearly two thousand years ago, was locked up in a password-protected portion of Becks's brain.

". . . so, that secret, it's right here, Foster, right inside Becks's head. I wanted you to hear it with me."

"What about Liam and Sal?"

She shook her head. "They'll be next . . . but I just feel I can trust you, because—"

"Because I haven't got long to live?"

Maddy winced. He was right. "No, that's not it. It's . . . The note said 'tell no one.' So whatever Becks has got to share with us, I guess I just want to hear it first."

He nodded. "Fair enough. You're quite right."

Maddy beckoned Becks to sit down on the bench on the other side of Foster. "Becks . . . I'm going to open your locked partition now; are you ready?"

"Affirmative," she said coolly.

"I'm sort of worried, Foster. It's something important. I'm sure it has something to do with the future."

"Or perhaps something the future knows about the past?" he added.

"Yeah . . . It could be anything, really. But this—what she's about to say"—Maddy laughed a little manically—"this secret is what the legend of the Holy Grail is all about." She looked at him. "I'll be honest with you: that kinda freaks me out a little. It's going to be a big thing, right? Big. It's gonna change things."

He nodded thoughtfully. "Possibly."

"I'm scared."

"It's just *information*, Maddy. Better to know something than not." He reached for her hand and squeezed it. "We'll figure it out together, so we will."

"All right." She leaned across the old man. "Becks. Listen very closely." She lowered her voice. "iPad—caveman—breakfast."

Becks's face suddenly became a blank canvas, expressionless. Her eyes locked on Maddy. "Hello, Maddy." She looked at Foster. "Who is this?"

"He's Foster, part of the agency. He can be trusted. Do you understand?"

"Affirmative."

"You remember you used that *cardan grille* to decode the Holy Grail document."

"Yes, Maddy, I do. It was a very interesting task."

"Good. I want you to tell me and Foster exactly what you read."

Becks's mouth opened to speak, then froze. She remained motionless for a good ten seconds before Maddy and Foster exchanged a questioning look.

"Becks? What's the matter?"

The question unfroze the support unit, and her gray eyes swiveled onto her. "I am unable to comply with your request," she said.

"I'm sorry?"

"I cannot reveal the message to you, Maddy. Not at this time."

"What? Who says?"

Becks's eyes flickered as she checked data. "I am unable to reveal that. But it is a higher authority than yours."

"A higher authority?" She looked at Foster. "A *higher authority*? Do you know who she's talking about?"

Foster frowned, puzzled. "No . . . no, I don't."

"Oh God, I don't like this," she whispered. "Secrets within secrets. I hate it! It means somebody's getting *used* here. And that somebody's probably *me*."

She turned to Becks. "Can you tell me anything about the message? Anything at all?"

"I am allowed to tell you it is a warning. That is all."

"But you said I can't know about it *yet*."

"Affirmative."

"Which, what, means you're going to be allowed to tell me at some point in time?"

"Correct."

"When?"

Becks tilted her head slightly, almost the way a dog does. Her gray eyes searched data, then finally settled back on Maddy. "When it is the end."

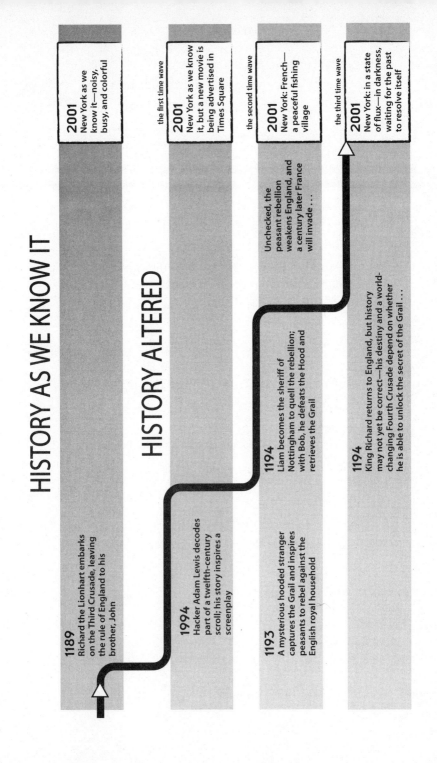

HISTORY AS WE KNOW IT

HISTORY ALTERED

2001
New York as we know it—noisy, busy, and colorful

the first time wave

2001
New York as we know it, but a new movie is being advertised in Times Square

the second time wave

2001
New York: French—a peaceful fishing village

the third time wave

2001
New York: in a state of flux—in darkness, waiting for the past to resolve itself

1189
Richard the Lionhart embarks on the Third Crusade, leaving the rule of England to his brother, John

1994
Hacker Adam Lewis decodes part of a twelfth-century scroll; his story inspires a screenplay

1193
A mysterious hooded stranger captures the Grail and inspires peasants to rebel against the English royal household

Unchecked, the peasant rebellion weakens England, and a century later France will invade . . .

1194
Liam becomes the sheriff of Nottingham to quell the rebellion; with Bob, he defeats the Hood and retrieves the Grail

1194
King Richard returns to England, but history may not yet be correct—his destiny and a world-changing Fourth Crusade depend on whether he is able to unlock the secret of the Grail . . .